THE PEOPLE
OF THIS PARISH

'What do *you* know of passion?' Guy rose and, putting his hands in his pockets, went to the window, where he stood looking down on the house he had rented to Ryder Yetman. 'You are but a girl of eighteen. Lord Thornwell may have been repulsive to you – and that I can understand – but you must behave correctly in public, Eliza. You must learn to control your temper. I think this scheme of going to Holland for a year is an excellent one. It will not be very exciting, but it will be interesting and it will give you the chance to think. I cannot but approve of it. With your interests at heart, my dear, I hasten to add.' . . .

Eliza said nothing. She didn't even look at her brother, because in her imagination she saw so clearly the figure standing on the roof, his hair the colour of the straw in his hands.

Slowly a plan, an idea whose audacity made her inwardly gasp, began to form in her mind.

D1312941

By the same author

writing as Nicola Thorne
The Girls
In Love
Bridie Climbing
A Woman Like Us★
The Perfect Wife and Mother★
The Daughters of the House
Where the Rivers Meet
Affairs of Love
The Enchantress Saga
Champagne
Pride of Place
Bird of Passage
The Rector's Daughter

THE ASKHAM CHRONICLES
Never Such Innocence
Yesterday's Promises
Bright Morning
A Place in the Sun

writing as Katherine Yorke
A Woman's Place★
Swift Flows the River
The Pair Bond

★*Available from*
Mandarin Paperbacks

The People of this Parish

Rosemary Ellerbeck

A Mandarin Paperback
THE PEOPLE OF THIS PARISH

First published in Great Britain 1991
by William Heinemann Limited
This edition published 1992
by Mandarin Paperbacks
an imprint of Reed Consumer Books Ltd
Michelin House, 81 Fulham Road, London SW3 6RB
and Auckland, Melbourne, Singapore and Toronto

Reprinted 1992, 1994

Copyright © Rosemary Ellerbeck 1991
The author has asserted her moral rights

A CIP catalogue record for this title
is available from the British Library
ISBN 0 7493 0554 1

Printed and bound in Great Britain
by Cox & Wyman Ltd, Reading, Berkshire

This book is sold subject to the condition
that it shall not, by way of trade or otherwise,
be lent, resold, hired out, or otherwise circulated
without the publisher's prior consent in any form
of binding or cover other than that in which
it is published and without a similar condition
including this condition being imposed
on the subsequent purchaser.

CONTENTS

PROLOGUE

Wenham was not exactly a village, not properly a town; too big for one, too small for the other. Yet with its market, its fine church, its cluster of shops in the main street and its growing population Wenham was, by the year 1880, more like a town than a Dorset village, a place on its way to prosperity.

During the day its inhabitants could be seen thronging the streets or in the shops, arguing over the price of cattle in the market, or the price of beef at the butcher's, the price of potatoes at the greengrocer's or flour at the grocer's. The menfolk made their way in and out of the taverns for refreshment, and there was a constant toing and froing as people called on one another or went about their business, rode their horses or drove their carriages – few of these – along the narrow main street.

Lady Woodville was seldom seen in the streets or shops of Wenham. If she needed anything it was sent for or, more likely, ordered from London, where the Woodvilles maintained a large town house. The country estate two miles from Wenham had its own farm, which provided all the vegetables and dairy produce that the members of the household needed.

Yet on Sunday the Woodville carriage could be observed stationed directly outside the church porch, its horses patiently pawing the ground or feeding from a nosebag, while the family attended divine service. They sat at the rear of the church in the Woodville pew, distinguished from all the others by the high, carved stalls and the cushions embroidered by the ladies of the parish.

Lady Woodville, a widow, was accompanied by her son,

1

Guy, her daughter, Eliza, and such relations or friends as happened to be staying. Latterly there had been another important addition to the household – a young Dutch woman called Margaret Heering to whom Guy was soon to be married. Sometimes her mother or father were with her, or her brother Julius and his wife, all of whom lived in Amsterdam.

The members of the Yetman family, on the other hand, were frequently to be seen on the streets, in the market and in the shops of Wenham. They occupied a large house in the centre of the town, but they had only lived in it for a generation, whereas Woodvilles had been at their mansion, Pelham's Oak, since the seventeenth century.

The Woodvilles were aristocrats, old money – what was left of it. The Yetmans were yeoman stock and their fortune newly made. In the previous century the Yetmans had served the Woodvilles in a menial capacity before Thomas Yetman, using his skills as a builder and master thatcher, had broadened his interests, extended his family, bought a fine house, thrust himself into any number of parochial activities, so that his son John now numbered himself equal to any man in the land.

It is with the Woodvilles, the Yetmans, the Heerings and the people of the small, mid-Dorset parish of Wenham, that this story is concerned.

PART ONE

A Woman from Holland

I

Eliza Woodville had promised her mother faithfully that she would be on her best behaviour at her brother's wedding. After all, next to the bride she had a most important role: she was chief bridesmaid, and such an onerous responsibility had sat heavily upon her for many weeks and caused her sleepless nights.

The fact was that Eliza was not the stuff of which good bridesmaids are made. Although a lady, she was not ladylike. She hated the whole idea of dressing up, being demure in church and holding the bride's bouquet. In truth she also hated taking second place, for everyone knew that all eyes would be on the one whose day it was: the bride. She would much rather that she had not been chosen; but as the only sister of the bridegroom her selection in a way was mandatory. As chief bridesmaid she was in charge of five others and two pages, who would hold the bride's long train as she walked down the aisle of Wenham parish church to become Lady Woodville.

Margaret Heering had been introduced to Guy Woodville by his uncle Prosper Martyn, who was a successful banker and businessman in the City of London. The Heerings were wealthy spice merchants from Amsterdam, customers of Martyns' Bank. The match was welcomed and was considered especially fortuitous because, at the time that Guy met Margaret, the fortunes of the Woodville family were at a low ebb and the very future of Pelham's Oak was at stake. The house was almost a ruin, both inside and out – evidence of years of neglect.

It was not unnatural that as Eliza stood behind her brother

and his bride during the wedding ceremony, conducted by the Rector, her thoughts should stray to this fact, because, although Margaret was by nature a cheerful and good-hearted girl, she was older than her groom and, despite a mass of Titian hair, she was otherwise astonishingly plain.

She had a large bony face with an especially protuberant nose and an overlarge mouth which, when she smiled, showed teeth too widely spaced. She had a long neck and a thin angular body, virtually bosomless like a boy's. She moved and even stood awkwardly as if overconscious of her lack of beauty and afraid that people were looking at her.

Guy, on the other hand, was so handsome he was god-like, almost beautiful, with perfect sculpted features. In addition he was tall and broad-shouldered, with dark brown hair that curled naturally and long luxuriant side whiskers. His eyes were brown, his complexion slightly swarthy. His bride seemed to clutch at his arm for support as they emerged from the church to face the world. Incredible as it seemed to her, the deed was done. They were man and wife.

Brides are traditionally considered beautiful, however, and that day Margaret's happiness made her almost beautiful too. As the bells pealed forth the sun broke out from behind clouds as if to cast on the pair, climbing into their carriage for the drive back to Pelham's Oak, a kind of benediction.

Riding in the carriage behind the bride, Eliza crossed her fingers and smiled kindly at Margaret's cousin Beatrix, who spoke very little English but who was much more attractive than the bride. What a pity, Eliza thought, that Guy hadn't chosen her.

The Woodville family seat was always referred to as Pelham's Oak rather than Pelham's Court, which was its proper name. It included a small hamlet, just a farm and a cluster of humble dwellings, which belonged to the big house. In the centre of the lawn stood a great oak tree, grown, so tradition had it, from an acorn from the oak in which Pelham Woodville's royal master lay hidden before his escape to France. The great oak

6

tree now dominated the lawn and was a feature on the skyline, visible for many miles around. Around this Pelham Woodville had started his mansion, which was continued and finished by his son Charles, named in honour of the Merry Monarch and later ennobled by him.

The mansion had originally been built of red Dorset brick, but an eighteenth-century Woodville faced it with stone from the nearby Chilmark quarry and gave it a porch and portico in keeping with the architectural tastes of that age of elegance. It was set on a hill between Blandford and Dorchester, and commanded a magnificent view of some of the prettiest countryside in Dorset. Across the River Wen atop a neighbouring hill, the little town of Wenham looked down upon the river which, just past Blandford, joined the Stour on its journey to the sea.

Anyone with a bird's eye view would have been astonished by the number of carriages which wended their way from the church, out of the town, over the bridge and along the winding road until they came to the great gates of Pelham's Oak and started to climb, a little more slowly and ponderously, up the hill to the house, which stood at the end of a long drive and was almost invisible from the road.

When his carriage arrived outside the portico, Guy was the first out. He put up a hand for his bride, whom he then scooped into his arms and carried over the threshold into the main hall, where the servants were lined up to greet the new mistress of the house.

One by one the other carriages drew up, allowed the occupants to alight and then drove away to await the end of the festivities. Henrietta, Lady Woodville, the bridegroom's mother, stood with the bride's parents, her brother Prosper Martyn, and the bride and groom welcoming the guests while Eliza arranged her charges, by now rather hot and thirsty, around the cascading folds of the bride's dress.

Then came the moment of great excitement when Mr Pond, the photographer from Wimborne, having mounted his elaborate camera on a tripod, disappeared under his cloth to photograph the bridal party, a memento which would adorn the drawing room wall for generations to come.

Eliza had been photographed before. First, with her mother, father and Guy when she and her brother were small and Mr Pond had first set up in business. Then she had posed, once again at the house, for her eighteenth birthday six months before. The result was rather stilted, rather artificial, its primness not seeming to capture the spirit of Eliza at all, and it had been banished to a room that was rarely used.

'May I change into my ordinary clothes now?' Eliza asked after Mr Pond had dismantled his apparatus and departed to develop the plates.

'Certainly not,' snapped her mother, flushed, not only from the exertions of the day, but also as a result of the glasses of champagne she had had recourse to in rather quick succession to soothe her nerves.

No longer would she be able to give commands which would instantly be obeyed, and expect to take precedence at all civic functions. Henceforward, she was the dowager, and would take second place to her son's wife. It was a prospect she viewed with dismay and alarm, and only now was its significance dawning on her.

Eliza knew what disturbed her mama and she made allowances for it. Since their father's death her mother had been anxious that Guy should marry: he must have an heir, but he must also marry well. The result was the inordinately plain but very cheerful and enormously wealthy Margaret Heering: a Dutch bride for an English baronet.

'Then *when* may I change into ordinary clothes?' Eliza persisted. 'You said "after the wedding", Mama.'

'I meant the wedding *day*. After the wedding *day*. Tonight there will be dancing.'

'I don't like dancing,' Eliza said petulantly.

Her mother sighed and, stopping a passing waiter, reached for yet another glass of the golden, restorative liquid that came from the banks on either side of the River Marne.

'If only you had been a boy!' she said, not for the first time. 'That's what you should have been.'

And that's what she would like to have been. Angrily Eliza tossed her curls, which had been twisted up in rags by her maid the night before and were now gathered up on top of her head in a cluster of long sausages. She hated them. She was about to turn her back on her mother and flounce away when the bride's father, Willem Heering, approached them, leaning jovially on the arm of the marriage broker.

Prosper Martyn was well named. The family were of humble origin. They had been boatmen from Poole who, during the revolution in France, had seized the opportunity to smuggle people and goods in and out of that beleaguered nation. Frequently it was dangerous work, but the greater the danger the higher the price. Soon the Martyns prospered, and they reflected their good fortune in naming the son who was to be the most successful of all.

Prosper, observing his niece in a petulant mood, put out a hand to bar her way.

'Now, Eliza, what is this? A temper tantrum on your brother's wedding day? Surely not!' he exclaimed.

'I want to get out of *this*!' Eliza said, tugging at her pale yellow muslin bridesmaid's dress. 'I want to put on my ordinary clothes. This makes me feel so foolish.'

Henrietta Woodville gave an exaggerated sigh and raised her eyes to the fine painted ceiling.

'I *said* she should have been a boy. If I say it once a day I say it ten times.'

'And yet she is a most attractive girl,' Willem Heering said. 'Why do you want to be a boy, Eliza?'

'Boys have more fun,' Eliza said. 'People think more of them. Who, in their right minds, would *want* to be a girl? Would you?'

Willem Heering seemed taken aback by the remark and looked for support to his friend, who was chuckling. Taking Eliza's hand, her uncle pressed it to his lips and smiled into her eyes.

'One day Eliza will learn the great advantages of being a woman: of being loved and protected, of never having to worry or want for anything. When you are in *love*, Eliza, you will forget any wish you ever had of being a boy in the joy of being a wife and mother.'

Eliza's face flamed with embarrassment and she wrenched her hand away.

'What . . . what *rubbish!*' she cried and went swiftly away to join the throng in the drawing room, many of whom were starting to drift on to the lawn now that the sun had established itself and the clouds had gone.

The two men and Henrietta watched the departing figure, rather at a loss for words, and then Prosper turned and shrugged his shoulders.

'She doesn't get any better, Henrietta. You can't have her behaving like that in public. I think she should be sent away to a finishing school to learn good manners. Willem here is a friend, he will understand. But others would be shocked. I am a little shocked myself to find her still so undisciplined.'

'Is that meant as a criticism of me, brother?' Henrietta asked, her eyes narrowing. 'If so . . .'

'Not at all, my dear, not at all,' Prosper said hastily. 'I know you have done all you can to make Eliza as decorous and genteel as a well brought up young lady should be. In manner and looks she is the pinnacle of refinement, a credit to you and poor Matthew. But this temper of hers – ' Prosper frowned ' – no man will tolerate it. We shall have a spinster on our hands unless something is done about Eliza.'

Spinster – everyone shuddered at the dreaded word. What worse fate could befall a young girl than to remain unmarried? Willem Heering shuddered perhaps the longest, because he had almost despaired of finding a husband for his adored Margaret, now twenty-nine years old. Long past marriageable age. The trouble was that she had resembled her dear mother whom, although he had come to love her very much, he had married for motives that had more to do with commercial advantage than with love.

Margaret, his only daughter. He would have done everything in his power to make her happy, and, when it came to it, he had. He had not felt demeaned at using money to buy his daughter a bridegroom. What luck it was to have chanced on the well-born but impoverished Woodville family. He had saved the Woodvilles, and they had saved his daughter from the years of loneliness, the lack of fulfilment that only unmarried women could know.

But as he looked at the bridal pair surrounded by their friends and the Woodville relations at the far end of the room, he felt a *frisson*, a moment of doubt. How could such a handsome, well-born young man possibly love his daughter? Would he remain faithful to her and make her happy? Margaret was clearly in love, but was Guy?

John Yetman had spent some time walking round the reception rooms admiring the paintings, which were old, and the splendid decorations, which were new: the painted ceilings freshly restored, gold leaf resplendent on the intricate cornice designs; the lozenges, *quatre foils* and heraldic emblems of the Woodville family. Some eighteen months had been spent on the restoration of the house, a fact of which he was well aware because most of the work had been done by his men. John was a master thatcher but also a general builder, though he no longer soiled his hands with the mundane tasks of his trade. Yetman's had become the largest firm of builders in much of the district between Wenham and the coast. He had offices in Yeovil, Blandford and Poole, and his business interests crossed the county boundaries.

A generation ago anyone connected with trade would never have been invited to a social occasion such as this. But times were changing, everyone knew that. The rich man remained in his castle, the poor man at his gate, but in between there was a mixture, a confusion of classes and class consciousness that had not occurred before.

Even now it was doubtful whether John Yetman and his family would have been invited to the Woodville wedding were it not for the important civic positions he held in the community. He was a Justice of the Peace, Chairman of the Parish Council and patron of many a good cause connected with the community: its widows, its orphans, its malefactors – fortunately few – waifs and strays.

Lady Woodville was tempted to take evasive action when she observed him approaching her with his family, but her brother immediately stretched out his hand in welcome and drew him by the arm towards his sister.

'My dear, may I introduce Mr Yetman?'

'Of course I know Mr Yetman,' Lady Woodville said, graciously offering him her gloved hand. 'He has several times been on inspection while his men were working on this house.'

'To your satisfaction I hope, my lady?' Mr Yetman said unctuously, propelling forward his beaming spouse and two comely young women. 'May I introduce my wife, Mrs Yetman and my daughters-in-law, Judith and Adeline?'

'How do you do?' Lady Woodville's touch was even lighter, her tone remote. It was possible to deduce from it that Mr and Mrs Yetman would never be invited to tea or any private social occasion held in the house.

'And my sons Robert and Hesketh, my daughter Agnes.'

Was there no end to them? Lady Woodville touched fingers, noting as she did so that the Yetmans, despite their lowly origins, had produced a fine-looking brood of children. None of them resembled country yokels who made their living thatching and toiling. Agnes was not only remarkably pretty but very fashionably dressed in the latest creations, not from Wenham or Blandford, or even Bournemouth but, surely, London?

The family were introduced to Willem Heering who, having been brought up in the traditions of true democracy, shook all warmly by the hand and fell into an earnest discussion of business with Mr Yetman, who still retained his soft Dorset vowels.

Willem Heering was interested in all aspects of business and so was Mr Yetman. The two wandered off, leaving Lady Woodville attempting to converse without appearing patronising with Mrs Yetman, her daughters-in-law and her daughter, while the sons discussed country matters with Prosper Martyn in an atmosphere of easy familiarity.

'What a lovely bridesmaid Eliza made, my lady.' Mrs Yetman tactfully eschewed mention of the bride. 'You won't have *her* on your hands for long.'

'Alas, I'm afraid we shall.' Lady Woodville gave a slight sigh. 'My daughter is a tomboy. Surely you have seen her riding over the fields dressed in men's breeches? Well, if you have not, everyone else has.'

Mrs Yetman permitted herself a smirk.

'There *is* talk, my lady . . . but a very pretty sight, I'm told.'

'You see how *really* pretty, how *feminine* my daughter can be if she wishes.' Lady Woodville pointed across the room. 'But what man of refinement would want to marry a girl who wears breeches?' She then raised her hand in the direction of the French windows, where two friends of hers happened to be conversing. 'Please excuse me, Mrs Yetman. I have just spotted some people I haven't seen for years.'

She bowed graciously, and Mrs Yetman and her daughter stood back, to be joined by the two Yetman sons, who appeared satisfied with their conversation with Prosper Martyn.

'He's thinking of buying a farm hereabouts,' Hesketh, the elder, said. 'I told him we'd keep an eye open.'

'So near his sister. You surprise me,' their mother said, but she had her eyes on Agnes, who was looking enviously at the bridegroom, circling the room with his bride on his arm.

Agnes Yetman was one of the prettiest girls in Wenham and she knew it; but even she, pretty, accomplished, able to sing and sew, ride and dance, had never had a chance with the glamorous, dashing Sir Guy. He was known to fancy ladies, but only of a certain kind and these he met in London. Everyone in Wenham knew that his marriage to the Dutch woman was a marriage of convenience.

But one day she would outstrip the new Lady Woodville, Agnes thought. One day she would do even better than Sir Guy, and her house would be even bigger and finer. Accomplished she might be, but the overwhelming yearning in her heart was not simply for love. It was for power and the desire to blot out from her life the mean and humble origins of her parents, which still betrayed them by their accents, their lack of fine manners. Agnes had been sent to a good school; yet she had too many memories of her father and mother looking countrified and out of place among the well-bred and genteel parents of her fellow pupils. Oh, how Agnes yearned to be thought genteel too. One day that wish would come true. She knew it.

Interested in everyone, everything, yet a little shy, Euphemia Monk stood on the far side of the great cream and gold reception room close to the Reverend Austin Lamb, Rector of the parish, who had performed the ceremony. He stood there in his clerical dress, complete with gaiters, a benign smile on his normally stern features, his eyes darting over the assembly as if checking on the numbers of his congregation eminent and respectable enough to have received an invitation to the grandest wedding in the district since Guy's father, Sir Matthew, had married pretty, wealthy Henrietta Martyn.

Euphemia Monk was also a wealthy spinster, and a regular worshipper at the church of St Mark. Her house faced the Rectory, and she was a particular friend of the Rector's wife, whom she assisted in many parochial duties.

She was in her early thirties, a comely and intelligent woman, but her life was almost ruined by her shyness, her consciousness of her position as a single woman who had been left a large house and a small fortune by her scholarly father, who had died the previous year. Euphemia's mother had died when she was born, and she had therefore been particularly attached to her father, and was desolated by his early death. At that time of bereavement the Lambs had been of great comfort to her, and she became even more religious and devoted to the church.

The invitation from the Woodvilles had been unexpected. She didn't really know them and was not in their circle. But a number of surprising names had been included in the wedding list, as though the family wished to rid itself of its reputation for being snobbish and exclusive, to be seen to broaden its horizons.

For weeks Euphemia had agonised about her dress, her style of hat, and now she stood wishing that she were not here but safe at home.

The Reverend Lamb was encouraging, expansive, protective of his charge, of whose nervousness he was well aware. At the best of times he was not a very perceptive man, but he was genuinely fond of Euphemia, having known her father well. Theobald Monk had not feared God, which had worried the Rector a good deal as his parishioner drew near to death. Yet seldom had he seen a holier moment, and he had closed the eyes of the dead man with wonder in his own and a sense of bewilderment. Theobald had seldom attended church, so why had the grace of God appeared to touch him at his last hour?

He turned to his timid charge and said encouragingly: 'Now, Euphemia, why don't you say hello to the Yetmans?'

'I don't really know them, Mr Lamb.' Euphemia pressed her handkerchief to her moist palms and screwed up her eyes in agony.

'Of course you know them!' The Rector beckoned to John Yetman, who was taking his leave of Willem Heering, an expression of satisfaction on his face.

'Good day, Rector.' John Yetman shook him warmly by the hand. 'What a very pleasant occasion, very successful if I may say so. *And* a beautiful sermon, Rector.' Mr Yetman briefly raised his eyes to heaven. 'It almost moved my wife to tears.'

'Oh, and it moved me too,' Euphemia said with fervour. 'The passage from the Scripture was *most* beautifully chosen, Mr Lamb.' Euphemia's bashfulness had vanished as she clasped her hands together.

'"Who can find a virtuous woman? For her price is far above rubies,"' the Rector intoned. 'Proverbs chapter 31, verse 10.' He knitted his fierce brows and looked steadfastly at the bride, who was being introduced by her husband to Lord and Lady Mount, old friends and near neighbours of the Woodville family. 'Yes indeed. I am *very* surprised at Guy's choice, but I approve of it. The new Lady Woodville looks a *most* worthy woman who will be an adornment to the family.'

'How nice to see you out and about again, Miss Monk,' John Yetman said, looking at Euphemia kindly. 'Your dear father would be pleased to see you moving about in society again. How charming you look today.'

Euphemia blushed at the unexpected compliment and put her hands to her face.

'Really, Mr Yetman. When you compare my looks to those of your daughter, Agnes, there is no comparison.'

'I do not *compare* them, my dear,' John Yetman replied. 'You are different types of women. But I may pay you a compliment, may I not?'

'Certainly you may,' the Rector said robustly on behalf of his timid charge. 'But take care that Mrs Yetman doesn't hear you.'

'Oh, my wife is not jealous.' John burst out laughing. 'She has far too good a hold of me for jealousy to have any part. Besides, I am old enough to be this good lady's father.' John bowed to Euphemia. 'I do hope we shall have the pleasure of entertaining you in our home, Miss Monk, now that your mourning is over.'

Euphemia Monk was too unnerved to reply.

'A little mouse,' Catherine Yetman said dismissively as soon as her husband joined her, her eyes still fixed on Euphemia. 'I never saw anyone so timid.'

'She was overprotected by her father.' John Yetman pursed his lips. 'But for him she would have been married long ago. He never let her out of his sight. Now it is too late. Then she had to mourn him for well over twelve months and cut herself off from society completely. I like Euphemia Monk,' he said firmly. 'We must ask her to dinner with the Rector and Mrs Lamb.'

'Very good, dear,' Catherine Yetman said with a sigh, taking her husband's arm. 'I wish we could find a husband for Agnes. She looks about her too freely. People will talk.'

'Nonsense.' Yetman patted her arm as he exchanged smiles with a fellow member on the Parish Council. 'There is *plenty* of time for Agnes. She should be in no hurry to find a mate. She will be well endowed and can afford to pick and choose. *I* would like her to travel a little, take more time for books and serious pastimes. She is too frivolous. In time, I promise you, Agnes will make a very good match.'

John Yetman fell silent as he and his wife continued their stroll through the crowded room, conscious of the importance of the occasion, of seeing and being seen, stopping to greet the many similarly honoured guests they knew.

Eventually the call went out that the bride and groom were cutting the cake, and everyone hurried into the dining room to participate in the joyful proceedings.

John Yetman, who had many things to be thankful for, tried hard to forget his immediate worries and enjoy what was left of the day.

Just after five the bride and bridegroom left to take the ferry from Portsmouth for a honeymoon on the Continent. The wedding night they would spend in Wimborne. The guests, in a flurry of excitement, had gathered on the steps of the porch and in the drive to see them off.

Margaret had changed into a travelling outfit of green moiré silk which, though a little unsuitable for the time of year, looked attractive with a matching toque which set off the colour of her hair, undoubtedly her greatest asset. She wore a fur stole against the cold. The bridegroom wore a grey suit, stiff collar, and a pearl-grey tie, not unlike the dress suit he had worn for his wedding. He carried a top hat which he waved to the crowd as they streamed forward to throw confetti over the departing carriage.

As the carriage rounded the drive Margaret hurled her bouquet into the throng. She had in fact aimed it at Eliza, who carefully sidestepped it so that it fell to the ground. For a moment it lay there until the youngest bridesmaid, Daisy Watmough, cousin of the Woodvilles, started forward and scooped it up, much to the amusement of the crowd.

'It was meant for you, Miss Woodville,' Mrs Yetman, who was standing beside her, said meaningfully. The two moved back from the crowd, some of whose members had begun to scamper down the drive after the departing carriage. 'I noticed you deliberately did not pick it up.'

'In fact the little girl who wanted it most got it.' Eliza looked at the happy smile on ten-year-old Daisy's face.

'But surely she is a little young to contemplate marriage?' Mrs Yetman ventured.

'So am I,' Eliza said with a bold glance. 'I have not the slightest intention of settling down, I assure you.' She looked around at the guests, many of whom were now strolling back up the drive having watched the carriage drive through the gates. Some were preparing to take their departure, some were accepting a fresh glass of champagne and looked as though they were settling in for the evening.

Relations and close family friends had been invited for dinner and a dance afterwards, for which the staff were already actively preparing, bustling in and out of the great rooms, discreetly rearranging furniture and removing soiled plates and glasses.

'Did Ryder not come today, Mrs Yetman?' Eliza ventured in the tone of one who cared little one way or the other. 'I noticed that your other two sons and Agnes were here.' In fact Agnes had been particularly active in trying to spot the point to which the bride would throw her bouquet, but had completely misjudged it.

'Oh no,' Mrs Yetman replied with a smile, 'Ryder doesn't like this kind of thing. He says he can make better use of his time.'

Much later that night, after the dinner and the dance which followed, Eliza lay awake, head on her arm, gazing at the trees of the park silhouetted against the moon. She was too nervous, too excited, too tired to sleep. Once again she had disgraced herself in public and, once again, been reprimanded for it. With justification. In her behaviour everyone saw a petulant schoolgirl rather than a young woman on the brink of adulthood. Time and time again she vowed to reform, and time and time again she failed. She was too impetuous, too wilful, too undisciplined. Unless she grew up, she realised, she would be tied to her mother's apron strings for ever.

But maybe there was an excuse. The last few weeks and months had been nerve-racking and also exciting. At times they were almost unbearable for the two women who knew that their lives were on the point of being changed, almost certainly for good. They were both to be supplanted, their place in the house taken by a stranger; a woman they liked but hardly knew. Not only a stranger but a foreigner: a woman from Holland with Continental ways.

Neither of them knew of the conversation between Guy and his uncle's friend Willem Heering which had taken place some eighteen months before in London.

It had been a very serious conversation, by way of being a commercial transaction, and Guy emerged as a partner in his uncle's business, and a man who had promised to become engaged to be married. When the announcement was made public a swarm of workmen descended on Pelham's Oak and began to restore and refurbish it inside and out in a way that had not been done since Charles Woodville had a small country house of the Stuart period turned into a great mansion worthy of a man of title and wealth.

Among them had been Ryder Yetman, acting as his father's foreman in charge of the work force.

Eliza had not been encouraged to hang around the workmen who gutted the house, nor had she wanted to. But Ryder had noticed her, and she could not help noticing him. He was a tall, strapping fellow who towered over most of his powerful workmen. He had not worn work clothes but a suit and tie, and he had always ridden to work on horseback. They scarcely ever exchanged a word in the long period of time it had taken to restore the house for Guy's wedding; but Eliza had promised herself that, when it was all over, maybe at the wedding, she would snatch the chance to talk to him, even if only to annoy her mother.

Maybe, she thought, that's why she had been in such a bad mood all day. Maybe the absence of Ryder, the fact that he hadn't even wanted to be there to see her, was the true reason for her ill temper.

Eliza got out of bed and wandered restlessly to the window, throwing it open so that the cool night breeze could fan her face. The soft tender buds on the trees emerging into leaf seemed to make an intricate lattice pattern against the sky and, at a distance, lit by the full moon, she could see the silhouette of Wenham standing on the hill above the River Wen.

She wondered why Ryder hadn't come, and if he lived with his family in the house in the middle of the town. He was quite a lot older than she was, fair with a rugged, weatherbeaten face, his hair bleached by the sun and constant exposure to the air. She, on the other hand, was very dark. Her skin was almost olive-hued because the Martyns had Portuguese blood in their veins. Eliza's straight black hair curved over her ears and flowed down her back when she loosened it. She knew that, with her dark colouring, her straight black brows and tawny eyes, she was striking, and for some years now, both in London and in the country, she had been aware of the glances that men gave her. Today at the wedding she knew that more eyes were on her than on the bride. But she was not interested except, just perhaps, in one.

And he had not been there.

2

John Yetman's grandfather had been an agricultural worker on one of the farms belonging to the Woodville estate. He had married a scullery maid from Pelham's Oak, and the eldest of their nine children had been Thomas, who rebelled against his family's poverty-stricken life. He forsook the land and went as an apprentice to a builder. In time he persuaded his brother Roger to join him, but the remainder of his siblings faded into insignificance, content merely to continue with menial work and swell the numbers of the population in which they lived.

Thomas had been born in 1800, the dawn of a thrusting new century which was to bring his native country great prosperity but also, among the less privileged classes, appalling poverty and degradation as well. The nineteenth century was an age of contrasts, but the young Thomas, born with the century, knew on which side of the divide he was going to be.

In 1821, a fully fledged master builder, he set up business in Blandford with his brother Roger, although Thomas was to continue as the stronger partner.

Five years later Thomas married the daughter of the man who had taught him his craft, who gave the young couple as a wedding present a house near the banks of the Wen half way up the hill that led from the river to the town at the top.

Riversmead was a fine house built of warm Marnhull stone and, as his business prospered, Thomas extended the house and made outbuildings for his carriage and horses. He had three sons: John, George and Christopher. George died of tuberculosis when he was still a boy, and Christopher tried a number of trades but became master of none, preferring to drift around the country and travel abroad. Occasionally he turned up at Wenham asking his brother for a bed for a few nights and, inevitably, a handout, which the generous, forgiving John, who took after his hard-working father, always gave him. But Christopher never settled and soon he was off until, like the proverbial bad penny, he turned up again weeks, months or even years later.

John had sometimes feared that his own eldest son, Ryder, would take after his Uncle Christopher, the family black sheep, the ne'er do well. The men were similar to look at: broad and muscular, tall and handsome, attractive to women.

However, Ryder's trouble seemed that he had too much ambition rather than too little. He wanted to achieve too many things. He ran away to sea at fifteen and mastered the mysteries of sail, even obtaining a mate's ticket. But he abandoned that in order to follow in his father's footsteps when both his brothers, who had shown academic prowess at school (which Ryder had not), decided on professional careers. Hesketh took up articles with a firm of solicitors in Bournemouth, and brother Robert, who was good at figures, went into a bank before starting up in business on his own.

Ryder, clever with his hands, showed great aptitude as a builder and quickly mastered all the aspects of the trade: brick-laying, roofing, thatching, plumbing, plastering and painting.

Then, out of the blue, he announced that he wished to travel again, to become a soldier, and he spent three years in the army in South Africa before being invalided out after fighting in the Zulu war.

At twenty-eight, he had packed a great deal into a short life. Since his return he had been working for his father again, but, somehow, it was apparent that his heart was not in it. He was restless, and it seemed that once more he might be off on his travels, when suddenly, to his family's relief, he announced his engagement to the miller's daughter, who was a schoolmistress in Yeovil. The family sighed with relief.

Ryder obviously wanted to settle down. Months before he met Maude he had rented a cottage on the Woodville estate from Sir Guy and was renovating it in his spare time.

John Yetman was a proud man – proud of his wife, his children, his capacity for hard work; proud above all of himself. He had extended the house by the river as his family had grown, six children in all, of whom two had died in infancy.

Now he stood by the window in his drawing room, his brow furrowed, his eyes brooding over the waters of the river which flowed past the bottom of the garden, about a hundred yards away. In his hands there was a letter which announced that his shiftless brother was once more going to pay the family a visit.

At that moment the maid appeared to announce that dinner would soon be served, and John put the letter in his pocket and turned away from the window as the maid stood back to show in Ryder with his fiancée, Maude, whom he had gone to fetch from the mill.

'Maude, my dear,' John said with pleasure, going up to plant a chaste kiss on her brow. 'How nice to see you. You look charming as usual. You have arrived just in time to dissipate my bad temper. Now let's have a glass of sherry before we go in to dinner. Ryder, would you see where your mother is?'

'Mother's downstairs in the hall, Father.' Ryder went to the great mahogany sideboard and removed the stopper from the sherry decanter. 'Some poor person from the parish wants a bed for the night.'

'And no doubt she'll find him one,' his father sighed. 'She can never turn anyone away.'

'It's a woman, Father, a vagrant.'

'Ah!' John Yetman raised his eyes piously to the ceiling. 'It will have to be the workhouse at Blandford. How I wish those poor creatures . . . Well.' John turned as his wife came bustling in. She was a small woman who had been remarkably pretty and dainty in her youth. She was still comely, but she had grown rotund with the years. 'And what have you done with the poor creature, my dear?'

'Given her a straw bed in the stables, as usual,' Catherine said briskly. 'And tomorrow Robin will take her to Blandford.'

'How does she come to be here, Mother?' Ryder passed his father a glass of sherry. The other he kept for himself as neither of the women would accept a drink, though his mother enjoyed a glass of port after her meal on Sundays.

'Some tale. I didn't understand it. It is usually the same – a cruel father or husband, or maybe no husband at all and a baby.' She smiled kindly at Maude. 'This is the sort of thing you will have to do, my dear, in time. Human nature is of infinite variety.'

'How do you mean, Mrs Yetman?' Maude enquired with a pleasant smile, taking her seat beside her father-in-law-to-be.

'When *you* are mistress of this house . . .'

'Not for a *long* time, I hope, Mrs Yetman . . .'

'Or *any* house.'

'Yes, Ryder, now that you are soon to be married you must start finding a proper house for yourself.' His father suddenly seemed struck by the thought.

'But I have time, Father.' Ryder sat down next to his fiancée and crossed his legs casually.

Catherine, glancing from one to the other, looked troubled.

'If you mean the cottage, dearest, I'm afraid *I* am not going to live in it,' Maude said firmly. 'I have told you that, but you insist on continuing to repair it. What will you do? Live there by yourself?'

'Perhaps.' Ryder gave her a detached, almost indifferent smile.

'Dinner is on the table, sir, ma'am.' The maid came in again and made the announcement with a bob.

John drained his glass and looked at his watch.

'Is there any news of our Agnes, Maisie?'

'The carriage is not back, sir. Robin took her to Sherborne.'

'Then we must begin without her.' John tapped his watch and popped it back in his waistcoat pocket. 'Come.' He pointed towards the door, and his wife rose and preceded him, Maude, her shoulders very stiff and erect, following. John put a hand on Ryder's shoulder and, as the ladies went through the hall, held him back.

'What *is* the matter with you, Ryder?' he hissed in his ear.

'The matter, Father? I don't understand you.' Ryder looked surprised.

'Of course Maude doesn't want to live in a farm labourer's cottage! You seem to be doing your best to discourage her.'

'She liked it when she first saw it, Father.' Ryder looked solemnly at his father from under thick, fair brows. 'But that was before I asked her to marry me. She only changed her mind afterwards.'

'I don't blame her.'

'It would seem that she set out to catch me, and when she thought the hook was firmly in my mouth she started to dictate her own terms in order to decide whether I should be knocked on the head or thrown back into the river.'

'Don't be so ridiculous,' his father hissed again. 'Maude is very suitable, and it is you who would be the fool if you let her go. Besides, you need to settle down.'

The two men crossed the hall together to find that the women were already seated. Catherine looked enquiringly at them as father and son sat down on their different sides of the table.

'Is anything the matter?' she asked.

'Nothing.' John Yetman shook his head and the maid moved slowly forward to serve the soup.

John and Catherine Yetman were people of the town, retaining their Dorset accents and, in many ways, their country manners and upbringing. Though her husband was ambitious they remained a relatively unpretentious couple and, compared to the Woodvilles, their establishment was neither large nor grand; but, for Wenham, it was still considerable. There was no butler or footman, but there were three indoor maids, a cook, and various outdoor staff who lived in the outbuildings: a coachman and his wife, two gardeners, a groom and a general boy.

'Miss Eliza Woodville asked after you at the wedding,' Catherine said as they began eating their soup.

'Oh yes, how *was* the wedding?' Maude cried excitedly before Ryder, who seemed astonished by the remark, could reply. Maude's demeanour was invariably grave and she smiled little, but the subject of the wedding clearly animated her.

'It was the most wonderful occasion.' Catherine sat back and sighed. 'I never saw such splendour, or expect to again. Certainly *your* wedding . . .'

'My father could never afford anything like *that*,' Maude said reproachfully.

'Oh, I don't mean on that scale at *all*, dear,' Catherine cried. 'The Woodvilles are the Woodvilles, and he has married money.'

'A lot of it,' John agreed. 'The Martyns were wealthy, but Sir Matthew got through that fortune in no time. Let's hope there is sufficient for this one to satisfy young Sir Guy.'

'Oh, I think he *will* settle down.' Catherine nodded sagely, and was about to continue when the door flew open and Agnes, out of breath, hurried in.

'Oh, forgive me, Mother, Father.' She made a little bob to each of her parents in turn. 'A wheel of the carriage broke and . . .'

'It is quite all right, my dear. Calm yourself.' Her mother, who was an imperturbable lady, nodded to the maid, who brought Agnes's soup. 'We knew Robin had not returned with the carriage and we did not worry. We were just talking about the Woodville wedding.'

'I thought you might be talking about Ryder's wedding,' Agnes said archly. 'When is that to be?'

'I think it should be soon.' John Yetman sat back and started to crumble his bread nervously. 'The sooner the better. Ryder is not young.'

'Twenty-eight is not old, Father,' Ryder protested laughing.

'I had two children by the time I was your age, young man. Tomorrow we will set about finding a decent establishment for you. Oh – I forgot.' An expression of annoyance crossed his face again, and he drew out a letter from his pocket. 'My brother Christopher is arriving at Blandford station. I shall have to meet him.'

'Oh *dear*.' Catherine looked crestfallen. 'I did so hope . . . He was only here a month or two ago.'

'He *is* my brother, dear.'

'Of course.' Catherine folded her hands and nodded for the maid to clear, her attitude apparently one of wifely respect and obedience. 'Only I hope he does not stay long.'

'Poor man, this *is* his home,' John protested. 'The only home he has.'

'Then I wish he would find another. I wish *he* would find a wife.'

And this time she did not attempt to conceal the exasperation in her voice.

After dinner Ryder and Maude went for a walk by the river while he smoked a cigarette. The couple had been encouraged to set out alone. John Yetman had gone, as usual, to his study to examine building plans, and Catherine and Agnes either sewed or read in the drawing room until it was time to go to bed.

For a long time the young couple strolled in silence, and Ryder wondered, as he so often did, why there was so little desire in his breast for the woman by his side. Maybe she wondered the same thing.

During his three years' service in South Africa, the only white women he saw were the wives of the officers. As a ranker Ryder had had no access to women because the only ones available had been the native women who serviced the troops, and Ryder had a natural fastidiousness about this as well as a horror of disease.

Though older, Maude Brough had been a friend of Agnes, and she was one of the first young, unattached women he saw when he returned home a year ago with a wound in his leg which was slow to heal. With her brown hair, parted in the middle, and her fair complexion, she had been reasonably attractive, and he felt he wanted to be married, to settle down, and the combination of emotions made him think, or imagine, he loved her.

Three months ago he had proposed. Maude agreed immediately, but almost at once they had begun to quarrel. Now there was tension in the air again.

'You're quite determined about the cottage, aren't you, Ryder?' Maude said after a while in an effort to bridge the constraint between them. She wanted Ryder – any woman would – and had boldly set her cap at him as soon as she saw him.

'My dear, you knew about it when we became engaged,' Ryder replied.

'Naturally I thought you would give it up.'

'But you told me you liked the cottage.' Ryder's voice was icily polite.

'I said it was a very pretty cottage, Ryder, in an attractive position . . . And yet . . .' By the light of the moon he could see the anguished expression on her face, and he felt both deceived and a deceiver.

Oh, if he could only unsay that proposal spoken in haste three months before!

'And yet I hoped,' she went on, as he gave her no help, 'as we *were* to be married, *you* would change your mind.'

'You want a bigger house, too.' His tone was derisive.

'Why, Ryder . . . I would have thought . . . the cottage is totally unsuitable. It is miles from anywhere. At least in the first year of our marriage – ' her words were heavy with meaning ' – I would wish to continue teaching. It was my hope that perhaps we could find somewhere between here and Yeovil.'

'Yet all those "hopes" you did not express at the time, Maude. This is the first time I have heard you say you wish to continue teaching.'

'Well – ' fretfully she twined and untwined her fingers ' – we did not know each other very well.'

'And still don't, if you ask me.'

'Oh, Ryder that will come. I'm sure of it.' And, as if fearful of saying too much, she tucked her arm in his and they walked silently back to the house.

After all, she didn't want to lose him.

Ryder was a young, healthy man, now recovered from his wounds, who normally slept well at night. But that night he slept fitfully.

He knew now that he was engaged to someone he did not love. He felt she knew it too. He also doubted if her feelings for him were any more passionate than his for her. Yet who would be the first to speak? Would they say nothing and, victims of circumstances, of convention, marry and spend their days in mutual antagonism, or, as she said, might love perhaps come?

Some people said it did.

Ryder got out of bed and looked for his cigarettes in the pocket of his coat, a thing he seldom did at night. He lit one and, half opening the window, leaned out, breathing the fresh night air. At times like this he was reminded of the torrid heat of Africa and, sometimes, his eyes closed and his heart pounded as though he were in the grip of a nightmare.

Sometimes he thought he was a man who had left his soul in Africa. Yet even as that thought came to him again, he knew he was wrong. It was not that war had made him incapable of feeling love. His passions had been woken, but the object of them was unattainable – now, and forevermore.

The house was hidden from view, but he turned his head in the direction from which the gentle breeze blew, down the hill all the way from Pelham's Oak.

Henrietta Woodville gazed around the elegant bedroom she had occupied since her husband, Matthew, had brought her to Pelham's Oak as a bride. He was a handsome man but, even then, he had been an invalid; a sickly person who was constantly visiting the Continent in search of a cure for his bronchial troubles. That he had lived as long as he had was largely thanks to her; that she had borne him two strong, beautiful children was largely thanks to her and the blood of the Martyns, yeoman stock.

Henrietta had been ten years younger than her husband and now, at fifty, she felt in her prime. Yet here she was, being cast aside as a widow, and not a wealthy one at that. Her inheritance was gone and she, along with her son and daughter, was dependent on the money of the woman who was supplanting her.

Her emotions were mixed because, on the one hand, she was grateful that the financial burden had been eased. However, she also knew that this marked the end of a long era. She wandered slowly over to the large bay window that gave such a beautiful view and looked at the valley, when her attention was caught by a rapid movement in the field below. There was her daughter, that tomboy, looking for all the world like a boy in her brother's old shirt and riding breeches, practising her jumps over the hurdles, each one a little higher than the one before. Well, all *that* would have to come to an end, and not before time. Margaret couldn't keep everyone, even though her fortune was considerable. She would not even *wish* to contribute to the upkeep of her sister-in-law. Whether she liked it or not, Eliza would have to be found a mate.

Or perhaps she should be sent back to school as her uncle, normally an equable, even indulgent man, had darkly hinted. Who would care to marry a girl with no money and such a violent temper – one who flouted convention and wore men's clothes?

Eliza, who should have been her mainstay now, seemed indifferent to the change in circumstances. How long did she think her brother and his new wife would tolerate having her in their house, doing exactly as she pleased, refusing to conform, demanding her own way in everything?

Henrietta looked at the fob watch which hung from her waist and gave an exclamation. Eliza was still riding her horse and Prosper Martyn was due for tea. Henrietta had particularly asked Eliza to look nice today as her uncle had something important to say. Just then Henrietta saw Prosper's light carriage bowling up the drive, drawn by two frisky horses and driven by himself.

A little flustered, Henrietta hurried downstairs to welcome him.

Prosper Martyn was the youngest of Henrietta's three brothers. She herself, the only girl, was the eldest of the family and there were ten years between herself and Prosper. Despite the age difference she was closer to Prosper than to her other brothers because he had remained a bachelor and they were married men with families. Since Matthew's death Henrietta had come to depend on her youngest brother a lot: he seemed to have a fount of wisdom, in addition to his natural abilities as a businessman.

Although Prosper had been the lover of many women in his forty years, he had never found one without whom he could not lead his life. He was still searching, if search it could be called, for that one special woman who most of his acquaintances now doubted would ever come.

When Henrietta got downstairs she found him in the drawing room, hands in his pockets, staring ruminatively out of the low bow window. Henrietta briskly pulled the bell for tea then joined him. She knew quite well what had caught his attention.

Prosper greeted his sister with a peck on the cheek, but his face remained thoughtful and unsmiling. He was a man of medium height, dark haired with long side whiskers, and he looked older than he was. His air of authority was instantly recognisable, and as instantly obeyed. People respected him, some feared him, yet those who served him and knew him best loved him.

Prosper had always regarded his only sister's children as his own. His two brothers had moved out of the county: one lived with his family in London, the other in Yorkshire, and Prosper was not close to their children. But he loved Guy and Eliza, and he worried about them.

He worried more particularly about Eliza. He felt that a

31

girl with such beauty, but undisciplined and untamed, could only come to harm. He had no idea where she had got her unorthodoxy from. It was a mystery to him.

'There *is* a man,' he said, putting his arm around Henrietta's waist, 'who might do as a husband for our Eliza.'

'Oh?' Henrietta's troubled countenance cleared and she put her hand over Prosper's.

'He is wealthy and he is a lord. In many ways he is ideal *if* she would have him.'

'*She* have *him*!' Henrietta exclaimed. 'She should jump at the chance.'

'Ah, but we know she won't, don't we?' Prosper looked affectionately at his sister, and as the maid entered with the tea tray they fell silent and continued to watch the skilful horsewoman outside putting her mount through its paces in the field next to the house.

There was no doubt that Eliza was an excellent rider. She cleared the fences easily and neither rider nor horse ever came to any harm. She didn't expect the overworked grooms to do everything and looked after her horses herself. If they were ill she nursed them with the anxious love of a mother.

Now she was putting her horse through the complicated steps of the dressage, each manoeuvre carefully planned and faultlessly executed. When she reached the edge of the field, unaware that she was being observed, she gave an unladylike whoop, stuck her heels gently into her horse's flank and flew through the gate and out of sight.

'His name is Lord Thornwell,' Prosper said, turning from the window after the maid had left the room. 'He is a merchant banker, a man of great charm with a town house and an estate in Leicestershire. He farms and he hunts. Eliza would like him. They would have a lot in common.'

'But – ' Henrietta raised an eyebrow as she went over to the table to pour the tea ' – there is a "but", isn't there, Prosper? I can tell by your tone of voice. Is he very ugly?'

'He is, in fact, considered a good-looking man – but he is fifty.'

'*Fifty!*' Henrietta cried. 'Why, that is my age.'

'Exactly.'

'Then perhaps he will do for *me*?' She smiled archly at her brother. 'Perhaps you should introduce me to Lord Thornwell and then I will not be a trouble to my children or you any longer.'

'Alas.' Prosper gave her a sympathetic smile. 'His lordship had the misfortune to lose his only son two years ago. The lad died of consumption at the age of fifteen. He is very anxious to have an heir to inherit his ancient title and considerable wealth. I fear, my dear, that in that respect you would be of little use to him.'

Henrietta, still smiling, passed her brother one of the fine porcelain teacups.

'I was only teasing. I don't think I could ever marry again, or change the style of life I'm used to here.'

'But when Guy and Margaret return?' Prosper sat down opposite his sister, taking two sandwiches from the plate she passed him.

'I believe they're going to spend a lot of time in London. The house in Mayfair is being refurbished. Guy, of course, now has his business there, thanks to you and Willem. I wonder if he will take to it?'

'He'd better,' Prosper said grimly. 'We have invested a lot in that young man. He carries all our hopes.'

Henrietta said nothing but continued to pour the tea. Suddenly there was a crash as the front door slammed, and with the force of a small hurricane Eliza rushed into the drawing room and dropped to her knees in front of the tea table.

'*Starving*,' she cried, cramming a sandwich into her mouth. 'Oh, Mother, I saw . . .'

'Kindly do not talk with your mouth full,' her mother said reprovingly. 'And what is the meaning of coming to tea in your riding breeches, Eliza? I have forbidden you to wear those unseemly garments. For a *woman* . . .'

Eliza waited obediently until she had finished what was in her mouth and then said in a ringing tone: 'I am *not* a woman,

33

Mother. I am a girl. You're always telling me that: I'm a girl, a child . . .'

'Well, you behave like one . . .'

'Therefore I dress like one. Good afternoon, Uncle Prosper.' Eliza rose to her feet and, popping a kiss on her uncle's forehead, took two more sandwiches.

'I saw the most *beautiful* little foal at the farm, Mama. I am determined to have her. Oh, she is such a darling and Ted says – '

'No more horses.' Henrietta shook her head firmly. 'You have three horses, two here and one in London. It is quite sufficient . . .'

'You must grow up, you know, my darling Eliza,' her uncle said, taking her hand and swinging it gently to and fro. His eyes brimmed with love and affection.

'But, Uncle, it is not childish to love horses or to want them . . .'

'I know it is not.' Her uncle released her hand and patted the place next to him on the sofa. 'Here, come and sit beside me.' Then he joined his hands in his lap and faced her, his expression now grave. 'My darling Eliza, you know I love you as my own child, and all I want for you is your happiness.'

'What has that to do with horses?' Eliza went on cramming the sandwiches into her mouth as she sat beside him, as though she had not eaten for a week. Then she picked up the crumbs from the plate like a scavenger and popped them into her mouth too, her wide eyes alight with mischief, the very picture of childlike innocence.

'I have come to talk seriously to you today, Eliza.' He put a hand on hers and glanced at Henrietta.

'Oh *dear*,' Eliza said with mock horror in her voice. 'I know, I am to be sent away to a school for young gentlewomen to correct my behaviour. Some of my classmates will be eleven or twelve; but that doesn't matter. I – '

'I have a serious marriage proposition for you, Eliza,' her uncle continued gravely. 'It is no light or laughing matter.'

'*Marriage!*' Eliza gave a gasp. 'Are you joking, Uncle?'

34

'No, I am not.'

'But I don't know anyone I wish to marry.'

'That's not important, Eliza. The person I have in mind is someone I think you could come to love. He is a man of wealth and distinction. He could give you everything you would wish for in life . . .'

'Even more horses,' her mother added helpfully.

Slowly Eliza put the plate down on the table and dusted her fingers.

'I simply can't believe this. Is it someone I know?'

'No, you have not met him,' her uncle said.

'And is this gentleman aware that he wishes to marry me, someone he has never seen, or that *you* wish us to marry?'

'He knows I have a very beautiful niece. We are good friends in business. He is also a farmer and very interested in horses. He has a famous stud near Newmarket.'

'Oh, he might not be so bad then,' Eliza said, reaching over for a piece of cake. 'Except that I have not the slightest desire to leave my home, which I love, and marry a man I have never seen.'

'His name is Lord Thornwell. You would be Lady Thornwell. It would be a match of great importance for you *and* your family. In addition I feel it will bring you, personally, much happiness.'

'Oh, *thank* you, Uncle,' she cried scornfully. 'I see that comes last.'

'I wanted to put the positive features of the marriage first. In many ways marriage is a business transaction. It is a contract.'

'I see the marriage of Guy and Margaret has affected us all,' Eliza said sardonically.

'That's a very crude thing to say, Eliza,' her mother cried. 'I believe Guy entertains a lot of affection for Margaret.'

'Well, I don't. I'll be frank, Mother. Guy married Margaret because he was told to, by Uncle Prosper and his old friend Willem Heering. I can quite see that Uncle views *all* marriages as business alliances. There is a sort of marketplace for people, like the one for cattle they have in Wenham.'

'Eliza, I *forbid* you to speak like that,' Henrietta said sharply. 'Besides your rudeness, you are hurting someone who cares for you greatly.'

'I *do* care for you greatly,' Prosper said gently. 'You know that. I love you as my own daughter. Harry Thornwell is an extremely nice man. I do wish, at least, that you would agree to meet him. We cannot force you, merely ask you.'

'And where will this meeting take place?' Eliza enquired haughtily.

'I suggest in London. Maybe at my brother's house. There is no hurry, my dear, you are not being pushed into anything. And if you do not like his lordship, if neither of you takes to the other, why then there is an end to the matter. But I must tell you that I think it an extremely advantageous match, and if Lord Thornwell is as taken with you as I suspect he will be I urge you strongly to consider it.'

Eliza got up and, sticking her hands in the pockets of her breeches, went over to the window and gazed at her beloved mare Cleopatra grazing in the field. Near her, never far away, was her daughter Lady, and below them lay the rolling countryside of Dorset which Eliza loved so much: the ranks of trees on the brows of neighbouring hills; the dips in the valleys through which ran the little twinkling tributaries of the Wen, like capillaries to the veins in the body. Beyond was Wenham and, above the town, the long escarpment of Wenham Hill, the highest point in the area. How often had she ridden through these valleys, over these fields, along by these streams until she was familiar with almost every inch? Slowly she turned and gazed at her mother and uncle, who were looking anxiously up at her.

'I will meet Lord Thornwell if that is your wish, but only as a friend of yours and the family's. I shall be embarrassed but I shall do it, to please you, Uncle Prosper, and to please Mother. But as for marriage – I would have to love someone *very* much to leave all this, and I must tell you both' – she paused to look at each of them in turn – 'all the gold in the world could never buy me happiness if it took me away from this place where I was born.'

She then left the room abruptly, and Henrietta and Prosper remained behind, gazing at each other with raised eyebrows.

'She will like him,' Prosper said after a while.

'But his age?'

'He doesn't look his age, and you certainly mustn't refer to it until she sees him.'

Eliza slept badly the night after the conversation with her mother and uncle. She kept tossing and turning in her bed, and every time she woke she thought she heard her horses whinnying. Once she nearly went to the stables to be sure that they were all right, but she knew it was her imagination, the effect on her mind of disturbed and troubling thoughts.

At first light she was up and dressed again in her breeches and shirt and, before breakfasting, she went down to feed and groom them, and then saddled Lady for a ride.

It was the first of May, a beautiful morning, and the air was balmy. The sound of birdsong seemed particularly sweet in the trees, and brought back memories of childhood: the smell of hay, of warm manure, of newly cut grass and wood fires.

' 'Tis going to be a fine summer they say, Miss,' Ted, the groom, said as he helped her saddle Lady. 'Maybe we'll breed from Lady this year.'

'I could never leave here, Ted,' Eliza said suddenly as tears filled her eyes.

'I didn't know you wus leaving, Miss Woodville,' Ted said looking puzzled.

'They want me to marry a man I've never met,' she burst out to this longtime companion whom she regarded as a friend rather than a servant.

'Who's "they", Miss?' Ted asked gently, taking a seat on a bale of hay and sticking a piece of straw in his mouth as Eliza adjusted herself in the saddle.

'My mother and uncle.'

'Well, 'tis good to wed. I'm thinking myself . . .'

'But Ted, you're older than me! I'm only eighteen. They want me to marry a lord with a lot of money.'

Ted scratched his head with the straw and then stuck it in his mouth again.

'He has a fine stable,' Eliza went on as though talking to herself.

'Ah,' Ted said brightening, 'then mebbe it might not be so bad a thing if you wus wed to him, Miss. You won't have no interference, *and* your own stable.'

'But it will be my *husband's* stable, not mine.'

'This baint yours neither, Miss.' Ted shook his head. 'And when the new Lady Woodville gets home who knows what changes there may not be?'

Who knew indeed? That was the question. If it hadn't been for the fact that change was in the air Eliza would have rejected her uncle's proposition out of hand. But now it was Margaret's house, not her mother's, and although she liked her sister-in-law well enough she didn't really know her. Nor did she know how much freedom Margaret would let her have. Marriage did strange things to people.

She made no reply, so Ted rose and gave Lady a friendly pat on the rump as Eliza rode her out of the stable yard. Then he watched her as she set off down the valley towards the farm that lay at the bottom. She might stop for a friendly word with the farmer and his wife, maybe drink a glass of milk fresh from the cow. Before she disappeared from sight Eliza turned and waved to him, and then dug her heels in Lady's flank and gave her free rein.

Eliza loved the early morning. The sound of hooves pounding on the earth made the blood course in her veins and filled her with exhilaration and a feeling that she would overcome everything – that the hated wedding would not take place and she would remain as free, as independent and as happy as she was now.

After a brisk ride she paused by one of the streams that ran into the Wen to allow Lady to take a drink. She went right to the edge of the stream so that Lady could stand in it and bend her neck down to drink from the clear, cold water. All was still. A magpie flew down and gazed curiously at Eliza then rose and darted swiftly into the hedge. Over her head the burgeoning leaves blew gently in the morning breeze.

On the far side of the stream was a cottage which belonged to the Woodville estate – as did most of the dwellings in the valley. In it had lived the farmer's mother until her death a few months before. Eliza could discern even from a distance that something was moving on the thatched roof, and once Lady had had her fill she crossed the stream and, out of curiosity more than anything else, cantered towards the cottage.

In the narrow track in front of the garden was a cart filled with straw. A ladder led up the wall of the cottage to the roof, where another continued up to the chimney. A man was kneeling half way up the roof, and as he stood up Eliza could see the leather knee pads, padded with horse hair, which were worn by a thatcher.

As the man straightened up, clasping a bundle of reeds under one arm, his corn-coloured hair was outlined against the deep azure blue of the sky. He looked like some god, standing gazing down at her, and as he raised his hand to greet her she suddenly realised who he was and it was as though she had been brought back to earth with a bump.

Ryder Yetman.

She still remained as if mesmerised as he released his bundle on the roof, turned his back on her and started to climb down, his long body lithe and agile, until he reached the last half-dozen rungs and landed at the bottom. In his hand he still held the leggit, a long piece of wood with which the bundles of reeds were dressed, or fitted in with the others.

'Miss Woodville,' he said smiling, then, as she sat on her horse, transfixed, he went up to her, his smile fading.

'Are you all right, Miss Woodville?'

'Perfectly,' she said and, emerging from the strange trance-like state the sight of him had induced in her, she shook her head vigorously. 'I didn't expect to see you, that was all.'

'What brings you out so early, Miss?' He put his hand to his eyes to shield them from the strong light behind her head.

'I like to take a morning ride, Mr Yetman,' Eliza said. 'I haven't seen you here before.'

'I just started this morning.' Ryder Yetman pointed up at the roof.

'Don't you have men to do your thatching?'

'I prefer to do it myself,' he replied, 'especially as the house is for me.'

'Oh!' Eliza looked startled. 'You are going to live *here*?'

'I hope so.' Unlike his brothers, who had worked hard to get rid of their accents, Ryder still retained his Dorset burr.

'It's a very small house, Mr Yetman.'

''Tis big enough for two.'

'Oh!' Eliza was aware of the burning sun on her cheeks or, rather, she hoped it was merely the heat of the sun. 'Are you getting married?'

'Yes.' Ryder put his leggit on the ground, then adjusted one of the straps on his knee pad.

'I hope you'll be very happy, Mr Yetman.'

'Thank you, Miss Woodville.'

He finished his task and, rising, looked at her.

'I may be getting married myself,' she said, tilting her head defiantly.

'Then I hope *you'll* be very happy too.'

'If I do I shall leave the valley.'

'Well, with your brother getting wed I don't suppose you'll find much to do round here now, Miss.'

'Why weren't you at the wedding, Mr Yetman?' Eliza demanded, her head on one side.

'I've got better things to do with my time than dressing up fancy and going to weddings of that kind.'

'Will you be married in the parish church?'

'I expect so, Miss.' Ryder turned as though he wanted to get on with his work.

'I'll be going along then, Mr Yetman.'

Ryder looked up at the roof and scratched his head. 'I want to get as much of this done today as I can before the weather turns.'

'Does it make a difference if the reeds are wet?'

'It makes it unpleasant, Miss Woodville.' Ryder gave a deep, throaty laugh. 'It makes it unpleasant to work in the rain.'

'Who are you going to marry, Mr Yetman?' Eliza thought it only polite to ask.

'Maude Brough, the miller's daughter. Do you know Maude, Miss Woodville?'

'I know the miller but not his daughter.'

'She was brought up by an aunt, the sister of her mother, who died. She's been teaching in Yeovil.'

'Won't it be very remote for her out here?' Eliza enquired.

Ryder paused, frowning. 'The cottage will do us until we can afford something bigger. Would you like to see inside, Miss Woodville?' he asked politely as if he'd forgotten about the weather. 'I should have asked you that before. Though I suppose you know it as it's your property.'

For answer Eliza quickly dismounted from Lady, and as she jumped to the ground Ryder reached out and took her hand, gripping it in his firm clasp. For a moment he stared into her eyes as if puzzled by her response.

'Thank you,' she said, and he released her hand. 'No, I've never seen inside and I'd like to.' At the door she waited for him to catch up with her, as he was carefully tethering Lady to the fence.

'She won't run away,' she called. 'I brought her up from a foal.'

'She's a beautiful horse,' Ryder said, appreciatively stroking Lady's nose. 'But you can't take risks, Miss Woodville. Something might frighten her, a dog maybe, or a rabbit. Catch her bolting over those fields and you'll be hard put to stop her. She might break a leg or damage herself in a fall.'

'You're right.' Eliza looked suddenly crestfallen as though she should have known better. 'Thank you, Mr Yetman.' She turned abruptly and entered the cottage which, she realised, was much larger than it looked from outside. It had a big downstairs room and a doorway that led to a kitchen, with a cool pantry beyond that.

It was empty of furniture and the bare floor was stone. She suddenly shivered and hugged herself, and Ryder said contritely: 'Sorry, Miss Woodville, I forgot how cold it was inside.'

'It *is* cold,' she said, 'but in the winter you'll have a lovely warm fire.' She looked over at the inglenook and could imagine Ryder there with his Maude, one on either side of the fireplace, enjoying the contentment of family life. Soon there would be children too.

A scene of utter domestic contentment, here in this remote place, rose in her mind's eye. How, she wondered, would it be with Lord Thornwell? She shivered again, but this time it was not on account of the cold.

'I'd better go back,' she said. 'My mother will wonder where I am.'

'Well, take a look upstairs now you're here.' Ryder pointed to the staircase which led straight up from the main room. 'There's a fine view which you'll appreciate.'

He stood back, once more offering her his hand to help her up as there was no banister. This time, however, she didn't take it.

The upstairs was as roomy as downstairs with three bedrooms, two of them quite large. These rooms too were empty, the walls freshly painted, the wooden floors swept clean.

She opened the window of the largest room and poked her head out to see, as Ryder had indicated, a magnificent view of Pelham's Oak. The gracious white house was basking in the sunlight, its windows open, and her labrador Rex was chasing something, maybe a cat or a rabbit, across the smooth lawn.

'We'll be able to wave,' she said, pointing. 'That's my bedroom window.' Suddenly she felt foolish as she saw the smile on his face.

'Well, not for long if you're getting wed, Miss Woodville,' Ryder remarked dryly, leaning against the wall, his hands in the pockets of his breeches.

'It's not *sure* I'm getting married,' Eliza murmured. 'I mean I haven't made up my mind.'

'Oh, I see, Miss.'

'I haven't even met the man, to tell you the truth,' she said woodenly.

'Not *met* him? I don't understand, Miss Woodville.'

'I'm to be introduced to him in London in a week or two. If we suit, if he likes me and I like him, well . . . It sounds a bit strange, doesn't it?' she said seeing the new, thoughtful expression on his face.

'It seems very old-fashioned, to my way of thinking, Miss. I thought arranged marriages were things that happened long ago. Maybe not in society,' he added as an afterthought. 'It seems a pity that a pretty girl like you should have to marry a man she don't love.'

'Have you known Maude long?'

'No I haven't, as a matter of fact.' Ryder scratched his head and frowned. 'Well, I've *known* her, like, since she was a little girl, but then when her mother died she went to live with her aunt. I met her again last summer when she came to see her father. She's a friend of my sister's.'

'Is she pretty?'

Ryder appeared to consider the question.

'No,' he said after a pause. 'Not 'zactly pretty, not like you, Miss Woodville. But I like her. She's a nice person. We'll suit.'

'I hope you'll be very happy,' Eliza said, closing the window. She could imagine this room when it had a wardrobe, a tallboy, chairs and a bed . . . She glanced again at Ryder and, from the expression in his eyes, it seemed to her almost as though he could divine what she was thinking.

'I hope you'll be happy with whoever it is you're to meet, Miss Woodville,' Ryder said. 'I truly do.'

'I don't *have* to marry him,' she burst out.

'Then don't unless you're sure, Miss,' he said softly.

Henrietta seldom came down for breakfast, so Eliza was surprised to find her mother waiting for her when she got back, though it was not yet nine o'clock.

43

Breakfast was served in the breakfast room, a sunny room not far from the kitchen. This made it easier for the servants to prepare and serve it, especially when there were only one or two members of the family in residence.

'I wondered where you were, dear.' Henrietta looked askance at her daughter's riding outfit. 'What kept you so long? I saw Lady standing for a long time outside the house where Mrs Crook used to live before she died.'

'Did you not see me talking to Ryder Yetman?'

'Ryder Yetman!' The expression on Henrietta's face changed immediately. 'What was Ryder Yetman doing in old Mrs Crook's house?'

'He's thatching it. He's going to live there.'

'You do surprise me,' Henrietta said. 'I thought the family had money.'

'He must have come to some arrangement with Guy, as the house belongs to us.'

'But why would he want to live in that remote place?' Her mother's tone was scornful.

'He likes it. He's getting married.'

'And I wonder what he thought of you, talking to him in *that* outfit!'

'Mother, don't be silly. I saw him by chance. I have a feeling Mr Yetman doesn't care about small matters of dress.'

'You could be right,' Henrietta sniffed. 'I've heard odd stories about Ryder Yetman.'

'Oh?' Eliza was immediately interested. 'What sort of stories?'

'He was a soldier, you know, and was wounded in the Zulu war. As the eldest son he disappointed his father, who wanted him in the business.'

'But he is in the business. He supervised the work done on this house.'

'He helps his father out when he feels like it. But Ryder pleases himself. The family aspires, but apparently Mr Ryder Yetman does not, or he would not wish to live in that mean little cottage with his wife.'

'It's a dear little cottage,' Eliza protested. 'So sweet and pretty in the valley. I envy him.'

'Really, Eliza,' her mother said crossly. 'I can't understand you at all. Here you are on the verge of great things, and yet you can talk like that. What nonsense.'

'I suppose you're referring to Lord Thornwell. You call marrying a man I don't love a great thing?' Suddenly Eliza stood up and brought her fist down angrily on the table. 'Mama, I will *not* be bartered for.'

'What *are* you talking about, my dear?' Henrietta put on her spectacles and began to slit open the envelopes of the letters by her plate.

'I'm not going to be sold to Lord Thornwell. That kind of thing does not happen now.'

'What kind of thing, dear?' Her mother stared at her coolly.

'Arranging a marriage.'

'Oh yes it does,' Henrietta said firmly. 'Make no mistake about that. *And* far more often than you think. It happens all the time. It's a question of suitability. Stuck here in the heart of the country, miles away from decent society, you are unlikely to find a suitable mate. Why do you think Guy and Margaret were brought together?'

'I thought it was for her fortune?'

'Please don't be crude, Eliza.' Henrietta winced visibly. 'It was a question of *suitability*. Guy, like you, was unlikely to meet the right sort of woman. He met plenty of the wrong ones, I know that. And yes' – her mother inclined her head – 'I will say that Miss Heering's fortune was not unwelcome; but then to have an English baronet for a husband, a house the size of this one, an established town house as well, was very attractive to her and her family.'

'Doesn't love *ever* matter, Mother?'

'My dear, I didn't love your father when I married him.' Henrietta smiled nostalgically. 'Of course he was attractive, but love came later. He was a very suitable match for me, and the dowry I was able to bring was not unattractive to him, or rather to his father, who could barely make ends meet. Alas,'

Henrietta sighed and began agitatedly to slit the envelopes of the few remaining letters. 'We got through my money very quickly. This estate had been allowed to decay, and your father was never a well man. Had he been, the financial predicament in which we found ourselves might have been very different.

'As it isn't – ' Henrietta reached over and affectionately took the hand of her daughter, who had resumed her seat ' – I do wish you to think very seriously about Lord Thornwell, my dear. I not only feel in all sincerity that he would make you very happy; but you would release your family from a great financial burden. With you happy and well taken care of we would all sleep easier in our beds. It would give Guy and Margaret a much better start in their married life. Believe me, my dear,' she said, looking deep into Eliza's eyes, 'you owe it to your family as well as yourself.'

3

Ryder Yetman climbed slowly back on to the roof after Eliza
had ridden away, but for a long time he stood watching her
until she was out of sight, his work forgotten. When she
finally disappeared around the sloping field between the farm
and the big house he sighed and turned reluctantly back to his
task, heaving the bundles of Abbotsbury reeds and savagely
patting them into place with his leggit to form a course across
the roof.

But although his professional expertise would never have let
him down, his heart was not in his work, and after a while he
scrambled down to the ground and went into the house to find
his cigarettes.

Eliza Woodville. He could picture her as belonging in this
cottage as he could picture no one else. Despite being a lady,
born in the great house from a long line of aristocrats, she
would be at home here whereas Maude, his betrothed, born
a countrywoman, a miller's daughter, would not.

He had known about the intensity of his feelings for Eliza
before he became engaged to Maude. However, even supposing
she felt anything for him, *could* feel anything for a man socially
her inferior and so much older than she was, he knew the very
idea was hopeless. She was young and she was beautiful. She
would be the prize for a much wealthier, much more suitable
man than he could ever aspire to be.

Ryder had first seen her when he was given the task of
supervising the work his father's men were doing at Pelham's
Oak. He was at that time still unfit for work himself, yet he

could supervise, and as he knew every aspect of the building business he was ideally suited for the task.

One day he had been standing in the front hall and the young daughter of the house had come running up the steps, dressed in her riding habit, a black coat and skirt, lace jabot at her throat, carrying her hat and riding crop in her hand. Her hair had been tucked neatly into a net and she looked decorous and, then, older than she was.

He hadn't known who she was at first. He had stood aside as, clearly in a temper, she rushed past him, her face flushed, her eyes glinting dangerously, her lips pursed. She'd slammed the door into the drawing room behind her, and there was the sound of raised voices as she confronted her brother. He never discovered what the row had been about, but he knew then who she was.

Ryder had seen little of Miss Woodville in those days because the big house, needing so much refurbishing, became a scene of such disorder that the family often went up to the London house and remained there as long as possible. But whenever Eliza was there he looked out for her and, slowly, he began to realise that maybe she was doing the same.

Now today she had sought him out. He was sure of that. Incredibly his feelings were reciprocated; but what could he do about it?

Cigarette in hand, Ryder went slowly up the stairs and into the room that was to be his bedroom. He stood by the window and let his finger run along the sill that she had touched.

Then he turned and imagined, as she had (only he did not know this), the great bed in the middle but, instead of Eliza lying beside him, there would be Maude.

Maude Brough, twenty-six years old, a clever woman, a schoolmistress and not unattractive. But there had never been a spark between them as there had been between himself and Eliza. He could imagine himself allowing his arm to encircle her waist as she stood by the window; he would gently bare her shoulders and then her breasts, and he would . . .

Ryder put his hands to his eyes, and his shoulders heaved in a great sigh of loss, of desolation.

Ryder knew what people said about his Uncle Christopher and himself – that they were alike. He didn't mind being compared to his uncle physically, because he was a fine-looking man and, in many respects, his nephew liked him. But he knew that Christopher was an idler, a loafer, and it was this aspect of the comparison that annoyed Ryder, who knew he would always work for his living and never be afraid of working hard. His uncle, on the other hand, was a sponger who was always asking anyone who would give it to him for money. But work for it? Never.

Ryder sat across the table from his uncle, listening to him as he entertained the company with tales of his recent adventures. These included a visit to the Continent, and an escapade with a beautiful woman in Rome, a widow, he said, with a fortune.

'But she was too quick for me,' Christopher Yetman concluded with a smile and a wink. 'She wished to hang on to her money if not her virtue, and while my back was turned I'm damned if she didn't pack her bags and leave. Left me to pay the bill too. But while she went out of the front door I nipped smartly out of the back, and as far as I know the hotel bill is not paid to this very day.'

'Really, Christopher!' Catherine exclaimed indignantly. 'Have you *no* shame, repeating such a story in front of my young daughter . . .'

'Oh, *Mother*, I am not as young as that,' Agnes protested. 'I am quite well aware that these things happen.' She looked pertly at her mother and only momentarily lowered her eyes.

Agnes was, in fact, twenty, and very well aware of the things that happened in society and out of it. The baby of the family, a pretty girl, but not particularly good-natured; but she had an allure, a quality that attracted men, though so far she had always kept them at a distance, finding none of them good enough for her.

'That may be,' her father said sharply, tapping his spoon on the table. 'But your mother is right. Christopher, you will kindly keep your bawdy stories for the smoking room, *if* you please, and *not* entertain us with them at table.'

But even he could scarcely suppress a smile, so good-natured was his brother, so comical in his attempts to improve his situation, which invariably ended in disaster. Christopher with his charm and his looks, his air of breeding, which contrasted with his own homely countrified air, could get away with anything.

If Agnes felt too worldly-wise to appear embarrassed, the man sitting to her right did. As the story progressed he had lowered his face and, as the outcome became more certain and the story took on a note of ribaldry, a flush slowly suffused his cheeks. His employer, noticing his discomfiture, gave him a good-natured smile.

'Come now, Herbert, you've heard worse tales than that, haven't you? You're a grown man, Herbert. Come now,' he said.

Herbert Lock fumbled with his napkin, and Agnes turned provocatively to him, eyes wide open.

'Why, Herbert, you're blushing!'

'There now, look what you've done to our guest,' Catherine chided her, vigorously ringing the bell to summon the maid. 'Spare his blushes, if not Agnes's.'

'I assure you I'm *not* blushing, Mrs Yetman,' Herbert stammered, giving a realistic cough while he held his throat and swallowed hard. 'A piece of bread went down the wrong way.'

'There, you've shocked Herbert!' Agnes pretended to frown disapprovingly at her uncle.

'Really, Agnes, I am *not* shocked.' Beside himself with confusion, Herbert thumped his chest and took a large gulp of water from the glass beside his plate as if to prove his point. 'I . . .'

'I won't repeat any more tales then,' Christopher promised. 'I'll save them, as you say, John . . .'

'But won't Herbert be in the smoking room?' Agnes looked

at him archly. 'You *are* old enough to smoke, Herbert, aren't you?'

'Please don't tease Herbert,' Catherine Yetman commanded sharply. 'He is one man we could not do without.'

'And I will second that,' Ryder said. 'Without Herbert the business would collapse.'

It was true. Herbert Lock had come to the Yetman business in Blandford as a callow youth of sixteen and now, twenty years later, he was one of the mainstays of the entire operation. All the accounts were under his strict control, and he knew everyone and everything; not an item escaped his sharp nose or enquiring eye. He could ferret out theft, deception, late payers and defaulters. So indispensable had Herbert become that John Yetman had made him a partner, with overall financial control of the business.

So, in a sense, Herbert was part of the family rather than a guest; yet the Yetmans always felt on formal terms with him. He always called them Mr and Mrs Yetman and referred to John in the office as 'sir'. He had begun as an inferior and seemed in his own estimation to have remained one.

Herbert was reserved, shy, pious and, until recently, he had lived with his widowed mother in an old Georgian house in the centre of Blandford. But his mother had recently died, and not only the house but the large legacy she'd left were his. All his, and no one to share them with: the money, the pretty house, his prospects at the still relatively early age of thirty-six.

Many a young woman in Blandford or thereabouts would have been glad of an offer from Herbert. Shy and pious he might have been, even withdrawn; but he was hardworking, presentable, not good-looking but not too bad and, of course, he was careful with money and had plenty of it to spare. Quite a prize, quite a catch. There was, however, one insuperable obstacle: hitherto Herbert was unknown ever to have shown any interest in women, and it was assumed that he would remain a bachelor to the end of his days.

After dinner the party went into the drawing room for coffee, where Catherine Yetman excused herself on the grounds that she had a headache and would go early to bed. Ryder accompanied her to the door and then stood looking anxiously into her eyes.

'Are you sure you're all right, Mother? I have not thought you looked well for some days.'

'I am quite all right, Ryder,' she said, smiling at him and briefly touching his cheek. 'Now, you have a good time and don't worry about me. What a pity Maude couldn't be here tonight.'

As Ryder took her arm to escort her to the stairs she looked anxiously up at him.

'Things *are* all right with Maude, aren't they, Ryder?'

'Of course, Mother, why should they not be?' Ryder let go of her arm and leaned against the newel post. Dressed in a suit with a clean white shirt and tie he looked so handsome that his mother wondered how he had escaped marriage for so long. But that was the trouble: Ryder was so hard to please.

'Are you *still* unsettled, Ryder?' she asked.

'What's the matter with you tonight, Mother?' Laughing, he touched her arm. 'You seem over-anxious.'

'Of course I'm anxious. My other sons are happy and settled. I want you to be happy and settled. Only, all the time . . .'

'Yes, Mother?'

'I *worry* about you, Ryder. Fancy taking that little cottage when you were on the verge of getting married.'

'When I took it I didn't know I was going to ask Maude to marry me,' he said carefully.

'Then you should have got rid of it immediately. But now you're doing it up! Your father says you spend hours there, sometimes days. You neglect his work for yours. He's unhappy about you too. We don't want you to be like . . .'

'Oh, I shan't be like Uncle Christopher, Mother. I'll always earn my bread, never fear.'

Catherine stood on the bottom step of the winding staircase and, putting both hands on his shoulders, looked earnestly into his eyes.

'Tell me, my son, *is* there something wrong?'

'Nothing wrong, Mother.' Ryder put his hands in his pockets and gazed at the floor. 'Nothing wrong 'zactly . . .'

'You don't love Maude, do you?'

Ryder didn't reply but traced a circle on the stone flags of the floor with his toe.

'She would be more suited to Herbert than me,' he mumbled.

'She's *such* a nice girl.' Catherine wrung her hands. 'But I have thought, watching you, she was not the one. You are not right for each other.'

'Then what must I do, Mother?' Ryder spread his arms out helplessly. 'She will sue me for breach of promise if I ask to be released – not that I mind *that* so much . . .'

'Your father would mind,' his mother replied quickly. 'He would hate the scandal. So would I. Maybe if you talked to her . . . maybe she feels as you do?'

'I don't think Maude loves me, but she wants to be married and settled. I can understand it. She is twenty-six. She will not let me go so lightly, I can tell you!'

'Then maybe we should introduce her to Herbert.' His mother appeared serious, but Ryder only laughed.

'Mother, have you not noticed that Herbert has eyes only for Agnes?'

'Agnes?' Catherine looked startled. 'Oh, Agnes would have nothing to do with Herbert. What an idea!'

'I like Herbert,' Ryder insisted. 'Frankly I think he would be good for Agnes. We don't want Agnes getting desperate, like Maude . . .'

'Agnes is too like you,' his mother replied. 'Hard to please. Restless . . . unsettled. Oh, *why* are my oldest and youngest not more like my middle children?'

Suddenly Catherine staggered slightly and, her face very pale, leaned against the banister.

'Mother, what is it?' Ryder demanded. 'You're not well, are you?'

'My dear, I am just tired,' she said firmly, drawing herself up. 'It has been a very busy time. The Woodville wedding was

53

exciting. I had to see to my clothes, and Agnes's. We had to look right as it was such an important occasion. It was an honour to be asked to the wedding. Even if you did not think so, we did, and we had to make a lot of preparations for it. I shall now rest up for a few days and I'll be as right as rain.'

She bent forward suddenly and kissed him gently on the brow. 'You sort out your own problems, my lad, and don't worry about mine.'

Then, briskly refusing his offer of help, she turned and went heavily up the stairs, while Ryder remained in the hall staring anxiously after her.

Back in the drawing room he found his father and uncle sitting by the fire smoking. Of Agnes and Herbert there was no sign.

'Gone for a walk,' his father said winking.

'Oh, *you've* noticed it too.' Ryder smiled and helped himself to coffee and brandy. 'Father, is Mother all right?'

'She has a headache . . .'

'I know, but she hasn't looked well for a while. She's lost weight and she's too pale.'

'It's her age,' his father said sagaciously. 'It comes to all women sooner or later, my boy.'

'Oh, is that all?' Ryder looked relieved, if a little unconvinced, and slumped in front of the fireplace.

'Christopher was asking me if there were any rich widows in the district.' John Yetman, with a smile, began to fill his pipe. 'He's thinking of settling down.' John chuckled as if amused by the idea and began slowly to draw on the tobacco. 'I told him, you see, I couldn't give him any more money. I can't go on supporting him when I have four children, two of them still unmarried.'

'But Ryder's getting married,' Christopher said. 'Couldn't I take his place, Brother? Father left us both money, you know.'

'But you spent all yours.' John Yetman looked earnestly at his brother. 'You wasted your substance, Christopher, whereas I husbanded mine. Husbanded it and made it grow. You sold your shares in our father's business and threw away your money. Even if I could help you any more I wouldn't . . .'

'Oh, Father, that is harsh.' Ryder jerked himself out of his reverie.

'Not harsh at all,' John replied. 'Now, if your uncle could put a hand to the business . . .'

'I am not fitted for it, Brother.' Christopher accepted one of the cigarettes Ryder held out to him. 'I can't add up a column of figures.'

'Herbert adds up the figures . . .'

'I couldn't put one brick on top of another. I haven't Herbert's brain or Ryder's practical skills . . .'

'There is no rich widow,' Ryder said as if thinking aloud. 'But there is a lady in the parish who has recently come into a lot of money. Am I not right, Father? Miss Fairchild.'

As he looked at his father for confirmation Christopher slapped his knee and roared with laughter.

'That old spinster with the hare lip? Do you think I'd so much as look at her?'

'That's a cruel thing to say,' John said disapprovingly. 'You could do worse. For one thing she's not old. But she'd be a fool if she had you, or the likes of you. She has such a sweet disposition that, frankly, I never notice her disfigurement. She is a kind and generous-hearted woman. Yet it is true she has just been left very well off by the death, one after the other, of both her parents, with the shop and all its stock at her disposal.'

'Euphemia Monk,' Ryder said thoughtfully. 'Another one with plenty of money.'

'Now *she* would never look at your uncle,' John said firmly. 'She is much younger than Miss Fairchild; besides, Euphemia's good-looking *and* has plenty of time to find a suitable man. But Miss Fairchild – ' he tilted his head ' – I'm afraid that poor woman, good though she is, will never be wed.'

As the bell on the inside of the door jangled, Victoria Fairchild turned sharply and seemed to hesitate, like a rabbit caught in a beam of light, uncertain whether to retreat into the safety of the back of the shop or stay where she was. When her parents had been alive she had seldom been seen in the front of the shop, preferring to remain in the storeroom at the back which was her domain. Here she had sole responsibility for the inventory, measuring out and cutting cloth, making the Dorset buttons for which the haberdashery shop was renowned, and keeping the books of the prosperous little business which her parents had run since the early days of their marriage in the 1830s.

Christopher Yetman, dressed in his best suit and carrying a top hat and cane, closed the door carefully before turning and peering into the gloom of the shop. Behind the counter bales of material of all kinds – cottons, poplins, silks, bombazines, worsteds, wools – in a variety of textures and widths, rose to the ceiling, while on the counter neatly arranged in boxes were spools of thread, ribbons, buttons, needles and pins.

Everyone used to laugh at Victoria Fairchild at school, until finally she was removed by her parents and educated privately. For Victoria had been born with a hare lip and, even though a compassionate and skilful doctor had managed to repair much of the damage, the scar remained, giving her a slight speech impediment. But the scar left on her mind went much deeper.

Christopher had only seen her about three times in the last twenty years, but they were the same age, forty-five, and he remembered her very well. He bowed solemnly towards her as her hands flew to her face and her eyes opened wide in surprise.

'I do believe it is Christopher Yetman.'

'You believe right, Victoria,' Christopher said smoothly, advancing into the shop. 'I am paying a visit to my brother and sister-in-law, and when I heard that your dear mother and father had passed away I wanted to call and offer you my condolences.'

'Oh, Christopher!' Miss Fairchild let her hands fall from her face and, hesitantly, came round the counter towards him. 'How *very* kind of you. *Such* a kind thought.'

'You will miss your parents, Victoria.' After placing his hat on the counter Christopher put both hands on top of his cane and looked at her gravely.

'Oh yes. Yes, I do. Very much. They went within a year of each other, and I am quite lost without them. They were so dear to me, so good.' The suspicion of tears lurked behind her eyes and she went on: 'Would you care to come in for a minute and sit down in the back, Christopher? We have comfortable chairs there and should not be disturbed.'

'Why that's very nice of you, Victoria,' Christopher said heartily. 'It would be good to have a chat with you again, about old days, eh?'

Victoria said nothing, but as she locked the front door and led the way through the shop she grimaced to herself. The only memories she had of Christopher Yetman were of the way he used to lead the bullies who mocked her in the playground and forced her parents to remove her from the local school. But that was a very long time ago, and she was touched by his generous impulse in coming to see her.

Christopher now looked approvingly round the back room, noting how neat everything was, how perfectly and meticulously kept. There was an air of diligence and prosperity about the place which appealed to him. On either side of the fireplace were two chairs, and on the hob a kettle boiled.

'I was just making tea,' Miss Fairchild said. 'May I offer you a cup, Christopher?'

'You may,' Christopher said, making himself comfortable in one of the chairs and undoing the middle button of his jacket. 'How kind.'

As Miss Fairchild bustled about, warming the pot before spooning the tea into it from a large caddy, putting out two cups and saucers, a plate of biscuits taken from a tin, he watched her appreciatively. Really, had it not been for the vertical scar between her lip and nose, she would have been considered comely. But no one had ever noticed her violet eyes, her peach-coloured skin, her shining golden hair and slender waist. All they noticed, those cruel children, was the one minor blemish that divided her from the bulk of her fellows. Even now he remembered with a sense of shame how he used to taunt her in the playground, and he shifted uncomfortably.

Victoria, however, seemed quite excited by his impromptu visit and smiled at him as she handed him his tea and offered him a biscuit.

'I haven't entertained in the back since my poor mother passed away,' she said.

'Travellers, people like that, don't you ask them in here?' Christopher accepted a biscuit and popped it into his mouth.

'Oh *no*!' Miss Fairchild looked deeply shocked. 'People of *that* kind are always seen on the other side of the counter. It would never do to receive them *here*.'

She helped herself to a biscuit and, as she crunched it, he could see that she was beginning to feel at ease with him. He sighed.

'You must feel very lonely on your own now, Victoria.'

'Oh, I do.' The biscuit finished, she clasped her hands together in her lap and her eyes assumed a faraway expression. 'I really don't know what to do about the shop, whether to carry on or to sell it. You see,' she blushed a little as she pretended to dust crumbs from her lap, 'my dear parents left me comfortably off. As well as the shop I have investments, trusts they made on my behalf and, of course, a large house. I would like to travel and see a little of the world. I would like . . .'

'I am very interested in buying the shop and its stock,' Christopher said urgently, leaning forward. 'I would like to settle down and it would be a good investment for me.'

'But, Christopher,' Miss Fairchild's expression was one of frank astonishment, 'you know nothing about the haber-dashery business.'

'But you could advise me, could you not, Victoria? If you like we could be partners.' He gave another deep sigh and leaned back in his chair, half closing his eyes. 'You have no idea how a man longs to settle down after a lifetime of travelling.'

The new Lady Woodville had no illusions that her husband had married her for love. Yet he was kind and charming, with

58

impeccable manners, and if their relationship lacked passion, for her it was more than enough. For the plain spinster from Amsterdam had long ago resigned herself to life without a man. Her wealth, she knew, would cushion her from the harsher realities of life, but she never dreamed that at twenty-nine it would buy her a husband.

Even to be seen with Guy Woodville made her feel beautiful. He had the presence of the true English aristocrat. People looked at him, not her; but she didn't mind. Although there was speculation as to the reason, *she* was the one he'd married, and many women envied her.

They had had a leisurely honeymoon travelling on the Continent in the style that her money was able to provide. From Venice they had crossed into the Balkans, and from there to the Levant and Damascus, where they were escorted across the desert by the Bedouin. It had been very exciting because they both loved exploring ruins and there were plenty of these. The ancient city of Palmyra at dawn or sunset was unforgettable. They found that they had more in common than they thought, and Guy, whose education had finished at Cambridge, was a delightful, knowledgeable, even erudite companion.

As for the intimate side of their life together, Margaret had much to learn and he taught her as gently and kindly as he could. She was grateful to him, and the more her gratitude increased so did her love. She returned to England completely enamoured of her husband and determined to be a good wife. She would not nag or question him; she would let him have his freedom to spend her fortune as he wished. All she wanted was to be his helpmeet; someone of whom he could be proud. Of course she wanted to be a mother too.

In the past eighteen months there had been so much to do. After their engagement, the wedding was postponed because everyone agreed there was much work to be done on Pelham's Oak and the house in Chesterfield Street, Mayfair, which had been in the Woodville family for a century. Margaret loved both houses, but especially the one in London which, in addition to its many splendid rooms full of fine eighteenth-century furniture, had a large walled garden in which a fountain played.

Margaret loved the shops, the theatres, the hectic social life in London. As Lady Woodville she had the entrée to almost every level of society, short of royalty, and although she admired the old Queen, she had little time for the raffish set that surrounded the by now middle-aged Prince of Wales.

Yet there was much in London that distressed her. The poverty was apparent in the streets, where ragged beggars, some quite young, crouched in corners holding out their hands for alms. Fallen women paraded themselves openly along Piccadilly, or lingered in the shadows of even the most exclusive streets in Mayfair. But Guy cared very little for social reform, and she was too new a bride to wish to engage in any undertakings of which he might disapprove.

She knew that Guy was not attracted to business, that he would rather have played the role of young man-about-town. But his uncle and her father had wanted him to work, and every day he rose, reluctantly and not too early, to go to his office in the City, where he arrived about eleven. He left at four and went to his club. Usually they dined together at eight, or sometimes he collected her to take her to the theatre and they supped at the Café Royal afterwards or, more usually, at the houses of friends.

Margaret always breakfasted with Guy, getting up before him and making sure that his valet had done his job properly and that his clothes were laid out and his toilet articles were ready. She had had a bathroom with hot running water installed in the house when it was refurbished.

When at last Guy came into the dining room to make his selection from a choice of hot dishes, she would be waiting for him to hand him the morning paper and any letters and discuss with him the programme of the day.

They had been back from their honeymoon about six weeks and had spent a third of that time in the country and the rest in London. It was beginning to be hot and soon they would leave for the country and stay there. Guy would take a month's holiday and concern himself with the affairs of the Dorset estate, even though a manager had now been appointed to run it for him.

Many things were different now, and not all of them were appreciated by Guy, who for most of his life had been a spoilt young man doted on by his invalid father and adoring mother. He knew that Margaret tried hard and that the marriage had been essential. But it had certainly curtailed his freedom, and he envied his young unmarried friends who were free to please themselves. He had to resort to lies when he wished to do this.

As Guy came into the dining room, Margaret rose and went over to the sideboard, presenting him, on the way, with the morning paper so that he could begin to read it as soon as he sat down. She liked to serve his breakfast herself, and he ate heartily while she had black coffee and toast and honey.

Guy pecked her on the cheek and asked her how she'd slept.

'As always, perfectly, my dear,' Margaret said with a fond smile. 'And you?'

'As always, perfectly,' Guy said, also with a smile. But he looked a little tired.

'Although you were *very* late home, I think.'

'I was playing cards at my club,' Guy said in an offhand way. 'The time just sped by.'

Of course she wouldn't dream of chiding him for not letting her know the previous day he would not be home to dinner. It was her firm intention not to nag, not to let him feel that his freedom was in any way constrained by marriage to a woman five years older than himself. In many ways at twenty-four he was young for his age, both in looks and manner.

'Anything in the post today?' Guy looked cursorily through the letters.

'An invitation from your aunt to dinner next week.'

'Oh yes.' Guy sat back and shook out his napkin. 'That is *the* dinner.'

'How do you mean, dear?' Margaret put before him a dish

of his favourite things: fried eggs, chops and country sausage.

'Don't you know about *the* dinner?' Guy's voice had a mocking tone. 'Aren't you in on the secret?'

'Not that I know of.' Margaret looked mystified.

'It is to introduce my wild young sister to a man my uncle wants her to marry. They haven't a chance, of course.'

'But I had no idea . . .'

'No, it's a very close family secret.' Guy looked with relish at his plate and rubbed his hands. 'Mother wishes to tame Eliza and get her to settle down.'

'But she is so *young*.'

'That's why she thinks she needs to be tamed. She is too fond of mannish activities like riding horses astride in men's breeches – an old pair of mine as a matter of fact.' The idea seemed to amuse him. 'Do *you* disapprove of that, Margaret?' He leaned over and looked at her, and she felt embarrassed by his gaze.

'Well,' Margaret stammered, 'it's not usual, but then Eliza has not had the benefit in recent years of a father to control her.'

'My mother thinks she behaves like a gypsy. They are anxious to marry her to Lord Thornwell, who has vast estates, a stable and considerable wealth.'

'Well . . . what does Eliza think of that?'

'She has never met Lord Thornwell.'

'Oh!' Margaret felt herself blushing. The fact that their own marriage had been arranged was never referred to between them, but the circumstances he was describing were very similar to theirs. The Woodvilles had wanted her money, and she had wanted a husband.

'Surely she doesn't have to marry anyone she doesn't want to?' Margaret ventured.

'No, of course she doesn't. I shan't let her,' Guy said firmly. 'Whatever my mother and Uncle Prosper say.' He appeared to hesitate and then went on: 'Not that I don't think it would be a very good idea for my sister to marry. She is headstrong and, in her way, a little eccentric. It's not very good for a woman to get a reputation for oddness.'

'I thought she only wore breeches on the estate?'

'Yes, she does; but she rides like a man and as fast as a man. Sometimes she behaves like a man. She loves messing about in the stables, grooming her horses herself. When she was younger she was always hanging around at the farm. She never hides the fact she would have liked to be a man.' Guy sighed and, for a moment, thoughtfully suspended his knife and fork over his plate.

'My poor little sister. Lord Thornwell, though rich and well-born, is fifty. She is in for a shock.'

Margaret gave a sharp exclamation. '*Fifty!*'

'He is, I understand, a very *young*-looking fifty. But that is still thirty-two years older than our Eliza. It is a big gap.'

'Does she know this?'

'I don't think so.' Guy shook his head. 'They thought it best not to tell her that, though the advantages of the marriage, from *every* point of view, have been outlined to her, carefully, of course. The fact is that Lord Thornwell is anxious to breed. He is a widower and had an only son who died at the age of fifteen. Who better than my nubile young sister to provide him with an heir . . .'

'Oh, that's monstrous.' Margaret looked shocked, then put a hand to her mouth. 'I'm sorry, Guy, I didn't wish to offend.'

'You don't offend *me*, my dear.' Guy smiled at her reassuringly. 'You have a lot to learn about our English ways. Now, how would you like to see Henry Irving at the Lyceum? I'm told his Shylock absolutely *must* be seen.'

'Anything you like, Guy,' Margaret said docilely. 'Anything you wish, you know I wish too.'

Guy looked at the clock. It was after ten and he gave a muttered imprecation and finished his breakfast. A cab would take him to his office and he would be there in twenty minutes.

Guy hated his work. He had no interest in business, no head for it either. At Cambridge he had immersed himself in the classics; besides, he couldn't add up. However, it was part of the bargain of the marriage contract and he would stick to it, for the time being.

He finished his breakfast, rose, kissed his wife and went into the hall, where the newly installed butler helped him on with his coat and hat.

'The cab is waiting outside for you, Sir Guy,' he said.

'Thank you, Bates.'

Guy took his cane, tipped his hat rakishly forward on his head and ran lightly down the steps into Chesterfield Street.

The cab driver removed his hat.

'To the City, sir?'

'Lower Thames Street,' Guy replied, leaning forward. 'Quick as you can.'

Gwendoline Martyn invited to her house in Cadogan Place men and women of every description. Newly rich men of business mixed with men of ancient title and wealth. Sometimes the two were combined. Trade might not be acceptable, but business and the Stock Exchange were, and there were many who had their feet in both camps. It was no longer possible to be idle and expect to see money grow. Rich men like Lord Thornwell belonged to the old nobility and yet ran a successful business to augment the family fortunes.

The Martyns were, quite blatantly, new money and made no secret of the fact. They had owned the house in Cadogan Place for five years and had bought it from an impoverished nobleman who had had to retreat to his Scottish estate in order to survive – a lesson to everyone, if one were needed.

There were some people in society who would not receive, or be received by, people like the Martyns, but they were fast disappearing. New money bought, as well as property, education, manners, refinement. Gwendoline Martyn, though not an educated woman (few were, for to be educated was to court spinsterhood), was intelligent, well informed, an accomplished horsewoman and needlewoman and, now, a successful hostess. Her frequent salons were notable successes.

Harry, fifth Baron Thornwell, was a business partner of

her husband's. He had been at Eton with Matthew Woodville and the two men had been introduced here in Cadogan Place. Edgar Martyn was even a better businessman than his younger brother Prosper, because he thought of nothing else, whereas Prosper liked to visit the theatre, to travel, to wine and dine and entertain ladies of a certain kind to intimate dinners in restaurants in Soho, Covent Garden and the Strand.

Edgar and Gwendoline Martyn stood at the entrance to their impressive first-floor drawing room as the names of their guests were called out by the butler.

'Mr and Mrs Augustus Wainwright.'

'How do you do?'

'How do you do?'

'Sir Peter and Lady Tree.'

'Lovely to see you again.'

'My dear, you look so *well*. How was the holiday?'

'Mr Prosper Martyn.'

'Fancy seeing *you*!' The brothers jocularly poked each other in the ribs, having been together in conference all day.

'How *are* you, my dear?' Prosper affectionately kissed Gwendoline, who squeezed his hand.

'Lord Thornwell.'

Formal handshake. Bows.

'So *good* of you to come.'

'Thank you for inviting me.'

'Sir Henry and Lady Tarrant. Lord and Lady Fisher, Mr Michael Lowry, Sir Guy and Lady Woodville and Miss Eliza Woodville . . .'

From the end of the room Lord Thornwell turned abruptly as the name was announced and drew in his breath in admiration as his eyes fell on the tall, beautiful young woman who stood behind her brother and sister-in-law waiting to greet her aunt and uncle. She had wisely dispensed with bustle and tight corsage and was simply gowned in light yellow muslin with décolletage and short sleeves – in fact it was her bridesmaid's dress altered for more formal evening wear. Her dark hair was caught up and fastened in ringlets at the nape of her neck, and her almost olive skin gave her a passing resemblance to a gypsy with her alluring tawny-brown eyes and straight, rather thick brows. Lord Thornwell knew that her pedigree was exceptional and she was certainly no gypsy, but from where he stood one could almost have imagined her to be Italian. There was a classical simplicity and elegance about her as she waited to kiss her aunt, who was fussing over the newly married Margaret.

Eliza stood patiently with a pleasant half-smile on her lips, lightly tapping the fan she held in one hand against the palm of the other. But what struck him nearly as much as her beautiful features was the graceful curve of her neck, her slim shoulders above the neckline of her simple yellow dress. In her hair were scattered flowers that looked like primroses or cowslips, undoubtedly artificial, but cleverly woven into her coiffure to produce an effect that was at once countrified yet elegant. He found her breathtaking, absolutely breathtaking . . . but, so young. She would have to be painstakingly wooed.

Lord Thornwell stood with his back to the fireplace, a glass of champagne in his hand, and raised it to his lips in a silent toast to his prospective bride. If the wedding came off he would never forget his debt to his colleague Prosper Martyn.

Margaret, of course, was the guest of honour. The party was ostensibly intended to introduce her to the society and business people with whom the Martyns associated.

Gwendoline made a great fuss of the bride, bestowing only a perfunctory kiss on her niece. Eliza was thus able to take her time, standing behind her sister-in-law and surveying the elegantly gowned ladies and the gentlemen in evening dress. To her chagrin and disappointment Henrietta had had to remain behind in Chesterfield Street with a chill that she was sure she had caught in the train. But Eliza had been dragged relentlessly round the shops for stockings and undergarments, and the flowers for her hair which had to match her dress.

Apart from her relations, Eliza didn't know a soul in the room. She couldn't help but be awed by the occasion, her first big social engagement in London. It was even just a little exciting to speculate about the identity of Lord Thornwell.

Surreptitiously she looked around the room for likely candidates. In a far corner, deep in conversation, were two young men, one or other of whom she decided must be the intended suitor. One was about Guy's age and had a look of restless energy that she found quite appealing. At that very moment the young man looked towards her, as though he were on the look-out too, and she quickly pretended to be interested in something else. But she felt a sudden sense of exhilaration: maybe the evening wouldn't be too bad after all.

Eliza was by far the youngest person present, and young ladies were not supposed to drink alcoholic beverages. She sipped barley water while her elders drank champagne. The constant movement and the murmur of voices began to get on her nerves, and she wondered how people could exist in such an atmosphere so often, as they had to do in town. She thought of Lady and the valley below Pelham's Oak, and suddenly unbidden in her mind's eye there rose the image of the strong, athletic figure of Ryder Yetman standing on the roof with his fair hair shimmering against the deep blue sky. It had been like an apocalyptic vision that kept returning to haunt her.

'My dear Eliza,' her aunt's voice broke into her reverie, 'I want you to meet Lord Thornwell, who is a friend of both your uncles and also knew your father. Harry, may I present to you my niece, Eliza Woodville?'

'How do you do, Miss Woodville?'

Lord Thornwell smiled at her and bent his head over her hand. She stared as if mesmerised at the thatch of iron-grey hair on his lordship's head. When he looked up his calm grey eyes were friendly and he kept her hand in his; but although quite handsome his cheeks were withered and she knew he was old. He was an old man.

'I've heard so much about you, Eliza. May I call you Eliza?' he enquired pleasantly.

'Of course, sir.'

'And I'm Harry.'

Harry – Harry Thornwell. He was tall and distinguished looking, his face immensely kind; but he was as old as her uncle, perhaps even older. As he saw her expression his eyes clouded momentarily. Well, he should have known it would not be an easy task to attract a beautiful, aristocratic young girl.

'I'm so sorry I missed the wedding of Guy and Margaret,' he said conversationally. 'That way we might have met before. But I was in Italy. Did you enjoy the wedding?'

'Very much,' Eliza replied woodenly. 'Did you enjoy Italy?'

'Very *much*.' His tone was enthusiastic. 'I have a villa near Genoa. Do you know Italy at all?'

'Not at all. I've never been abroad.'

Lord Thornwell kept his voice deliberately casual.

'I must say your brother looks astonishingly happy,' he remarked.

'Doesn't he?' Eliza glanced at Guy. She too was puzzled by how happy he was.

'He is obviously rapturously in love. Lucky man.'

Had he gone too far? Lord Thornwell was about to explain himself when the butler appeared and announced dinner.

'My dear Harry, *would* you take in Eliza?' Gwendoline murmured at his elbow, giving her arm to Guy, while Margaret was partnered by Edgar.

'Gladly.' Lord Thornwell offered his arm to Eliza, who put three fingers through it. She felt very nervous, even rather giddy.

The procession seemed to form itself naturally to go into the dining room, led by Edgar and Margaret, who already seemed to have struck up a rapport. As a mature woman Margaret had learned to overcome shyness.

'Such a pleasant woman, your sister-in-law,' Lord Thornwell said. 'I found her most charming.'

'She is.'

His arm seemed to press intimately against her. He patted her fingers in an avuncular manner. Yet she knew that he knew: this was not a chance encounter. By no means. How could he *presume* to think she could care for a man of fifty or more, even though he had a seat in the House of Lords and large estates? What did she care about wealth or status? Guy might have had to sell himself to a woman much older than him, but she didn't. Slowly her anger began to mount at the presumption, the indignity that had been forced upon her. She was to be sold, as Guy had been sold, and no one had told her! Was there no end to the rapaciousness of her mother and uncles? Were they all in this conspiracy?

In front of her the dining room glittered with gas lamps on the walls and candles in silver candlesticks on the table. There were black-coated servants everywhere, and a string trio played Schubert in the corner.

It was a grand occasion, and as Lord Thornwell's wife there would be many of them – any number. She would be stifled by them. She would hate them. She would have to arrange them and invite all these pompous, stuffy people, who would ogle her or fawn upon his lordship's young bride.

A footman showed them to their places at table. As he drew back her chair, a feeling of panic rose in Eliza's breast and the faces round the table, all of whom seemed to be smiling at *her*, swam and once again she felt giddy.

She looked at Lord Thornwell who, still smiling, was pointing to the chair beside him and preparing to sit down.

Eliza looked at the seat, at the face of the footman, which appeared puzzled, at Lord Thornwell, who now showed traces of concern, and then at her aunt who, at the head of the table, was smiling encouragingly at her.

It was a trap, a carefully planned, cunningly laid trap from which she would never, ever be able to withdraw. She must do it now before the painful clamps fastened round her ankles. Suddenly Eliza seized the back of her chair and flung it away from her.

'No,' she cried, 'no, no, no.'

Then, gathering up her skirt, she ran helter-skelter from the room.

4

Maude Brough stood in the centre of the playground while her small charges swirled about her, each little girl holding on to the hand of her partner. Round and round they went, their high voices raised in unison:

> 'Ring a ring of roses
> A pocket full of posies
> A tishoo a tishoo
> They all fall DOWN!'

The last syllable was uttered in a shout as they collapsed on the ground, their skirts billowing in the air, and their waving legs, encased in blue woollen stockings and black shoes, looking like the feet of tiny beetles.

Maude had worked for two and a half years as assistant teacher at a small private school for girls run by Mr and Mrs Pope in their large family house in a village near Yeovil. It could accommodate up to fifty young scholars and was set on high ground which afforded a beautiful view of the Somerset countryside; with its deep valleys and wooded hills. As a school it was well equipped, and its extensive grounds enabled its pupils to participate to the full in all kinds of outdoor activities. The Popes were very keen on the benefit to mind and body of rigorous exposure to the open air.

Mr Pope had formerly been a master at Eton College and he was well qualified as a teacher and disciplinarian. He only took pupils up to the age of eleven, after which they transferred to a bigger school with every expectation of doing well, as Heather

Hall School imbued most of its girls with the foundations of a good academic education. Mrs Pope, herself a mother of four, supervised the domestic side.

Maude was grateful for the opportunity that had enabled her to rise above her station and become a professional woman, and thus advance several steps up the social ladder. All five children of the miller of Wenham had been ambitious, but Maude, the middle sister of three, was the only one to become a professional teacher.

She was, however, always torn between her aspirations and her love for the town where she was born, especially the sleepy river that rolled past it, and the mill which, it was claimed, ground the best flour in the district, on the bank near the bridge.

It was this maybe, as much as her fear of remaining a spinster, that had made her agree to marry Ryder Yetman. He was a man of the town, his love for it as deep as her own.

Moreover, Ryder, as an older man who had been abroad, was attractive to a woman who had never been further south than Southampton. For a short time she was swept off her feet by Ryder, but that mood of elation did not last long.

In a very short time she had realised that their temperaments were incompatible.

'Maude dear – ' Mrs Pope appeared at her side, a bell in her hand ' – have you forgotten that recreation should have ended five minutes ago? You are dreaming, Maude, dreaming.'

'I'm sorry, Mrs Pope,' Maude said colouring and, taking the bell from the headmaster's wife, she gave it a vigorous ring. Immediately her little charges obediently formed themselves into a docile line in front of her.

It was not like Maude to daydream. Mrs Pope frowned. Their favourite teacher had become engaged, was due to leave them in the summer. While they regretted the fact, they were happy about the cause; yet that perceptive mother of four was sure that all was not well. Maude had never introduced them to her fiancé, and seldom spoke about him.

She certainly did not act like a woman in love.

'Maude, we are having a little soirée next Tuesday,' Mrs Pope said as she accompanied Maude and the line of children back to the school. 'Would you like to bring Mr Yetman?'

'Oh no thank you, Mrs Pope,' Maude said quickly.

'We would love to meet him.'

'Well, you will . . . one day.' Maude's voice trailed off lamely.

'But why would you not like to bring him next week, Maude?'

'I'm sure he would not be free, Mrs Pope. Besides, he does not really enjoy those entertainments. Not like Mr Westwick . . .' Maude gave a deep sigh.

Mr Westwick was a man of great sensibility, delicacy and education, as unlike Ryder as it was possible to be. He taught mathematics in the school and had been educated at Cambridge. It was, of course, a position far beneath his capabilities; but he had a tendency to chest complaints and had been told not to strain himself.

'You like Mr Westwick, don't you, Maude?' Mrs Pope was a woman who did not mince words.

'I think everyone likes him, Mrs Pope.' Maude smiled. 'It would be hard not to like him.'

'But I think *you* like him particularly.'

'Mrs Pope, I am engaged to be married,' Maude said primly.

'Then we must talk about your replacement,' Mrs Pope murmured, and with a little wave she turned off in another direction.

From the window of his room Samuel Westwick watched Maude Brough deep in conversation with the headmaster's wife. As they ushered a line of small girls back to the house they looked like two mother hens with a brood of chicks. He was the only male member of the staff to be resident, because he was a friend of the family – a fellow student of one of the Pope boys at Cambridge – and was here as much for his health as anything else, to take advantage of the beneficial effects of the pure Somerset air.

Suddenly Maude looked up and their eyes met. Samuel waved

and tapped his finger urgently against the window pane. Maude shook her head and smiled, giving a meaningful glance towards Mrs Pope.

Samuel felt his heart flutter in his breast. His breath came in short gasps and he put his handkerchief to his mouth, inspecting it anxiously for tell-tale signs of blood.

Eliza gazed round at the members of her family who surrounded her. Their expressions registered various degrees of disapproval. Her mother looked the most angry. Margaret seemed to feel sorrow rather than anger, to show a degree of compassion that might be to Eliza's advantage on another occasion. Guy carefully studied his nails, rarely looking at his sister and yawning from time to time as though to indicate his embarrassment.

It was Guy, nevertheless, who, as head of the household, spoke first. He finally finished examining his nails, gave them a polish on the lapel of his coat and stood up.

'You know, my dear Eliza, how upset the family are at your outburst the other evening, when only the best was intended.'

'Only the *best*!' Eliza exploded. 'To marry me off to an old man.'

'Tush, dear,' Henrietta said reprovingly. 'He is my age exactly. I do not consider myself old.'

'But still old enough to be my father, Mama.'

'Nevertheless your behaviour was inexcusable,' Guy intoned, and, raising his chin and putting his hands behind his back, he fixed his eyes sternly on Eliza. 'You might have sat through the dinner and been polite. Nothing you did not wish would have been forced on you.'

Yes, it was inexcusable, rude.

Eliza, momentarily crushed by her family's united attitude, hung her head. 'I'm sorry,' she murmured, 'I don't know what came over me.'

Although the family knew what was behind Eliza's sudden exit – and probably Lord Thornwell did too – it remained a

73

mystery to most of the other guests, except for the inexplicable cry: 'No, no, no!' That had done most damage. The obvious explanation, the one most people accepted, was that Eliza had felt unwell; the unaccustomed heat had made her rush from the room. Lord Thornwell had sent flowers. Although kindness itself, he had the wisdom not to make a personal enquiry. Doubtless he had correctly divined the expression in Eliza's eyes as she'd looked at him.

'You know perfectly well what came over you!' her mother burst out. 'A sheer *wilful* display of bad manners. Poor Gwendoline. She prides herself on her successful parties. The shame and humiliation of the evening will take her weeks, if not months, to recover from.'

'Yes, I'm particularly sorry about Aunt Gwendoline.'

'It need never have happened, Eliza,' Guy went on censoriously. 'For a girl of your breeding, quite unacceptable . . . so we have decided . . .'

At the last minute his nerve seemed to fail him, and he looked to his wife for support.

'We thought it might be in your interests, Eliza dear.' Margaret quickly took up her cue. 'You must believe us when we tell you we only have your interests at heart.'

Eliza was about to make a rude retort when she changed her mind. She divined that Margaret, after all, meant well. She had no axe to grind, unlike her mother and brother. She wished to get on with her sister-in-law rather than antagonise her. So she stayed silent, though her expression was still rebellious.

'I have, as you know, family in Holland,' Margaret continued. 'Your mother and brother and I have discussed the matter with your Uncle Prosper and my father. We think . . .' Margaret's voice faltered under Eliza's gaze but, with a quick glance at Guy, she went on: 'We think that in *your* own interests, with *your* welfare at heart, you should spend some time in Holland.'

'Holland!' Eliza gasped. 'But I don't want to go to Holland.'

'It is a very good opportunity,' Henrietta butted in. 'There is an academy in Amsterdam, a finishing school for young ladies. There is the kind Heering family to stay with . . .'

'A finishing academy!' Eliza could not contain herself. 'You think *I*, who have been free to do what I want, ride my horse over the countryside at will, would want to go to a *finishing academy* . . .'

'Only for a year.' Guy tried to sound reasonable.

'A *year*!' By now Eliza was slightly hysterical. 'Have you all gone mad, taken leave of your senses. A *year*!'

Then, running her hands wildly through her hair, she turned her back on her family and, as she had done a few days before, stormed from the room, banging the door after her so hard that the large, well-built house appeared to shake.

Guy found he was trembling, whether with anger or nerves he wasn't sure. It was an ordeal to confront Eliza, whose temper was well known. Margaret had gone very pale, and Henrietta got up and began to pace around the room, her small, trim figure quivering with indignation.

'This is too much.' She raised her finger in the air. 'That rebellious child will have to be disciplined. If she were not younger and capable of overpowering me I would beat her. Guy . . .'

'I shan't beat her,' Guy said quickly, stepping back with a nervous laugh.

'You must go and talk to her, put some sense in her head. You and she have always been close. Tell her that if she does not do as we suggest . . .'

'Yes?' Guy asked as his mother seemed to hesitate.

'Well, she must do as we suggest,' Henrietta concluded lamely. 'She is a minor and she has no choice. Put the truth to her, and do it forcefully, Guy.'

'Yes, dear,' Margaret said, giving him an encouraging smile. 'Do as your mother asks.'

It was true that, despite the difference in their ages, Guy and his sister had always been close. They were both instinctively rebels, though as the man, and now the head of the family, Guy invariably got his own way. He was six years older than his sister, two other children having died in infancy in between, victims of the same bronchial weakness that had afflicted their father. Maybe it was the fact that Guy and Eliza had survived that had drawn them together.

Now Guy walked slowly along the corridor, his head bent in thought. He stopped and knocked at the door.

'Eliza,' he said softly.

He said her name again, this time louder, and then again, but there was no reply. He turned the handle, but the door was locked.

'Let me in,' he whispered, his face close to the door. 'I only want to help.'

He stayed there for a few seconds more and was about to walk away, when the door was flung open without warning and he nearly fell into the room. Eliza stood in front of him, her face stormy and streaked with tears.

'I . . .'

'How *could* you?' she cried. 'How *could* you let them send me to Holland – to that awful, stuffy, pious family?'

'My dear sister.' Guy put out his hands placatingly. 'Just allow me to come in and talk to you.'

Eliza stood back, and Guy walked into her bedroom, observing the crumpled bed where, doubtless, she had flung herself in a fit of weeping. Momentarily he was overcome by pity for his sister, and as he turned round he opened his arms and she ran into them, leaning her head against his shoulder.

'Oh, Guy. I *wish* I were a man.'

'You've always said that, my dear,' he whispered, stroking her hair back from her brow and looking tenderly into her eyes. 'Believe me, it isn't always the advantage it seems. Don't forget I have had to do something in which I had very little choice. I had either to marry Margaret or face selling this house. Ruin was just round the corner. We would have been destitute had I not done so, Uncle Prosper made that very clear to me. How do you think I feel about *that*?'

'I hate Uncle Prosper sometimes.' Eliza broke away from

him and banged her fist into her palm. 'All he thinks about is
. . . position . . . influence . . . money.'

'When you have none it is the most important thing in the
world.' Guy drew her down on to the crumpled bed. 'With
Margaret's fortune I can hold my head up again. I am a man
of substance, of consequence. If only I didn't have to go to that
dreadful office' – he put his head in his hands – 'I would be the
happiest man in the world . . . even with Margaret.'

'You do not . . . love Margaret?' Eliza whispered.

'How can I *love* Margaret?' Guy said scornfully. 'She is five
years older than I am; she is ugly and she has a will of iron.'

'But there *is* something I like about Margaret,' Eliza insisted.
'I do not see her with your eyes, but in her expression today
I saw sympathy for me in my predicament. Of course, she is
at odds with Mother about her position in the house. It is not
easy for her.'

'I don't dislike Margaret either,' Guy said hurriedly. 'Like
you I find her very sympathetic. She is very kind. But you
know, my dear' – he put a hand on her shoulder – 'I am a
man who has known love, passion. It is very hard for me to
have as my life's companion someone who has none at all.'

'Then you know why I could never have married Lord
Thornwell,' Eliza said mulishly.

'What do *you* know of passion?' Guy rose and, putting his
hands in his pockets, went to the window, where he stood
looking down on the house he had rented to Ryder Yetman.
'You are but a girl of eighteen. Lord Thornwell may have been
repulsive to you – and that I can understand – but you must
behave correctly in public, Eliza. You must learn to control
your temper. I think this scheme of going to Holland for a
year is an excellent one. It will not be very exciting, but it
will be interesting and it will give you the chance to think.
I cannot but approve of it. With your interests at heart, my
dear, I hasten to add.'

He sat down again and took Eliza's hand gently in his own.
'Who knows what will happen in Holland? Wouldn't it be funny
if I were married to a Dutch woman and you were wed to a

Dutch man? If he were like Margaret, *he* would be sure to keep you under control.'

Eliza said nothing. She didn't even look at her brother, because in her imagination she saw so clearly the figure standing on the roof, his hair the colour of the straw in his hands.

Slowly a plan, an idea whose audacity made her inwardly gasp, began to form in her mind.

Guy knew a great many young, titled or wealthy men, most of whom had titled or wealthy wives. There were a few bachelors in his group, a few men-about-town who Margaret feared, not without reason, might lead him astray.

A few days after the family conference with Eliza (who since then had spent most of her time sulking in her room or riding Lady disconsolately round the fields correctly attired, at the family's insistence, in riding habit and using a side saddle) Guy made his escape to London. There he intended to enjoy a few days in the company of his friends while making a pretence of doing some work.

How Guy hated his days of drudgery in the warehouse overlooking the Thames where he was being taught the rudiments of the vast Heering and Martyn business. How he looked forward to going home to Chesterfield Street in the evening. There he would bathe and change, before going to his club, or maybe to a less reputable establishment where he could play for high stakes and meet women whose virtue was less than perfect.

One night Guy visited a gambling club in Covent Garden where bezique, chemin de fer or ordinary card games were played for high stakes, where gin or whisky could be had for tuppence a tot, and where a woman, or a man, could be hired for the hour or the night. He had dined well at Quaglino's in the company of three of his friends, all of whom were unattached, dissolute and as rich as Croesus. For a long time when his own prosperity foundered Guy had had to shun their company. It was good to be numbered in their circle again.

They were all drawn to the card tables by the high stakes

offered and the fact that there were a number of pretty women sitting, or standing, idly about watching the game.

Guy was about to sit down and take his chance at bezique, to attempt to bring the elusive knave of diamonds and queen of spades together, when he caught the eyes of a young woman who seemed to be in the company of an acquaintance of his, Caspar Moss, who was the heir to an earldom.

For a moment he was transfixed. She could not have been more than twenty. Her eyes were a brilliant blue, her complexion was a flawless cream, and golden curls in an elaborate coiffure tumbled about her head. She wore a décolleté gown and he saw the mounds of a pair of most beautiful breasts rising enticingly from the froth of tulle.

Guy gulped and asked for his cards, but under that disturbing, curious gaze his play was erratic and he lost a lot of money.

Finally he withdrew, and after paying his debts and buying himself a whisky he sauntered back to the bezique table. The young woman wore a look of boredom because Lord Moss excelled at the game and did not appear to tire of it. Guy didn't know how he could keep his eyes on his cards in her presence.

He stood behind her, admiring the sweep of her shoulders, the graceful curve of her neck. Slowly she seemed deliberately to turn and gaze at him and, as he smiled, he lifted a finger as if enticing her over to him.

Caspar was so absorbed in his game that he didn't notice that his companion had left his side and, as the woman rose gracefully and sauntered to the edge of the crowd, Guy withdrew to the back of the room and she followed him.

For a moment they stood smiling at each other and then Guy said: 'Haven't we met before?'

'I don't *think* so,' she murmured, her voice low, musical, as lovely as her face.

'I'm a very old friend of Jelly Moss.'

The fact that he knew the Viscount's nickname was a way of establishing his credentials.

'I hardly know him at all,' the woman said dismissively. 'My name is Lally. Lally Bowyer.'

'And mine's Guy Woodville.'

Later he escorted her back to an address just round the corner in Drury Lane. It was a shabby house in a shabby street patrolled by pimps, prostitutes and a variety of rogues and ne'er-do-wells who were sometimes apprehended by the patrolling bobbies from nearby Bow Street and hauled off to the cells.

It was a far from salubrious area and Guy's heart sank. She had told him she was an actress, but now he thought that maybe she was nothing better than a common prostitute.

The entrance to the house was dingy and there was an all-pervading smell of fried fat. Guy's nostrils twitched as he followed Lally up the stairs right to the top, where both paused while they caught their breath.

'It's only temporary,' Lally said, with a fetching smile that completely turned his heart, stifling all criticism, 'while I find my feet.'

Impulsively Guy leaned towards her and, before she had time to open the door, kissed her.

Margaret found her role as the new Lady Woodville a difficult one. She had not foreseen how much Henrietta would try to interfere in the running of the house, or the moods and capriciousness of her young sister-in-law, Eliza. In her innocence she had thought her husband's mother would be content to take a back seat, and she had scarcely thought about Eliza at all.

For a woman who, approaching thirty, had been resigned to the idea of lifelong spinsterhood, the advent of young Sir Guy had been like a dream. He was handsome and aristocratic. His manners were exquisite. To all and sundry, high and low, equals and servants, he was the same courteous man whom many people not only respected but also loved.

Margaret was, however, aware that there was another side to Guy: she knew he liked to play cards, to patronise the gaming tables. She did not wholly approve of some of the friends he introduced to her in Chesterfield Street, and she regretted the fact that so many of them were aimless, footloose bachelors.

But she had made up her mind not to nag, and she would

not nag. Despite his economic dependence on her family, she would allow Guy his freedom; in that way she hoped, in time, to win his love.

In those first months of her marriage Margaret was in love and wanted everyone to love *her*. She soon discovered that the reality was different and that, as a foreigner, many people regarded her with reserve, even suspicion.

Wenham was a small place and, in her eyes, the attitude of its citizens narrow and small-minded. She knew she was an object of curiosity and that the servants showed their allegiance to her mother-in-law rather than her. Despite her almost perfect English, some people professed not to understand what she was saying.

It was all rather distressing, but Margaret was not one to let things get her down. She had too much to be grateful for: an entire new existence, a husband she adored and the possibility of a child one day. In fact, everything to live for.

Despite Henrietta's dominating presence and her interference, she had little to do with the actual running of the house, or the estate. She objected to someone usurping her place, but she had never bothered herself with mundane matters and now it was too late. Margaret was there, the reins very much in her hands.

Margaret assumed control more and more, especially when, the honeymoon over, Guy started to spend a lot of time in London. Margaret spent days, weeks going over inventories with the bailiff and the estate manager with the aid of a map of the locality until she felt she knew every building on the Woodville estate.

To everyone Margaret was gracious and polite, but she wanted no one to be under any misapprehension as to who she was. She went over all the accounts, visited all the tenanted properties and either negotiated new terms with the tenants or gave them orders to quit. In cases of genuine hardship, however, she suspended payments of rent altogether, and would look after the sick and the poor and send clothing for their children.

Finally she turned her attention to the farm just two fields away from Pelham's Oak. Again she examined the accounts and the returns. She saw that the yield of eggs, milk and dairy produce was low; her conclusion was that the tenants were unsatisfactory. She decided to pay them a visit.

As her carriage stopped outside the farmhouse she sat for a few moments examining the scene before her. She observed that the house and outbuildings were in a bad state of repair; the cattle thin and undernourished.

Sir Guy's mother had never dirtied her shoes by coming to the farm, and the farmer was understandably astonished when the Woodville carriage stopped outside his door and the new Lady Woodville alighted, unaccompanied. She stepped carefully across the muddy farmyard, picking her way between the cackling, excited hens and curious cats, and introduced herself to the farmer who was washing his boots under the pump in the yard.

He knew nothing about her, except that she was a foreigner, and her appearance surprised him because she looked so much older than Sir Guy.

Excited by a personal visit from the great lady herself, Martin Crook summoned his wife from the kitchen, and together they conducted Lady Woodville over the house. She paused for some time in each room to make copious notes, showing shock here, concern there at the state the place was in. When she saw the bedroom where the couple's six children slept she was appalled.

'The baby died of measles in the spring, my lady,' the farmer's wife said, sniffling pitifully. 'But for that we'd've had seven.'

Margaret offered her condolences, but thought she noted a look of relief on the face of the harassed mother. However, as a method of birth control it was a drastic remedy.

'Sir Matthew and then Sir Guy never took any interest, my lady,' the farmer whined. 'When we asked the bailiff for help we were sure it never got passed on.'

Margaret nodded grimly. It was true that some of the rooms were uninhabitable, and when it rained water poured in through a hole in the roof.

When they returned to the main room Mrs Crook scooped a crying toddler off the floor with a deft movement and, tucking it under her arm, wiped its nose vigorously with her sleeve. Margaret instinctively winced and looked around for somewhere clean to sit down.

The little speech she had been going to make about the need for the family to find somewhere else to live was forgotten. Instead she said: 'I have made a careful inventory of all the work that needs to be done here, Mr Crook, and I will see that it *is* done, and soon. When the farm has been properly restored I shall not raise the rent for the time being but will give you the chance to improve your produce. It may be that I will lend you the money for new equipment, because new methods of farming are being invented all the time. In Holland we have some excellent farms,' she said with pride, 'and employ the most advanced methods. But I am told that your milk is sometimes sour on delivery, the eggs bad; I could count the ribs in some of those poor beasts in the field.' She put her pencil under her chin and appeared to consider the matter with great care. 'I will give you two years to put things right; then we shall review the situation. Now.' A flea-ridden cat made a leap for her lap – maybe sensing a chance to escape with so bountiful a patron – but brushing it aside she got quickly to her feet and prepared to take her leave. 'The problem is where will you live while the repairs on your house are being carried out?'

'Can't we stay here, my lady?' Martin Crook tugged at his ear. 'There baint nowhere else we can go.'

'I saw a house along the valley.' Margaret pointed in a westerly direction. 'That belongs to the estate, does it not?'

'It does, my lady,' Mrs Crook said. 'My husband's mother lived there until her death last year.'

'Well, that would seem ideal . . .'

' 'Tis let, my lady,' the farmer said. 'And the new tenant is just about to take up residence.'

'And who may that be?' Margaret looked puzzled. This piece of information had escaped her careful investigations.

''Tis a man called Ryder Yetman, my lady. He belongs to the Yetman family in the town, but he don't seem to have much to do with them.'

'And what does he do?'

'He was a soldier, my lady; but he'm a thatcher now. His family is in the building trade, but grown so rich now that they don't soil their hands with that sort of work no longer.'

'Of course, Yetman,' Margaret murmured. 'They worked on Pelham's Oak, did they not? And Ryder Yetman was in charge. He did very well. Maybe we can persuade him to work on the farmhouse. I shall go and see him straight away.'

'Thank you, my lady.'

With much deference to her superior social status the farmer and his wife saw her to the door, to which her coachman drew as close as he could to prevent her dirtying her dainty shoes in the mud.

Seeing her sister-in-law's carriage outside the farm, Eliza had chosen another route and circled the fields, sticking close to the river until she came to the cottage on the far side of the stream.

Her mother was in Bournemouth for the day visiting her brother Prosper – no doubt to discuss her – and Guy had gone up to London by train. Not infrequently he spent a night or two in town before he returned.

The shirt and breeches she had worn had been spirited away, and she dared not disobey her mother now that all the family were united against her. They had tried to break her spirit, as yet without success, but she was sufficiently afraid to give in to small things. She didn't know whether she was strong enough to resist them completely.

She wore a simple riding habit with a long skirt, and high boots underneath. Because it was so hot she had removed her jacket and, instead of the normal shirt wore a chiffon blouse with billowing sleeves.

When they came to the stream she let Lady drink awhile, all the time gazing at the cottage on the far side of the field, now dressed with a bright, shiny golden thatch. The walls gleamed with new white paint and the door and the woodwork were black. Nestling in the valley, it looked like a cottage from a fairy tale and, spurred on by curiosity, Eliza crossed the stream after Lady had drunk her fill and trotted slowly across the field until she came to the path that led from the farm.

The house appeared to be deserted. The door was shut and she could see no movement inside. She felt a strange sense of disappointment, almost loss, and was about to turn and go back when she heard a sound from behind the cottage; the sound of a shovel entering the earth.

She slid gracefully to the ground and tethered her horse to the gatepost. Then she walked cautiously round the side of the house and stood for a moment, unobserved. Half way down the garden, Ryder, stripped to the waist, was digging the soil over, turning the sods then plunging his spade deep into the ground again.

She was a little embarrassed by the sight of a half-naked man and was about to retrace her steps, when just then he looked up. Quickly he threw his spade on the ground and reached for his shirt. Shrugging it over his head and then tucking it into his breeches, he came towards her, his expression if anything as embarrassed as hers.

'Miss Woodville!' he cried. 'Please forgive the state you saw me in.'

'That's perfectly all right, Mr Yetman.' Eliza remained cool and composed. 'I happened to be passing . . .'

'Come in, Miss Woodville, please.' Ryder threw open the back door. 'And please also overlook the fact that I'm not prepared to receive visitors.'

'The cottage looks beautiful now,' Eliza said with enthusiasm, stepping into the cool kitchen. 'I couldn't help but admire it.'

'I haven't seen you for a long while, Miss Woodville,' Ryder said. 'I thought maybe you'd gone away.'

'No, but I'm going away soon.' She looked round the pretty

kitchen with its fresh green check curtains, a bowl of flowers on the scrubbed deal table.

'I thought maybe you wus married,' Ryder ventured.

'No.' She paused.

'Please come this way, Miss.' He pointed to the main room. 'Can't have you standing in the kitchen.'

Eliza followed him into the sitting room, where pretty chintz curtains billowed in the breeze coming through the window. There were rugs on the stone floor, and two comfortable chairs on either side of the inglenook, which bore traces of a recent fire. Against the back wall was a low sofa covered in the same material as the chairs.

A large bowl of flowers stood on the deep window ledge, and everything gleamed and shone with polish, signs that a woman had been at work.

'Well!' Ryder stood in front of the empty fireplace, his hands in the pockets of his breeches. 'Not married, eh?'

'No.' She looked at him for a long while and then said, 'Are you?'

'No. Not yet.' He set his mouth in a stubborn line as though he did not wish to discuss the subject.

'I changed my mind,' she went on. 'About the marriage.'

'Oh, *you* didn't like the man your family wanted you to marry?' Ryder chuckled and took up his pipe from a cleft in the wall near the inglenook.

'He was fifty years of age,' Eliza exclaimed indignantly, leaning forward. '*Fifty!* And *I* am not yet nineteen.'

'That is too bad, Miss,' Ryder said, again with a chuckle. 'And what did you do?'

'I ran out of the room where we were to dine. I don't know what came over me. I felt a kind of madness. I was so angry, so humiliated, as though they'd mislead me and made a fool of me. People assumed I didn't feel well; but I simply couldn't bear to sit next to *him*.' She paused and sat down, uninvited, in one of the chairs. Ryder began to light his pipe in a slow, measured way, staring at her thoughtfully.

'My family knew what was wrong, of course, and so did

Lord Thornwell. He was very nice, though, and sent flowers. I feel I *had* behaved badly, and my family were furious. I am to be exiled abroad as a consequence . . .'

'Oh, I'm sorry to hear that. You'll miss your riding.' Ryder put his pipe in his mouth and started to puff at it to get it to draw.

'I'm to be taught to be a lady.' Eliza's voice was heavy with sarcasm. 'To go to *school* again. That's why I'm not allowed to wear breeches when I go riding. In fact I'm not supposed to be here. But my mother is in Bournemouth and my brother in London. Doubtless there'll be someone spying on me.'

'It sounds like they keep a pretty strict eye on you, Miss Woodville.'

'They do. And yet I'm *nineteen* in a few weeks' time. Isn't it shocking that I'm treated like a child?'

'I'm surprised you take any notice of them, knowing you.'

'How do you mean?' She looked at him with interest. ' "Knowing me"?'

'Well!' Ryder contemplated the bowl of his pipe. 'I've had a good opportunity to observe you about the house and riding in the fields. You may not know it, but I have. I've observed you a great deal, Miss Woodville, and the conclusion I've reached is that you are an independent spirit. You do not like conventions, and you are not conventional.'

'But how can I break away from *them*, Mr Yetman?'

Ryder shrugged, then he knocked his pipe on the side of the inglenook and put it back in the cleft in the wall.

'Marriage is the only way for a woman. That's what I find unfair. Marriage or spinsterhood – there's no other choice. There *are* woman of learning, but people are afraid of them. I've travelled a great deal, you know, Miss Woodville. I've known and met people of all kinds.'

In the corner of the living room was a bookcase full of books, and in another corner a great globe stood on a stand. Ryder went over to it and began to revolve it with his hand.

'I travelled the world. I fought in a war. I've been wounded, left for dead. When I came back here I knew I didn't fit in no more, but I loved the land and I had no place else I wanted to go. I thought maybe I'd settle when I met Maude Brough again. She seemed to like me and I liked her . . . but, well, enough said,' he concluded rather lamely.

He looked into her eyes and he wanted to tell her that he thought he loved her, not Maude Brough. He wanted to tell her that he was obsessed by her; that her beauty had haunted him ever since he'd first seen her in the big house.

But he didn't dare. Not yet. Not, perhaps, ever. He would not, however, have told her that he felt a physical passion for her the like of which he had never felt for Maude Brough. The idea might have shocked her as it sometimes shocked him; the depth of his feelings, his sense of frustration as he thought about her in all his waking hours. Frequently he dreamt about her as well.

But from the way she looked at him now he thought maybe she knew it with her woman's intuition, and he was about to take a step nearer her when suddenly the noise of a carriage outside interrupted the silence that had fallen between them. Ryder went to the window and looked out.

'I'm afraid 'tis your sister-in-law, Miss Woodville. I think she must have come after you,' he said.

Eliza remained where she was. She felt a little nervous, but unafraid. Ryder's presence gave her courage. He was strong, and his strength seemed to pass into her. She knew that a situation had arisen between them that was as far-reaching in its implications as it was unexpected. It was frightening, but thrilling too.

'Open the door,' she said, and there was a command in her tone. 'Ask her to come in. She's already seen the horse. There's nothing we can do. Anyway, we've nothing to be ashamed of. A man and a woman can talk, can't they?'

Without answering, Ryder went to the door and, opening it, stepped outside. Eliza heard him greet her sister-in-law and then she heard her name. She remained where she was, sitting upright, and it wasn't until Margaret entered the room that she got to her feet and greeted her without smiling.

But Margaret had a smile on her face; her manner was gracious as though she wanted to make them feel at ease.

'Fancy seeing *you* here, Eliza! I didn't know you and Mr Yetman were so well acquainted.'

'Well, we are,' Eliza said, a note of defiance in her voice. 'As I happened to be riding here, I looked in. Does *that* satisfy you, Margaret?'

Margaret raised her hand defensively.

'Please don't misunderstand me, Eliza. I haven't come here to see you, but Mr Yetman. Naturally I saw Lady at the gate and realised you must be here. But I was not spying, I assure you of that.'

'That's good,' Eliza said. 'In that case I think I'll be going.'

'Oh, pray don't go,' Margaret said, pleasantly enough. 'I merely came to ask Mr Yetman if he could advise me on some repairs necessary at the farm. Perhaps we could ride back together, Eliza?'

'As you wish.' Eliza sat down again while Ryder invited Margaret to do the same.

'You know how pleased we were with the refurbishment to Pelham's Oak.' Margaret removed her gloves in a leisurely manner and placed them on her lap.

'I don't do that sort of thing any more, ma'am,' Ryder said, leaning against the wall and beginning to fill his pipe again.

'Oh? What do you do?'

'I haven't decided yet, Lady Woodville. I've been doing up this cottage, see?'

'I do see. It looks very pleasant.' Margaret gazed round appreciatively. 'I'm sorry you can't supervise the repairs to the farm for us.'

'I don't do much work for my father any more, Lady Woodville. I prefer to work for myself. I'm going to start a little smallholding here, growing flowers and vegetables, maybe have a few hens. Then I'm going to do some thatching. I like that.'

'He did this roof,' Eliza said as though it were something she too was proud of.

'You're very capable, Mr Yetman,' Margaret said, getting to her feet. 'If you would like to reconsider my proposition, please come and see me; but let me know soon, because I want it to be done quickly.'

'I can tell you now for sure that I won't do it, Lady Woodville,' Ryder said, blowing smoke into the air. 'Once I make my mind up I don't change it. Besides, I've too much to do here before winter sets in. Best see my father, ma'am. I'm sure he can help you, or knows someone who can.'

'Well, in that case I'll consult him.' Margaret now looked sharply at Eliza, who got reluctantly to her feet.

'It was very nice to see you again, Mr Yetman.' Margaret turned graciously towards him at the door.

Eliza thought how quickly, yet how subtly, she had transformed herself from Miss Heering to Lady Woodville.

'And *you*, my lady.' Ryder bowed his head, politely but not in the least obsequiously.

'Goodbye, then.'

'Goodbye.'

He nodded to Eliza, who nodded to him. No message passed between them, but already they seemed to have an understanding that precluded any need for formal farewells.

Eliza on Lady trotted behind Margaret's carriage all the way back to the house. The spring in her horse's step seemed to find an echo in her heart. She was so happy she felt almost delirious. Was she, perhaps, a little bit in love? Was it possible? When the groom came out to look after the horses, while the coachman unharnessed the carriage, he gave her a startled look. She didn't know it, but the expression on her face was beatific.

Margaret paused to chat to the coachman and give him further instructions, while Ted took Lady's bridle and led her round to the back. Although Eliza thanked him she didn't seem to see him. He wondered what had happened to her on that short journey. Mystified, he removed Lady's saddle and began to rub her down.

'Shall we have lunch outside on the terrace?' Margaret said. 'It's such a lovely day. Would you like that, Eliza?'

'Lovely,' Eliza said, not caring where she ate, or when. 'I'll go and change.'

She ran quickly upstairs to her room and stripped off her riding habit. Her heart was racing and she felt like bursting into song. Was it possible to fall so quickly, so easily in love with a man she scarcely knew? The fact that her family would consider him most unsuitable didn't matter in the least. If anything, it added to his attraction. She splashed her face with cold water from the jug on the washstand and combed her hair. Then she put on a summery dress, a pretty floral cotton with a square neckline and short balloon sleeves that her dressmaker had made for her the previous summer.

When she got downstairs the table was already laid in the shade of Pelham Woodville's great oak tree which had given the house its name. Its thick branches swung gracefully across the lawn, touching at one extremity the ornamental fish pond and, at the other, the terrace made of blocks of Purbeck stone on which stood classical statues in bronze and marble, imported in the eighteenth and nineteenth centuries from Italy.

Two or three miles away, as flown by the crow, lay Ryder's cottage, shimmering now in the haze of noon. The windows were closed and it looked as though Ryder had gone out. It was impossible from here to see round the back, but Eliza could imagine him stripped to the waist again digging, a film of sweat across his brow matting his blond hair as though he'd been swimming.

The footman had finished setting the table and held out a chair for Eliza who, thanking him, sank into it. He was someone new she had never seen before. These days the house seemed full of strangers.

'Lady Woodville will be here in a few minutes, Miss Woodville. Would you like something to drink?'

'A glass of water, thank you,' Eliza said to the footman, who bowed and made his exit in precise, measured steps across the terrace. The table had been laid with a white linen cloth, and the Woodville family silver sparkled in the sunshine.

The family, hidebound by convention, had been unaccustomed to eating outside unless it were for a picnic, but as she put her head back and closed her eyes against the sun, Eliza thought what a good idea it was – one of many that Margaret had introduced. As a Dutchwoman brought up in the ways of industry and frugality, Margaret had immediately made changes to the running of the household. She didn't mean to annoy her mother-in-law, but, inevitably, she did. Henrietta found more and more occasions to be away from home, spending much of her time in Bournemouth or its environs, where she was seeking to purchase a property.

The footman brought a jug of water and glasses on a tray just as Margaret arrived, having changed her dress. As she sat down he sprang forward to spread a napkin across her knee.

'Shall I serve luncheon now, my lady?'

'Yes please, Arthur.'

Margaret not only personally engaged each new servant but she remembered their names and knew all about them. She had no need, or desire, for a housekeeper, having been trained by her economical mother to run a large household: to see to everyone's wants and needs from the head of the house right down to the humblest servant.

Luncheon was a simple affair of cold meats and salads, with newly churned butter and freshly baked bread. There was a summer pudding to follow, delicious with fresh cream, and they drank water.

At the beginning of luncheon with the servants present they discussed trivialities, but over the pudding, when they were alone, Margaret got down to what was on her mind.

'This cream from the farm is very good,' she said after tasting it. 'One of the criticisms I had of the farm was the quality of some of its produce. If you see the state of some of the animals you do not wonder. Half-starved cows do not produce good milk. The farmer then brought my attention to how much needed doing, how poor his facilities were. His spirits are very low. I'm afraid your family let everything decay for too long, my dear Eliza. It was as well I came along when I did.' Her lips pursed disapprovingly.

Eliza knew exactly what she meant: Sir Matthew and Sir Guy had been sadly derelict in their duties.

'*That* was the purpose of my visit to Mr Yetman,' Margaret said firmly. '*Not* to spy on you.'

'I'm glad to hear that,' Eliza said, but she kept her eyes on her plate. She was afraid their sparkle might give her away; that the joy she was feeling might reveal itself.

'However, my dear, I must tell you just the same how concerned I was to find you there, alone in his house, with a man. Supposing it had been someone else who discovered you and not I? Supposing it had been your mother?'

'I would not have gone if my mother had been here,' Eliza replied. 'I know that she stands at her window spying on me.'

'Nonsense, you must not say such a thing of your mama . . .'

'But it's true. She also asks the servants to spy on me. I know because they tell me.'

'Tut tut, Eliza, I don't think you should be so familiar with the servants.'

'Some of the servants are my best friends,' Eliza said defiantly. 'Those, the very few, who have been here since I was a child. Ted in the stable was a young lad of about eleven when he started looking after our horses. Ted would *never* spy on me.'

Margaret rose and, pressing her hands to her slender corseted waist, began to pace back and forth. Finally she paused in front of Eliza and gazed down at her. Margaret was tall for a woman so, standing over her, she seemed to Eliza formidable, to have grown in stature.

'My dear Eliza, I think you know that I am genuinely fond of you and want to be your friend. I am a good deal older than you, but I have never had a sister. This is a foreign country to me. Dearest Guy, as you know, has to spend a lot of his time in London. I am delighted he takes the business so seriously, for he has much to learn. I know that Guy was brought up with no need to work. Unfortunately so was his father before him, and the Woodville fortune has practically vanished. Guy is a capable man, but not a man of business. The men in my family were brought up to be frugal and hardworking from their youth. Hence the rewards,' Margaret said with a smile. Then impulsively she sat down next to Eliza and placed her hand over that of the younger woman. 'Oh, I know quite well why Guy wanted to marry me, or rather why his family did. But it was advantageous for me too. Besides the fact that I genuinely love Guy, I wanted to marry and get away from my family. So I know how you feel, my dear, how confined and restricted. We all thought Lord Thornwell an exceptionally fine and attractive man.'

'Fine for you perhaps, but not for me.' As soon as she had uttered the words Eliza regretted them. 'I'm terribly sorry,' she said, clasping the hand that still lay across hers. 'I didn't mean to be rude.'

'I know what you mean.' The practical Margaret nodded her head emphatically. 'Lord Thornwell would have been nearer *my* age than yours; but believe me, my dear sister – for I think of you as that – age is immaterial. Lord Thornwell presented for you what Guy presented for me: a chance to change one's life, change it completely, and for the better. I'm afraid you may well come to regret that you turned down the opportunity.'

'Well, I *don't*,' Eliza said, just as emphatically. Her gaze turned towards the cottage that lay in the valley, and in her mind's eye she could see Ryder leaning against the wall filling his pipe. There was a repose, a strength about him. But it was more than that; much, much more.

'I see.' Margaret got up and resumed her pacing. The footman and a maid came and cleared away. Coffee was brought out in a silver pot, and *petits fours* which cook had baked that morning. Margaret thanked the footman, told him to go, poured and handed Eliza her cup.

'I think your rebellion will be the undoing of you, my dear, if you do not take care. I see a lot of Guy in you; but Guy is a man. You would do well to take advantage of your stay in

Holland to overcome this impulsiveness which I think of as a family weakness. As you are a woman yours will do you more harm.'

'I'm not even sure I'm going to Holland,' Eliza burst out.

'But what do you mean? *That* is all arranged.'

'Yes, I know it is, but not with my consent. Am I a child? No, I am a woman. Had I consented to become engaged to Lord Thornwell I would be nearly a married woman as well, like you.'

'Yes, but under the control of your husband.'

'You are scarcely under the control of *Guy*.'

Margaret acknowledged the justice of the remark and gnawed anxiously at the corner of her fingernail. After a while she put her hand down, and when she looked at Eliza she was no longer smiling.

'Fortunately your brother is so unconcerned about what happens here that I have a free hand; but, essentially, when a woman marries she forfeits her independence. Yet what independence has she before? I loved my father, but I didn't want to be under his control for the rest of my life. Far rather a husband I love and cherish than an ageing father to whom I am subservient. There is also the hope of children to bring joy to our lives and an heir for Guy.

'You see, Eliza, that is the truth of the matter, and if you think anything else you are deceiving yourself. My advice to you is to be obedient to the wishes of your family, which are made in your interests not theirs. Obviously a renewed acquaintance with Lord Thornwell is now quite out of the question, so you must profit as much as you can from your stay in Holland. From what I have seen this very day, I think it should be brought forward. I think you should leave next week and not linger here another moment.'

'Whatever for?'

'I believe you know what I mean, Eliza. Mr Yetman is an attractive man, but he is far beneath you socially. In Holland we would call him a peasant. I did not like to see a lady of quality so much at ease in the company of such a person. I must tell you, my dear, that if you do not agree to go to Holland as soon as possible, I shall be forced to tell your brother and mother exactly what occurred today. Believe me, that will cause a family row of the first order – one that you will surely live to regret.'

5

The late afternoon sun cast its long beams across the shining, polished flagstones of the downstairs room as Ryder took one last look round the cottage. Everything was ready for his bride: the house spruce and spotless inside and out; the thatching finished; the garden, back and front, neat and tidy, with vegetables and flowers already showing their heads above the ground. Beyond the garden was an orchard and, beyond that, the fields where Ryder thought he would keep his few sheep and a cow to provide fresh milk in the morning.

But Maude still showed no enthusiasm for living there, even though he had shown her round two days before. She had been solemn, unsmiling, detached, uninterested. He felt there was more of a gulf between them than ever, but there was no way of telling how she really felt about him. Reserved Maude had always been, and this was the way she continued. However, that very evening they were to see the Rector to discuss the plans for the wedding, the reading of the banns, the date for the marriage itself.

Loving one woman, Ryder was being forced into marriage with another. He had no choice.

Carefully he locked the front door and strode over to Piper, his horse, who was tethered to the post where Eliza had tethered Lady. Every moment that she'd spent with him in the house was precious; everything she'd touched was sacred.

With a deep sigh he unhitched Piper and, springing on to his back, rode off, making a sharp detour so that he could see as much as possible of Pelham's Oak, serene on top of the hill. Its grandeur seemed to symbolise the gulf between himself and Eliza. He was the son of a countryman, a builder; she, the daughter of a baronet.

Ryder completed the circuit of Pelham's Oak wondering if Eliza had looked out and seen him. Once the house was out of sight he gave Piper a sharp tap on the flank and cantered home. Waiting for him at the gate of Riversmead was Agnes, her hat in her hand as though she had just returned from a walk, or a trip to the shops.

'I saw you coming,' she called, swinging open the gate, and as he passed through he smiled at her and held out his hand.

Ryder was eight years older than Agnes, and for most of her adolescence he had not lived at home. Although she loved and admired him, she didn't feel entirely at ease with him. Hat still in her hand, she followed him up the drive and round to the stable, and as he jumped off Piper and unsaddled him, she leaned against the stable wall watching him.

'Have you been at your cottage?'

'Yes.'

'Father seems upset you're not working for him so much.'

'I have to get the cottage ready,' Ryder said, beginning to rub Piper down, his mind clearly on his task.

'For *Maude*?' Agnes gave a brittle laugh.

'I don't know why you laugh like that, Agnes,' Ryder said reprovingly, looking round. 'She's got to live there.'

'She won't.'

'I think she will. She was there two nights ago and made not a squeak of protest.'

Ryder finished his work on the horse. Then he went over to a tub that stood by the wall and, taking several handfuls of oats, began to fill a bucket to feed Piper.

'I don't think you want to wed her,' Agnes said slyly.

'I asked her, didn't I?'

'If you really wanted her you'd do what she wanted.'

'If she really wanted *me* she'd do what I want. She'll have to.

I love that cottage.' Ryder stood up, his eyes glinting as though he were seeing it in his mind's eye: seeing it with someone very different living there with him.

'Anyway, Maude'll be here soon,' Agnes said. 'She sent a message.'

Ryder nodded. 'We're going to see the Rector. See? It's all fixed.' With a heavy heart Ryder finished his task, and as the horse greedily munched its feed he put on his coat and prepared to go into the house.

'Ryder,' Agnes said, a note of urgency in her voice.

'Yes?'

'It's about Mother.'

'What about Mother?' Anxiously he screwed up his eyes.

'She's not well. I can tell.'

'Then she must go and see the doctor.'

'He says it's nothing. It's her time of life.'

'But is there anything really to worry about?'

'It's not like Mother to be so weak, to spend so much time in her bed.'

'I know nothing about women's problems,' Ryder said gruffly. But he was worried. If Agnes had discerned enough to mention it, why hadn't he? Maybe because he was too preoccupied with his own problems, too self-absorbed.

'You are a good girl, Agnes.' He reached out to touch her. 'I wish you could be happy, married to a man you loved. Now Herbert . . .'

Agnes gave a wild laugh and flung back her head.

'Oh, don't mention that silly man's name.'

'But he's *not* silly. He's clever and he's nice. His prospects are excellent.'

'But I don't *love* him.' Agnes stamped her foot peevishly. 'And, what's more, I don't think I will *ever* meet anyone I can love here in Wenham.'

'There are plenty of nice men in Wenham, and hereabouts.'

'Hm!' Agnes snorted derisively. 'It depends what you mean by "nice". I don't find any of them "nice" enough to attract *me*.' She caught at the lapel of his coat and gently pulled him towards her. 'I would *so* like to go to London, only Mother and Father won't let me.'

'London?' Ryder looked surprised. 'Why, it's an awful place.'

'You think so, but I don't.'

'You've never been there.'

'But I'd *love* to go.' She let him go and clasped her hands together, her eyes gleaming. 'I could stay with Aunt Emma. I'm sure that there I'd meet someone I really liked, could really love, someone worthy of me . . .'

'Worthy of you!' Ryder gave a snort.

'Yes, *worthy* of me, Ryder. I don't consider any of the men here are really worthy of me.'

As they resumed their walk and rounded the stables, Ryder drew her to a bench on the lawn and, sitting her firmly down, he sat next to her and looked at her earnestly.

'We are country people, we Yetmans. Our great-grandparents tilled the soil,' he said.

'Our grandfather was a builder . . .'

'But before that, humble folk.'

'Not any more.' She thrust her chin defiantly in the air.

'Father may have made money, but we are simple ordinary folk.'

'*I* don't feel ordinary,' Agnes protested. 'I feel special, and I want to marry someone special. Like . . . like Sir Guy.'

'Guy Woodville!' Ryder gave an explosive laugh and jumped up. 'You are getting ideas above your station, my dear sister. Anyway, he already has a wife.'

'Someone like him.' Agnes's pert little tongue darted out, moistening her lips. 'Rich, titled and very good-looking.'

Just then they were interrupted by a noise at the gate. Peter, the gardener, who had been weeding in one of the herbaceous borders, went over to open it and Maude drove through in her small pony and trap. She drew up in front of the porch just as Agnes and Ryder reached her. She looked pretty and summery in a muslin dress and a straw bonnet, and as she looked at Ryder she smiled at him. He opened the door of the trap and, taking her hand, helped her out.

'Peter, there are some oats in the yard. Give a handful to the horse and water him. Miss Brough will be some time.'

'Yes, sir,' Peter said smartly, leading the pony and trap round the side of the house.

'Tonight is *the* night,' Agnes cried, kissing her future sister-in-law on the cheek.

'What do you mean?' Maude looked at her coolly.

'Very exciting.' Agnes looked surprised. 'Aren't you *excited* about going to see the Rector and having the banns called?'

'Very,' Agnes said, but her expression remained impassive. 'What time are we expected, Ryder?'

Ryder took his watch from his pocket and studied it. For a moment his eyes seemed obscured by a mist which was slow to clear.

'Six o'clock.'

His expression, too, was wooden, but his heart was beating rapidly. The die was about to be cast.

'Ryder spent all day getting the cottage nice for you,' Agnes continued a little maliciously. 'In fact our father says he spends more time there than on his work.'

'I know Ryder, he's very thorough,' Maude said with a schoolmistressy smile of approval.

'You mean you don't mind going to live there now?' Agnes looked surprised.

'A woman must be obedient to her husband,' Maude said primly. 'It's in the marriage vows.'

The Rector of Wenham, the Reverend Austin Lamb, looking across his large desk, decided he had rarely seen a less likely pair of lovebirds. They sat at a distance from each other, scarcely glanced at each other, and when questioned replied in monosyllables: 'yes', 'no', 'perhaps', 'maybe'.

Frequently there were long silences during which the Rector gazed at them keenly as if wondering whether they were too timid to speak. Engaged couples were usually alert, excited, a little apprehensive, shy; but here he had a mature pair – a man and a woman who seemed curiously unmoved by the thought of their impending union.

The Reverend Lamb was not at all like his name. He was a fierce, bigoted, rather frightening man who had few of the charitable virtues extolled in the Bible which he cited so often. He was a man of fire and brimstone. If he were to be believed, there would be few places in heaven for the majority of his docile, blameless congregation, who cowered in front of him, Sunday after Sunday, victims of his hour-long perorations on doom and perdition.

Rather than listening to engaged couples, candidates for confirmation or the ministry, he preferred haranguing his innocent flock from the pulpit, gazing down at them as though they were lost sheep penned up in their pews.

The Rectory, next to Wenham church, was a huge stone house which had been built in the early years of the century. Some would have said it was more fitting for a nobleman than a servant of God, since it had twelve bedrooms, four or five reception rooms, and accommodation for sixteen servants in addition to the family. The Rector incumbent when the house was built had eighteen children and had been married twice.

Even today the Reverend Lamb, who had but one small daughter, kept a good table and enjoyed living well.

Finally in exasperation he broke the silence by looking at the heavy clock which ticked loudly on the mantelpiece.

'Well, if you have no further questions . . . Mr Yetman?'

'No, Rector.'

'Miss Brough?'

'No, Rector.'

'Then we have to fix the day. The important *day*.' The Rector drew his diary towards him. 'Let me see, if we call the first banns next Sunday. How about . . .' He ran his finger down the calendar. 'September? Is September a good month?'

'September is excellent,' Ryder said, surprised he could speak, because his throat felt dry and his lips parched. 'You think September, Maude?'

He turned to his fiancée and looked, at last, into her eyes.

Her expression was unfathomable but she smiled. Somehow Ryder felt that she couldn't trust herself to speak. Was she happy, sad, nervous, frightened? It was hard to know. Her behaviour was very strange.

'Well, that's all,' the Rector said, closing his diary with a thump and, joining his hands, he gazed at them. 'I have explained everything to you, I think. The meaning of marriage, its purpose, above all its solemnity. God made it a sacrament. Now, all I can give you, my children, is my blessing and wish you well.' Coming round the desk, he placed a hand on the head of each and muttered a few inaudible words.

Then he escorted them to the door and stood in the porch watching them as they took the path along by the churchyard to the river. He shook his head. Had he not known Maude Brough so well, had he not been so *sure* her virtue was impeccable, he might have wondered if she were being forced into marriage by necessity. But no, not Maude. Besides, as a practical matter, her figure was too trim.

For a while Maude and Ryder walked side by side without speaking. It was a beautiful evening, the air vibrant with the sound of bees, with the song of birds in the lush green trees. In front of them the Wen cut the valley in two, and beyond was Wenham Hill and the wood where Ryder and his brothers had played as children.

'Ryder!' Maude stopped abruptly, and as Ryder stopped too he could see on her face the signs of some inner struggle. Her expression surprised, almost shocked him.

'Maude . . .'

'Ryder. I . . .'

She seemed to have difficulty in finding words to express what she wanted to say, and Ryder gently prompted her.

'Do say what you have on your mind, Maude. Is it the cottage?'

'No, Ryder, it's more important than that. In fact . . . I don't know how to go on . . .' and to Ryder's consternation Maude slumped to the ground and put her head in her hands. Anxiously he sat down beside her.

'Maude, are you not well?'

'Oh, *Ryder*,' she gasped looking up at him. Suddenly she put her head in her hands again and tears started to trickle down her cheeks. Why someone normally so impassive should behave like this he was at a loss to explain.

'I don't know how I can tell you this, Ryder . . .' she said, trying to control herself. 'You have been so good, done so much, the cottage, everything . . .'

'The cottage . . .' He attempted to smile.

'It's simply that . . . there's someone else,' she burst out, not allowing him to finish. 'I have been so weak allowing it to go this far, and to break the news to you today, when we have actually seen the Rector, arranged for the banns to be called . . . just because I had not the courage to speak before . . . I feel so ashamed.'

'You mean you love another man?' Ryder asked incredulously. 'You don't *wish* us to be married, Maude?'

'How can I when there is another?' Her tears had dried up, but now she began to wring her hands. 'I don't expect you to understand, or even forgive me. I know the humiliation for you will be considerable, but you must blame me not yourself. *I* will take the blame and make sure that everyone in the town knows it. You are so good, Ryder – ' she managed a tearful smile ' – so correct . . . a little stubborn on the matter of the cottage, I'll agree, but one can only admire firmness in a man. I have deceived you, misled you . . . But you see, there is someone at the school . . . he is not at all like you . . . a scholar, indeed an invalid . . . but . . .'

'Maude, I *do* understand,' Ryder said, his hand closing over hers, trying hard to keep the relief from his voice. 'Please don't distress yourself.'

'Then you will release me from our engagement?'

'Of course.'

'But an engagement is a solemn undertaking.'

'I will not hold you to it. I would not *dream* of it . . .'

'But the little cottage was so perfect, you put so much love into it . . .'

'Ah yes.' Ryder hung his head, but only because he did not wish to hurt her by letting her see the joy in his eyes.

Lally . . . she wore her hair like a crown round her head, tight little blonde curls in front and a mass of tiny ringlets behind. Her skin was the texture of a softly ripened peach: flawless. Her eyes were the colour of cornflowers, and as for her figure it defied description.

Since their first meeting in the gambling club he had learned more about her; a little, not much, because his darling was very secretive. She was a dancer at the Alhambra Theatre of Varieties and she told him very little about her origins or her past; but she had aspirations, that was clear. She was ambitious and wished either to climb higher in her profession or make a very good match.

But what she was or where she came from didn't matter at all, because he loved her: deeply, passionately, sometimes he wondered if it were irrevocably too. Guy had had many affairs with loose women and chorus girls; but there was something about Lally that touched his very depths, a mysterious intangible quality that he had never discovered in a woman before. She gave herself, but only so much, and her smile was as enigmatic as the Mona Lisa's. She kept something of herself back and, because of it, he gave her his heart.

Lally's boarding house in Drury Lane was mainly occupied by ladies of the acting and other professions. One of the professions was known as the world's oldest, and many girls who wanted to be dancers or actresses were forced to join its ranks in order to make ends meet. Some never left it. Thus in the tall Georgian house with its crumbling paint and peeling wallpaper, people were coming and going all day and all night.

The cab stopped in Drury Lane and Guy, looking anxiously up at Lally's window, threw a few coins at the driver and then sprinted up the stairs and through the front door, which always remained open.

He ran up the stairs two at a time to the third floor and tapped on the door before slowly turning the handle.

Lally lay almost as he had left her: clothes tossed on the floor, the bed crumpled from their lovemaking, her golden hair spread across her pillow, fast asleep.

It was a tiny room that, in other days, had been a servant's attic before the area began to decline as the better off moved further west. Apart from the rickety iron bedstead there was a washstand with a jug and basin on top and a wardrobe leaning on three legs, its door half open to disclose an unsightly mess inside. The floor was bare except for a rag rug, the curtains were too short for the window and failed to meet in the centre, and there was a great damp patch in the corner of the wall from which a loose piece of faded wallpaper was dejectedly making its way down to the floor.

But none of this mattered to the impetuous lover who, blind to anything but his mistress, tiptoed over to the bed and crouched beside her, gently blowing at her face until she opened her eyes. Then he wafted in front of her a bunch of violets he had bought from a flower seller at the corner of the street as the cab turned into Drury Lane.

'Oooo . . .' Lally began, stretching out her hand, but he immediately stopped her mouth with a kiss.

That day there was no lunch because there was no matinée. Guy sent the old hag who ran the house out for sandwiches from a nearby public house and a bottle of champagne.

They made love and they ate, made love again then slept in each other's arms. At five he looked at his watch, lay on his back and sighed. Lally ran a hand lightly over his face.

'What is it, my love?' she asked, her deep blue eyes shining trustfully.

She had a very soft low voice, an educated voice. She protested that she was a girl of good class who had run away from home because she wanted to be an actress. Guy wanted to believe her, but it was difficult. It was true that she had an air of breeding, but he felt that it could have been acquired, like her cultured voice. He had an idea that she came from the East End and a past she was anxious to obliterate. But he didn't mind. That Lally should remain in some ways mysterious was part of her charm, the essence of desirability.

Guy took her hand and caressing it, brought it to his lips.

'I have got to go down to Dorset to look after my estate. We shan't be able to meet so often.'

'Oh, Guy.' She gave a deep sigh and leaned her cheek against his. 'For how long?'

'For a month, my darling. I shall try and come up to town once in a while. With my wife in the country it may be possible to meet at our house. But my love – ' he kissed her hand and looked seriously into those deep, deep blue eyes ' – we must get you away from this hole. I want you, while I'm gone, to look for a place, maybe a little house in St John's Wood.'

'But I could never *afford* such a thing, Guy,' she protested.

'No, but I can. You find somewhere nice for us, my darling. It will be our little love nest, and I will visit you there often.'

'But a *month*, Guy. I don't think you can love me very much if you can stay away a *month*.'

'My darling, I adore you, you know that,' he protested. 'But since my wedding I have only been in Dorset a few days, and there is a lot to do.'

'If only we'd met before.' Lally sighed deeply, locking her arms round him. 'I might have been Lady Woodville. What a cruel, cruel thing fate is.'

Knowing better, Guy remained silent. If there had been no Margaret, there could have been no love nest for Lally. At five o'clock he took her out to dinner, and afterwards walked with her across Leicester Square to the stage door.

He then hailed a hansom cab which took him to Chesterfield Street. Margaret was waiting for him with a meal carefully chosen, beautifully cooked and exquisitely presented.

As he sat down opposite her, flicked his napkin across his lap and blew her a kiss, Guy thought he was a very lucky man indeed to have two women who adored him.

'How was work today, dear?' she asked, nodding to the butler to begin serving the meal.

'As always.' Guy stifled a yawn. Lally was an energetic

mistress and their love-making, though delightful, made him tired. He would prefer to have gone to the club for a few hands of bridge and then an early night, but he and Margaret had an engagement with Aunt Gwendoline, whose feathers were still ruffled after the scandal caused by Eliza's rejection of Lord Thornwell.

While dinner was being served with slow solemnity, Margaret said nothing, but as soon as the staff had left the dining room, she leaned across the table and said in an urgent whisper: 'It is most important that you make a success of the business, Guy.'

'*Why* is it?' he demanded petulantly, taking up his spoon to eat his soup.

'Father says that the well of money is not limitless. He talks of it drying up . . .'

'Now listen, Margaret, I will not be blackmailed.' Guy scowled. 'I made that very clear at the start.'

'Of course, dear.' Margaret bent her head submissively to her plate.

'I'm a man of quality. I am not used to work and, frankly, I don't like it. However, I have agreed to put *some* hand to the business, because I realise that these days having money is not enough. It must be made to work. The good old times when a gentleman was simply intended to be a gentleman have gone. But don't expect too much of me, Margaret.'

His wife did not look at him, but inwardly she sighed. Maybe a little of that ephemeral gold dust of first love was beginning to fall away from her eyes . . .

John and Catherine Yetman sat at the dining table, heads bowed in an attitude of prayer. But really it was because they could think of nothing to say. Agnes fidgeted with her knife and fork, but she had guessed the news already. The only one who appeared unperturbed was Christopher Yetman, who went on making a hearty meal.

'You are no longer to be wed?' John asked at last, raising his head. 'Is that what you are saying? She has thrown you over?'

'She loves someone else, Father.'

'But she promised; a betrothal is a sacred, *solemn* undertaking.' John's voice rose with indignation as he proceeded.

'Well, Father, not from the point of view of the church. In law maybe, but I shall not sue Miss Brough for breach of promise. I would not wish to marry someone who loved another.'

'I think she was a hussy,' Catherine said vehemently, 'shameless and brazen. Engaged to one man, making eyes at another.'

'Oh no, Mother, I don't think she was. This fellow is a teacher at her school, a scholar, a gentleman. She considers they have more in common than she and I would ever have. I dare say she's right.'

'I must say, you don't seem very crushed.' Christopher Yetman gave his nephew a knowing smile. 'Maybe it was not a very hard sacrifice to allow Miss Brough her freedom?'

'There were differences,' Ryder acknowledged. 'She did not want to live where I did, nor, I think, *as* I did.'

'For that I can't blame her,' his father said bitterly. 'I told you you should give up all idea of living in that cottage once you were married. I was prepared to assist you financially to find something more suitable. Really, Ryder,' woefully his father shook his head, 'this will look very bad in the town. To be thrown over by Miss Brough! Not good enough for the miller's daughter.'

Ryder seemed only too willing to concur.

'Indeed. I felt therefore that I should go away for a time, Father. Besides, I am restless. I thought I was to be settled. Now I am not. In this mood I am no good to you or myself.'

'But where will you go?' His mother's voice was quiet, anxious. 'Not abroad again, I hope?'

'I don't know, Mother.' Ryder pushed his plate away and folded his arms, his brow furrowed in thought. 'Sometimes I don't feel I belong in Wenham. I am like a stranger here. I hoped with Maude, a local girl, I could settle down, but it was not to be . . .'

'I can understand that, dear,' his mother said, but his father gestured impatiently. He pushed away his half-empty plate, rose from the table and threw his napkin on it, like someone throwing down the gauntlet.

'Run away, will you? I'm ashamed of you, my son. It makes the deed of being jilted by Miss Brough all the worse.'

'I don't look at it in that light, Father.'

'Then if *you* don't, everyone else will.' His father's tone was harsh. 'They will think you have been driven out of town by a petticoat. Besides – ' his father sat down again and reached for the water jug ' – did you ever think that you are leaving *me* alone again? I am to work on the business by myself?'

'There's Herbert, Father, and Perce . . .' Perce was the head builder.

'Two men who do *not* take the place of my son.' His father thumped the table. 'I need you, Ryder. You are good at what you do. I'll make you a full partner. I'll buy you a house in Blandford where you will be away from all the gossip. I'll . . .'

'I *am* going, Father,' Ryder said quietly. 'I have made up my mind.'

'Oh, my ungrateful sons!' John Yetman raised his fist to the ceiling as if calling on God to strike them down. 'What did I do to deserve such sons, none of whom will be here to help me in my old age . . .'

'You are exaggerating, John,' Christopher, who had been listening to the proceedings with interest, interrupted calmly. 'You told me only the other day how proud you were of your sons. You said Hesketh and Robert had done well, that Ryder was a "real man", one after your own heart – and now you ask what you have done to deserve them. It doesn't make sense.'

'What my husband *means* – ' Catherine came rapidly to her husband's aid ' – is that now he is alone in running the business. He is not getting any younger. A man with three fine sons would have hoped that at least one of them would have been prepared to carry on the family firm started by their grandfather. We *are* proud of Robert and Hesketh; they are professional men, the first we have had in this family. As for you, Christopher,' she curled her lip contemptuously, 'the sooner you stop hanging round poor Victoria Fairchild and filling her head with all sorts of ideas . . .'

Christopher leaned back in his chair, a satisfied smile on his face.

'My dear Catherine . . . *I* am not giving Miss Fairchild ideas. If she entertains false hopes that's her fault. *I've* said nothing.'

'I hear that you are in that shop every day . . .'

'If you *will* listen to gossip, my dear . . .'

'In fact it *is* true, isn't it?' she challenged him. 'What else do you do with your time?'

'True only in the sense that I am interested in investing in the business . . .'

'With *what*, may I ask?' John burst out contemptuously. 'What will you use for money?'

'Ah, that's where I was hoping you could help me, Brother. If I were to buy . . .'

'You know absolutely nothing about haberdashery.' Catherine angrily seized the bell and shook it to summon the maid. 'I never heard such nonsense . . .'

'You know nothing about anything,' John said. 'Everything you have touched has been a disaster.' Then, as the maid entered and started clearing the dishes before serving the sweet, they stopped their discussion and began to talk instead of general matters, prospects for the harvest and so on.

But later, in the drawing room, they continued the conversation. The oil lamps were lit, and the windows shut and curtains drawn against the insects which, with the advent of summer, came up from the river. Catherine sat upright in a chair sewing; the men sprawled with glasses of brandy or port in their hands. Agnes had gone to her room to read.

Despite the discord Ryder thought that it was a domestic scene that he would miss when he went away; the closeness and devotion of home, no matter what his father said; the comfort of family ties.

But go he must. Not on account of his broken engagement; that he didn't mind at all. But now that he was free, the person

III

he had to get away from was Eliza, before he enmeshed them both in what could only be a hopeless passion. *That* was the test of his love.

'To return to the theme at dinner.' John still sounded angry, but he was by now a little more mellow thanks to the brandy he had drunk. 'Miss Fairchild is of the opinion that you are interested in her, and not her money *or* her business. She has said as much to her friend Miss Bishop, the schoolmistress, who came to see Catherine the other day.'

'Oh *did* she?' Christopher cast a jaundiced glance at his sister-in-law, who kept her eyes on her work. 'And no one told *me*.'

'It was not your business.'

'But it is my business.' Christopher got up to help himself to another glass of port. 'That is the thing I hate about a small town. You can't put one foot in front of the other without *everyone* knowing what you're up to.'

'When the penniless younger brother of one of its leading inhabitants starts making overtures to a middle-aged spinster of means, it is *not* a trivial matter,' Catherine replied in a low, calm voice, determined not to lose her temper. 'This is a very close-knit community. You are an outsider, Christopher . . .'

'Me an outsider!' Christopher exclaimed. 'But I was *born* here. In this very house. If anyone is an outsider, Catherine, it is you.'

Catherine was a girl from Wimborne, twenty miles away, when she married John Yetman.

'If you marry into a family you become part of the community,' John retorted. 'Catherine has lived here for over thirty years. She knows every single person in Wenham and they know her. We *care* for Victoria Fairchild because she's a woman with a disadvantage, despite her comparative good fortune, and we don't want unscrupulous people taking advantage of her.'

'Oh, *that's* how you see me, is it?' Christopher seemed saddened rather than annoyed by his brother's attitude. 'Unscrupulous.'

'You have never given us the opportunity to think anything

else, Christopher.' As though sensing his sadness, Catherine kept her tone of voice reproachful rather than angry. 'You never come here unless you are out of money, and now you have been with us for over five weeks, eating our food, using our linen and, apparently, taking advantage of Victoria Fairchild.'

'Supposing I loved her?' Christopher asked. In the profound silence that followed, he casually produced a cigar from his inside pocket and began the elaborate process of lighting it. As no one seemed able to find words, once he had got it drawing he went on: 'Victoria Fairchild is a *very* comely woman. She has a very minor disfigurement, which I don't find all that displeasing. She is forty-five, my age. We have known each other since we were children. It is true that she has a fortune and I have not. But I would not be the first man to marry to his advantage – nor, I suspect, the last. You should be happy on my behalf and keep your judgement for others.'

'Then you are really serious?' John could not hide his amazement. 'What Miss Bishop said was *true*?'

'Five weeks is only five weeks.' Christopher contrived to look mysterious. 'We shall see what we shall see.'

Because it was ready for habitation, and the atmosphere at home – what with his own and his Uncle Christopher's revelations – was tense, Ryder decided a few days later that he would take up residence in the cottage he had prepared for his bride. He would stay there at least until he had completed his plans to leave the district; at the moment he did not know where he would go. If Eliza left for Holland before him, it might not even be necessary.

The truth was, of course, that he did not really want to leave or to lose the chance of those meetings with Eliza, whose casualness did not deceive him. He hoped that maybe she would make at least one last visit before he packed his bags for a journey he did not want to make. The trouble was that, like his uncle, he had no money and he was too proud to ask his father for any. Besides, he didn't feel he deserved it. He had not worked for it, and he had let his father down.

Ryder was a complicated man. At the age of twenty-eight, he was not satisfied with life, nor particularly proud of the part he had so far played in it. He knew that the family sometimes compared him to his uncle, but he would never marry a woman for her money as his uncle seemed prepared to do.

Even if Eliza would have him, he was in no position to marry or support her. In a few years that might change. She was only eighteen. Who knew what the future, and a change of fortune, would bring?

Ryder put a bed and some rudimentary furniture in his cottage, driving it over himself in his pony and cart. He knew he would not be there long, but it was a quiet place in which to make plans. He was sitting one evening at his back door smoking a peaceful pipe and watching the last rays of the sun disappear below the distant hills, when he heard the sound of a horse approaching which then came to a stop directly behind him.

He knocked out his pipe and went round the side of the cottage to see who the visitor might be.

'My goodness, Miss Woodville. You startled me,' he exclaimed.

'Did I, Mr Yetman?' Eliza seemed intent on making sure that Lady's bridle was secure on the hitching post before she turned to him. 'I'm sorry about that.'

' 'Tis very late, Miss.' Ryder looked at the sky and scratched his head doubtfully. 'After the reaction of your sister-in-law that day I didn't think you would want to come this way again.'

'I've come to say goodbye,' Eliza said, walking towards him. 'I'm to be sent to Holland next week.'

Ryder stepped back and Lady whinnied, as though she had understood the importance of what was being said.

'I'm very sorry to hear that, Miss Woodville. I'll miss you.'

'I'll miss you too – Ryder. That's why I came.'

Ryder looked hesitantly towards the door.

'I don't think I should ask you in, Miss. I don't think your sister-in-law would like it, nor your mother. Don't forget that I'm your brother's tenant. He could have me out of here just like that.' Ryder snapped his fingers above his head.

'You're not a poor man, Ryder,' Eliza said. 'Your family is wealthy. I wonder that your fiancée is prepared to live in a cottage as small and humble as this. Did you not tell me that she would rather you lived elsewhere?'

Ryder turned away, apparently absorbed by the size of the giant hollyhocks which framed the pretty porch of the cottage.

'That is all in the past, Miss Woodville,' he said at last.

'What is in the past? I don't understand.'

He took his eyes from the blooms and turned towards her.

'I'm no longer to be married to Miss Brough.'

'Oh, I'm sorry to hear that.' Eliza put a hand to her mouth as though she had been caught out in a lie. Her eyes, which had looked troubled, suddenly seemed to sparkle.

'Don't be sorry, Miss. It's better not to marry than to marry a person you don't love.'

'You didn't love her?' Eliza gasped.

'Nor she me, Miss, though it was she who broke off the engagement. I don't profess to be a gentleman, Miss Woodville, in the way, for instance, that your brother is, but I would never humiliate a lady I had asked to marry me. I hope you understand that. It was *her* choice, but I am glad she chose it. Now do you understand?'

'I understand,' Eliza said, and as their eyes met in mutual recognition he thought for a moment that she was going to run to him and embrace him.

Instead she leaned towards him and there was an urgency in her whispered communication:

'They want to send me abroad at once. I thought you would never know what had happened to me if I didn't come now. The only time I could get away was at night. My brother and sister-in-law are in Holland making arrangements for my stay.'

'And your mother?'

Eliza laughed. 'My mother would never think that even I

would dare venture out at night; but she watches me like a hawk during the day. Ryder, may I come in for a few minutes? I'm getting cold.' Eliza rubbed her arms and gave a realistic shiver. 'And please – ' she looked at him appealingly '– call me Eliza. I feel we know each other well enough for that.'

With a show of reluctance he did not feel, Ryder opened the door and crossed the room to light the oil lamp, which flared into life, making the shadows dance upon the walls. Then he bent down and put a flame to the kindling wood that lay under the logs in the grate.

Eliza knelt in front of the fire. She was still shivering, but she knew it was from fear as much as the cold.

Ryder gazed at her in some concern.

'You don't seem well to me, Miss Woodville – Eliza. That shivering isn't natural.'

'I'm afraid, Ryder.' She continued to rub her arms and he knelt beside her.

'What of, Eliza?'

He put his arm around her to warm her and pressed his lips against her cheek.

She snuggled close to him, feeling very peaceful, as though, finally, she belonged.

6

The Heerings were Dutch burghers of repute who lived in a prosperous merchant's house overlooking the Prinsen Gracht, one of the many canals bisecting the city of Amsterdam. From here Willem Heering went daily to the warehouses where his spices were stored. They were imported in bulk from China, India and the East Indies; and from Amsterdam were shipped to the rest of Europe and the Americas, and to the vast London warehouse – overlooking the Thames by London Bridge – whose intriguing and tantalising odours permeated the maze of tiny streets.

The Heerings had made their fortune in the spice trade as long ago as the seventeenth century; but they were not greedy, avaricious people, just prosperous, God-fearing men of business to whom home and family were also important.

Of Willem Heering's four sons, one was a lawyer, but the others all worked in the business with their father. In the present century the family had extended their interests into banking and other forms of imports such as silk, tobacco and rice, also from the East. They had even acquired a small fleet of ships.

The Heerings had ties of business and friendship with the Martyns that went back many years. Both families were solid citizens; they understood one another and had much in common.

The Woodvilles, however, were a completely different matter. Willem Heering didn't understand Guy Woodville at all, and even less did he understand his father, Matthew, who had let his family fortune dwindle away to nothing while he sought cures for real or imagined illnesses in all the spas in Europe.

No, Willem Heering had little time for such as the Woodvilles, and would much have preferred his daughter to have married one of the honest, hard-working Martyns, had a male member of the family of the right age been available. He adored his only daughter, and would have sacrificed his soul to see her happy. Instead he did the next worst thing: he sacrificed his judgement, and when he saw she had fallen in love with a handsome feckless man, he allowed himself to be swayed by Guy's old and distinguished name, two large houses and a thousand workable acres, and did not discourage her.

In the months since the wedding Guy, in the opinion of his father-in-law, had not improved one iota. He was seldom seen in the offices in Threadneedle Street or in the warehouse in Lower Thames Street, and yet he spent money at a prodigious rate. Willem wondered if he drank, or gambled. So far the problem was not serious enough to take up with his daughter. He had no wish as yet to disillusion her about her new husband, with whom she was still clearly enamoured.

There was also the matter of the heir. Willem hoped an heir, with at least half of him full of good Dutch bourgeois blood, would prove a more capable man of business than his father or grandfather.

As for Guy Woodville, he enjoyed very little about his visit to Amsterdam. He considered his in-laws pedestrian and dull, bourgeois to the core, lacking any interest whatsoever.

His wife's charms palled compared to those of the delectable Lally. Margaret, worthy daughter of a worthy family, had neither the beauty, the innocent wit nor the passion of his little dancer. He knew that Margaret was good, diligent, frugal and rich. She also loved him and did everything she could to please him – though why he scarcely knew, for he was aware that since Lally had come into his life he was cantankerous, ungrateful, like a bear with a sore head.

'I know you are longing to get back, dearest,' Margaret said one morning as the two lay together in bed.

Puzzled, Guy looked at her hard, wondering whether she were teasing him; but her face bore a pleasant, even a serene expression. In fact he looked at her twice before once again setting his mouth in a grimace.

'You will be anxious to return to your business,' Margaret continued as if in explanation.

'Well, I don't like to abuse your parents' hospitality,' Guy said, stifling a yawn. 'And, frankly, my dear, I do find Amsterdam a dull place. Why, it's hard to find a place to get a decent game of cards, or see a show. I . . .'

'Guy,' Margaret said with uncharacteristic timidity, putting a hand on his arm. When he looked at her again, her expression was so strange, so diffident and yet, at the same time, appealing, that he was at a loss to understand it.

She repeated his name, and this time her voice faltered.

'What is it, dear?' Guy shifted uncomfortably to the far side of the bed.

'I have something to tell you. I hope you will be pleased.'

From the expression on her face it could only be one thing. His Herculean efforts in this direction were not unrewarded. His face relaxed into a smile.

'I came to Holland also because I wished to consult my own physician. It was he who delivered *me*. It is my earnest hope that you will allow him to deliver *our* child, dearest Guy – the child that I am happy to tell you I am now expecting.'

For once champagne, instead of good Dutch beer, flowed in the frugal Heering household. Guy was toasted, fêted, as if his wife's pregnancy were a condition he had accomplished solely by himself.

He felt that he could now insist on returning to England, pleading pressing business. Margaret would have liked to stay longer with her parents, but Guy was anxious to be off. Besides, he said, he wished his wife to travel before the autumnal storms set in. It was also arranged that, when the time came, her *accoucheur* would come to her. It would never do for the heir to the Woodville name to be born a Dutchman.

On their last evening in Amsterdam, after a good dinner, the ladies repaired to the drawing room to entertain one another with chatter, a little singing or sewing. Margaret, in particular, wished to be with her mother; for didn't a woman need her mother at a time like this?

Willem took Guy into his smoking room, where he offered him a cigar from the Dutch East Indies, imported by his firm, and some fine old Napoleon brandy. He stood in front of the fire while his son-in-law sat in a chair, his legs elegantly crossed, a cigar in one hand, a balloon of brandy in the other. He had a smug, rather self-satisfied smile on his face and he felt a contented man: rich, about to be a father by his lawful wife, with a lovely frolicsome mistress to whom to return.

'Cheers, Father-in-law,' he said, holding up his glass. 'May it be a boy.'

'Boy or girl, as God wishes,' Willem said piously. 'But yes, Guy, I'll own that a boy first time will be very nice for you, and your family. The succession would be secure. I hope, however, that you will go on to have several children of both sexes. My sons have given me pleasure; but my daughter has given me joy. There is a fine distinction, as you are perhaps aware.'

'I understand you, sir.' Guy's tone was respectful. 'Both Margaret and I desire a large family.' He took a sip from his glass then held it aloft again. 'May I say, Mynheer Heering, how grateful I am that you have entrusted me with the well-being of your daughter? I cherish her, and I always shall.'

'I'm very glad to hear that,' Willem said; but there was a note of caution in his voice, and he put down his cigar and glass carefully on a table before resuming his position in front of the fire, hands clasped behind his back. 'I am sorry, however, to introduce a discordant note into this otherwise happy occasion.'

'Oh?' Guy felt a flicker of apprehension as he carefully placed his glass beside his father-in-law's. 'And what is that?'

'It is the rate at which you are getting through Margaret's

dowry, *our* hard-earned money. That is worrying us all. We are a wealthy family, thanks be to God, but our money is not limitless. There is no bottomless pit. I have taken care of all the bills for the repair and refurbishment of your two houses to a high standard of excellence. That alone cost a small fortune. I would very much like to know, sir, on what you are spending such an enormous additional sum of money.' His tone was polite; the expression on his face courteous, even kindly, and a little mystified.

Willem Heering was a man of about sixty who carried his years well. He was not tall, but he seemed to gain inches from his erect, self-confident stance. He was prosperous, successful, someone to be reckoned with. Guy, though well aware of his father-in-law's authority, his wealth and power, was not overawed by it. After all, was he not now a man of wealth and power too?

He appeared now to consider Willem's question at his leisure. Finally he said: 'There are many small matters of business for which I am in need of substantial funds, sir. These I am not at liberty at the moment to divulge, nor would I wish to. In England a woman's money belongs to her husband. It is the law, and I am not accountable to you, or anyone, as to the manner in which I spend it. You can be sure it is in good hands, safely invested in property and the like.'

'I wish I could,' Willem said, gazing sternly at his son-in-law. 'Unfortunately I am not so convinced. As I understand it from your uncle, you are seldom seen in our London offices, or our warehouse. In fact you have not been seen for weeks; nor have you been known to undertake any business on behalf of the firm. Therefore I must tell you that I find your explanation unsatisfactory.'

'I still don't propose to answer you,' Guy said loftily. 'In fact I consider it a gross impertinence on your part to question my integrity. As to where I go, or what I do with my time, is that not my own affair?' Slowly he rose to his feet, his tall, athletic body by now towering over his father-in-law.

'Now, I think we shall join the ladies, and tomorrow we take our leave. I should inform you, sir, that Margaret is in my care; she is my responsibility and so is her money. She is carrying my child. If you attempt to interfere in our lives I shall prevent you from seeing her again. I shall feel it my duty. So take heed sir.' He pointed a finger at Willem, whose face was plum-coloured as the veins bulged in his neck.

'And *you* take heed, sir, and *you* take care,' Willem thundered. 'The money is *not* limitless. If you continue on your profligate way and get through my daughter's dowry, there will be no more. As for her rights, there is a move in England to redress these wrongs. You may find yourself in not such a fortunate position in a few years' time, but accountable to her and to me for money that is no longer there. I have given my daughter's happiness to *your* care, Sir Guy. I am answerable to my maker for it.'

The journey back to England was a difficult one. The autumn winds had turned the Channel into a boiling sea, and Margaret spent the crossing confined to her bunk. Guy was a good sailor and he paced the deck restlessly, enjoying the buffeting of the winds that cleared the cloud of uncertainty and confusion that seemed to envelop his mind.

Conscious of Margaret ill in the cabin below, he almost wished that she would miscarry, lose the baby they both wanted so much. Maybe then he could make a fresh start with Lally, beloved Lally. He would divorce Margaret and make his mistress his wife. In time people would forget her origins.

But they would be penniless. He would be thrown out of the business. Willem Heering might even hound him through the courts to try and recover some of his funds, in his chagrin that they had not produced happiness. Guy sensed that his father-in-law could be a vindictive even vengeful man.

The wind roared, the boat rolled. Guy put his hands to his head: nonsense, it was all nonsense. The wind was making him deranged. He staggered below to make sure that his wife of six months was all right.

Eventually the dreadful journey came to an end and the boat limped into Bournemouth Bay. As soon as the calm waters of Poole Harbour were in sight Margaret recovered, chided herself for her display of weakness in front of her husband, and did her best to put on a cheerful front.

But Guy was all consideration, concerned and even tender, anxious that she had not harmed herself, or her precious burden. She thought he looked unwell himself; he was pale and careworn. But he was quick to reassure her.

'I am a very good sailor, my dear. It was concern for you that made me anxious. Never mind, here we are.' He pointed towards the quay. 'There, my uncle's carriage awaits us, if I am not mistaken, to take us home: and to rest and safety.'

Prosper Martyn did indeed stand on the jetty, his coat fastened to the neck against the cold wind, his hat clasped in his hand. He looked grim, and his face only briefly broke into a smile as he bent to kiss his niece-by-marriage after she was carefully escorted down the gangplank by her husband. His expression worried Guy, who didn't doubt that his father-in-law's information about his neglect of his duties as a director of the business came from Prosper; but he made no comment. In any event, Willem had promised to say nothing to his daughter, as long as Guy mended his ways and the mysterious out-flow of money ceased.

Margaret was still very pale, but Prosper's suggestion that they should delay their return for a day or two and stay in Poole was rejected. Guy was anxious to deposit his wife in the care of his mother and make haste to London and the arms of his Lally.

'As you wish,' Prosper said. 'However, I will accompany you back to Pelham's Oak and make sure you are comfortably installed – ' he looked anxiously at Margaret ' – especially in view of Margaret's condition.'

'There is no need, I assure you, Uncle,' Guy said testily.

'Nevertheless, I intend to do it,' Prosper said. 'I have a

reason which you will understand by and by.' He refused to say more.

The party stopped at the Martyn house, a large double-fronted structure overlooking the harbour, for refreshment. Margaret changed her clothes and had a short rest, after which she pronounced herself recovered. The colour had indeed returned to her cheeks, and with a fresh change of clothes she looked perfectly restored. Guy, on the other hand, continued to look troubled and careworn. Margaret put it down to anxiety on her behalf, and her love for her spouse grew deeper than ever. All the way to Wenham she clung to his arm, but he was unresponsive, gazing moodily at the passing countryside, lost in thought.

Prosper too said very little, but stared grimly out of the window on the other side. Clearly he had something on his mind. Guy of course thought it was his extravagance and wondered how much his uncle had told his mother.

Margaret, pleased to be feeling herself again, remained cheerful. She kept up a constant stream of chatter about their stay in Amsterdam until at last the welcome sight of Pelham's Oak appeared on the hill before them.

Prosper, however, began to appear more agitated than ever and sat at the edge of his seat, straining forward.

'What *is* it, Mr Martyn?' Margaret said, after gazing curiously at him for some time. 'Have you something serious on your mind?'

'There's nothing wrong with Mama, I hope?' asked Guy, suddenly anxious. 'You haven't been hiding anything from us, have you, Uncle Prosper?'

For answer Prosper opened the door and leapt out of the carriage as soon as it stopped by the front entrance, before the footman who was hurrying down the steps had time to open it for him. Guy jumped out on the other side and carefully handed Margaret down, while the footman went to the rear to get down the luggage.

Feeling more anxious than ever now, Guy looked towards the house, but of his mother and sister there was no sign.

'How is Lady Woodville?' Prosper enquired of the footman as he began to heave the trunks to the ground.

'As well as can be expected, sir.'

'Then she *is* ill?' Guy, by now thoroughly alarmed and anxious, turned angrily on his uncle. 'And you have been hiding it from us.'

'It's not as you think,' Prosper began. 'Your mother is not exactly unwell; but she is upset. However, I wanted us all to be together before I broke the news.'

'What *is* it? What *is* it, for God's sake? You will make Margaret most unwell if you keep us in suspense like this.'

'Well, I suppose I'd better get it over with,' Prosper said. 'Maybe I should have told you before. The very mention of it sends your mother into hysterics. But you both looked so unwell on the quay, I wanted to give you time to recover.' He put a hand on Guy's arm and looked into his eyes. 'It's Eliza. I'm afraid she's run off with that rogue Ryder Yetman. They have completely disappeared.'

Henrietta lay as she had for the past three days since the news was brought to her, partly on her bed and partly off it. She refused to undress and go to bed properly and be comfortable, or yet to be dressed and sit upright in a chair.

She was suffering from what was popularly known as 'the vapours' – outbursts of hysterical weeping punctuated by real, or simulated, fits of swooning. Her condition had given rise to some anxiety, and the doctor called twice each day.

As Guy approached her, she began to weep again, flinging her hand across her face as though to shield her eyes from the sight of him.

'Mama, Mama,' he cried, kneeling beside her and trying to put his arm round her. 'You must not take on so or you will make yourself very ill.'

'I *am* ill,' Henrietta moaned. 'In fact I think I am near death. How *could* my daughter do this to me, to us, to the family? How can I show my face in London, never mind Wenham, again? What will people say?'

Prosper stood anxiously behind Guy, gnawing at a fingernail. Margaret, greatly shaken by the news, had gone to her room to rest.

'I'll have that scoundrel hunted through England,' Guy said. 'I'll have him publicly whipped. I'll have him thrown into prison. I'll . . .'

'*If* you are wise you will do none of those things,' Prosper said trenchantly. 'You had best put your sister right out of your mind, as though she had never existed. She's nothing but a strumpet, a harlot.'

'Oh, oh, oh!' Henrietta wailed. 'My daughter, my beautiful daughter . . . How *could* she do this to her mama?' She glared balefully at her son. 'We are disgraced in the eyes of the world, of society. Do you realise that, Guy? Every time anyone sees us in public they will snigger, if not openly then behind their hands. We will never, never get over the shame that Eliza has brought upon us.'

However, the sight of her son seemed to act as a restorative to the distraught mother, who slowly realised what a ridiculous spectacle she was making of herself. Three days of grief was enough anyway. Now that she had the support of her son, his wife and her brother, she felt stronger. It was time to take stock.

She asked them to summon her maid and then to leave her. She would join them downstairs presently.

By dinner time both female members of the family were sufficiently recovered to come downstairs and join the menfolk. The meal, the first solid food Henrietta had eaten for several days, became an occasion for an account of what had happened as well as a council of war.

Eliza had been missing one morning a few days previously. Ted first gave the alarm before dawn that her horse was not in the stable. Her maid found her bed had not been slept in, and some personal items were missing. Henrietta immediately fainted and the family physician was sent for. He also gave some sound practical advice and the police were alerted. Ted scoured the vicinity for signs that there had been an accident,

Lady riderless, for example; but there was nothing. There was also the fact of the missing personal items, which included some pieces of jewellery, underclothing, a dress or two, a valise.

Shortly after noon the suspense had been relieved by a letter from Eliza. This, in a voice trembling with indignation, Prosper now read to the group gathered at table, after the servants had withdrawn. ' "Dearest Mother," ' (the letter ran), ' "Because I know how anxious you will be about me I make haste to let you know that I am well. However, I have also to tell you that I have left home and gone away with Mr Ryder Yetman.

' "He and I have met on many occasions in the last few months and came to realise that we were completely and utterly devoted to each other, and neither of us wished to have anybody else. We also realised that, because of our differing stations in life, our love was doomed. I would be sent to Holland and might never see him again.

' "I know how much grief and pain this will cause you and my family, but I cannot live without Mr Yetman. I am sure that if you knew him as I know him for the splendid and upright man he is" – ' here Henrietta gave a fresh shriek and stuffed her handkerchief in her mouth ' – "you would grow to like him," ' Prosper continued, frowning at her.

' "Please forgive me for causing you pain, Mother, but you always did say I was not like other girls. However, I have no wish to be a man. I know now that I am a woman like other women, and I am in love.

' "Ryder and I have gone away for a time to be out of the district, but I shall write to you again in a while telling you of our plans. For the time being our address must remain secret . . ." '

' "*Our* address," ' Henrietta wailed. 'They are living together in *sin*. Eliza doesn't even attempt to hide it.'

'Hush, Henrietta.' Prosper looked at her severely. 'Please let me finish.' He cleared his throat and continued: ' "I hope you can find it in your heart to forgive me, Mother, and that shortly we shall meet again." '

'*Never!*' Henrietta shook her head vigorously. 'Never.'

'"Your devoted daughter,"' Prosper concluded, '"Eliza."'

As he pronounced the name, he looked round the table and saw that the eyes of his companions were fixed on him, as if drawn by magnetic force.

'Well, that's it.' Prosper let the letter flutter on to the table. 'Couldn't be clearer.'

Guy, who had appeared dazed by the news, suddenly leaned forward and laid his head on the table. Anxiously Margaret rose and went to him.

She put a comforting hand on his head. 'I can see this has been a terrible shock to you.'

'Terrible, terrible,' Guy said. 'How *could* she do it? We have always been so close. How could she do this and not confide in me when she knows the pain it must cause?'

No one knew the answer. Slowly Guy recovered his composure; his expression changed from despair to wrath and he banged his fist on the table.

'It's the fault of that man who has seduced her. *He* is the one to blame, not my sister . . . my little sister.' His voice faltered. 'That brute of a man has taken her away. If he dares show his face here again I'll have him flung into gaol. I'll see that he rots there for ever.' Suddenly he locked his arms around his body and put his head on the table again, as though in an agony of pain.

'Oh, Eliza, Eliza, how *could* you do this? How could you inflict such a terrible, terrible wrong on a family who loved you?'

The town of Blandford stood on the River Stour at the edge of the Blackmore Vale. In 1731 it had been partly destroyed by a dreadful fire and had been rebuilt in the Georgian style. In the course of its relatively uneventful history the name 'Forum' had been added to it, perhaps because of the importance in the town of the central marketplace, dominated by the Town Hall and its imposing church, whose distinctive baroque cupola was a landmark for miles around.

Salisbury Street, ran out of Market Place, the main thoroughfare, up a hill and out of the town. On it stood the large and important premises of Yetman Bros (Est. 1821), the name blazoned in gold paint edged with green on the imposing front window.

Thomas Yetman had acquired the premises towards the end of his life. They had remained the headquarters of his business, though there were smaller branch offices in other towns in the area.

John Yetman had worked here since he was first apprenticed to his father as a boy of fourteen. A young, beardless lad, he had started in accounts then progressed to orders and building specifications, gradually learning the practical side of the business and becoming in time a master builder.

He now sat at the desk that his father had occupied and which he had inherited on his death. It was the desk belonging to the head of the firm and of the family, and he hoped this was how it would continue to be for generations to come. He had hoped, above all, that it would suit his eldest son, Ryder; but Ryder had gone away with only the briefest of calls to inform them that he was going. He told them he would write and give them his address. He would tell them then what his plans were and when he intended to return. He had kissed his mother long and hard and gazed into her face.

His father still hoped that the deep love he had for his mother would make him return soon. Since Ryder's departure John had been depressed and uneasy; uncertain about the future, concerned about his children Agnes and Ryder. Above all, he was worried about the health of his wife. The doctors now seemed to think that there was more wrong with her than the normal women's problems they had dismissed as being part of her time of life.

The Yetman office was on the first floor of the building, over the main room where Herbert worked, along with another youth and two young women who attended to the clerical and secretarial side of the business.

Although Herbert was a partner and indispensable, he liked to keep at the heart of things, to see what was going on, though he had a right to his own office and would have been given one had he asked.

He frequently saw his superior in the course of a day's work, and as his head now appeared on the other side of the frosted glass door, he didn't knock but came straight in, a sheaf of plans in his hand.

'I have the latest report on the new development in Dorchester, sir, and our architect there says that the proposal will be very favourably received by the Council as providing necessary homes for the poor.

'Very good, very good.' John waved the plans away as soon as Herbert tried to put them in front of him. 'I leave all that kind of thing to you, my boy. I know I can trust you, and you are good at it.'

'But, sir . . .'

'I said I *trusted* you, Herbert.' John looked at him, his expression a mixture of irritation and fondness. 'Oh, Herbert, if only you were my son. If *you* were to succeed me, I would be a happy man.'

'I'm sorry, sir.' Herbert moved back a step or two. 'I'm sure Ryder will soon be back. It's the distress of losing Miss Brough . . . one can understand how hurt his feelings were.'

'I hope you're right, Herbert.' John screwed up his eyes and gazed out of the window towards an identical set of buildings on the other side of the street. 'Sometimes I think I don't understand my son. With his mother not well you'd think he'd want to be near her.'

'But does he know how unwell Mrs Yetman is? I always understood him to be a kind and thoughtful man.'

'Well, she is not *seriously* ill. Not ill enough to detain Ryder, to be quite honest. Some days she is better than others. I dare say my real grief is that he's left me. No, if my boy wished to go away for a time I could not blackmail him with unnecessary worries about his mother's health to keep him here.' John shook himself and leaned forward to examine a set of figures before him on his desk. He had already added them up a dozen times that day. 'Now, where was I?'

'Sir,' Herbert tried again.

'I said see to details of that kind yourself . . .'

'It was not about that, sir, that I wished to talk to you.' Herbert cleared his throat loudly, and John Yetman looked up.

'You wish to talk to me about something else? I hope to God it's not to say *you're* leaving?'

'Oh no, sir, no. On the contrary . . .' Herbert cleared his throat again, and his employer observed a deep flush slowly suffusing his face.

'Go on then, Herbert. It sounds serious.'

'It is, sir, and I hope you don't think me presumptuous. If you do, sir . . .'

'Go on, man, get it out. What is it? You're a partner. Do you wish to be head of the company?'

'No, sir, I wish to marry your daughter. I think you know how fond I am of her, Mr Yetman.'

Slowly John spun round in his swivel chair.

'I'm sorry, sir. I see you're shocked.' Herbert began to stammer. 'But I . . .'

'Not *shocked*, my dear boy – but surprised, yes.. I'm surprised you didn't ask me before. I would like nothing better than for my daughter to be married to a man of your calibre. However –' slowly he shook his head ' – how she will respond I cannot say. I know she likes you, but she has never confessed to any deeper emotion . . . but then, there is no reason why she should tell us, her parents, or wear her heart on her sleeve, is there? Maybe this is the very thing she's been waiting for.'

John Yetman rose from his chair with surprising agility for one bowed down by so many woes, and grabbed his employee by the shoulders.

'My dear, dear, Herbert. I feel a new lease of life. Let us hope Agnes consents. Nothing would give me greater joy, and I'm sure to Mrs Yetman too, than to welcome you as a member of this family. Indeed, as my son-in-law I should regard you

131

as my son and would feel very happy that, whatever happened with Ryder, the business was safe and secure in your capable hands. Blessings on you, my boy, blessings.'

John was about to embrace Herbert again when there was a respectful knock on the door, and one of the junior clerks from downstairs put her head round it.

'Mr Martyn to see you, sir,' she said, passing him a card. 'Says to apologise for arriving unannounced, but it's *most* urgent.'

John Yetman gazed at the card, and immediately his face lit up with renewed pleasure.

'Well, this *is* a happy day,' he cried. 'First I am to acquire a son-in-law I like and respect . . .'

'You *hope*, sir,' Herbert murmured, but John appeared not to hear him as he walked swiftly over to the door, throwing it open just as Prosper appeared at the top of the stairs. 'And here is my friend Mr Martyn.' John flung out an arm in welcome. 'Welcome, sir, welcome. It is very good to see you.'

If John was surprised by the frosty smile of greeting, he gave no sign of it – perhaps, indeed, he did not notice it – but drew up a chair for his guest as he prattled on.

'We have not met, I think, since your nephew's wedding? *Then* I believe you were thinking of purchasing land in this area. Is that what you have come to see me about? May I dare hope that we are to be entrusted with the building of your country home?' John beamed and, as Prosper was about to speak, drew the bashful Herbert forward.

'May I introduce to you Herbert Lock, Mr Martyn? He is not only my right-hand man in business *but* today he has asked for the hand of my daughter, Agnes, in marriage. I cannot tell you how happy that makes me.'

'Indeed!' Prosper's demeanour was one of a man who had come on a grave mission, yet John Yetman still appeared not to notice it. Moreover, his guest remained standing, twirling the brim of his top hat in his hand. 'I wish you much happiness, Mr Lock,' he said politely.

'Thank you, sir,' Herbert stammered and began to back towards the door. 'But the lady in question has yet to agree.'

'Oh, she will, she will.' John affably patted him on the shoulder. 'If she has sense, she will.' Then he thrust a bundle of papers into Herbert's hand and directed him towards the door. 'Now back to your plans, young man. Mr Martyn and I have work to discuss.'

'Indeed!' Prosper coughed, and as John, still all smiles, seated himself behind his desk, his guest tentatively took the seat that had been offered him.

'Now, sir, how may I assist you?'

'I see you do not know why I am here,' Prosper said gravely.

'No, but I can guess.' John Yetman rubbed his hands together. 'More business, eh? What a happy day this is for me. You have no idea how fond I am of young Herbert, how much I wished to have him for a son-in-law. He has a first-rate mind, but he is a diffident lad . . .'

'Mr Yetman,' Prosper said in a voice loud enough to drown the torrent of speech from the other side of the desk, 'your son has eloped with my niece. I take it you do not know this, or I doubt you would be so pleased to see me.'

John Yetman's mind still seemed to dwell on the happiness of his daughter, but at Prosper's words he blinked rapidly and the smile left his face.

'I *beg* your pardon?'

'They have eloped, gone away. Her mother is a nervous wreck, the whole family is distraught.'

'But it cannot be.' Slowly John rose from his desk, keeping one hand on it, however, as though for support. 'My son has only recently ended his engagement to another lady.'

'Then he is quite a fellow, is he not?' Prosper observed dryly. 'I too heard he was engaged to be married, and found it hard to believe what I heard.'

'It *cannot* be,' John murmured again, as Prosper thrust the letter Eliza had written to her mother into his hands.

'Read this, Mr Yetman.'

John fumbled for his reading spectacles and then slowly sank back into his chair. His hands, holding the letter, were now shaking.

Prosper, stern and upright, a hand on the head of his cane, watched him attentively.

After a while John let the letter flutter on to his desk and rested his chin on his hand.

'I cannot believe it,' he said flatly.

'You knew he had gone away?'

'He said it was to get over Maude. She broke the engagement and he didn't wish to be the laughing stock of the whole town.'

'Where has he gone? Do you know?'

John shook his head. 'He said he would write when he was settled. I cannot *think*, Mr Martyn, that when my son took his leave of me and his mother and sister *this* was in his mind . . .'

'Of course it was in his mind!' Prosper leaned over and angrily banged the desk. 'Don't be a fool, man. He has been planning it for weeks, months maybe.'

'But he was *devastated* by Miss Brough's request. They had only just seen the Rector and fixed the date for the wedding. The banns . . .'

'Then you have a blackguard for a son, I'm sorry to tell you.' Prosper rose abruptly and reached for the letter. 'I shall have to have that as evidence; because when he is found, Ryder Yetman will be apprehended and prosecuted for seducing a minor. Miss Woodville is but *eighteen* years of age.'

'I know.' John's lower lip trembled. 'Oh, Mr Martyn, you have *no* idea what this news has done to me. A moment ago the sun shone; now there is nothing but black clouds. Oh, how can I break this news to Mrs Yetman? What will my poor wife say?'

'She will probably disown her son,' Prosper said in a low, vibrant voice, 'as Eliza's mother has disowned her daughter.'

For many weeks after the news spread that Ryder Yetman had eloped with Eliza Woodville, that he had deceived not only his ex-fiancée Maude Brough but his family, the town of Wenham was in a state of shock. As far as the townspeople were concerned, it was a pleasurable shock. What was agony for the respective families was meat and drink to the gossip mongers who thronged the High Street on market days, who went from shop to shop, tavern to tavern, or who gathered in one another's cottages behind closed doors.

A scandal of such proportions had not happened in Wenham for years, and the good people of the town made the most of it.

There was, of course, genuine sympathy for the well-liked parents of the truants. There were those who felt real distress on the Woodvilles' account and were genuinely concerned about the effect on Mrs Yetman's health. For days John Yetman could not bring himself to go to his office because so many people wanted to stop him in the street and commiserate with him.

One whose grief on behalf of the family was real was the schoolmistress Miss Agatha Bishop, like Catherine Yetman a native of the town by adoption rather than birth. She was fond of the Yetman family; she had taught all the children, for she had first come to the village school as a young woman in her early twenties and was now nearly fifty.

Agatha Bishop was a good, wise woman. She was one of the many who liked Ryder Yetman and found it hard to believe he had done what he had. She hurried to the Yetman house to console her friend Catherine whom, knowing her nature, she was not surprised to find sitting composedly by the window overlooking the river doing her needlework.

Miss Bishop was shown in by the maid and greeted with great cordiality by the mistress of the house, who, however, did not rise to greet her guest.

'I hope you will forgive me, my dear,' she said, pointing to the chair the maid had put next to her. 'This is not one of my better days.'

'I quite understand.' Agatha Bishop put a hand on her arm. 'I came as soon as I heard.'

'I knew Ryder was not happy –' Catherine put aside her work and removed her spectacles ' – but I did not know *why*. If only he had spoken to me. I thought we were so close.'

'I am sure he would have wished to speak to you, Catherine.' Agatha pulled her chair a little nearer to her companion. 'But he must have known what you would say. He could hardly have told you he wished to elope with Miss Woodville and expect you to approve. He was in the grip of a passion that, clearly, he was unable to control.' Miss Bishop's face was a little flushed as though the thought excited her too.

'I had no idea he was even well acquainted with her,' Catherine went on. 'Apparently she had been secretly visiting him at his cottage – the cottage he was supposed to be preparing for his bride! Now that it is out it appears the servants knew all the time. Ted up at Pelham's Oak is a cousin of Peter, our gardener. Everyone knew but us.'

'It's always the way.' Agatha nodded sympathetically. 'In fact Ryder *and* his uncle . . .'

'Oh, don't mention that man to me!' Catherine said, picking up her needlework and stitching rapidly. 'If only he'd go away.'

'He spends more time with our dear Victoria than is good for *her* reputation.' Miss Bishop pursed her lips. 'If he does not declare himself I am afraid he will compromise her.'

'Goodness, is it as bad as that?' Catherine looked appalled.

'She is besotted with him. She doesn't even have to hide her fascination.'

'But he has said *nothing* to us.'

'I think John should talk to him.'

'John has no influence over his younger brother, Agatha. Anyway, he has too many things on his mind. He is devastated by Ryder's elopement. He feels it reflects on the whole family. It *does* reflect on the whole family. Hugh Brough, the miller, is furious. He says Ryder has made a laughing stock of Maude. I can't tell you the damage all this has done to our name in the town of Wenham. I don't think the Woodville family will ever speak to us again.'

Agatha Bishop sat back, her face thoughtful. She was a tall, comely woman with smooth skin, dark brown eyes, and iron grey hair which she wore in a bun.

In her youth she had been very pretty, and several of the local men had sought her company. But, rather like Agnes Yetman, she thought at the time that none of them were quite good enough for her. She rejected them all and, since then, had set out to win the reputation of someone wedded to her work.

Miss Bishop was always sought out by people in need of counsel; those who found the Rector too fierce, his wife too forbidding, parents unsympathetic or spouses too close. They would go to Miss Bishop, who had known them all for years, taught most of them, and was sufficiently detached and level-headed to offer good advice.

'Did you consider calling on Lady Woodville?' she asked after a while.

'Lady Woodville?' Catherine looked at her in horror. 'I would not dare. I last saw her at her son's wedding and she was so kind to us. How could I have imagined *Ryder* . . . I would not *dare* approach her ladyship. She will never forgive us.'

'It's not as though it were your family,' Miss Bishop began, but just then the door opened and Agnes put her head round.

'Oh, Mother, I didn't know Miss Bishop was here.' Agnes came slowly into the room. 'Am I disturbing you?'

'Of course not, dear.' Miss Bishop beckoned her in, noting to herself how well Agnes looked, as though the scandal about her brother had not touched her.

'Mother wanted me to get something from Blandford. Herbert Lock is taking me in his pony and trap.'

'Oh, is Herbert here?' Her mother looked round with interest.

'He has business in the town, Mother. He is picking me up in about an hour and Father will bring me back.'

'Such a nice boy, Herbert,' Catherine murmured encouragingly.

'Not a *boy*, Mother, a man,' Agnes corrected her.

'Well, such a nice man. He has been with us so long I still think of him as a boy.' Catherine ferreted about in her work basket and produced several cards on which there were the remnants of different coloured wools.

'If you would take these to the wool shop and ask Mrs Best to try and match them for me,' she said, 'I would be so grateful, dear. And do try and cheer up your father. There is nothing we can do about Ryder. Nothing. Life has to go on, has it not, Agatha?'

'Oh, I agree, Mother,' Agnes said and, nodding politely to Miss Bishop, she made for the door.

'Agnes looks well,' Miss Bishop remarked after the door had shut behind her. 'Did the business with her brother not upset her?'

'Maybe she is a little envious.' Catherine looked rueful. 'Agnes lives in a dream world. I'm only hoping she will agree to settle down with a nice boy like Herbert Lock – it would be the making of her.'

For a while, as the pony pulling the trap trotted briskly along the well-worn road between Wenham and Blandford, neither driver nor passenger spoke. Herbert was aware of a tightness around the collar, a constriction in his chest, and breathing, even in that pure clear air, seemed difficult.

Agnes was clearly preoccupied with other things – probably the business about her brother. But she looked cheerful enough as she sat holding on to her hat, staring ahead of her, humming a tune he didn't recognise. Preoccupied with her brother, but maybe not upset in the same way as the rest of the family.

As they crossed the bridge and climbed the hill out of Wenham, reaching level ground at the top, Herbert brought the pony to a halt just off the road at a spot overlooking the river. It was a sultry day, and though the sun still shone the sky overhead looked ominous. Herbert got out his handkerchief and mopped his brow.

'Why, Herbert is the drive too much for you?' Agnes asked with a mocking smile.

'It's warm for the time of year.' Herbert tugged at his collar.

'Take your coat off,' Agnes suggested, her eyes on the road again as if she were in a hurry to be off.

'Would you mind?'

'Of course I wouldn't.'

She smiled at him, and he felt encouraged by her concern. His spirits soared. Agnes had never given him the slightest hint that she was interested in him; but her father said she might be. She had been too well brought up to betray emotion. Herbert cleared his throat.

'Agnes . . .'

'Herbert,' she said impatiently, 'would you start up the pony again? I have to be in Blandford before the wool shop shuts.'

'There's plenty of time, Agnes. There is something I want to ask you.'

'Ask away,' Agnes said in a merry voice which renewed Herbert's hope, and, taking off her hat, she began to fan it back and forth across her face.

'Would you marry me, Agnes?'

Agnes went on fanning for a while as if she hadn't heard him; but he saw that her expression had changed. She finally stopped fanning and looked at him.

'Can you be *serious*, Herbert?'

'I'm very serious, Agnes,' he said stiffly, feeling so hot that he thought his collar would throttle him. 'I hoped . . .'

'I cannot marry you, Herbert,' Agnes said before he had time to tell her what it was he hoped. 'I don't love you.'

'You don't *know* me, Agnes.' He let the reins drop and tugged at his collar and tie. Misinterpreting the signal, the pony stepped on to the road again and recommenced its brisk trot towards the town.

Seeing his opportunity slipping away, Herbert seized the reins and tried to stop the pony, who took no notice, as if he too were keen to get to the shops before they closed.

'Whoa, whoa there,' Herbert called desperately.

Agnes started to laugh. She jammed her hat on her head and, carefully holding it with one hand, she went on laughing until her face was red. Herbert finally managed to get his pony under control, and the beast came to a stop where the Wen joined the Stour about a mile further on. Angry, red, confused, Herbert gazed at Agnes.

'Why are you laughing, Agnes?' he demanded.

'Because it's all so funny,' she said.

'Why is it funny? *I* don't find it funny.'

'Oh, it *is* funny,' she insisted, slapping her knee, but her smile disappeared. 'You're trying to propose marriage and the pony bolts. He thinks it's funny too.'

'I don't see what's funny about it,' said Herbert, looking very aggrieved.

'You mean you were serious?'

'Marriage is a very serious thing. I wouldn't attempt to joke about it. Look, Agnes.' He turned towards her, the reins still loose in his hands. 'I realise you're upset about Ryder. Perhaps it was not a good time to choose. But I *am* serious, and I will ask you again. I have asked your father . . .'

'Who of course said yes,' Agnes exclaimed, 'because he would do *anything*, especially after what has happened to Ryder, to have me settled.' She took a deep breath. 'I tell you one thing, Herbert: if I have to go to my grave as a spinster I would never marry you. You are a clerk, and you will remain a clerk in my father's business . . .'

'I am a partner,' he spluttered. 'A full partner.'

'You oversee all the clerical work. You have a clerk's mentality. And if you ask me what *I* think of my brother, I admire him. I am not upset at all. He had the courage to reach out and grasp happiness when he had the chance, instead of marrying that boring Maude. Boring, like you, Herbert. I wouldn't marry you if you were the last man on earth. Now, please drive on, or I shan't be able to carry out my mother's errand.'

John Yetman was sitting in his office attempting to summon up some interest in his work. He knew that he could not grieve forever about Ryder, and, in many ways, he hoped he never saw him again; that he and the woman he had seduced, had vanished from sight and would be seen and heard of no more.

He looked at his watch and wondered where Agnes had got to. It was after half past five and the shops would be shut. He heard footsteps running up the stairs and locked his drawer.

Getting up, he took his hat from the hatstand and was about to put it on his head, when he saw the face of Herbert through the frosted glass door and flung the door open.

'Is Agnes finished, Herbert?' he asked jovially. Then seeing the expression on his partner's face, he clasped him by the shoulder.

'Whatever is the matter, man? Agnes is not hurt, is she? There's been no accident?'

'Agnes is *very* well, Mr Yetman,' Herbert gasped. 'She was laughing fit to bust when *I* last saw her. She thinks I am an ass, sir, the funniest fellow in the world; a donkey if ever there was one.'

Herbert collapsed on to a chair, his arms hanging limply.

'She would not marry *me* if I was the last man in the world, Mr Yetman.' He paused for a moment and gazed at him. 'You could have spared me this, sir, you could have warned me.'

Quickly John Yetman put his hat back on the stand and, crossing the room, knelt by Herbert's side.

'My dear Herbert, I had no idea. None at all . . .'

'You could have spared me the humiliation, the indignity, Mr Yetman. You could have prepared the way and found out how she felt. You *told* me she liked me . . .'

'Of course she likes you.'

'I thought you might mean in another way. As a future husband. She does not like me in that way at all. She says I am a clerk, with the mentality of a clerk. You could have spared me all that, Mr Yetman, if only you'd asked her how *she* felt. That was the reason I spoke to you.'

'Herbert, I had no idea.' John got to his feet and ran his hand agitatedly across his brow. 'Of *course* I would have spared you this humiliation. But the news of Ryder – it came the same day, you remember, that you spoke to me – it drove everything out of my head. Oh, my poor fellow. I am so sorry. I had no idea you would declare yourself so soon. Look, let *me* speak to Agnes. I will talk to her tonight and . . .'

'I never want to see her again, sir.' Awkwardly, wearily, Herbert got to his feet; his face was covered with a film of perspiration and his thick blond hair stuck to his forehead. His Adam's apple wriggled uncomfortably over the knot made by his tie. 'You introduced me as your future son-in-law. You gave me every hope. It was not fair, not just. I never want to see any of your family again. I am giving my notice from this very minute, Mr Yetman. I will leave today.'

'But, *Herbert* . . .'

'You Yetmans know how to humiliate people, don't you, sir?' Herbert gasped as he made his way to the door. 'You know how to put the boot in and make a person feel really small. Ryder did it to Maude Brough, pretending he loved her and wanted to marry her. The moment she released him he ran off with someone else. He never loved her at all. Now Agnes . . . oh, how she laughed at me. And you could have spared me the whole thing, sir. But you didn't. Now, Mr Yetman, I am going to clear my desk and, as God is my witness, I will never darken your door again. Never.'

7

Ryder Yetman lay on the grass, his back propped against the wall of the cottage, warmed by the sun, gazing at Eliza as she put Lady through her paces in the field next door. He had his old felt hat tipped over his eyes to keep out the strong rays of the late summer sun, and the heat, the feeling of peace and fulfilment, made him somnolent; but still he couldn't take his eyes off her. Her graceful seat on the horse, her poise, recalled the first day he had seen her – over two years before – at Pelham's Oak.

From then on he observed her, though he never betrayed it by a glance, and he never spoke a word other than to pass the time of day.

In time he met Maude Brough, who was more attainable, who would help fill a cold, empty bed. Then, like some mirage, Eliza had come riding up to him as he thatched the roof, and soon after that he knew she felt the same as he did.

Eliza. *His* Eliza.

She glanced at him and, aware of his gaze, waved. He waved back, pretended to close his eyes, and soon the sounds of Lady's trotting stopped and Eliza, dressed in her man's shirt and riding breeches (this time an old pair of his), flopped down beside him. Dressed like a man, but very far from being one.

He reached out to encircle her waist, and their mouths touched. A lock of her hair fell over his eyes. He unbuttoned her shirt and cupped her breast in his hand; the large nipple at the tip grew erect and hard. Her tongue brushed his mouth and he slowly pulled down her breeches, and then his.

They coupled like animals in the field with no one except, perhaps, a stray bird or two to see them. Their breeches lay at their feet, the sun was behind them and they started to laugh.

'If Mother could see me *now*,' Eliza began, but he put his hand over her mouth.

'Ssshhh,' he said. 'Don't spoil it.'

He thrust more deeply, spurting his seed into her, and she closed her thighs so tightly over his that they seemed like one flesh.

Eliza moaned a little, and he kissed her eyes, his hands encircling her face.

'I love you,' he said. 'Love, love, love.'

Eliza said nothing, but her rapid breathing grew slower, calmer. She opened her eyes and they were moist with tears.

'It is the most perfect thing, being with you,' she murmured. 'I will never leave you, Ryder. Never.'

'Even if your brother comes after me with a whip? Even if he has me thrown in gaol for corrupting a minor?'

'Let's get married,' she said, eyes suddenly wide open. 'Let's get married *now* and nothing can ever separate us.'

'My darling,' he replied, 'no one would marry us, because you are too young.'

'We can go to Gretna Green,' she said.

He lay on his back. It was quite impossible to believe in such passion and to know that, with her, it would happen again and again. He would never let her go either. He could never let her go.

'Are you serious?' he said at last. 'It is not recognised in law. It can be undone if we get married at Gretna.'

'Not by us. I will *never* return to have my brother or mother undo our marriage, even if we never see Wenham again.'

'You wouldn't like it as a wanderer, a vagabond, my Eliza.' He pulled aside her shirt and gazed at her breasts. She lay exposed, lewd, legs outstretched. Her dark hair cascaded over her shoulders, and desire still glowed in her eyes.

Could such happiness last for ever?

'We can work,' she suggested, putting her hand over her eyes to keep out the sun.

'What work can *you* do?' His tone was gently mocking. 'You were brought up as a lady.'

'I can ride. I can break horses. We can be like gypsies. *Ryder!*' Suddenly she turned on her stomach – thus denying him a priceless sight – and leaned on her elbows. '*You* can thatch. We can travel the country with Lady and Piper. I would *like* to be a roving gypsy.'

'You would not, my darling,' he said emphatically. 'You would hate it. But . . .' Reluctantly he sat up and dragged on his breeches. His action made her aware of her nakedness and she quickly covered herself too. 'My Eliza, we are running out of money. I have to find work or we can't pay the rent of the cottage. If we have nowhere to sleep and not enough to eat you will soon get tired of this wandering life. You will begin to hate me and want to go back to Mama.'

'Never,' she said. 'Never.'

Ryder knew she meant it, but he was worried. Their impulsive act had weighed on his conscience ever since the night they became lovers. It had been useless to try and pretend he didn't love her, especially when she made so clear the extent of her affection for him: that she was prepared not only to sacrifice her virtue, but her reputation, her upbringing, her position as a Woodville.

She had admitted to loving him completely, and he returned that love.

A few days later, spurred on by the knowledge that she was about to be sent to Holland and that no time must be lost, they slipped away.

They left before dawn with the minimum of belongings and taking only their two horses, Lady and Piper, with them and, skirting Wenham, made their way over to Sherborne, where they stayed in a hostelry for a week as man and wife. There Eliza sold some of her jewellery.

From Sherborne they went to Yeovil and then they looked

round for a cottage to rent. They found one near the small stone-built village of Montacute, which surrounded the beautiful ancient house of that name, seat of the Phelips family, but gradually crumbling into a ruin because, like the Woodvilles in another valley thirty or so miles away to the east, the Phelipses had not husbanded their fortune carefully enough.

Ryder got occasional work on one of the farms; but it would soon be winter and Eliza might soon be pregnant. For all they both knew she was even now.

That night, over their supper of freshly baked bread and ham cured at the farm, they talked seriously about the future. Eliza was happy enough simply to be with him; she seemed unwilling, or unable, to see into the future. But she was only eighteen and inexperienced.

Ryder, on the other hand, was older and had known many women. He had behaved irresponsibly with Eliza, though by nature he was not an irresponsible man. He had fallen deeply, responsibly in love, and he wished to make Eliza aware of the consequences.

They had not set out on an easy path. He knew that if she tired of the life, she would tire of him. She might dress like a boy and behave like a boy, but she was a woman, a gently reared woman. Above all, she was a lady: accustomed – however much she might rebel – to comfort, luxury, servants to do her bidding. The harsh cold nights would be too much for her; the rough life would, perhaps, make her ill.

'If you are serious,' he said when she had demolished all his arguments, 'we *could* go to Gretna and have the blacksmith wed us over his anvil.'

'Oh, Ryder, I am serious,' she cried, jumping up and rushing round the table to hug him.

'We have a bond as it is,' Ryder said gravely, putting his arm around her waist. 'And for me it's for life; but for you, Eliza . . . You're much younger than I am. You're from a different station in life . . .'

'I want to hear no talk like that,' she cried, flinging her arms round his neck. 'We have a bond and we always will have. We know it.'

'The way I reckon is,' Ryder said slowly, 'that, although it won't make the marriage legal, it *is* a marriage. It might make a difference to how your mother and brother felt about you.'

'You know that I don't care at all how they feel about me,' she cried, falling on to his lap.

'Now you don't; but later on you will.' He put his hand up and stroked her cheek, gazing into her luminous eyes. 'You will tire of poverty and the wandering life, my Eliza. Maybe we will have a child, and you'll want a home for it and security . . .'

'Oh, don't think of things like that,' she burst out. 'Don't even *say* them. It is too late. What's done is done.'

She was right. It *was* too late; far, far too late to repent of their action. Now they had to face the consequences, but with their mutual love, and her ebullience, perhaps they would win in the end.

The journey to the Scottish Borders took much longer than they expected. Autumn was approaching and the weather was wet and cold. Gallant Piper and Lady struggled along uneven, poorly made roads, but feeding them was costly and shelter hard to find. Near Appleby in Westmorland they sold Piper to a band of gypsies.

It nearly broke Ryder's heart, but it was better to sell Piper while he could still get a good price. He was a young horse and, despite the journey, in fair condition. He knew that Eliza would never part with Lady, and for the rest of the journey he walked beside her leading the horse.

Finally at Gretna, over the blacksmith's anvil, they became man and wife. Their new life together began.

From the window of the small cramped room at the top of the warehouse in Lower Thames Street Guy had a splendid view downstream past London Bridge. All day long the river traffic plied up and down, loading and unloading goods at the wharves which lined either side of the Thames.

Though he did not appreciate the view, Guy spent a lot of time looking out of the window, far more time than he did bending over his books, his ledgers, his stocktaking cards and the firm's accounts.

Guy hated work. He hated the warehouse and the dingy room that the senior partners had allotted to him, which was a steep climb up more than a hundred stairs. He felt that it was a punishment intended to demean him, for the main offices were in Threadneedle Street, five or ten minutes' walk away. They were attached to the Martyn-Heering Bank, were sumptuously appointed in mahogany. In the dining room an excellent lunch was served, and business was discussed over port afterwards with the many foreign bankers and men of affairs whose trade was expanding like that of the astute Heerings and Martyns.

But Guy was scarcely ever invited to lunch. Instead he ate in a chophouse along Lower Thames Street, or in one of the many winding lanes that ran like capillaries around the teeming, bustling body that was the City of London.

He knew he was on probation, carefully watched, his figures gone over in minute detail. Sometimes he spent hours in the wind and rain, supervising the unloading of the barges that lumbered slowly up the Thames from the ports at the estuary. Sometimes he felt he stank of spices, and he would go thankfully home at night and, after a bath and a change of clothes, go to his club until it was time to pick up his Lally from the stage door of the Alhambra.

It would soon be Christmas, and a thick fog hung over the murky reaches of the river, the hooting of the barges punctuating the eerie stillness. Although it was eleven o'clock in the morning it was almost dark, and he worked by lamplight. There was a tap on his door, and when he called 'Come in' Uncle Prosper put his head round, smiling cheerfully. Guy got reluctantly to his feet. He blamed Prosper for this state of drudgery to which he – a baronet of the realm – had been reduced. He knew that Willem was no admirer of his, but Prosper could have done much to make his lot an easier one.

'Good day, Uncle,' he said stiffly, pointing to a rickety chair by his desk. 'Please sit down. Be careful, it's *very* dusty.'

Prosper looked carefully at the seat of the chair, and before sitting down lifted the tails of the morning suit he always wore for business.

'I see I do not find you in a very happy frame of mind, Guy.'

'What would you expect in a place like this?' Guy said with a shiver as he glanced towards the pale embers in the grate. 'It is like something out of Dickens.'

'Come, come, it's not as bad as that!' Prosper protested. 'At least you have a future, a home *and* a title. The young men in the novels of Mr Dickens had none of these. You are serving your apprenticeship, Guy, learning the business the hard, and proper, way. Your future will be a bright one, *if* you work hard. You are shortly to be a father. Surely you have pleasure at least in *that* achievement?'

'Of course.' Guy's reply was perfunctory, unenthusiastic.

'And how *is* dear Margaret?'

'Quite well, I think.'

'Then you do not see her very often?' His uncle looked at him shrewdly.

'My dear Uncle,' Guy burst out petulantly, 'as I am made to work so hard, when do I get the chance to see my wife? Besides, these days she spends most of her time in Dorset, while I, as you know, am forced to waste my time in this pitiless hole.'

He stared round bitterly, and Prosper leaned forward, his face grave.

'My dear Guy, I feel it is my duty to urge you to be serious about your work, *and* about your marriage. I have often called to see you late at night in Chesterfield Street and you have not been at home.'

'God in heaven,' Guy cried, looking up at the ceiling and slapping his forehead, 'do I have to account to you for how I spend my spare time as *well* as my working time?'

'Of course not, my dear boy,' Prosper replied, leaning back and gazing at his watch suspended from a gold chain across his waistcoat. 'I am merely commenting on the fact. People who go to bed very late do not work well. Sometimes it was well after midnight when I called.'

'Then what were *you* doing up at that time, may I ask?'

Prosper tilted his chin and stared down his nose at Guy.

'My dear boy, I consider that remark impertinent. I am forty years of age. I have served *my* apprenticeship. I have made a lot of money and helped to boost the fortunes of the firm. *I* am a senior partner. I am talking to you now as your uncle, a close relation. I hope you also regard me as a close friend, one who has your interests and those of your family at heart. Talking of the family – ' Prosper examined the tips of his well-manicured fingers ' – what news, if any, of Eliza?'

'None that I know of.'

'None at all?'

'No.'

'She never writes?'

'Not to my knowledge. Not to me.'

'Are you not concerned about her?'

'I'm very concerned about her; but I am also disappointed. I thought Eliza above that sort of behaviour. She was, after all, born and brought up a lady, and Yetman is undoubtedly a rogue – seeking to better himself at the expense of my sister.' Guy shook his head. 'I'm afraid I have to tell you, Uncle Prosper, that if my sister ever came back to Wenham, I feel I could not receive her at Pelham's Oak. That would look like condoning her behaviour. She has humiliated us, made us a laughing stock and, because of the harm she has done to my mother and our family, I could never allow her access to the family home again.'

'I find you a strange man, Guy.' Prosper looked perplexed.

'And I find *you* a strange man, Uncle.' Guy rose to his feet again and, crossing the room, stood gazing out of the grim, curtainless window, turning over the loose change in his trouser pocket. '*I* am a man of twenty-four, a baronet. I have been well brought up, accustomed to the highest standards. I am well educated, my father was a scholar.' He turned and looked accusingly at his uncle. 'Yet he was an invalid and our financial affairs declined. For this reason I am penalised and, I must tell you frankly, I resent it. As you yourself observed, I am a married man, and my wife is shortly expecting a child. I find it humiliating that I am not only spied on in my personal life, but am reduced to the circumstances of an impoverished clerk in order to learn the business. A business, incidentally, in which I have absolutely no interest.'

'*That* is quite obvious,' his uncle said, shaking his head. 'What *are* we to do with you, Guy?'

'What do you mean, "we"?' Guy turned slowly to face him.

'My fellow partners and I. We can see you have no interest in the business, no head for figures. In many ways all the hours you spend here are a futile waste of time.'

'Good! Then may I go?' Guy said, snapping shut the ledgers which lay piled on top of one another on his desk.

'And do what?'

'What I am accustomed to do, what my father did . . . be a gentleman.'

'*And* keep a mistress?' his uncle interjected quietly. 'Is *that* what the money is going on?'

Guy sat down abruptly. Then he drew a case out of his pocket and, lighting a cigarette, blew a stream of smoke arrogantly into the air and crossed his legs.

'My wife is scarcely a beauty. Even *you* will admit that.'

'Still, she is a good woman, a clever woman.'

'I do what I can by her. I have fathered a child.'

'Isn't it a little *early* in your marriage to take a mistress, Guy?' Prosper leaned forward, the expression on his face not unfriendly.

'How did you find out?'

'I happened to be passing the stage door of the Alhambra and saw you coming out with a remarkably pretty girl on your arm.'

'And what was *your* business in passing the Alhambra, may I ask?'

'Very similar,' Prosper replied with a smile. 'I was in the vicinity of Leicester Square. But *I* can afford my pleasures.

Look, Guy' – he got to his feet and, in his turn, took his place by the window, gazing down into the murky waters of the Thames – 'I am here to help you. I am your uncle and I love you. As you know, I have always regarded you and Eliza as my own children. That is why your apparent indifference to Eliza distresses me. For all we know she might be dead.'

'I'm sure we would have heard if she were.'

'What I can't understand is your attitude towards your sister.' A frown crossed Prosper's face. 'She only did what you are doing; she fell in love. She with a farmer, a thatcher, you with a dancer.'

'It's quite different and you know it,' Guy replied tetchily. 'A man is permitted a lover. A woman, especially one as gently reared as Eliza, is not.'

'Well, I want to find Eliza.' Prosper wandered from the window and resumed his seat. 'I thought by now she would have written. As for *you*, young man – ' he gazed solemnly at him ' – I am keeping a very careful eye on you. We will not continue to employ you if you do not work harder. I doubt if even a wife as besotted as Margaret will continue to worship an indifferent husband who does not work, and yet keeps a mistress solely upon her fortune.'

'You would never tell her, Uncle!' Guy gasped. 'You would never *dare*.'

'I *would* dare, but it would distress her too much. However, I have no intention of blackmailing you. I will continue to treat you as one man of honour treats another.' Prosper rose and clapped an avuncular hand on his nephew's shoulder. 'You must show more mettle, Guy, more spirit, or, believe me, you will lose not only your wife but your mistress as well.' He removed his hand and straightened up. 'No woman wants a man without a fortune – unless perhaps it is your sister Eliza – and in her spirit, her disregard for wealth and position, her defiance of convention, I find much to admire.'

Margaret Woodville lay on the chaise-longue in the drawing room, her back supported by a pillow, doing her tapestry.

Unlike most of the women of her time, she did not enjoy sewing. She had been carefully trained in the domestic arts, to perform each task correctly – sewing, cooking, embroidery, dressmaking – but she did not enjoy them. What she preferred were organisational skills – managing a house and seeing to the accounts, ensuring that everything worked and ran well, allotting servants their tasks and generally taking charge; but the minutiae of domestic life bored her. She had rather large, clumsy hands and was not deft enough to be a good needlewoman.

However, while awaiting the birth of her baby, there was little else to do on a cold February morning, with her mother-in-law absent and Guy, inevitably, in London.

There was a tap on the door of her sitting room, and her maid entered with a tray on which there was a cup of hot chocolate. She also dropped some letters on the table by Margaret's side, retaining one in her hand. Margaret glanced at it curiously.

'What is that, Ethel?'

'It is a letter for her ladyship,' Ethel said, tucking it under her arm as she carefully arranged the chocolate with a pot of thick cream beside it. The odour was enticing; but Margaret was intrigued by something about the letter and peremptorarily held out her hand.

'Let me see it, Ethel.'

'It is for her ladyship, ma'am.'

'I know that; but show it to me.'

Reluctantly Ethel passed her the envelope with its large girlish handwriting which Margaret had immediately recognised.

'It is from Miss Woodville!' Margaret cried excitedly.

'Yes, madam.' Ethel reached for the letter but Margaret held on to it.

'How *very* exciting. Her ladyship *will* be pleased. I'll give it to her and we will read it together.'

Ethel gazed at her feet, and her cheeks slowly went crimson.

'Why, Ethel, what is it?' Margaret looked curiously at her as, placing the letter firmly in front of her, she spooned into the chocolate a plentiful supply of cream and mixed it well into the red-brown liquid.

'Oh, delicious,' she murmured, tasting it. 'Now, my good woman. You have something on your mind. What is it?' As she again put her cup to her lips she looked at Ethel over the rim.

'Well . . .' Ethel caught up her starched white apron and began to knead it anxiously in her hands. 'I don't think her ladyship will be very pleased with me, madam.'

'Nonsense. She will be *delighted* to get a letter from her daughter. The family is frantic with worry.'

'I don't think so, madam,' Ethel insisted, still crimson, drawing up the apron almost as far as her waist, so that Margaret, ever house-proud, cried sharply:

'Be careful of your apron, girl! It will be unfit to wear this afternoon. Economy in all things, you know.'

Ethel knew. The whole staff knew only too well what great store the new mistress set by economy, forever counting the pieces of silver, the linen, the knives and forks, to make sure that nothing was missing.

It caused a certain amount of resentment, but in other things the younger Lady Woodville was very fair. The staff were clothed, fed and paid well; their wages were among the best in the district. If they had to live under suspicion of stealing it was a small price to pay. They put it down to the fact that her ladyship was foreign.

Ethel attempted to straighten her crumpled apron by smoothing it with her hands.

'Sorry, m'lady,' she mumbled. 'May I go now?'

'Not until you explain what you mean by saying why you think that my mother-in-law would *not* be delighted with this letter from her daughter.'

'Because she has had a number of others, ma'am.' Ethel's voice was almost a whisper.

'Oh, surely not, girl! She would have told us.'

'She has had them regular, ma'am. Her ladyship never opens them, but keeps them in a cupboard.'

'What nonsense!' Margaret finished her chocolate and delicately wiped her lips on the linen napkin that had been provided with it.

'No, ma'am, 'tis true. She has had half a dozen letters from Miss Eliza and has opened none of them. I know because when I was sorting through her ladyship's underclothes one day I saw them all there, unopened, ma'am.'

'I must see this for myself.' Margaret kicked back the stool and made a valiant effort to stand. She felt so huge and cumbersome that she nearly toppled over, and Ethel put out a hand to steady her.

'Careful, ma'am,' she said respectfully.

'Take me to her ladyship's room and show me the cupboard. At once,' Margaret commanded.

'I *dare* not, ma'am.'

'I insist.'

'But I *like* it here, ma'am.' Ethel, who was one of thirteen children from a poor home in Cornwall, was on the verge of tears. 'I've always done me duty proper and behaved well.'

'Indeed you have, Ethel. Your position is not at all in danger, I can assure you of that.'

'But if her *ladyship* knew I'd sneaked . . .'

'She will not know. I will say that I intercepted the letter and then see what her ladyship makes of this. I promise your secret will never be revealed.' Margaret gave Ethel a gentle push. 'Now, show me the cache, my girl, or else you may well find yourself without employment in this house.'

Henrietta, Lady Woodville, leaned back against the cushions as her carriage carried her home from a visit to Bournemouth. One hand held firmly on to the strap as the horses jogged along at a fair pace to be back before dark, while the other restlessly tapped against the rug that covered her knees.

The visit to Bournemouth this time had been ostensibly to see her aunt, her dead mother's sister, who was in her eightieth year.

In fact she hadn't been anywhere near Aunt Nora, but had spent the whole time doing what she always did these days on her many forays to Bournemouth: seeking a property to live in so that she could move away from Pelham's Oak and the company of her overpowering, demanding daughter-in-law.

More than anything else she was irked by the secrecy necessary to the success of her enterprise. For she had no money – her dowry having been spent by her husband even sooner than Guy had wasted his. Prosper knew of her desire to leave Pelham's Oak, but did not approve of it. To him, stern man of business, it was an unnecessary extravagance, and he declined to help her find the money. She could probably have raised it by selling her jewels, but this she did not wish to do. One had to hang on to one's jewels as security against one's old age.

Oh, if only Guy had been like the Martyns, with their gift for making money; for turning, it seemed at times, stones themselves into gold. No, he was a Woodville through and through; thriftless, a spender.

Thus, for the moment, her search was for a property that would be suitable for her station, and the only way she could do that was by finding something to rent. So far a property grand and yet inexpensive enough had not been found. Unlike her daughter, she had no intention of ending up in a cottage.

Even the thought of Eliza made Henrietta shudder. She also felt guilty. The letters put, unopened, into her linen cupboard bore the postmark Keswick. She could only guess at what Eliza was doing there, for open them she would not, could not. In the act of taking the paperknife to the first missive, delivered well before Christmas, her hand froze; since then there had been several more.

Perhaps Eliza was in need, in distress. No matter. Henrietta did not wish to know. Eliza had become a fallen woman, an outcast, someone of whom her mother was deeply ashamed.

She was glad when the welcoming lights of the house on the hill came into view. Once again her quest had been fruitless, and she was cold and tired. Someone had had the temerity to offer her a tiny house on the sea front. As though *Lady Woodville* could even consider such a hovel! Sometimes the humiliation was as hard to bear as the desertion of her daughter and the overbearing presence of her daughter-in-law.

Ted had driven the carriage, because the regular coachman was ill. As he brought the carriage and pair round to the front of the house, alighted from his seat, put down the steps and opened the door for her ladyship, he took off his hat and bowed.

'Thank you, Ted,' Henrietta said, fastening the astrakhan collar of her coat tightly around her neck and preparing to run to the shelter of the porch out of the cold east wind.

'Is there any news of Miss Eliza, my lady . . .' Ted began, looking at her diffidently but, at the very mention of the name, Henrietta fled without even the courtesy of a reply.

Solemnly Ted drove the carriage round to the stables. As he unharnessed the horses and began to rub them down, he thought of Miss Eliza and Lady, and wondered, as he often did, what had become of them.

The footman Arthur was already helping Henrietta out of her coat when Margaret, with the slow, cumbersome walk of the heavily pregnant, came into the hall. Henrietta looked up but scarcely bothered to smile.

'Did you have a good visit, Lady Woodville?' Margaret enquired politely. The time had not yet arrived, nor did it seem that it ever would, for Margaret to address her mother-in-law by a more informal or endearing title.

'Thank you.' Henrietta acknowledged her with a frozen smile.

'And how was your aunt?'

'Very well. Arthur, would you see that tea is served in my room?' Henrietta asked the footman, rubbing her hands together. 'I am perished with cold.'

'I have asked for tea to be served in the drawing room,' Margaret said pleasantly. 'I thought we could take it together. There is a large fire and I have, in addition, some very good news for you.'

'Oh?' Henrietta's face brightened. 'And what may that be?'

'Come and see,' Margaret said with a beckoning finger and a smile and, turning, she led the way.

Henrietta followed her daughter-in-law into the drawing

room and, hurrying up to the fire, held her hands out to its welcoming heat.

'Lord, I was perished in that carriage,' she said. 'I shall be thankful for my warm bed tonight. Now, what is the good news you have for me?' Still with her back to the room, her hands extended to the fire, she turned and gazed at Margaret, who had resumed her seat on the hard chaise-longue at one side of the fireplace.

At that moment Arthur and one of the maids entered with the tea tray, which was put on a table drawn up to the fire.

Very correctly, decorously and slowly, Arthur poured from the silver pot into the cups of Sèvres porcelain (needless to say, part of Margaret's dowry), while the maid added milk and handed the cups to the two Lady Woodvilles. Margaret then said they would help themselves, and dismissed them.

Henrietta rose from her place by the fire and turned her back so as discreetly to warm her behind.

'The surprise?' she asked again, this time rather impatiently, and Margaret produced a letter from her pocket which she held up in front of her.

'A letter. A letter from your daughter! I wanted to give it to you myself. Is that not *thrilling*, Lady Woodville? Please *do* open it quickly.'

She was smiling eagerly as she held out the letter. Henrietta snatched it from her and thrust it into her bosom.

'Oh *dear*.' Margaret feigned surprise. 'Do you *still* have no wish to know the whereabouts of Eliza, and her circumstances?'

'Of course I don't,' snapped Henrietta. 'She is *no* daughter of mine, and where she is or what has happened to her I care not.'

Margaret rose with difficulty from the chaise-longue and walked slowly over to Henrietta, her hand outstretched.

'Then may I have the letter, Lady Woodville, and your permission to open it? I have a strong regard for my sister-in-law, whatever her misdeeds, and I would like to know that all was well with her.'

'The letter is addressed to *me*,' Henrietta replied obstinately.

'Yes, but you will not open it . . . nor the others that you have tucked away in your bedroom somewhere.' Suddenly Margaret's expression changed from one of cool calculation to outrage. 'Do you *realise* that poor girl might be ill, or in need? Six or seven letters you have had, I understand, and the contents of not one of them communicated to the family.'

'None of them have been opened.' Henrietta stared at her defiantly.

'Precisely.' Margaret's mouth snapped shut and she held out her hand again. 'The letter please.'

'No. Not this, nor any of the others. They are addressed to me and are my property.'

'Then I shall summon Guy from London and demand that, as the head of the family, he procures them. I am very concerned about Eliza and her well-being.'

'Then you should have done something to stop her leaving.'

'There was nothing I could do,' Margaret retorted. 'Indeed, at the time I shared the disapproval of the rest of the family. But, as time has gone by, I should think we have all had the chance to reconsider, to feel a little less harshly about her. I for one wish her no harm, and I would dearly love to know whether she is well, or if she needs help. After all, she is still very young.'

For answer Henrietta moved away from the fire and made as if to leave the room. Despite her clumsiness Margaret managed to run ahead of her and, standing in front of the double doors to the drawing room, barred her way.

'No. Not until I have the letter, or you will read me its contents,' she said.

'I refuse. Please let me pass. As soon as I'm out of here I shall tear up that letter and all the others. I would also very much like to know the source of your information, so that I can dismiss the servant concerned from my service.'

'From *my* service. All the servants here, including your maid . . .'

'Ah!' Henrietta cried, 'It was *she*.'

'I did not say it was,' Margaret replied. 'But even if it were, you have no right to dismiss her. *I* pay her wages.'

'My son's money pays her wages.'

'It is *my* money, Lady Woodville,' Margaret pointed out coldly. 'Mine, or rather my father's. Do not think he does not know in what condition the Woodville finances were, or that he will go *on* pouring money into an impoverished, nay, bankrupt household. I would rather live here in penury than have my father continue to pour money like an endless stream into this family . . .'

'Ha! I would very much like to see that!' Henrietta exclaimed, tossing her head. She sank on a chair as though she were out of breath, one arm flung casually over the back.

'My dear Margaret, you may as well know that the Woodvilles soak up money like a sponge. Matthew did, and Guy is no different from his father. With Matthew it was a ceaseless round of spa resorts, consultations with doctors, quacks of all description. With Guy, I imagine, it's gambling or some such. The Woodville men have no concern about money and will spend all they get. In time you too will be reduced, as I have been, to an unenviable state. Why,' she said, throwing up her arms, 'do you not think I would love to leave this detestable house, where I have felt myself scarcely tolerated ever since *you* stepped through the doors? Of course I would; but I can't. I have nowhere else to go.'

'But you can *leave* any time you like, Lady Woodville.' Margaret's tone was icily polite.

'Oh, but I can't. I have no money to buy somewhere that is suitable to my station.'

Slowly Margaret sat down again, her hand pressing on her belly. Her breath seemed to be coming in short bursts, and there was a look of distress on her face.

'Is your mind made up, Lady Woodville? Do you *really* not desire to live here any more?'

'Yes, I do *not* desire to live here any more.'

'Then I think the feeling is mutual.' Margaret gave a long-drawn-out sigh, but she still seemed to be in pain. 'I am quite willing to lodge enough funds, or have my father lodge them for you, to buy a residence which, while not opulent, will enable you to live in the fashion and comfort to which you are accustomed. There is one proviso, however.'

'Yes?' Henrietta said, in sudden elation; aware that her heart was beating wildly. Margaret held out her hand.

'Give me the letter and the others you have concealed. When they are in my possession I will complete my part of the bargain. Now – ' She pressed her hand to her stomach, her face once again contorted in pain. 'Now, would you be very kind and send Ted for the local physician? I think I may have gone into labour before my time.'

At four the following morning, assisted by the local doctor and a midwife – as her own *accoucheur* from Holland was not due until the end of the week – Margaret Woodville gave birth to a healthy son who weighed over eight pounds. He was to be named George. As he was ushered into the world he gave a lusty cry. In the eyes of his parents, he seemed to have the sensible looks of the Heerings rather than the dashing looks of the Woodvilles, though of course it was rather too early to tell.

Meanwhile in her bedroom nearby, his grandmother sat looking with satisfaction at the grate and the ashes of all the letters from her daughter, which she had burned, one by one, still unread.

8

Titus Frith was a rough, bluff man who, like Willem Heering, had an only daughter whom he adored. His was, at only seventeen years of age, of quite exceptional beauty, and he could deny her nothing. She was never allowed to go anywhere without a chaperone. Even from the house she was spied on in case one of the farm hands was tempted to be familiar with her. Farmer Frith was terrified that his precious daughter would fall for the wrong man; but there was little chance of any man so much as touching her, because her father scarcely let her out of his sight.

Titus Frith knew nothing of the history of the couple to whom he had rented a cottage by the shores of Lake Ennerdale, Mr and Mrs Yetman, or he might have taken even more care of his daughter than he did already, were that possible. He did not know that the beautiful, pregnant Mrs Yetman had been disowned by her family for running off with a man they considered unsuitable.

To him Ryder Yetman was an honest man he employed to do odd jobs around the farm. He could turn his hand to anything, and in the few months since the Yetmans had occupied the humble dwelling, the pair had become indispensable. Farmer Frith's meanness, and the bleakness of life on the farm, didn't worry them. Indeed, they seemed to thrive on their isolation, a fact which the farmer and his dyspeptic, equally disagreeable wife found curious.

The Yetmans were a self-contained couple, disinclined to socialise even in the tiny Lakeland community in which they found themselves. They had arrived there by chance on the back of Lady as the winter was settling in, looking for accommodation for themselves, and grazing and shelter for the horse.

They were almost in rags when they arrived, and the flanks of the horse were thin. But they wanted work not charity, and Farmer Frith, who found it hard to get workers because of his reputation, or keep them because of his harshness, eagerly offered it to them: a cottage and five shillings a week, part of it to be paid back as rent. In addition – a big inducement, this – there was one full hot meal a day.

The Yetmans did not feel they were in a position to bargain. The north of England was not an easy place in which to find work. Their money was almost gone and they were hungry. Both were desperately afraid of the effect this might have on the baby Eliza was expecting in the spring.

They had been intending to go south to a warmer climate when they heard of Hunter's Hill farm and the chance of work.

Unlike her thrifty sister-in-law, Eliza had never been taught how to manage a house; she knew nothing about cooking, cleaning or laundry work, but she learned quickly. The farmer's wife, Bessie, would tolerate no sloppiness. She was quick to chide and reprimand, and desperation made Eliza a good pupil. She knew how fortunate they were to have secured shelter, warmth and a reasonable pittance to see them through the winter.

Each week Ryder went to Keswick, sometimes with Mr Frith and sometimes alone; but all the letters he had posted to Lady Woodville remained unanswered. This continued rejection increased his feeling of guilt about the harm he had done in taking a gently reared, innocent girl from her home. He had dishonoured her, made her pregnant, illegally wooed her and, now, cast her up on a lonely Lakeland fell far away from her loved ones.

It was not what he had intended, and his shame would have been greater were it not for the joy she gave him, the love they bore each other. Eliza refused to let Ryder take the blame, claiming that she had forced herself on him. He was all she ever wanted. Not for a moment did she regret what she had done and, although she missed the gentle landscape of Dorset, she soon fell in love with the steep slopes, the high lonely crags and the wide expanses of Lake Ennerdale, one of the remotest parts of Lakeland.

Every morning at six Ryder and Eliza rose from their bed, sluiced themselves in water – sometimes so cold that the ice had to be broken – had a hunk of bread and hot tea in the kitchen, the fire still unlit. They then hurried to the farm, still in darkness, to begin their duties. Ryder served as cowman, milkman, shepherd, carpenter, doing with cheerful efficiency and much skill every job that came to hand. Eliza began the morning by cleaning out the grates and lighting new fires downstairs; this had been done upstairs by a maid who rose earlier and was even more hard pressed than she was: a pathetic, underfed little mite called Beth. She then washed up the dinner dishes of the night before, the breakfast dishes and then, going along to the washhouse, sorted through the soiled linen not only of the family, but of the other farm workers who lived in outbuildings on the lonely isolated farm. Much of this was foul and exceedingly dirty, unpleasant to handle. Sometimes Beth assisted, and sometimes she didn't. There were many equally unpleasant tasks for her to do.

Eliza's day was full, and as her pregnancy advanced she grew very tired. Her back ached and her ankles swelled. Ryder worried about her, but she would take no rest. The day began at the farm at seven, and it ended at seven when she served the family their dinner.

Then she and Ryder would eat with Beth and the farm hands in the kitchen before creeping home, thankfully, to bed.

There was a false spring in Lakeland which brought out the daffodils; the lambs were born early and the air was balmy. But, as sometimes happens, it was followed by snows and harsh winds. At times the snow, which nearly always covered the distant peaks – some of the highest in Lakeland – fell on the slopes of Bowness or the lower ground.

One morning Eliza lay in bed while Ryder slept, breathing gently beside her. It was bitterly cold in their bedroom, and she clung to him for warmth, recalling the days when a housemaid would creep into her room around dawn and light the fire as carefully and quietly as she could so as not to disturb her young mistress.

Eliza could hear the new-born lambs bleating pitifully in the field. Even though they were the sturdy Hardwick sheep of Lakeland, on those bleak slopes they could have scant chance of survival. As if in response, her baby moved in her womb, and she put a hand on her belly, trying to imagine its tiny limbs, what sex it was. It didn't matter: boy or girl, it would be wanted and loved.

Ryder stirred and groped for her, and she bent to kiss him.

'Why are you awake?' he murmured in the darkness.

'It's nearly time to get up. The cock at the farm has started to crow.'

It was their signal to rise, far more accurate than any clock.

'I heard the lambs bleating and felt my baby move inside me. Oh, Ryder – ' she kissed him gently on the mouth again ' – it will soon be here.'

The answer was a loud sigh, and, in the dim light of dawn, she tried to see the expression on his face.

'What is it, Ryder?'

'This is no place for you, Eliza, or our baby. I have a feeling we must soon be gone from here.'

'But are we not happy here, Ryder? The Friths are not very pleasant, but at least we have a roof over our heads, work to do.'

'Do you think that is the sort of work I want you to do?' he asked roughly. 'You were born a lady and, through me, you are reduced to this.'

'But *I* chose it, don't forget. I was not abducted. I chose to leave home in order to be with you, and therefore I accept this life with you.'

'But it is not what *I* want. Eliza . . .' Ryder struggled up, his teeth chattering with cold, and lit the candle by the bed. Then he snuggled down under the bedclothes again and placed his own hand against her belly. 'Eliza, I have a mind to go home.'

'Home?'

'Back to Wenham. I will throw myself on my father's mercy and ask him for work. The way Farmer Frith treats his men and animals disgusts me. I can't make a decent life for us, and our child, on these pitiful wages. We will never be able to save or have our own home.'

'We cannot go back to Wenham,' Eliza said slowly. 'Wherever we go, it cannot be there.'

'But why not? It is *our* home, the people and the land we love.'

'Do you think the people will love *us*?' she retorted. 'My mother has not even replied to my letters. I shall not write to her ever again, or have anything to do with her.'

'But if we go back we need not see her. We can live in a village on the far side of Wenham.'

'What makes you think that your father will give you work?' she asked after a pause.

'Because he knows I'm good at what I do. I can but ask him, and if I don't succeed, I can get work elsewhere; but at least it is a gentler land, a milder climate.' He put his arm round her and hugged her fiercely. 'Oh, my darling, beautiful as this landscape is, it is a harsh, cold place in which to live and work, and bring up a child.'

That morning after breakfast Mr Frith appeared at the door of the kitchen and asked Eliza if she would come into his office, where he kept his records, ledgers, and did his accounts.

His room was a comfortable one, and from his large desk at the window there was a magnificent view of Bowness, Herdus Scaw and Great Bourne. Not only the tops of the crags surrounding Lake Ennerdale but the slopes beneath had a thick covering of snow. Although it was bitterly cold elsewhere in the house, a big fire roared up his chimney. On either side of this were two large leather chairs. Farmer Frith pointed to one of them.

'Sit down, Eliza, and warm yourself. Have you got enough logs in your cottage?'

'Yes thank you, Mr Frith,' Eliza replied, somewhat astonished at his concern for so lowly a creature as herself.

'You must take care of yourself at a time like this.' He looked at her almost anxiously. 'If the roads are impassable the midwife will not be able to get to you.'

'I have no fear, Mr Frith,' Eliza said, throwing back her head. 'If the midwife cannot get here Ryder will be able to do everything necessary.'

'Has he been a midwife, then?' Farmer Frith looked puzzled.

'Oh no, sir.' She shook her head and smiled. 'But he has delivered many a calf. He will know what to do.'

'You have great confidence in your husband, Eliza,' the farmer said almost gently.

'I have, sir.'

'It does you credit.'

'Thank you, sir.'

Eliza was about to rise from her chair, still surprised by this apparent concern on the part of a man she considered harsh and unfeeling, when he indicated that she should remain seated. He began to light his pipe and, regardless of its effect on her delicate stomach, blew a thick stream of smoke into the air, sucking at the stem until he was satisfied.

'Don't go, Eliza,' he said between puffs. 'I want to ask you something.'

'What is that, Mr Frith?'

'You know I have never asked about your origins, nor do I wish to. Your past is your secret, and you may prefer to keep it that way. Doubtless you have good reasons which I do not enquire into. However, it is obvious to me that you were born into much better circumstances than the ones in which you find yourself here. Now that you are so near your time, I dare say that you could do with a little more money, something to put by, perhaps, for your child's future?'

'Why, we can always do with more money, Mr Frith,' Eliza

replied with a smile, wishing she could add, 'On the wages you pay,' but not daring to.

'I want to make you an offer for Lady,' the farmer said bluntly. 'My daughter covets her and, as you know, I can deny her nothing.'

'Oh no, sir, Lady is not for sale,' Eliza said firmly, shaking her head. 'She is the oldest friend I have; the best, apart from my husband. I could never part with her.'

'But you cannot ride her, my dear, in your condition,' the farmer protested, leaning forward. 'What use is she to you?'

'Ryder takes her to market. When I have rid myself of this burden' pointing to her stomach, 'I shall ride her again. No, Lady is not for sale. Never. She is part of my family.'

For a moment the farmer didn't reply. Reflectively he began to tamp down the tobacco in his pipe, which had gone out; then he relit it, and Eliza felt sick and began to cough.

'Jenny has her heart set on Lady, Eliza. I will give you a lot of money for her.'

'I'm sorry, Mr Frith.' Eliza now struggled to her feet. 'I will never sell her.'

'Then I may have to give you notice, my dear, to repossess the cottage.'

His words gave her such a shock that the baby lurched in her womb.

'You cannot be so unkind, Mr Frith. You couldn't dispossess a woman with child and a man who have both served you well for pitiful wages, just for a *horse*.'

'It is not for me, my dear,' he replied unctuously. 'It is for my daughter. She tells me that if she doesn't have Lady she will want to go away to Windermere or Carlisle. She is bored here. She wants her own horse.'

'Then buy her another.'

'She has set her mind on Lady, Eliza. She is used to getting what she wants.'

'But she may ride Lady *any* time.' Eliza felt a mounting sense of panic. He seemed so determined to have his own way.

The farmer took another puff of his foul-smelling briar and emphatically shook his head.

'Lady, or eviction. It is up to you.'

'Then we go,' Ryder said that night when Eliza, who could still hardly believe it, told him the story. 'We pack up here and go. And Lady goes with us. It is a sign that we are meant to go. I have felt it in my bones for some time that it was not right for us to stay here. We will pack up and go as soon as we can.'

'But we have no money.'

'I have a little put by.' He looked at her unhappily. 'It is the journey for you on horseback in this weather that bothers me. If we get as far as Keswick I think we shall have to stay there until the baby is born.'

'Maybe we can *plead* with Mr Frith. He cannot be *such* a bad man.'

'What he has done *is* the act of a bad man,' Ryder said savagely. 'An evil man. It is in keeping with his character. As for that daughter, she gives herself so many airs she is detestable. I shall be glad to see the back of them all. Tomorrow we will pack up, and the next day we shall creep away before dawn, without saying goodbye.'

However, when they woke the next morning the snow was so deep that they could scarcely get out of their cottage door, and Ryder had to dig a path to the farm. Lady was warm and safe, stabled with the other horses belonging to Mr Frith. While Ryder went off to the fields to help try and rescue what new-born lambs he could, Eliza went about her work in silence; but she felt sick and unwell. Mrs Frith was curiously quiet. The farmer was in the fields with his men, and of Jenny there was no sign. If her father had told her the outcome of his offer she was probably sulking in her bedroom.

Mrs Frith noticed that Eliza seemed to be in distress, and as she helped her with the baking in the afternoon she looked at her speculatively.

'When is your baby due, Eliza?'

'Not for another two months, Mrs Frith.'

'Yet you appear to be having pains.'

'I have some pain, Mrs Frith, but I have had them before.' Eliza paused and touched her side, and the sweat poured down her face.

'Sit down, girl,' Mrs Frith said. She was a practical country-woman, used to dealing with servants and animals and treating both about the same. Kindness from Mrs Frith was most unusual. As Eliza sank thankfully into a chair, the farmer's wife bade Beth make a pot of tea, and then she handed a cup to Eliza.

'You'd better go home for the rest of the day and lie down, Eliza. Be sure, though, that you're here sharp at seven tomorrow.' And with that she left the kitchen to take her own tea in the parlour, probably with her daughter.

'Cow,' Beth said scornfully when the door was shut, wiping her nose on her sleeve. 'You could die in your job for all she'd care.'

'I think you could,' Eliza said, looking at the door. 'How long have you been here, Beth?'

'Too long,' Beth said, snivelling again. 'I came here when I was eleven, and I'm now fifteen.'

'*Eleven!*' Eliza said, aghast. 'That's terrible.'

'It's quite common in these parts, Miss,' Beth said. She never called Eliza by her Christian name, perhaps because, in her peasant bones, she knew instinctively that she was in the presence of someone very superior. 'Some never go to school, and start work as soon as they can do useful tasks. I miss me mother and father, though,' she said, as two large tears fell out of each eye.

'Oh, Beth,' Eliza said, struggling to her feet. 'Where do your mother and father live?'

'Dead, Miss,' Beth said, by now openly sobbing. 'They both died of fever a short time after each other, and me and my brothers and sisters were taken to the workhouse.' She looked wanly at Eliza. 'We were parted there. So, happen I shall be here the rest of my days, Miss.'

'Oh . . .' There was a sharp spasm of pain on the left side

of her abdomen, and Eliza felt her first real pang of fear that all was not well with her baby.

'Help me back to my cottage, Beth,' she said, 'and then try and find my husband.'

'But Miss, Mrs Frith . . .'

'I don't care *what* Mrs Frith says,' Eliza said, with a note of panic in her voice. 'Do it, and do it now, or it may be too late.'

The poor dead little thing lay wrapped tenderly in a blanket as if it had been a living child. Though perfectly formed, its skin was like wax, and it was scarcely more than the size of a doll. It had never uttered a sigh. The baby came eight weeks early, and the midwife who arrived when Eliza's ordeal was over looked at it without pity and said it would never have had a chance.

She was as kind to the bereaved mother as she – brought up in a harsh climate – knew how. Eliza lay inert in her bed, while Ryder wept quietly by her side.

The midwife washed Eliza and changed her, and then she stood back and looked critically at her.

'This is no place for you, you know, my girl,' she said, shaking her head. 'I can see that you're used to a far, far better life. You shouldn't have kept working so long, or so hard. You're not made for it. Fine bones, you have, and a delicate constitution.

'Now, you had better go back to where you came from and do the sort of work you were used to doing – a governess, was it? – before you lose another baby.' She looked dispassionately at the small corpse. 'Do you want me to take it with me, or will you dispose of it yourself?'

'It's a *boy*,' Ryder said angrily. 'My son. Please don't refer to him as "it".'

' "It's" not a person at seven months, my love,' the midwife said with grim practicality. 'They don't even register them.'

That night Ryder dug a hole in the snow, and tenderly he placed the small, perfectly formed infant, wrapped in the shawl they had bought for it, in a deep grave. In the fields the new-born lambs bleated as if fearing for their own fragile lives, and the wind howled. Ryder filled in the small grave with his shovel, and then he knelt and said a prayer, the tears which ran down his face enough to soak the ground beneath, were it not for the fact that it was so wet already.

From the window of the cottage Eliza, leaning against the sill for support, watched him working by the light of the storm lamp. She was so blind from weeping that she could hardly see him, but she felt that she had to be present at the pitiful obsequies. Without prayers or ceremony, it was like burying a dog; but it was their child. Together, though dead, they had baptised him and given him a name:

Thomas. Thomas Yetman.

Not yet a human being.

It took Eliza a week to recover from her miscarriage, and even then she was weak and bled heavily. Ryder had made up his mind that they would not linger in that inhospitable valley, but would make for the warmer, gentler climate of the south.

He sought out Frith to tell him that they were leaving and asked for the wages due, but Frith hummed and hawed and shook his head.

'Well, you haven't worked the full month,' he objected.

'What do you mean, I haven't worked the full month?' Ryder snarled. 'I have given you far more than you paid me for, you unprincipled rogue.'

'Unprincipled rogue! How *dare* you address me thus?' Farmer Frith spluttered. 'As for your wife, who has lain about all the time doing nothing . . .'

Ryder just managed to control himself, to prevent his fist coming in contact with the farmer's great overhanging chin.

'My wife even had to give her tea,' Frith went on truculently. '*She*, the mistress, making tea for a mere servant.'

'My wife is no servant and you know it,' Ryder said menacingly.

'Then what is she?'

'I can't say, but she's no servant.'

'I knew you two were up to no good,' Frith said contemptuously. 'Skulking up here, away from civilisation; to avoid authority, I'll be bound.'

'What do you mean by that?'

Frith, feeling bolder now that the threat of violence seemed to have receded, put his hands on his hips and stared at Ryder, a mean look in his eyes.

'If you ask me what I mean, I'd say you're a pair of thieves; maybe escaping from gaol or on the run from the authorities. It would, for instance, interest me to know how you came by a horse of such breeding, if you did not steal it . . .'

Ryder's fist was just about to connect with the farmer's chin as Frith stepped back and extended a placatory hand.

'Now look, Yetman . . . don't get angry. Maybe you came by the horse by fair means, I'm not asking. That your wife *is* a lady I have no doubt, and I have never asked questions about your past, have I now? I gave you work *and* a roof over your heads . . . so I will strike a bargain with you.' Frith pulled himself to his full height, which was still a good few inches shorter than Ryder. 'I have offered to buy the horse from your wife, but she will have none of it. I make the offer again.'

'She will still refuse,' Ryder said between clenched teeth. 'All we want is our wages and we'll be off.'

'Ah, but I am not going to give you any wages.' A look of cunning returned to the farmer's eyes. 'You have not stayed the full month, you have not earned them . . .'

'Of course we've stayed the full month, you blockhead.' Ryder reached out and, clutching him by his coat collar, shook him. 'We've stayed *many* months.'

'Yes, but *this* full month. You have not worked a full month.' The farmer began to claw at Ryder's hand. 'I can see that, whatever your wife is, *you're* no gentleman. Now let go of me, there's a good fellow, and I'll bargain with you.'

Reluctantly Ryder dropped his hand in case he throttled the man, who anxiously, ran his finger round his collar and retreated a few steps further back.

'I'll buy the horse. I'll give you a good price, enough to get you where you're going in comfort, in view of your wife's condition. I know she's very weak. She's no good to us any longer, and you're too violent. You can both take yourselves off; but I want that horse. My daughter has set her heart on it. I'll give you good money. I can't say fairer than that. Take it or leave it, but you'll never get that horse over these hills in this weather. I know this country and the treacherous snows that can come down on the hills, blocking the paths. Both the horse *and* your wife will die . . . you too, perhaps, though maybe that's too much to hope for.'

Lady seemed to be expecting Eliza, who crept round to the stable after the rest of the household had gone to bed. She whinnied gently and put her nose between Eliza's extended hands as if she wanted to be kissed. In the pale light of the lamp her beautiful eyes looked sad, almost as though she knew.

'Oh, *Lady!*' Eliza's voice was thick with tears. 'Oh, my darling; my dear, dear horse . . .' She struggled, but no more words came. Lady gently nuzzled, almost as though she could speak. Eliza ran her hands along her sleek, dark back.

'I know you will be looked after,' she said. 'But I'll come back for you, Lady. As sure as God is here to judge me, I will come back for you, and take you home where you belong.'

She then leaned her face against the horse's head and gave full vent to the tears that had never been very far from the surface ever since she had lost her baby.

First the baby, then Lady. There was now only one priceless, precious possession left, and she must never lose him. Only Ryder gave her the strength, the will to go on.

Suddenly she felt a hand on her back, and she jumped away from the horse so suddenly that she nearly upset the oil lamp on the straw-covered stable floor.

'Oh, goodness, Beth, you frightened me,' she cried.

'Can't you take me with you, Miss?' the serving-maid said, clearly struggling herself against tears. 'You've been so good to me, the only one who ever spoke nice or treated me right. I'll do *anything* for you, Miss, not ask for wages. Please . . .'

'Oh, *Beth* . . .' Eliza bent down to the poor stunted creature and clasped her hand. 'I hate to leave you behind, but it is impossible for you to come with us. We have no money, no place to go . . .'

'I don't care, Miss.' Between pitiful sobs, Beth squeezed her hand. 'I can't stand it here . . .'

'I know,' Eliza said in an urgent whisper. 'They are forcing me to leave Lady behind, but I am determined to get her back. If you look after Lady for me I promise you that, one day, the three of us will be reunited.'

'Oh, *Miss* . . .' Beth knelt on the floor and clasped Eliza's knees. 'I don't know who you are, but you're much better than me. Braver too. I'd give my life for you . . .'

'That won't be necessary, Beth.' Eliza gave a shaky laugh. 'Just you look after Lady, and one day we'll be together. As soon as we have an address I'll write to you, and you can write to me.'

'I can't write, Miss.'

'Well, maybe someone in the village will help you. My *poor* girl.' She stooped to kiss her and realised that, once again, the tears were flowing. Flinging her arm round Lady, she briefly leaned her head against her velvety flank. Then abruptly she turned her back and, her lamp swinging in the darkness, casting grotesque shadows before her, she fled.

As the train pulled out of Carlisle station Ryder put his arm round Eliza, who leaned her head against his shoulder. Soon the town was behind them, and to their right they could see the high crags of Lakeland like an impenetrable barrier against the skyline. From where they sat looking, silently, it seemed like a passing dream; or was it a nightmare? They had gone by cart to Cockermouth and then by carriage to Carlisle. By the time they had purchased their tickets to London they had scarcely any of the money left that Farmer Frith had paid for Lady, a fraction of what she was worth.

'We could never have ridden her back to Dorset,' Ryder murmured, aware of her thoughts; her eyes mesmerised, like his, by the sight of the distant mountains, which gradually vanished from sight as though they had been nebulous clouds in the sunlight. 'Frith was right. The journey would have killed her. I'm *glad* to get away,' he continued in a harsh voice, as Eliza made no reply. 'I felt those mountains were closing in on me.'

'But our baby lies there.' There was a catch in Eliza's voice. 'Poor little thing, he is all alone.'

'He is with God.' Ryder's lips brushed her cheek. 'He is not there at all. We must believe that. We *must* believe, and we must believe, above all, that we will have others; that all will be well once we are among our own kith and kin.'

Eliza, whose heart felt almost bereft of emotion, could only hope he was right.

It was a long journey. They had an overnight stop in London, and then they went by coach to Dorset, arriving at Blandford six days after they had left Ennerdale. They put up at a small hotel in Blandford, where Ryder sent immediately for a doctor, because his wife was weak and bleeding heavily.

The doctor also was a stranger, although he seemed to look at Eliza with curiosity. He said that she must rest and not leave her room and, as well as prescribing a restorative, he recommended a diet of red meat and nourishing food. Ryder could barely scrape together enough money to pay his bill.

The following day, while Eliza was still asleep, he set out to see his father.

It was seven miles from Blandford to Wenham, and he walked all the way, arriving just after lunch at his father's house. He knew there was a chance that he would not be at home, and he dreaded the questions that his mother would ask, the reproach he would see in her eyes because, since his elopement, he had not written to his family at all.

However, as he opened the heavy gates of his old home he saw his father alone in the garden, the paper on his lap, having a snooze after what had probably been a good lunch. Unlike the weather they had left behind, the sun shone on this land of plenty, the trees were in leaf and the birds sang. It was like leaving one world for another.

Ryder thought the unexpected beauty of the day was a good augury as he walked slowly up the path and then on to the lawn where his father sat, mouth open, emitting gentle snores.

Ryder crouched at his father's feet not wishing to disturb him. Hunger nudged at his vitals, but he had made arrangements at the hotel for Eliza to be well looked after. He had said that the probability was that he would not be back until the following day.

He looked up at the large house made of Marnhull stone in which he and his brother and sister were born. Below them ran the River Wen, and on the far side of the bank was Wenham Wood, where he had played as a boy with his brothers.

Those seemed like nostalgic, happy days: the days of his youth.

With an inward shudder Ryder recalled the past months of his life: the hard work and unremitting toil of the farm; the dark mornings, short days and even darker, longer nights in the Ennerdale valley. He recalled burying his stillborn son and the painful leavetaking between Eliza and her beloved horse.

Yes, the nostalgia of childhood was one thing, but it was a better, happier man who had money to feed and clothe his wife and children, and provide them with a warm house and a secure future. If his father gave him a chance his wandering days were done.

As if able to divine his thoughts, his father suddenly stirred and, opening wide his blue eyes, stared blankly at Ryder as though in a dream.

Ryder didn't rise but stared back at him, an unfathomable expression on his face.

'Ryder?' John Yetman said, blinking his eyes rapidly three or four times. 'Is it really you, Ryder?'

'It is I, Father.' Ryder got slowly, wearily to his feet.

'Oh, *Ryder*.' John Yetman held out his arms, and his eldest son embraced him, kissing him on both cheeks, his arm round his father's shoulders.

'Oh, *Ryder*,' John said again, now with tears in his eyes. 'Your mother is dead. There was no way we could let you know it. Why did you not keep in touch, son, let us know where you were?'

'Oh, *Father*,' Ryder cried, his heart almost too full to speak. If he had been close to anyone in his family it was to his mother: a gentle, unassuming, docile woman, totally lacking in the aspirations or ambitions of her husband. He knelt on the ground beside his father and, covering his face with his hands, wept as though his heart would break.

'Was it my fault, Father? Was she grieving over what I'd done?'

'No, no, lad,' John Yetman replied. 'She had a lump in her breast as big as a ball. It had nothing to do with you, though of course she was unhappy. However, the good God spared her the agony of lingering. She asked for you, Ryder, though. She missed you.'

Ryder continued to kneel where he was, shaking his head from side to side, tears pouring down his cheeks. He was weeping now not only for his mother but for his baby, for the suffering of his wife, for the misery of the last six months, for his wrongdoing.

'Father, Mother, forgive me,' Ryder murmured, removing his hands from his face. He took a handkerchief from his pocket and gave his nose a hearty blow. His father, leaning forward, gazed anxiously at him.

'Have *you* been ill, Ryder? You're very thin, and your suit is threadbare . . . And where is the lass, the young woman you took with you? 'Twas a big scandal in this neighbourhood, Ryder.' For the first time his expression was reproachful. 'I didn't know where to hide my face.'

'I know, Father.' Ryder hung his head. 'I made a terrible mistake. I committed a great wrong.' He raised his face, so stricken with sorrow that his father provided his own handkerchief and dabbed at his eyes. 'But I love Eliza, and she loves me. We are wed, man and wife . . . and we have suffered. We lost a child, we experienced great hardship, bitter cold and poverty. We were mistreated. She is not well, even now . . .'

'Then where *is* she, son?' John Yetman demanded agitatedly, getting to his feet. 'You must fetch her here, bring her home. Your wife? Wed to a *Woodville*? Oh, Ryder, my son, my son,' he cried, throwing his arms around him and weeping, as David wept for Absalom, only with gratitude that his son was alive, and restored at last to him.

9

Christopher Yetman was a man who came and went; a trial
to his family, a puzzle to the woman he wooed. Or *was* he
wooing? Miss Fairchild was never quite sure. He blew hot and
cold. She knew one didn't hurry these things, especially with
people of a certain age. It would never have done to rush into
things as Ryder Yetman had with Eliza, or Herbert Lock with
Agnes. It hadn't taken long for *that* piece of gossip to get round
the town, because Agnes thought it was terribly amusing and
told all and sundry.

Poor Herbert, bowled over by the humiliation of unrequited
love, eventually sold his house in Blandford and moved out of
the district.

When Christopher Yetman's nephew returned home with
his common-law wife, Christopher quickly put space between
himself and the family. He disappeared for weeks while Ryder
and John tried to sort things out. As far as John was concerned,
he was eager to forgive his son because he needed him. Herbert
had left a very big gap. He had not been able to replace him
and desperately wanted help.

As for Miss Fairchild, she didn't quite know what to do: sell
the shop or hang on to it. Was Christopher serious or was he
not? It was so hard to tell.

Ryder's return home, though it was a relief, was an upheaval.
No one except Victoria Fairchild really missed Christopher
when he went away; he would be sure to turn up again,
in a week, a month, a year. Despairing of him ever putting
any of his many promises into practice, Miss Fairchild decided

eventually to put the shop on the market. Or would she? Well, not just yet.

Miss Bishop counselled her as best she could; but it was difficult, even for a woman as tactful as she was, as skilled in preparing people for bad news, to say precisely *what* she thought about Christopher Yetman. He was a good-looking man, he came from a well-known local family, he said he had means . . . but one never knew. Personally she neither liked nor trusted him, but she felt that if she said so outright Victoria might think her jealous.

Miss Fairchild lived beyond the church and the Rectory in the last big house in the village. Lower down was the home of Miss Monk, and Miss Fairchild considered herself fortunate that Christopher Yetman had not cast his cap at *her*, for she was younger, prettier, she had no facial blemish, and she had as much money as Miss Fairchild, if not more.

Miss Fairchild stood at her garden gate waving to Miss Bishop, who had been in for one of her motherly chats. No *use* waiting, no *purpose* in hoping. Put the shop on the market, maybe take a few trips around England and abroad. No use pining.

With a shrug of resignation – after all, Miss Bishop was almost always right – Victoria closed the gate, giving a farewell wave as Miss Bishop vanished down the hill on her way to see another of her great friends, Mrs Lamb. Miss Fairchild had never been much of a gardener: so much of her time had been given to the shop. A man came in to look after the garden, as he had in her parents' time. It was put mostly to lawn, with a few rose bushes, and a small orchard at the rear.

The Fairchilds had never kept pets and, especially since the death of her mother, there were many occasions when Victoria felt lonely. It would be nice to have a cat to stroke, a dog to pat . . . or a husband with whom to share one's bed.

A little *frisson* went down her spine at the audacity of such a notion. But Christopher had given her hope. In time, he seemed to say, just a little more time.

She knew that Christopher was fearful of anything unpleasant.

He found it difficult to face hard facts, bad news of any kind. He took off like a rabbit from a gun when Ryder arrived home, and then she had a letter from him from Brighton to say he missed her and would be back soon.

That had been three weeks ago. Meanwhile one lived on hope. Victoria knew that one problem was money. She had tried to convince Christopher how unimportant that was, but without success. He had his pride, and she admired him for it. He insisted on investing in the shop, so that they were equal partners.

Miss Fairchild sat on the bench in the garden and wished she had something she could take in her arms, like a cuddly cat, or a baby . . . But it would be too late for babies anyway. If only Christopher hadn't given her *hope*.

A little breeze sprang up, and she was about to go into the house when a voice hailed her. It seemed to come from very far away and, for a moment, she thought it was her imagination playing tricks with her.

She turned round and saw it was no trick. There he was, large as life, striding up the hill from the church, his arm raised in a cheery wave.

'Oh, *Christopher*,' she cried and, running along the garden path, rushed headlong into his arms. He reached out for her and then tossed her high in the air, as if she were a small child, before planting a kiss on each of her cheeks.

Victoria didn't care if anyone saw them.

Miss Fairchild had never had Christopher round to the house before. She always saw him in the shop because, ostensibly, they had met about business. She got into the habit of entertaining him to a cup of tea or coffee in the back room. She knew it was pretence, but it was decorous too. Several times he had walked her to the gate of her cottage, and, once, he had got as far as the porch.

Now here he was. She had thrown discretion to the winds and invited him in, given him tea and suggested he might stay for supper.

Christopher seemed very happy in her house, very much at home. He sat in her best chair in the front parlour, his legs crossed, smoking a cigarette, at ease with her and the world.

'I missed you you know, Victoria,' he said with a chuckle as she poured him more tea.

'And I missed *you*.' She stood very straight, the pot in her hand, and gazed at him. 'Where do you *go* when you go, Christopher? Why are you so *mysterious* about it all?'

'I'm not mysterious at all, my dear,' he said, smiling at her. 'I am a man of business, you know, a man of affairs.' He put down his cup and leaned forward. 'As a matter of fact I went to London, and then to Eastbourne and Brighton on matters of business to see if I could raise the capital to purchase the shop. You know that my brother has never been accommodating about *this*. Anyway, his mind is now full of Ryder.' Christopher made a clicking noise of disapproval. 'There is no room for me any longer in that household, I fear. Ryder is jealous of me.'

'Jealous?'

'Well, something's the matter. Victoria . . .' Christopher looked round. 'How would it be . . .'

'Yes, Christopher?' Her voice trembled slightly as, very carefully, she put the pot down upon the stand.

'Well, did you ever think . . . This *is* a nice house. But I don't want you to imagine for a moment that it's just for that. It's you. I miss you . . .'

'Christopher, are you saying . . .'

Abruptly he held up a hand.

'I'm saying nothing *yet*, Victoria. But I think we have an understanding.'

'Oh, indeed we have,' she breathed.

'But first I want to raise the money as I said I would. It has taken a long time – ' he sighed loudly ' – but these things do. I want it to be a proper partnership, because I don't want people to think I asked you to marry me merely for gain.'

During the Great Plague of London, those who were able to flee to the outskirts of the city or the country did so to try

183

and escape the hideous, contagious disease. In the centuries that had passed since then, London itself had spilled out into those parts which were once green meadows or ploughed fields. Some northern areas retained their countrified aspects – ponds, fields and woodland – and by 1881 Hampstead was a fashionable and desirable area in which to live because of its proximity to the open heathland which enclosed its pretty streets and winding lanes.

Every day nursemaids could be seen pushing perambulators containing the offspring of the nobility, the gentry or the well-to-do. Those of their charges who could walk or toddle ran along by their sides playing with their balls, their skipping ropes or hoops, sometimes accompanied by barking dogs, the family pets let off their leash for a good long run.

In summer the fair came to the Heath, and then the children were carefully watched because of the gypsies and the rough crowd from the London slums whom the fair attracted. But for most of the year the Heath was for those who liked fresh air and the out-of-doors and, although it was so vast that it could never be called crowded, on Sundays and holidays the numbers who appreciated its facilities swelled as the populace of overcrowded London came by public transport to take advantage of the clean, country air.

Not far from the High Street was a cluster of dwellings on the Heath itself known as the Vale of Health. There, so it was said, the fugitives of plague-ridden London had sought refuge for their animals and themselves and gathered in great numbers.

In one of these small houses, tucked away behind a walled garden, a young couple looked around with a view to purchase. It had taken them some time to find it, but now they knew it was exactly what they wanted, and they threw their arms around each other in delight at such a find.

The solicitor who acted for the vendor accompanied them on their expedition and was as pleased as they were that it filled the bill. It was small, but not too small.

'You see, I have a place in Dorset,' Sir Guy said, twirling his cane. 'This is perfectly adequate for Lady Woodville and myself when we visit London. My wife's chest is weak,' he said, looking anxiously at his partner. 'I want her to have the best air in London.'

'You could have nothing finer than this, Sir Guy,' the solicitor assured him. 'Why else is it known as the Vale of Health?'

It was true that Lally's constitution was not strong. She tired easily, and the long hours at the theatre sometimes left her prostrate. That, and walking up and down the three steep flights of stairs in Covent Garden, had made Guy determined to get her away as soon as he could.

The little house he bought for her in the Vale of Health was ideal, and he lost no time in completing the purchase, after which they spent many happy days together looking for suitable furnishings for their love nest.

By the beginning of summer Lally was able to move in.

'You have made me the happiest woman in the world, dearest Guy,' she said as they stood together at the window looking at the pretty little garden, with a fountain playing, all enclosed by a high wall.

'And you have made *me* the happiest man.' Guy bent to kiss her and, twining his arms round her, said: 'Lally, I want you to leave the theatre. I want you to stay here and wait for me. The theatre's not good for your health. Besides, I don't *like* you dancing. I don't like the way the men ogle you. I want no one to desire you but me.'

'But Guy, dearest, I shall be very *lonely* here,' Lally said doubtfully. It was true that she would miss her friends and the life of the theatre. She would also miss the suppers that she got from her many admirers when Guy was away. For Guy was not the only man in her life, though he was the most persistent. In many ways she did love him, but perhaps not *quite* as much as she said she did.

Lally was in the habit of lying to all and sundry about her past. In fact she had known neither mother nor father, but had been brought up in a foundlings' home from which she had made her escape at the age of fourteen. She was gifted with outstanding good looks and a quick, agile mind, and she put both to good use.

But Lally was not accustomed to a stationary life or to fidelity. The last thing she wanted was to be stuck in a small house on the outskirts of London pretending to be someone she was not. Who of her friends would be able to visit her in a place so inaccessible? Maybe a few of her wealthy men friends who could afford a hansom or who had carriages of their own; but she would not dare risk that because of Guy. If he found out, she thought, he might kill her.

'Let me continue in the theatre just a little longer, dearest,' she pleaded standing on tip toes to kiss him. 'Then in the winter when the fog starts I will do as you wish and remain in my little nest.'

'Oh, Lally,' Guy sighed, 'how can I refuse you anything? I love you so much.'

Lally kissed him with all the fervour of which her faithless little heart was capable, and as she broke away from him she asked: 'Won't your wife wonder why you spend so much time in London away from her?'

'She thinks I'm busy in the family business,' Guy replied with a chuckle. 'Little does she know I have not stepped inside the premises for weeks. I have no head for business and I do not like it – I was not brought up to work.'

Lally was alarmed. Stupid she was not; she was a sharp, intelligent Cockney girl who had lived by her wits for most of her nineteen years.

'But don't you work with your uncles?, and *her* father? Don't they miss you?'

A shadow passed over Guy's face. Despite the warnings of his Uncle Prosper, in his ardour he seldom thought through the consequences of his actions. In fact it never occurred to him to tell his uncles, or his father-in-law, where he was and what he was doing. He was master of his wife's fortune, and he knew she adored him. He did his best to make her happy when he was with her. He was a man who found it very easy to serve two mistresses. 'The very *last* thing my wife would do would be to question my behaviour or my whereabouts. Besides, she is very happy in Dorset, where she rules the roost. Now that we have a son, her happiness is complete.' He looked around him with an air of satisfaction. 'She has done her duty and I have done mine.'

Guy encircled his beloved's tiny waist with his arm and drew her even closer to him. He never thought that his words might hurt Lally, who, though she knew her station in life, continued to hope that, one day, it might change.

'Might she not find out about this purchase, Guy?' she enquired anxiously. 'After all, six hundred and fifty pounds is a lot of money.'

'Not to Margaret,' Guy said confidently. 'She brought an enormous dowry. Thanks to her I am now a very wealthy man, and you will never want for anything, my little love. It would never ever occur to Margaret to question anything I did. Now, my darling,' he said, bringing her hand to his lips and looking meaningfully into her eyes, 'we have perhaps time for a little rest before I have to go.'

Ryder looked round the office in Salisbury Street, at the portrait of his grandfather in a place of honour on the wall, at the shelves piled high with papers, documents, plans and ledgers and, finally, at the desk opposite his father's with its back to the window. John stood watching him anxiously, his hat still in his hand, as though he expected his son to take off again at any moment. Ryder felt a constriction in his throat as a wave of intense emotion swept over him, and he saw, from the expression on his father's face, that he knew quite well what was going through his mind.

'A full partner, Ryder,' John said, placing his hand squarely on his son's arm. 'My successor, my right-hand man.'

'I don't deserve it, Father,' Ryder said, bowing his head. 'After what I did, I don't deserve it.'

They had been to his mother's grave to lay flowers, and there he had knelt for several minutes mentally begging her forgiveness. This poignant moment was still fresh in his mind.

'I deserted you. I was not there when you needed me. I didn't even know my mother was dying. You are too good to me, Father . . .'

'You have been through a lot, my boy,' John said, finally flinging his hat on the hatstand and sitting down behind his own desk. 'You have been punished for what you did; but God has been good to you. He has given you a lovely, loyal wife. That you have earned the respect of a woman such as Eliza raises you in my estimation. I am prepared to believe that, rightly or wrongly, you were in the grip of a powerful emotion you could neither understand nor resist. I also know now that, despite loving another, you were prepared to honour your word to Maude. That alone was the action of a good man.' John Yetman put his head in his hands and sighed. 'I realise how difficult it was for you to tell us, your mother and me, about Eliza. I wish you could have written to us to let us know all was well.

'But I realise why you didn't.' He took a handkerchief from his pocket and blew his nose vigorously. 'Your mother loved you and trusted you to the end; but to have known where you were and what was happening to you, while it would not have prevented her death, would have eased her mental suffering.'

As Ryder raised his head his father saw the agony etched on his face.

'Put it out of your mind now, Ryder. She is in heaven and her sufferings are over. I believe that, even if she cannot see us, she will know that all is well. Indeed, she may have sent you to me in this hour when I needed you – and I *do* need you, Ryder . . .' John indicated the papers which lay in disorderly piles all over the room. 'Since Herbert left me I have scarcely been able to cope. My business is going to ruin; that business started by my father, continued by me, and to be passed on to you and, I hope, to your son. You are an essential link in this chain, and I'm sure your dear mother had some hand in your return. Today, kneeling at her grave, I thanked her for it.'

'Then, Father, as you say, to work,' Ryder said, sitting briskly at his desk and passing his hands over the smooth shiny surface. 'Tell me everything you have in hand, what you plan, and what you wish me to do. I will carry out every request to the letter, to the best of my ability.'

'Well done,' John said warmly, bending over the plans which lay on his desk. 'Pull up your chair and I will show you this new development we plan in Dorchester, or rather planned. We were just about to go ahead with it when Herbert left, and since then it has been in abeyance. Now I feel vigorous and confident enough with you beside me to continue it.'

Willingly Ryder rose to his feet and, with a pencil in his hand, sat beside his father while they talked, studying the draughtsman's plans and making notes.

At lunch time the two men went down to the Crown Hotel near the bottom of Salisbury Street for lunch. The bar was full of farmers, traders and local businessmen, some of whom greeted Ryder with varying degrees of cordiality, while others seemed deliberately to turn their backs on him.

Ryder had known it would be like this. The people of Blandford would be no different from those of Wenham, and this ambivalence would continue for some time.

'If only Eliza's mother would give us permission to marry,' he murmured to his father as he passed him the glass of beer he had bought for him at the bar, 'the dirty looks would soon stop. People would soon forget.'

'Lady Woodville has a nasty streak,' John nodded as his lips touched the foaming froth of his beer. 'They say the son would be prepared to forgive his sister, but *she* will not. Maybe you should go and see Sir Guy. He is a reasonable sort of man.'

'I think Eliza has a mind to deal with her brother.' Ryder drained his glass. 'She must persuade him that the deed is done, and the sooner we are married in church the better. Now, Father shall we go in to lunch?' Ryder looked at his watch. 'I am anxious to go over to Dorchester and inspect that site.'

They were about to proceed into the dining room, which was already nearly full, when John felt a tug on his sleeve. He called to Ryder, who had gone on ahead, and they both turned to look at a man neatly but nondescriptly dressed, with cold eyes peering through steel-framed spectacles, mutton-chop whiskers, and a bowler hat in his hand.

'Mr Yetman?' he enquired.

'Mr John Yetman,' John replied.

'Ah!' The man looked from John to Ryder. 'And would *that* be Mr Christopher Yetman?'

'That is my son Ryder. Have you business with us, sir?'

'I wonder if I may have a few words in private, Mr Yetman?' the man murmured, glancing furtively around. 'What I have to say is of a confidential nature.'

'You can say anything you like in front of my son,' John said gruffly. 'Get on with it, man, we are anxious to eat.'

'It will take a little time, Mr Yetman,' the stranger continued. 'Do you think I could call and see you in your office?' He looked at the heavy watch which hung from a gold chain across a grimy waistcoat that had seen better days. 'Say two o'clock? I am anxious to return to London.'

'You have come from *London*? Well then, you'd better sit down with us' – John hospitably indicated the dining room – 'and have something to eat.'

'I have had a bite already, sir. I went to your office and was told you had left and where to find you. I shan't detain you, sir; but what I have to say is a matter of some importance.'

'Come, then.' John beckoned to the waiter and asked for a table for three. He offered the stranger a drink, but the man would take nothing.

'Hollis, sir,' he said, extending a hand across the table. 'Michael Hollis of 201 Southampton Row, London.'

'And what is your business, Mr Hollis?' John shook out his table napkin and tucked it into the top of his waistcoat. 'Are you in the building trade?'

'Oh no, sir.' Mr Hollis seemed to find this amusing. 'I am by profession an enquiry agent.'

He stopped talking while John and Ryder, having studied the menu, ordered their lunch: beefsteak pie with vegetables and a pint of bitter each.

Mr Hollis watched them with a hungry look in his eyes, and Ryder formed the opinion that he had not, in fact, eaten, and that as soon as his business was completed he would make for one of the meaner hostelries in the town. He didn't seem nervous, but there was something shifty and vaguely disreputable about him that made Ryder uneasy. For some reason he thought of Farmer Frith.

'You seem to imply that your business concerns my uncle, Christopher Yetman.' Ryder looked at him intently.

'Yes,' Mr Hollis murmured. 'Would you happen to know where I might find him?'

'And why would you want to find him?' John took up the questioning.

'Well, he is wanted on a bigamy charge, sir. It would appear that Mr Yetman has a wife in Brighton, and another in south London. It would also appear that he may be in search of a third, as he has disappeared, having divested both ladies of all their money and left them in great distress. When Mr Yetman is apprehended he will face very severe charges – if proved, of course.' He paused and gazed at them calmly as John and Ryder stared at him open-mouthed from across the table. 'I see I've shocked you and your son, Mr Yetman . . .'

'A bigamist!' John took out his handkerchief and mopped his brow. 'I know nothing of my brother's activities. He comes and goes.' John glanced quickly at Ryder.

'I take it Mr Yetman has been as unsatisfactory as a brother as he was a husband.' Mr Hollis's sympathy was veiled. 'I realised immediately that this had nothing to do with you; but if you could kindly let me know *where* your brother is. Considerable sums of money are involved. Some, I understand, that he has purloined ostensibly for the support of his family . . .'

The focal point of the town of Wenham was the High Street. Here news and gossip of all kinds was exchanged, whether it was of a serious nature or something of the utmost triviality. In the centre of the High Street was the Baker's Arms, which was run by a family with an Irish name, McQueen, though all their progeny had been born and bred in Dorset.

The bar at the Baker's Arms was perhaps the most important place in Wenham for the exchange of information, as well as misinformation, about its inhabitants. Many of these were unable to defend themselves, for no respectable woman would be seen in the bar, which was presided over by an attractive woman called Annie who, although married, was always known by the name of her parents: McQueen.

Annie McQueen knew Christopher Yetman very well. He spent a lot of his time in the bar of the Baker's Arms and, as Annie was kind and sympathetic, he frequently confided in her.

Despite his mysterious past, the uncertainty as to his exact occupation or means, Christopher, with his fair, slightly greying hair, his rugged, weatherbeaten good looks, his hearty laugh, his formidable six-foot frame, was an engaging character. He had made several passes at Annie, but she had quite rightly deflected them on the grounds that she was a married woman with two children and her husband was a drover with a wicked temper.

It was Annie, apparently – no one could be quite sure – who passed on the information that Christopher Yetman was on the point of making Miss Fairchild the happiest of women.

However, the rumour that went round the town about Christopher's intentions towards Miss Fairchild might quite properly be laid at Annie's door because she told it to Mr Hibbert the butcher, who passed it on to his son Alfred, who told his girl friend Gertrude, who told *her* sister Mary, who worked at the greengrocer's. From there it circulated rapidly: to the baker's, the saddler's, the ironmonger's, round the market, until finally, inevitably, it reached the ears of Lily, Miss Fairchild's maid. Unable to contain her glee, she dropped a curtsy when she brought Miss Fairchild's breakfast one morning, and started blushing.

'Whatever is the matter, Lily?' Miss Fairchild enquired as

she opened her letters, gazing censoriously at the girl above her pince-nez.

'Nothing's the matter, Miss,' Lily said, still giggling and blushing.

'Something *is* the matter, Lily.' Miss Fairchild removed her spectacles and sat back. 'You are behaving like an idiot. Please tell me what is the matter.'

'Don't like to say, Miss.' Lily put a hand to her mouth.

'Does it concern me?' Miss Fairchild fixed her eyes sternly on the girl, who started spluttering.

'*Ever* so pleased for you, Miss,' she said at last.

'*Pleased*? What about? What on *earth's* the matter? Oh!' Miss Fairchild's eyes suddenly lit up with pleasure. 'Have I won the church raffle?'

Lily thought this very amusing and guffawed afresh until Miss Fairchild once again grew angry.

'Lily, please tell me what this nonsense is all about.'

'They say you are to be wed, Miss.' Lily dropped her hands and gazed at the floor. '*Ever* so pleased for you, Miss.'

'Wed?' Miss Fairchild gasped. 'To whom?'

'Why, to *him*, Miss,' Lily said meaningfully.

'Do you mean Mr Yetman?'

Lily nodded. 'They *say* he went to see the Rector about the banns – or *was* going to see, perhaps. I baint quite sure, Miss.' She looked at her lamely.

'Oh, can it be true . . .' Miss Fairchild rose quickly from the table, breakfast and morning post abandoned completely, and then, forgetting herself, she threw her arms round the serving girl and embraced her. 'Can it *possibly* be true? Where did you hear this? How long ago?'

Lily looked puzzled.

'The whole town knows about it, Miss, but I *believe* Mr Yetman mentioned it first to Annie McQueen at the Baker's Arms – '

'He mentioned it to her? He actually *said* he was going to see the Rector?' Miss Fairchild was by now quite beside herself.

'I believe so, Miss . . .' In the face of such enthusiasm Lily felt a spasm of doubt. 'Best check *yourself*, Miss – but that's what I *think* he did say.'

Trembling with excitement, after all there was no smoke without a fire, Miss Fairchild managed to assume a semblance of decorum long enough to finish reading the morning letters, which still contained items from solicitors about her parents' will. But continue with her breakfast she could not, and when Lily removed it she raised her eyes at the amount of toast that was left, the butter untouched, the top still on the pot of marmalade. Her mistress was in love indeed.

Miss Fairchild hastened to her room where, humming under her breath – Beethoven's 'Ode to Joy' – she discarded the prim grey blouse and skirt she had been going to wear in favour of a pretty floral print, a dress that swept to graceful folds round her ankles and was ruched at the neck and wrists, rather like an afternoon tea gown. She selected a hat which left most of her hair exposed, because Christopher had often admired what he called her 'crown'. Once he had touched it.

She put her watch, and a gold necklace her mother had given her, round her neck, and then she twirled several times in front of the mirror in order to inspect her appearance carefully for what could be her day of days.

Her cheeks were pink, her eyes shone. She knew that the love she felt in her heart for Christopher had transformed her. It had made her beautiful.

Miss Fairchild then skipped down the garden path and walked quickly along the road that led past Miss Monk's house, past the Rectory (she glanced in at the window in case the Rector or Mrs Lamb might be there to confirm the good news, but there was no sign of them). She walked past the church, imagining it on the day the doors would be open and she and Christopher would emerge arm in arm . . . This very day, she told herself, she would have her solicitors draw up a document making him an equal partner with her in the business on their marriage.

She turned left past the church, and hurried up a row of ancient thatched cottages where she imagined the people behind the windows all saw her pass and shared her joy. She knew them all, she could name almost everyone in every cottage or house in Wenham.

She came to the High Street, and the butcher waved at her from behind the carcase he was carving; the greengrocer, arranging a pile of apples on the stall outside his shop, gave her a grin, and the baker looked through his window above his loaves of bread and stacks of scones, buns and cakes and smiled brightly at her.

They knew. They all knew.

Outside the Baker's Arms Annie McQueen was washing the pavement with a mop that she kept dipping into the bucket beside her. Miss Fairchild paused as Annie, seeing her, leaned on her mop for a moment, a knowing smile on her lips.

But Annie was a woman with a reputation, even if she did have a jealous husband and two children, and Miss Fairchild kept carefully to her side of the road, hurrying on until she came to her shop and, putting the key in the lock, flung open the door.

Then she went quickly to the windows and let up the blinds. The sunlight flooded in over the display of goods in the window, the polished floor, across the counter, with all its boxes and jars, and up to the bales of material on the shelves, enhancing their brightness.

She went into the back room, removed her hat, put on a white apron and began to dust, still humming the 'Ode to Joy'. She had already counted the takings from the till the previous evening and put them, about fifty pounds, in a bag in the tea caddy. Removing the bag, she placed it on the table until she had time to go to the bank. Maybe then she would pop into the solicitor's and see about the arrangement she had in mind for Christopher.

Oh, *when* would he be here? All morning she looked up eagerly every time the bell rang as the door opened, but each time her hopes were dashed. Sales, however large or small, no longer interested her. Some of the customers wanted to linger and chat – oh yes, they knew, they *all* knew – but she was much too agitated. Besides, she was cautious by nature; who *wouldn't* be in her situation?

Feeling a little disappointed, she was about to close for the lunch hour when the door opened once more, and there he stood – a large bunch of flowers in his hand, his face wreathed in smiles.

'*Christopher*!' she cried, running from behind the counter. 'I was just closing shop . . .'

'I hoped I'd catch you in time,' he said, thrusting the flowers at her. 'Unfortunately I have to go up to London this afternoon, and didn't want to miss you.'

'Oh, Christopher . . .' Now her tone betrayed profound disappointment. She couldn't conceal it. She took the flowers, but let them hang apathetically by her side.

'But what *is* it, my dear?' He looked concerned.

'Oh, I did so hope . . . How long will you be away?' She looked so crestfallen he thought she was going to cry.

Christopher sighed and frowned. Upon closer inspection she thought he looked haggard, and a little drawn around the eyes as though he had not slept.

'Are you unwell, Christopher?' she asked anxiously. And then she went over to the door and locked it before returning to the counter, which she opened so that they could go as usual into the back room.

'Is something *wrong*, Christopher?' She stopped to gaze at him. 'You really don't look well.'

'My dear, I'm as right as rain,' he said, but he was all too clearly making an effort to smile. 'I have to go away on business . . . I don't quite know when I'll be back.'

'*Christopher*,' Miss Fairchild said breathlessly, having scarcely given herself a moment to think. 'There *is* something I wished to say to you. Please sit down.' Rather reluctantly he sat opposite her as she continued: 'My dear, if it's *money* you're worried about, please don't. I have enough for both of us. I don't need it, and if you do . . .'

'Oh, Victoria, you dear little thing.' Looking genuinely moved, Christopher rose and stood gazing down at her. 'If *only* I could . . .'

'Then do, Christopher, *do*.'

'I'll think about it,' he said, backing away. 'You're too generous, much too generous. You're too good. You're an angel.' His voice faltered, but even as he spoke he saw the bag of money in front of him waiting to be taken to the bank.

'Victoria,' he murmured, glancing behind him, 'should you not draw the front blinds? You know what the gossip is in this town.'

'Oh, I know what it is,' she said, laughing delightedly. 'I'll do that at once, Christopher. Then perhaps we could have a cup of tea?'

She hurried into the shop and drew the blinds, but when she returned Christopher stood at the door of the store room, barring her way, his hat in his hand.

'I must go now, my dear,' he said urgently. 'I haven't time for tea. John is taking me into Blandford to catch the London train. I said I'd only be a few moments. But I did want to take my leave of you.'

'Oh, you make it sound so *final*,' she said, a note of anxiety entering her voice. 'There's nothing wrong, is there?'

'Nothing at *all*, my dear,' he said, bending his face to hers. 'Nothing to worry your pretty head about.'

Then very gently, and for the first and perhaps last time, he kissed her.

Miss Bishop sat with her arms locked tightly round the weeping woman, feeling for all the world as though she were dealing with one of her small charges rather than someone only a few years younger than herself. Indeed, she had just returned from school when Victoria Fairchild came bursting into her sitting room without even giving her maid time to announce her, and flung herself on her in a torrent of weeping.

She had elicited the story bit by bit, as if dragging the truth from a truant schoolgirl.

'It's not the m-m-oney,' Miss Fairchild sobbed. 'I was going to g-give him *mine* – much, much more. It's the way he did it, behind my back.'

'And you're *sure* there was no one else there, no other way it could have been taken?'

'No other way,' Miss Fairchild insisted. 'The back and front doors were locked, and the money was on the table in the leather bag I always take it to the bank in. I cash up the day before, but the bank is closed in the evening. I nearly always go to the bank the following lunch time, and I can't help thinking . . . that C–Christopher . . .' Here words once again failed her, and she leaned her head against Miss Bishop's corseted bosom clad in shining black bombazine which was already moist with tears.

'He knew this, of course, and came to see you before he left.' Miss Bishop sniffed with disapproval, though her arm tightened round the shoulders of the stricken woman.

'We *never* went into the back room again, or I should have seen that the money was gone. He came to the door and swept me out, and we walked down the High Street almost as far as the Yetman house.' Miss Fairchild paused at the thought of that kiss, but she did not mention it for fear of shocking her friend. Quickly she went on: 'I was hoping that he would . . . speak, you know, declare himself. But he said nothing. I thought he looked sad, and now I realise there was a note of finality in his voice. But I never guessed *why*. Oh, Agatha, how shall I ever live this down? What will people *say*?'

'The people of this town will be very sorry for you, my dear. They will take you to their collective bosom,' Agatha Bishop said gently. 'They all knew what Christopher Yetman was like. *I* knew what he was like.' Miss Bishop prised Victoria from her very gently and looked into her eyes. 'He is a ne'er-do-well. He always has been. There were very few people who thought that his courtship of you was genuine . . .'

'Because I am too old and disfigured,' Miss Fairchild said, but even as she did she fingered the scar on her lip and recalled once again the soft touch of those other lips that had kissed it.

'No! Not because of that. But you are a woman with money and he had none. His family disapproved of him.'

'Then why did they keep on having him back?'

'Because John Yetman is a *good* man and he loved him.

Catherine knew better, but Christopher was John's flesh and blood.'

Agnes Yetman stood hesitantly outside her father's door and then tapped on it with a diffidence unusual in her.

It was the time of her father's afternoon nap, and she had in her hand a cup of tea. She tapped again, and then stealthily opened the door. Her father was lying on his bed fully dressed, fast asleep. She stood for a few moments looking down at him. Always a vigorous and industrious man, busy in civic affairs, he had suddenly seemed to grow much older in a very short time after the death of his wife. He had resigned from the bench and the Parish Council; his interest in his business had waned. He had never realised, and nor had Agnes, how much he depended on the woman who had been his companion for over thirty years.

John Yetman stirred as Agnes set the cup quietly by his side. He opened his eyes, rubbed them and smiled.

'Ah, Agnes. What time is it, my dear?'

'It's four o'clock, Father.'

John Yetman sat up, still rubbing his eyes. Then he reached out towards the steaming beverage and put the cup to his lips. Agnes noticed that his hand was shaking, and yet he was not an old man.

'Thank you, my dear,' he said, carefully replacing the cup. 'Excellent.' He put his hands behind his head and stared up at the ceiling, his blue eyes wide open, their expression troubled.

Agnes sat on the chair next to his bed and gazed at him.

'Did you sleep well, Father?' she asked.

'As well as I could with the crimes of that blackguard of a brother of mine in my mind.'

Uncle Christopher had left under a cloud – and what a cloud – much, much bigger than any of the ones he had left under before.

'You mustn't blame yourself, Father,' she said prosaically. 'You didn't know he would steal Miss Fairchild's money. Or that he was a bigamist,' she added as an afterthought, as if this were the lesser of the two evils.

'Fifty pounds! That was all there was in the bag, Miss Bishop told me. *I* would have given him that, to be rid of him. As it was I gave him money because I told him he must never come here again after he had so deceived us. Poor, poor Victoria Fairchild. I cannot bring myself to go and see her, but I must.' John reached out and took his daughter's hand. 'My dear Agnes, my consolation. What *would* I do without the support of my children?'

'Father,' Agnes said, leaning forward with an air of urgency.

'Yes, dear? What is it? You look worried.'

'I *am* worried, Father.' Agnes pressed her hands together in her lap. 'I'm very worried about the presence of Eliza in this house.'

'But she is your brother's wife,' John said in surprise.

'She is *not* Ryder's wife, as you well know, Father,' Agnes replied severely. 'I cannot think why you persist in deceiving yourself. They were married at Gretna Green, which no one regards as a legal marriage. Ryder could be locked up for what he has done if Sir Guy Woodville had a mind to it. But that is not why I am talking to you.' She was avoiding his eyes, but her voice all the time was becoming more emotional. 'I object to sharing a house with a woman who is notorious in this town. I scarcely dare show myself in the street.'

'Come, come, Agnes,' her father said, getting to his feet, 'that is a very serious thing to say.'

'Nevertheless it is true.'

'But where is your *Christian* charity, my dear? Eliza is a sick woman. Would you put her out in the street?'

'I'm not saying what I would or would not do, Father, except that I wish she were not here. I am sorry about what has happened, but she brought it on herself. It is God's punishment for her sin. Mrs Lamb says it is no more than she deserves.'

'Oh!' John leaned back on the bed again and crossed his arms. 'So that's it. You've been talking to the Rector's wife.'

'*She* talked to *me*, Father. She left me a note asking me to go and see her, and I did so this morning. She didn't need to tell me what people thought about *us*, in the town. Oh, I have suffered, Father. I have. I am mortally ashamed to be in any way associated with Eliza.'

'I'm surprised to hear you talking like this, Agnes,' John said sadly. 'I thought you had more charity.'

'Charity is not enough,' Agnes replied. 'Uncle Christopher made off with all Miss Fairchild's money, and look how much charity you gave *him*.'

'Not *all* her money by any means, only a part of it,' John protested feebly. 'I intend to make full restitution; but I cannot mend her broken heart. Ryder's beside himself with indignation too at your uncle's behaviour.'

'He's a fine one to talk,' Agnes snorted. 'As if you haven't enough to cope with without him bringing his whore here . . .'

'Don't you *dare* refer to your sister-in-law by that name.' John's voice was thunderous.

'She is *not* my sister-in-law.'

'They did what they could by going all the way to Gretna. If the Woodvilles would only give permission for the marriage, it could be made legal. But they won't, so they condemn them to live in sin.'

'They don't wish her to marry someone so far beneath them. The Woodvilles! You know how high and mighty they always were, despite a pressing shortage of money.'

'Agnes!' Her father looked at her in surprise. 'You seem to have become very bitter. I don't understand you. You could, for instance, ask your friend the Rector's wife to have a word with Lady Woodville. If the couple were wed in church the town would soon forget its disapproval, and we would all be happier.'

'If I do it, may I go to London, Father?'

'What do you mean, "may you go to London"?'

'*If* I help, *if* I speak to the Rector's wife, may I go and live with Aunt Emma?'

'Are you serious, girl? You wish to leave Wenham?'

'Yes I do, Father. I don't think I will ever find a suitable husband here.'

'Ah, that's it,' he said, wagging a finger at her.

'I don't wish to remain a spinster all my life looking after you, much as I love you, Father. If Eliza and Ryder regularise their position, maybe Eliza will stay here and help look after you while Ryder sees to the business.'

'So that's your plan. You have it all worked out, have you?'

'It's only a *suggestion*, Father,' Agnes said with a slight, simpering smile on her face; but already her heart felt lighter.

She could smell victory.

Miss Fairchild sat very stiffly in her chair and did not rise when John Yetman was shown in. He stood before her like a suppliant, feeling very awkward indeed, not knowing where to begin.

'Do take a seat, Mr Yetman' Miss Fairchild said coldly, pointing to a chair.

'Miss Fairchild, Victoria . . . We have known each other for a good many years. I think you know how *I* feel in my heart and why I am here . . .'

He saw her chin quiver, but she gave no other sign. Perhaps she found it difficult to speak, for she merely indicated the chair again without saying anything.

John Yetman drew an envelope from his inner pocket and placed it on a small table by the side of her chair.

'I come to make restitution, Victoria,' he said in a humble voice.

'If it's *money* you can take it away.' She continued to look straight in front of her. 'I have sufficient. If *he* had wanted it I would have given it, I would have given him . . . anything,' she burst out and, her shoulders shaking, put her head between her hands.

Swiftly John crossed the room and leaned towards her.

'He was a bad lot, Victoria. We all knew it, but we were helpless.'

'You mean he meant to steal from me all along?' She gave him a stricken look between her fingers.

'Not only that . . .' John turned away and took the seat she had offered him, avoiding her eyes. 'Victoria, he was married. We did not know it, *you* did not know it. There is even a suggestion that he was a bigamist. He preyed on woman for their money. He was traced as far as Blandford by – I believe, though he did not say so – a gentleman who was a police officer. I was able to persuade him to return to London by telling him I had no idea where my brother was.' John paused and looked at the ground. 'Maybe I did wrong; but I loved Christopher, as I think you did, Victoria. I didn't want him to go to prison. I think he has enough on his own conscience, but I had to tell him I knew because I felt he *was* pursuing you for your money and I did not want him to end up committing bigamy a second time!'

Victoria was still crying quietly, as if unable to take it all in, but John felt unable to help her, so deep was his own grief.

'I am *sure* he loved you,' he went on gently. 'He always spoke fondly of you. But my brother was an unscrupulous man who did not know right from wrong. I'm sure of that. He is his own worst enemy. If he had confided in me I would have helped him. But we had no idea – no idea at all.' John shook his head. Then, rising a little reluctantly, he went over to her again.

'Believe me, I know how you are suffering, Victoria, and I shall take the blame for my brother's deeds and carry them on my back for ever. I wish you *had* been my sister-in-law, because there is no nicer person in all Wenham. Now, my dear, will you regard me and my family as the relations you might have had, and always let us know when you need help, when you are lonely, or just when you want company?'

He leaned down to take her hands, and suddenly she pressed his tightly to her chest and, through her tears, nodded her head quite violently two or three times.

The following day the Rector of Wenham received an anonymous donation of fifty pounds, to be distributed among the poor of the parish.

10

Mrs Lamb considered it the duty of the Rector's wife always to concern herself with other people's business, and she had been one of the first to hear, through the servants, that Eliza and Ryder had returned to Wenham to live with John Yetman, newly widowed.

As news spread like wildfire in the small town, it didn't take long for people to ferret out the fact that the couple's alleged marriage was not in fact recognised by the law. And if the law didn't recognise it, God, represented by the Reverend Austin Lamb, certainly would not.

Although she pretended not to listen to servants' gossip, Mrs Lamb was well aware of what was being said. The prospect of having such immoral people for near-neighbours weighed heavily on the mind of the Rector's wife, for her husband had assured her that the die was already cast and their souls were destined for hell.

The Woodvilles regularly attended divine service in the parish church named after the Apostle Mark, but scarcely ever all together. It was known that the new Lady Woodville, despite presenting her husband with an heir, did not see eye to eye with her mother-in-law. When Sir Guy was in London one lady or the other attended church, but not both. When Sir Guy was at home the whole family attended, including, of course, both ladies. For little George's christening there was a full complement of relations from England and Holland, but both Lady Woodvilles kept far apart.

Like Margaret, Mrs Lamb had married late, and she and

the Rector had one daughter, Sophie, who was now six. Mrs Lamb was in her mid forties. She and Lady Woodville were acquaintances rather than friends, despite having lived in the same community for most of their married lives. Henrietta considered the Rector too evangelical, in the tradition of the Wesleys. She preferred the vague and pious type of clergyman favoured by the Church of England for country livings, who did not dwell too much on the wrath of God or punishment to be endured in the hereafter.

When Mrs Lamb felt it was time to speak – and that time came quite soon after Eliza's return thanks to the power of gossip – she drove over in her carriage to call on the fallen one's mother in the hope that she could be induced to put an end to such a shocking state of affairs.

It so happened that the senior Lady Woodville was on one of her frequent absences in Bournemouth. After she broke the bargain with her daughter-in-law and destroyed Eliza's letters, Margaret had not only declined to provide her with a separate establishment, but hardly spoke to her. In the large mansion the women led separate lives, one scarcely ever knowing the whereabouts of the other.

Mrs Lamb was disconcerted to find that the elder Lady Woodville was not at home, but gratified when the current mistress of the house agreed to receive her. Margaret was a member of the Dutch Reformed Church, and the tenets of the Church of England, especially as exemplified by the Reverend Lamb, did not appeal to her, though the Calvinist tradition of her church had much in common with the hellfire beliefs expounded by the Rector.

Margaret had been writing letters at her desk in the drawing room when the Rector's wife was announced by Arthur. She went to the door to receive the unexpected guest, holding out a hand in greeting.

'How very nice to see you, Mrs Lamb.'

'It is good of you to receive me, Lady Woodville. It was your mother-in-law who was the object of my visit.'

'She will be sorry to have missed you. Won't you stay and have a cup of tea?'

Mrs Lamb appeared undecided. The subject of her call was a delicate one, and the new Lady Woodville was, in addition, a Dutchwoman. Could she be expected to grasp the nuances of the customs of her adopted land? Would she even *understand* about such matters? Yet she seemed a sensible, down-to-earth woman.

Finally Mrs Lamb made up her mind.

'Well, that would be *very* nice, Lady Woodville. Thank you.'

Margaret asked her to sit down and rang for tea. The two women sat in the window embrasure commenting on the view, which was, indeed, very fine. In the distance they could see the square tower of St Mark's Church, Wenham, and, in between, the cottage from which Ryder and Eliza had eloped. For some reason this seemed to hold both their attentions, and they were both aware of it. Then the tea arrived, Arthur bearing the tray, as usual, accompanied by a maid in starched white apron, white cap and streamers, who bobbed self-consciously when she saw the Rector's lady staring sternly at her as if asking herself when she'd last seen her in church. Margaret, sensing that her visitor was here on an important matter, said that she would pour, upon which the servants withdrew.

Mrs Lamb sat ramrod straight, her buxom figure encased in whalebone, tightly laced. Despite her girth, she was a handsome woman, with strong features.

'Milk, Mrs Lamb?'

'Thank you.' Mrs Lamb nodded her head. The town was a little mystified by this foreigner, who was not young, not beautiful, and yet had captured the affections of a young, handsome man with an ancient name. Everyone, of course, knew *why*, just as, in a very short time, everyone knew that the knot between Ryder and Eliza had been tied, not by a priest in front of an altar, but by the blacksmith across the anvil at Gretna Green. There was always a source, of course, but the seeds of gossip at times seemed borne aloft by the wind.

'Was there a specific purpose to your visit to my mother-in-law, or is it rude of me to ask?' Margaret handed Mrs Lamb her cup with a smile and then offered her a plate of small, freshly baked angel cakes.

'Of course it's not rude of you to ask, Lady Woodville,' Mrs Lamb said. 'You are quite entitled to ask. In fact, you *may* be able to help. It concerns your sister-in-law.'

'Ah, yes.' Margaret sighed and added sugar to the tea in her cup.

'Have you seen her since she came back?'

'Alas, I have not. I fear she may be too afraid. My husband remains fond of her – they were always very close – but her conduct was quite shocking, and he cannot bring himself to go and see her, for fear that it will offend their mother. I am hoping that in time all this will change.'

'Of *course*.' Mrs Lamb nodded. 'We *all* hope that.'

'I am, however, very *fond* of Eliza,' Margaret continued. 'But for me to do anything at the moment is difficult.'

'You know, presumably, that she is living openly with a man to whom she is not married?'

'I believe there *was* a form of ceremony . . .'

'Not recognised by God *or* the law.' Mrs Lamb warmed to her theme. 'It is in fact a scandalous situation and one that is causing grave concern. Mr Yetman's daughter Agnes is quite distraught with shame and worry.' Suddenly Margaret knew where the seed of this particular piece of gossip had come from. 'The people of this parish,' Mrs Lamb went on, 'quite *rightly* expect its members to conform to the decencies of society. For an unwed woman and man to live *openly* together . . .'

'Then what do you want me to do?' Margaret sighed and took a cake. From somewhere upstairs she could hear the sound of her baby crying, but she knew that one of the nursemaids would rush instantly to his side.

'I wonder if *you*, dear Lady Woodville, could bring yourself to go and see your sister-in-law and prevail upon her, upon *him*, at least to be married in the sight of God – though, alas, I'm afraid the stigma will never leave them.'

'But first of all my mother-in-law and husband have to give their consent. Eliza is still under age, not yet twenty.'

'Of course they will consent!'

Margaret shook her head.

'I think not. In their eyes she is no longer a Woodville.'

'But they would give permission for a *proper* marriage and stop the scandal?'

Margaret shook her head again.

'I doubt it.' She got up and, walking to the window, crossed her arms. 'I am a Dutchwoman, as you know, Mrs Lamb. We are supposed to be a stern race, but perhaps we are a little more tolerant of the failings of others. I *would* like to see Eliza happy and properly married.' She turned to face the Rector's wife. 'However, I would offend my husband if I went to see her. I would incur his disapproval. Would *you* wish to displease *your* husband?'

To her surprise Mrs Lamb did not immediately agree with her, but appeared to consider the matter.

'That would depend,' she said at last. 'Of course, he need not know. I believe Sir Guy spends much of his time in London . . . and Lady Woodville is frequently away . . .'

'You mean I should go and see Eliza . . .'

'And *then* prevail upon your mother-in-law,' Mrs Lamb said with a gentle motion of her head, 'to do the *right* thing.'

She had returned to her beloved Wenham, yet in many ways Eliza still felt like an exile. Sickness and weariness had brought them home, yet the townspeople shunned her. Ryder, who quickly entered his father's employment, was finding social attitudes easier; but then he was a man.

Society was much more tolerant towards the misdeeds of men than women.

Despite the generosity of her father-in-law Eliza longed for the little cottage where she and Ryder had first known of their love for each other, but that was now occupied by someone else.

Eliza had also hoped for her sister-in-law's affection, but she did not get it. The unconventional Agnes, who spurned the local men, had turned very conventional in her attitude to her brother. Maybe she was jealous, or maybe she had an ulterior motive, using the anomalous situation to get her own way.

Nothing fell faster than an idol, and the image of the aristocratic, beautiful Miss Woodville – although she had always been considered a little eccentric with her habit of riding a horse dressed as a man – now lay smashed on the ground.

Eliza, however, went about her duties with dignity, smiling when someone smiled, which was hardly ever, and speaking when addressed. Usually it was merely 'Good day'. The shopkeepers took her money across the counter, but increasingly she sent a maid to do the shopping.

One day Eliza was standing in the garden of the Yetman house, watching the antics of her father-in-law's two dogs on the lawn, when she saw a carriage stop at the gate, and a woman descend and begin briskly to walk up the drive.

Margaret.

'Oh, *Eliza*,' Margaret exclaimed joyfully and took her in her arms.

An hour later Margaret sat quietly, a hand over that of her weeping sister-in-law. Her face was strangely composed though the tale Eliza had told was a chilling one. The weeping had begun with the account of the burial of the dead baby, and even Margaret, who had little imagination, could visualise the horror of that night with the wind whistling through the snow-covered valley and the new-born lambs bleating with cold.

Margaret's Calvinist upbringing told her that Eliza was getting no less than she deserved. God rewarded the righteous and punished wrongdoing, and from the very beginning Eliza and Ryder had been guilty of sin. Yet Margaret was also capable of compassion and pity, and these emotions now came to the fore for this girl-woman still in her teens.

'It is all over now,' she said gently. 'It is over. You can make a new life.'

'Mother will never forgive me,' Eliza murmured, shaking her head. 'No one speaks to me in the town. Ryder doesn't care what people think, but I have to shop around here. I am ignored or sniggered at from across the street.'

Margaret told her about the visit of Mrs Lamb.

'Mrs Lamb came to see Mama?' Eliza said in horror, drying her eyes.

'Your mother was not there. When I heard what she wanted I decided to come instead, because I wanted to see you, Eliza.' She put a hand tenderly on the young woman's cheek. 'I am very fond of you, you know, and what has happened has not lessened my affection, though I must confess I was shocked. I think it is more Ryder Yetman's fault than yours. You are only a girl, more sinned against than sinning. Are you quite certain he is the man you wish to spend the rest of your life with, dearest Eliza? *Is* a person capable of behaving like that the right man for you?'

'Oh yes,' Eliza breathed. 'He is a marvellous man. He has such courage.'

'And yet he seduced you.'

'But I would never leave him. I ran away. *I* seduced *him*. We thought then that a form of marriage was better than none. We intended to return here straight away, but the weather worsened. I knew then that I was expecting a child. There was nothing we could do. Oh no, I cannot live without Ryder. He is a good man and I love him.'

'Well, that's it then,' Margaret said briskly. 'We shall have to see what we can do. I will *have* to try and prevail upon your brother and mother to give the marriage their blessing.'

'Mama will never do it.' Sadly Eliza shook her head. 'I sent her six letters from Ennerdale, asking her forgiveness. She never answered a single one.'

Margaret sat for some time gazing ahead of her. She wore a pretty dress of blue organdie with a draped skirt and bustle, and a large cameo brooch at her throat. Her hat was made of the same material and set at an attractive angle on her Titian hair. She looked stylish, even handsome. She was one of those women who, never having been beautiful, would age well.

'Eliza,' she said at last, 'there *is* something I feel I must tell you. It will make you unhappy, but I feel you ought to know.'

And she told her about the unopened letters and about her bargain with Henrietta and what happened on the night George was born. After she had finished, Eliza was silent for a long time, and the tears, never far from the surface, welled up in her eyes again.

'Mama *never* opened my letters. Why?'

'I'm afraid she has rejected you as a daughter. I fail to understand it, because I know she loved you. Of course I considered she had broken our bargain, and relations between us are very bad; but I will try and reopen negotiations with her. There.' She patted Eliza's hand once more, smiled and got up. 'I have a plan that might succeed.'

'But what do you mean?' Eliza demanded, mystified.

'Trust me,' Margaret replied. 'Trust me to do what I can. You may never see your mother again, but you may at least be able to marry in church the man you love.'

'Never!' Henrietta once again began to pace agitatedly around the room. 'Never will I give permission, although in two years' time she will not need it. She can marry whom she likes when she is of age . . .'

'But *why* make her wait? Why cause her to suffer?'

'Because she must suffer,' Henrietta said implacably, putting her handkerchief to her mouth. 'She must suffer as she has made her *family* suffer.'

'You have not suffered,' Margaret said scornfully. 'She is the one who is suffering. She is an outcast in the town.'

'Good. She deserves it. In the olden days she would have been pilloried for less.'

'I can't understand you at all, Lady Woodville.' Margaret had an expression of distaste on her face. 'You are a most *unnatural* parent.'

'I will thank *you*, madam, to keep a civil tongue in your head,' Henrietta snapped. '*You* talk about being unnatural.

What is more unnatural than a daughter behaving as she did, and bringing shame on her family . . .'

'The Woodvilles have suffered no real shame,' Margaret burst out. 'It is your pride that is hurt. You can't honestly say that people have ignored *you* in the street, that you have been refused admission to houses because of what Eliza did.'

'People *know*,' Henrietta said bitterly. 'That is the point. They *know*. They may not *say* anything, but they know, and they look. That is why I long to get away from this neighbourhood . . .'

'Then you may do so,' Margaret said suddenly. 'I have decided to change my mind even though you reneged on your promise, and to buy you a house of your choice, so long as . . .'

'So long as *what*?' Henrietta asked, her eyes flashing.

'So long as you give your permission to the marriage of Ryder and Eliza, and persuade Guy to give his. That way your wish will be granted immediately. Eliza may have to wait eighteen months or two years; but you, Lady Woodville, will have to wait for ever.' Margaret lifted her head defiantly. 'I will never relent, never change my mind if you refuse this time. You will be bound to me and this place by an invisible chain that will hold you fast to Pelham's Oak, Wenham, the places you hate, for the rest of your life.'

If the righteous folk of Wenham had snubbed Eliza while she was living with a man to whom she was not legally married, they had no hesitation in peeping out of windows, peering round corners or loitering along those parts of the route which lay between the Yetman house and the church on the date of the official wedding. The ceremony was timed for 10 a.m., and the distance between the Yetman house and the church was only a third of a mile; but it was astonishing how many people, who one might have supposed would be otherwise engaged, managed to be out of doors or to find business in the vicinity.

Some of the good women of the parish (who had been among

212

the most critical) even found work to do *inside* the church, and others openly hung about outside gawping.

This was, however, no fancy society wedding; it was a matter of business between man and God, sanctioned by the law. Eliza did not wear white, but a pretty oatmeal-coloured dress with a slight bustle, chastely ruched at the neck and with long sleeves, again ruched at the wrists. She drove to the church in the carriage with John Yetman. Ryder, accompanied by Prosper Martyn, who, disgusted by the attitude of his sister, had insisted on being best man, had gone before her to await his bride at the altar. The Rector waited too, staring sternly at them above his pince-nez, while in his hand he held the Book; the word of God.

There was no music, and at a sign from the verger John Yetman and Eliza began their slow march up the aisle. No guests had been invited, so the congregation was a pitiful one. There was the witness from the Registrar's office, prescribed by law, and two of the women who had been cleaning the church stopped their labours while the ceremony was on and leaned on their mops watching the proceedings with interest.

It was a beautiful day and the sun shone through the ancient stained-glass windows upon the bride, whose heart was full of tranquillity, her eyes on the man she already called husband. As he stepped forward to take his place by her side there was the sound of a commotion outside, and the church doors were thrown open, causing the ladies propping themselves up on their mops nearly to fall flat on their faces. Both Ryder and Eliza, about to take their vows, turned expecting some disaster, but their expressions relaxed as they saw Margaret Woodville walk quickly down the aisle followed by Ted the groom, his hat in his hand. As Margaret took her seat in the front pew Prosper Martyn turned to smile at her approvingly. Ted sat a respectful two pews' distance behind. Across the aisle, as though anxious to keep her distance, Mrs Lamb never took her eyes from her prayer book.

'Dearly beloved . . .' the Rector intoned in the time-honoured ritual of the wedding service according to the Established Church.

It did not take very long. Ryder replaced on Eliza's finger the ring they had used at Gretna and only removed that morning. It seemed a bit farcical and they smiled at each other as if in secret amusement. But the ring felt like an old friend, and they clasped hands firmly as the Rector pronounced them man and wife. Then, removing his pince-nez, he raised his noble, craggy head towards the rafters as if to pronounce a benediction over them. Instead he joined his hands in front of him, lowered his eyes and began in the plummy voice he used for preaching:

'Dear children of God, the Gospel of St John tells us how Jesus sat preaching in the Temple when the Scribes and the Pharisees brought to him a woman taken in adultery. They set her before Our Lord saying "Master, this woman was taken in adultery, in the very act. Now Moses in the law commanded us, that such should be stoned: But what sayest thou?"'

Ryder and Eliza stood impassively before him, their hands still tightly clasped. Behind them Prosper Martyn looked daggers at the Rector, who ignored him. He also ignored Lady Woodville, who shook her head at him in violent disapproval. Meanwhile a small crowd had silently gathered at the rear of the church, and the Rector seemed, by the way he projected his voice, to be addressing them as much as the couple before him, as though he wished to distance himself as far as possible from the ceremony he had been required to conduct, clearly against his better judgement.

'Jesus, you will remember,' he went on, 'wrote with his finger on the ground. And this is the remarkable thing that he said: "He that is without sin among you, let him first cast a stone at her."

'Whereupon they all departed, one by one, until the woman and our Blessed Lord were left alone together. He asked her where were all those who had condemned her? "Hath no man condemned *thee*?" he said. And she replied "No man, Lord." So Jesus said "Neither do I condemn thee."'

The Rector's pause was almost as resonant as his preaching.

His silence filled the air. It was a protracted one, and then, fastening his eyes directly on Eliza, he intoned in a deep, sonorous voice: '"Go, and sin no more."'

Mr Lamb abruptly turned his back on the congregation and, approaching the altar, bowed. Then, clutching the hem of his surplice, the golden stole around his neck, he disappeared into the side chapel.

From the back of the church the crowd slunk silently away as though they, too, did not wish to be seen.

After the ceremony the bride and groom left by the side door, avoiding the Rector and any of those who lingered outside the front of the church. They were not ashamed or afraid, but they wanted to be by themselves. Ryder put his arm round Eliza, a gesture of familiarity and protectiveness that Prosper approved of. He smiled at Margaret Woodville, walking by his side, and she smiled back.

Ted had brought the carriage round and driven John Yetman, to whom the whole thing was an ordeal, back to his home.

Agnes had left for London the night before. She had hardly addressed a word to her sister-in-law in the weeks she had been in the house. Meals had been taken in silence, and it was a relief when her trunk was put on the carrier's wagon, which happened to be going to Blandford, and she went with it. Back at the house a small collation had been prepared, which was more in the way of being breakfast, because neither bride nor groom had felt like eating before they set out.

'I would like to have that man defrocked,' Prosper said as he stood by the open window in the drawing room drinking a welcome glass of sherry.

'He was only trying to make a point,' Eliza said. 'He was within his rights, I suppose.'

'*I* felt like making a public objection,' Prosper said grimly.

'*I* thought you were going to.' Margaret smiled at him. No wonder her father liked him and liked doing business with him. He had risen greatly in her estimation.

'I expected nothing better from the Rector,' John Yetman

said. 'I think I shall be praying with the Methodists in future. I will never set foot in that church again while the Reverend Lamb is the incumbent.'

'Oh, I think we should forgive the Rector.' Ryder smiled broadly at his bride. 'That will make us even better than him, because we shall be more charitable.'

It turned into a happy party, five people welded together by affection and love. John Yetman seemed the most affected, and perhaps the most bitter. He had been part of the parish all his life, much longer than anyone else present. He had been baptised in the church and married there. Now he called for silence and turned towards them.

'Friends,' he said, 'we few are met here to celebrate the marriage of my son and a woman I have come to love very much in the short time I have known her. What Ryder has told me about her, about the past, has made me love and admire her more and more. This feeling was increased today as she stood, with such dignity, by Ryder's side while the Rector gave his sermon, which was as uncharitable as it was unscheduled.

'I want to thank *you*, Lady Woodville, and *you*, Prosper Martyn, for showing that Christian charity so conspicuously lacking in the Rector, and others we could name.' He then raised his glass and, in a voice that shook with emotion, said: 'To Ryder and Eliza. May they be happy, forever more.'

When the time came for departure Eliza, with tears in her eyes, said to her sister-in-law: 'It was *very* good of you to come.'

Margaret seemed surprised by Eliza's emotion. 'I'm only sorry we were late and thus gave the opportunity for those gawpers to enter the church. But one of our horses went lame and we had to go back for another.'

Eliza held out her hand to Ted, who, cap in hand, was creeping slowly towards her.

'Oh, Ted,' Eliza said taking his hand, 'it is so lovely to see you again.'

'And you too, Miss,' Ted said in a shy, faltering voice. 'How is Lady, Miss?'

'I had to leave her behind.' Eliza's voice was tremulous. 'But she is well taken care of.'

'You left her behind?' Ted sounded incredulous. 'But you and Lady wus inseparable, Miss Woodville.'

'Mrs *Yetman*, Ted,' Margaret corrected him gently.

'Can't get used to it yet, ma'am,' Ted said. 'Honest I can't. I always spoke of her, and thought of her, as Miss Woodville. I reckon I always shall.'

'Ted,' Ryder said suddenly, 'if your mistress gives you permission, how would you like to go on a journey with me?'

'A journey, sir?' Ted looked at him uncomprehendingly.

'Why yes,' Ryder said, slapping him on the back. 'Just the fellow I need to help me fetch back Lady. I promised her to my wife as a wedding present.'

Looking round the valley, so balmy in the sunshine, with the meadows full of cowslips and buttercups, it was difficult to believe that it was the same place he and Eliza had left in a gale, blinded by a snowstorm. The sky was the cerulean, almost Mediterranean, blue of high summer, and the fells were lush green, covered with wild flowers. The fields of corn and hay were ripening, and the lambs who had bleated so pitifully in the cold were gambolling as if with joy at the end of winter. The pellucid waters of Lake Ennerdale, surmounted by high crags still capped with snow, were ruffled here and there by tiny wavelets caught in the soft breeze. Overhead gulls circled, giving their shrill cries, and from the chimney of the farmhouse low down in the valley a thick column of smoke spiralled lazily upwards.

Ted, who was not an emotional man, drew in his breath sharply.

'What a lovely place, sir,' he exclaimed. 'It's like paradise.'

'You should have seen it four months ago,' Ryder said. 'It was like hell, if hell can be cold. When my wife and I left here it was in a driving blizzard. That's when we had to leave Lady behind.'

'I can see it would be grim in winter,' Ted nodded.

'And *that* is the house where we lodged.' Ryder pointed through the window of the hired carriage to the humble shack, scarcely a cottage, by the side of the lake. Ted was unable to stifle a whistle.

'Miss Woodville lived *there*?'

'Aye, *and* suffered.' Ryder's face was grim. 'Drive on,' he called through the window to the coachman, and they completed the short journey to the farm in a few minutes.

There were a few hands at work in the farmyard, and they looked up curiously as the well-dressed man sprang down from the carriage. Ryder was an imposing figure clad in a frock coat, a shirt with a high, stiff collar, a carefully tied bow-tie and a top hat with a curling brim, and carrying a cane. He strode over to the group of men cowering in the yard, one or two of whom recognised him instantly.

'Is Farmer Frith here?' he asked, and without speaking one of them pointed inside.

By this time Ted had also got out. He was dressed in a smart check travelling coat, a newly bought bowler on his head. He went round to have a word with the coachman who had been engaged, after a night spent in Cockermouth, to drive them to the farm.

Ryder rapped sharply with his cane on the door of the farm. It was flung open by Beth, who failed to recognise him. She wore her habitual look of abject terror.

'Is your master inside, Beth?' Ryder asked, and the girl looked astonished that such a smartly dressed gentleman should know her name. She bobbed and stood back, and at that moment the farmer appeared at the far end of the room and looked intently at his visitor.

'Can I help you, sir?' He came as close as he could, something about Ryder appearing familiar.

'I have come back for Lady,' Ryder said without preamble, and as he removed his hat both Beth and the farmer simultaneously recognised him. Beth started gibbering and pointed to the carriage and servant in the yard.

'Well I'm damned,' the farmer said, slapping his thigh. 'Got yourself fine airs, have you, Mr Yetman? Is it a confidence trickster you are now?

Ryder stretched out his cane and struck him lightly on the cheek.

'I am itching to bloody your nose, Frith, and I'll not hesitate. I don't think *one* of your men will move to save you. Now go and saddle that mare you stole from my wife, because I have come for her.'

'I paid good money for her. She certainly does *not* belong to you,' the farmer said, gingerly feeling his cheek. 'I'll still have the police . . .'

'You will be so bloodied by the time I have finished with you, Frith, that even your wife will not recognise you. Do as I say and open the stable door. I have come to claim Lady in lieu of the wages you owed my wife and me. Now saddle her quickly because my man will ride her back, and see – ' he put out his cane again until the tip came to rest like a rapier at the unfortunate man's throat ' – that you do it now. We want to be back in Cockermouth by nightfall.'

Frith stared at him, knowing he was beaten. He backed nervously away from the point of the cane and, straightening his jacket with all the dignity he could muster, went into the yard, where he barked orders to the goggling farm hands.

Ryder strode to the door to watch him and, feeling something tickling his palm, turned to see Beth crouching at his side.

'Please take me with you, sir,' she whispered. 'I've looked after Lady, sir, as I promised. I've given her extra hay. I'll work for no wages. I . . .'

'Run and get your things,' Ryder hissed. 'Quick now, before he organises his men. They'll soon come to their senses, even if they hate him. If he orders them to attack me, in the end they will do it.'

Beth gave a squeak of alarm and scurried away, while Ryder walked into the yard, ordering Ted to follow him. Frith was struggling angrily with the bolt on the stable door.

'This is theft, Yetman,' he called out. 'I'll report you to the magistrate . . .'

'And I will report *you*,' Ryder said, seizing him once again by the scruff of his neck and spinning him round. 'I will report *you* for maltreatment of the people you employ here, the low wages, the disgusting conditions. Now let me see if my wife's horse is in any way damaged . . .'

Pushing Frith roughly to one side, he drew back the bolt and stepped into the darkened stable. It seemed that Lady recognised him at once, because she whinnied and pressed her muzzle into his hand.

'I've come to take you home, Lady,' he said softly, 'back where you belong. Now . . .' He ran his hand along the horse's flank. She was in good condition, perhaps because the daughter of the house had seen to it that she was well looked after.

'Come on, man, saddle her,' he said, poking Frith in the ribs again with his cane.

'Oh, but the cost of the saddle . . .'

'That is in the back wages too. However, there *is* something I'll give you.' He took out his wallet from his breast pocket and extracted some notes which he kept in his hand. 'I'm relieving you of the services of Beth. Doubtless you owe *her* wages and have mistreated her for far longer than you had the chance to mistreat us.' He held up the notes so that they could be seen not only by Ted and the coachman but by the farm hands who stood around staring, open-mouthed. 'This is payment of a kind. Not for the girl, because we do not buy or sell human flesh, or the horse, or the saddle. It is so that I am not called a thief – taking what does not belong to me.' He thrust the money at the farmer who, grabbing it, began to shake as though he were on the verge of an apoplectic attack.

Ted, meanwhile, having shed his hat and coat, was greeting Lady. He stroked her silken nose and murmured to her as he lifted the heavy saddle and bridle off the wall and put them on her back. Murmuring soft endearments, he led her into the yard and expertly ran his hands over her, checking her hooves to ensure she was properly shod for the ride to Carlisle where they would all board a train.

'She seems in good condition, sir,' he said to Ryder. 'Nothing much wrong there.'

Suddenly Beth appeared at the door, a ragged coat over her dress, and nothing but a bundle in her hands.

'Is *this* all you have, girl?' Ryder demanded in astonishment.

'Yes, sir,' Beth said with a bob.

'Get in there then.' Ryder pointed to the carriage and, without a backward glance, Beth scuttled up the steps and collapsed on the seat trembling. Ted's face appeared at the door and he grinned at her.

'Take no notice of my things, Miss,' he said, pointing to his fine new coat and hat, of which he was rather proud. 'Just make yourself comfortable.'

Beth went scarlet, and when Ted withdrew his head he looked pleased with himself.

By this time one or two more of the hands, interested in the commotion in the yard, had come back from the fields, and Ryder knew it was time to be off.

He saw Ted onto the back of Lady and gave a gentle slap to her rump as she was ridden out of the yard on to the road outside.

Then he turned towards the farmer, eyeing a butt that stood by the side of the stables to catch rainwater. With a sudden, dexterous move, he seized Frith simultaneously by the collar and the seat of his pants and tipped him head first into it. Then, dusting his hands together, as at a job well done, he strode towards the carriage while the farm hands, gaping at the master's legs waving frantically in the air, burst into spontaneous laughter.

'You'd better remove him from there,' Ryder called, 'else he'll be dead.'

And then he jumped into the carriage, smiled at Beth cringing beside him, and commanded the driver to be off.

'I want to be in Cockermouth before nightfall,' he said.

As they drove out of the yard on to the road Ted preceded them on Lady, trotting gently, her mane tossing in the wind.

Behind them in the farmyard Farmer Frith's men moved, somewhat reluctantly, towards the water butt to put him out of his misery.

Henrietta, Lady Woodville, looked round the bedroom where she had slept during all the years of her married life, where her four children had been born – two, sadly, to die in infancy – and where she had spent the unhappy years of her widowhood. Or rather, they had not been unhappy until Guy had married the woman from Holland and everything had changed.

Who would have thought that docile, rather plain Margaret would turn into a force to be reckoned with? Would be changed by the mere act of moving from one side of the Channel to the other? Would become a woman who wanted to be powerful as Henrietta had once been powerful; who wanted to rule not only her home and her husband, but her mother-in-law as well?

Finally Margaret had forced her to agree to the unsuitable alliance of her daughter with a man who traded as a builder! Eliza had been married in the sight of God to an ordinary, working-class man of the people whose hands were calloused and whose accent lacked the refined tones of a public school education.

By that time Henrietta had herself forgotten her own origins in trade because only by marrying a Woodville had she, in fact, become one.

Now she was to leave. Her boxes were packed, the drawers and closets emptied, the bed stripped. Most of the furniture was to go in due course to Bournemouth, to the house that Margaret had bought for her there. It was not too far away from her Martyn relations, and it was close to the sea. But it was a mere red-brick villa built only a few years before when Bournemouth began its expansion as a seaside resort to rival Brighton. It was not a mansion. It was not Pelham's Oak, ancestral home of the Woodvilles.

She was to stay with her brother while the house was

refurbished. She would have every comfort: a butler, a maid, a cook.

But it was not the life she wanted – and not the life she had envisaged when her son had married a woman for her money.

There was a movement behind her, and she turned with a distant expression on her face, expecting to see Margaret; but it was Guy. He crept in rather sheepishly, as he used to do when he had committed some misdeed as a small boy. The years seemed to slip away, and in her mind the image of the youthful Guy came vividly to life again. His mother, in a sudden rush of sentimentality, wanted to enfold him in her arms; but he was a husband now, a father, the head of the family. The years had put him out of reach.

'The carriage is ready, Mother,' Guy said quietly. 'But take your time. I know how you feel.'

Henrietta, dressed in her hat and furs, sat down suddenly on one of the upholstered brocade chairs, staring in front of her.

'Do you, Guy? Do you *really* know how I feel?' Wearily she passed her hand across her brow and gazed at him reproachfully.

'I think so, Mother,' he said contritely, as though he carried the blame for Margaret's behaviour. 'I'm sorry it came to this.'

'Had you not married *her* . . .' Henrietta began scornfully.

'We would not be *here*, Mother, if I had not married Margaret. It is only her money that has allowed us to continue not only to live, but to live well.'

'You could have found some other woman, an English woman who understood.'

Guy shook his head. 'An English woman from a good family would have had an English father who would have sent me packing. It was only a foreigner in search of an English title whom we were able to impress. Willem Heering is a great man in many ways; but he is venal. Thank God for that.'

He held out his hand, but Henrietta seemed disinclined to rise.

'You will come back, Mother. There will be holidays. It is not as though you were going for ever.'

'I shall *never* come back to this room,' she said with a shudder. 'There are too many ghosts.'

'As you wish, Mother.' Guy hung his head. 'But try and forgive.'

'Forgive?' Henrietta's head came up sharply. '*I* am thrown out of my own house by trickery. *I* am blackmailed for acting in the best interests of my own daughter. You think *I* should be the one to forgive? Do you know that Margaret actually *attended* Eliza's wedding?'

Guy nodded, but said nothing.

'She went back to the house afterwards for the reception. It's a wonder she didn't force you to go too.'

'She tried,' Guy said cravenly. 'But I knew how you felt.'

'And I'm very glad you did, Guy.' There was a triumphant glint in his mother's eyes.

'I didn't want to upset you, Mother, but, eventually, I *would* like to see Eliza again.'

'I hope it will be over my dead body, Guy.' Henrietta fixed a stern eye on him. 'I hope you will *never* receive your sister as long as I am alive. Please don't forget what she did. She dishonoured you, she dishonoured me, she dishonoured your father – but, most of all, she dishonoured the ancient family pride: the pride of the Woodvilles.

Springing from her chair, Henrietta advanced upon Guy, shaking her finger, and, suddenly, he realised how very afraid of his mother he still was. At the same time, he understood that he'd married a woman rather like her: someone who would always keep, or try to keep, him under control.

Henrietta saw the fear on his face and took advantage of it.

'You are a weak man, Guy – you know it and I know it. Never give in to that weakness and allow your sister to enter this house again. If you do, you will never forgive yourself – and *I* shall never forgive you.'

PART TWO

The Master Thatcher

II

Lally lay in the large double bed in the house in the Vale of Health, the tiny baby in her arms. She looked so pretty, so vulnerable, that Guy decided his love for her hadn't really changed despite the shock she had given him.

To Guy, Lally was an object of love, a beautiful thing for his delectation: someone who could remove, by her caresses, the cares of the world; with her kisses, the frustrations and anxieties of everyday life.

The last thing he had wanted from his goddess had been a child.

He had been so angry when she had told him the unwelcome news that, for many weeks, he didn't go near her. Wisely she made no attempt to contact him, and her silence eventually worried him. He realised how much she meant to him, and how bereft he would be if anything happened to her.

Very soon he was back with her again, but not quite on the same footing. There was a wariness now.

Six years had now passed since Guy had married Margaret Heering at the church in Wenham. He was the father of three children: his first-born, George, a daughter, Emily – and now a third child, a love child, a boy yet to be named. He was a pretty baby, tiny, almost like a girl, because he had been premature. Lally had been so determined to maintain her figure throughout pregnancy – as much to keep the curious neighbours away as anything else – that she had laced her corsets too tight. The miracle was that the baby had lived at all.

Guy sat down on the bed next to Lally and tentatively put

227

out his index finger, which was grasped by the tiny hand. The baby smiled winsomely at him and tried to put his finger in his mouth. His eyes seemed to plead for his father's love; but Guy didn't love him at all. As far as Guy was concerned, the baby was unwanted and unloved.

'Aren't you *glad* we had him?' Lally asked anxiously, seeing Guy's expression.

Guy said nothing but, his finger still held tight in the tiny fist, he stooped and kissed Lally. For a moment, she clung to him desperately, also wanting reassurance of his love.

'I wish we could be married, Guy,' she said, voicing a thought that was constantly on her mind.

'One day,' Guy murmured unconvincingly. 'Maybe. I am not yet financially independent of Margaret. Unfortunately the new Act of Parliament gives her some control over her money.'

'But I thought you were working so hard?' She pouted prettily, but the reference to work irritated him and he rose from the bed. Moodily he jangled the coins in his pocket and, walking over to the window, gazed out on to the Heath. It was autumn and the leaves were beginning to fall. In the distance some children, well wrapped up against the keen north wind, trampled through them under the watchful eye of their mother. It was a happy, domestic scene and, momentarily, Guy was envious. How nice it would have been to be part of such a carefree picture, instead of a man weighed down by anxieties, and fear for his future: a mistress he couldn't afford, an unwanted child and a domineering wife who was beginning to question everything he did.

The truth was that all had not gone well for Guy. In six years he had progressed from the mean little room in Lower Thames Street to one as small, but not as mean, in Threadneedle Street. He wore a frock coat to work with a top hat, and a gold watch and chain across his waistcoat. He was considered rather a dandy, his hat at a jaunty angle, and carried a cane. He usually smoked a cigar in the cab taking him to work. He was, after all, Sir Guy Woodville, baronet, though the company

228

seemed still to regard him as little more than a clerk. He had few responsibilities, and although he had made no losses for the firm he had made no profits either. He was a little more punctilious than before, but still undeniably bad at his job. He had no understanding of the complexities of the business world, of the fluctuations of the market, the movement of stocks and shares.

If Guy Woodville's life at the age of thirty had to be summed up in one word, that word would be boredom. He was a bored young man who felt he had lost his way; he envied others who always found things to do. Even though he never saw him, he envied his brother-in-law, Ryder Yetman. In five years, Ryder had turned a failing business into a profitable one. Under him Yetman Builders had boomed. He could imagine Ryder out walking with his family like the family up on the Heath now. Did Ryder have a mistress, Guy wondered; a woman of the lower orders tucked away in a little cottage in some hidden vale of Dorset? Did he, perhaps, have more progeny who, like Lally and the baby, were kept well hidden?

He doubted it. It was many years since he had seen Ryder, but from what he had heard he was the epitome of the contented man: loved, loving, and now wealthy. Some fellows had luck they surely didn't deserve.

'What are you thinking about, dearest?' Lally asked from the depths of the bed. She looked so delightfully languorous that, were it not for the unwelcome, tiny pink form in her arms, he would gladly have jumped in beside her.

'Oh, this and that,' Guy said, strolling back to the bed. 'I was thinking how I wished we *could* be together.'

'Would you divorce Margaret if you could?' She gazed at him keenly, taking careful note of his reaction to her question.

'Of *course* I would,' he said with conviction and, sitting by her side, again took her hand. 'But whether she would let me go is another thing. She is very happy at Pelham's Oak. Now that my mother has gone she rules the roost there like a fine lady. She gives dinners and parties, even a ball is planned for next week. She is an expert manager and looks after the finances, the accounts. The servants seem to like her and work well for her.'

'Then she will *never* let you go.' Lally's voice was desolate.

'Oh, darling!' Guy knelt on the floor by her side and, taking her hand in his, brought it up to his lips. 'Take heart. We must *never* despair. Never. Anything can happen.'

Tenderly Guy stroked her hair away from her hot, damp forehead. She looked so enchanting, yet he had never seen her face so unhappy. If she had wanted this child, which he doubted, so far he had brought her little joy.

'But dearest,' he said, continuing to stroke her hair as though she were a sleek animal, 'you know that I have two children of my own. I cannot at the moment acknowledge this baby. What is more, beloved, your own name and reputation will be compromised.'

'It is compromised already,' Lally said in a sulky voice. 'Don't think people don't know you visit me here.'

'A woman with a *child*, living alone, will be ostracised by everybody.' Guy went on. '*Now* you have some friends; and you speak to the neighbours whatever they may think. You will see.' He rose and, hands in his pockets, began restlessly pacing round the room. 'No one will speak to you. I know what happened to my sister. She is scarcely accepted in the town, and *she* has been legally married for five years *and* has three legitimate children.'

'Well, *you* weren't much help to her were you, Guy? Not much support?' Lally said waspishly. '*You* never spoke to her either. Still don't, I believe.'

Guy halted and, shrugging his shoulders, turned towards her.

'Sometimes I feel I would *love* to see my sister and speak to her, believe me. But I doubt now that she would receive me. It is true that my mother and I were greatly offended by her elopement with a man who had no class, and no money then either, though I hear he is now making a fortune . . .'

'Maybe that will influence your attitude.' Lally looked at him archly, gratified to see that his face had changed colour.

'There's no need for *sarcasm*, my dear,' he replied with dignity. 'Eliza's behaviour *was* disgraceful. The amount of suffering she brought upon my mother was enormous. *That* I cannot forgive, no matter what has happened since. Well – ' Guy crossed the room and, taking his hat, ran his fingers uneasily round the curved brim ' – I think we have no more to say to each other at the moment, Lally. But ponder over what I have said, my dear.'

Then, without kissing her or looking at his son again, Guy left the room.

Half an hour later when her maid entered Lally was still weeping. Abby was a good-hearted servant girl who had been with Lally ever since she first came to Hampstead. She was the same age as her young mistress, and she knew almost everything about her, what went on in her mind and in her life. She reached tenderly for the little bundle beside Lally and hugged him.

'What is it, ma'am?' she asked, rocking the baby back and forth in her arms. 'Is *he* not pleased?'

'He is not interested in the b-b-a-a-by,' Lally sobbed into her pillow.

'You didn't *expect* it, Miss, surely, did you?' Abby asked, peeking into the baby's blue eyes.

'I know Guy didn't want him, but I hoped that when he saw him he'd love him. He won't even give him a n-n-a-a-me. He has no h-h-h-eart. He says I will lose people's respect and no one will speak to me. Oh, *Abby* . . .' Lally sat up and ran her hands through her thick golden hair. 'I'm sure I will lose Guy. He has been too much of a gentleman to reject me, but now . . .'

'No loss if you *ask* me, Miss . . .'

'Mind your tongue!' Lally said sharply, but her voice lacked conviction. She knew quite well the contempt in which Guy was held by her maid. Maybe Abby felt the same about her too.

'He loves only himself, not *you*, and certainly not the baby,' Abby insisted.

'But *what* shall I do? Oh, Abby . . .' Fresh tears poured down Lally's cheeks, leaving ugly streaks on her beautiful face; her large eyes were like limpid pools. Abby, who knew nothing about the theatre, always thought that her mistress would make a fine actress. One minute she presented this face to the world, the next another. Smiling one moment, tearful and melancholy the next. Abby loved her mistress, but she found her vexing. Now she looked sadly into the eyes of the most beautiful baby she had ever seen. Beautiful, but unwanted and unloved, even by his mother.

'Abby, I don't *want* to lose Sir Guy. What's more, I would like to resume my career in the theatre. I can't have a baby *as well*, can I, Abby?'

'You have him now, Miss.' Abby held the baby closely to her as though to reassure him that at least one person loved him.

'Well . . .' Lally tossed back her head and examined her nails. 'One can always *give* babies away, can't one?'

'Oh, you *wouldn't*, Miss?' Abby felt so angry that she sat down, uninvited, on her mistress's bed. 'That *would* be a cruel thing to do. He's so beautiful . . .'

'Yes, but I don't *like* him much either, and that's the truth,' Lally said petulantly. 'I didn't want him. I did everything I could to prevent him happening. But Sir Guy is very impetuous. Men never think it's their responsibility to prevent babies happening. Then they get cross. It is *so* unfair. Now my career is ruined too. And all for what?' She threw up her hands in despair. 'Sir Guy was very angry when I became pregnant, but he stood by me. I know that it is really his wish that I should give the baby away.'

'I expect it is,' Abby said shortly. Then she rose, tucking the baby's shawl round him. 'I don't know how you could *give* your child away, Miss, and as his father is a nobleman I don't suppose you would send him to a foundlings' home.'

'But what shall I do?' Lally wailed, looking weak and appealing.

'My sister would look after him. You would have to pay her, of course, but she would love him, and if you ever wanted him back you would know where to find him. When he is grown up and tall and strong and looks like Sir Guy you may regret what you did to him as a baby. On the other hand – ' Abby gave her a withering look ' – you may not . . .'

'Oh, but Abby, that is an *excellent* idea,' Lally said as if an enormous weight had been lifted from her shoulders. 'Of course I love him a *little* bit, and I may even grow to love him more. But what you suggest is an *excellent* plan. Only – ' Lally's voice took on the wheedling note that Abby knew well ' – I haven't a lot of money, you know. How much do you suppose your sister would charge?'

It was true that Margaret Woodville felt, at last, a happy woman. She had two fine children, a boy and a girl, two nice houses; she had got rid of her mother-in-law, who now dwelt in comfort but not luxury – or not as much as she would have liked – on the cliffs overlooking Bournemouth Bay.

The only flaw in Margaret's life was her husband, Guy: that beautiful young man she had fallen so badly in love with, she had now come to despise. He had not lived up to her expectations. She supposed that it was foolish to have had any, but she had been in love, uncritical, and, despite the evidence, one always hoped that people would change.

Instead of pining, however, instead of wishing things were other than they were – as a Lally or a Henrietta might have done – Margaret busied herself with many interests. She had cultivated a number of acquaintances in the area and had made one or two close friends. There were Lord and Lady Mount, (old friends of the Woodvilles), who lived outside Blandford and had children a little older than hers. There were Mr and Mrs Sudbury, who owned a magnificent, historic home near Milton Abbey, not more than five miles or so from Wenham. They were about the same age as Margaret, but their children were older. The Sudburys were cultivated, wealthy and gregarious. There were Mr and Mrs Abbot of Field House near Wimborne who, some said, were the wealthiest people in the county. Again there was a houseful of delightful children. But probably her favourite people of all were Mr and Mrs Yetman. The Yetmans, of course, were not in the same category as the Mounts, the Abbots and the Sudburys – all county families like the Woodvilles. They were in a special category all of their own.

People have short memories, but the community in Wenham was slow to forget what had happened to Eliza in the year 1880. To the end of her life she would carry about her the whiff of scandal, an element of notoriety that some found shocking and others attractive. She was certainly different. She was direct, straightforward, uncomplicated and, like Ryder, she was by now completely indifferent to what people thought of her, or what they said behind her back.

Nine months after their church wedding a son was born, who was given the name Laurence. Then came Dora and Hugh in the next five years. With three young children under five, Eliza had plenty to occupy her, but she was ably assisted by Beth, who had come home to her with Lady as part of Ryder's wedding present. What a memorable, miraculous day that had been when they all arrived together with the tale of what had happened to Farmer Frith.

Like Guy Woodville, Ryder was often away from home, but for different reasons. He was committed to restoring his father's business and began to build houses, parish halls, even a church. He built a new factory in Blandford and a school in Yeovil. He took on regular workers and paid them well. He saw that they were well housed and looked after; that their children went to school and had enough to eat. In this he was a singular employer, and his workers loved him.

One day Margaret sat at her desk looking carefully at the statements from the bank, reconciling expenditure with income. She enjoyed accounts and thought it must be because business and banking were in the family. Yet one item, or, rather, a series of small items, puzzled her. Regular small amounts of money were being paid to a bank in Hampstead, London. Twenty pounds a month. Twenty pounds a month?

Her eyes narrowed, and she went along the corridor into Guy's study, which was on the first floor next to his dressing room. On the way she lingered in the nursery, where George was playing with his baby sister under the watchful eye of the nursemaid, Ruth. Her underling the nursery maid was tidying up, and it was a pleasant, domestic scene which brought a smile of pleasure to Margaret's face.

After chatting to the nursemaids and patting the children on the head (she was a conventional upper-class mother who saw them at certain times of the day: in the morning, after tea and at bedtime), she went into Guy's study and began to rummage through his desk. Twenty pounds a month – what could that be for? She looked for a clue and found none. She suspected gambling. The best thing would be to ask him or, better still, write to the bank. Margaret was the sort of direct, undevious woman who would do a thing like that. She would never let a suspicion rest. It might, she thought, be some error and they could be losing money. Twenty pounds a month was, after all, two hundred and forty pounds a year.

She was about to close the drawer of Guy's large untidy desk, promising herself that one of her tasks during the next few days would be to tidy it for him, when some papers were disturbed by the act of shutting the drawer. She looked closely and saw, lying right at the bottom, a legal document bound with tape and stamped with a seal. Curious, she pulled it towards her and sat down in Guy's chair to study it.

It was a lease.

On closer perusal she discovered that it had to do with the freehold purchase of a house in the Vale of Health, Hampstead. And it was dated just a year after she and Guy were married.

When Ryder and Eliza had eloped, Euphemia Monk had been thirty-two. She was considered timid and very, very shy, largely because she had lived a sheltered, secluded and, in truth, uneventful and rather lonely life.

Their elopement had seemed to her quite gloriously romantic, though, of course, she had not dared tell a soul. She knew neither of them personally and learned everything by hearsay; but vicariously she had shared the excitement of their exile, the humiliation of their homecoming. To her it was like a novel from the circulating library which nice girls were not supposed to read.

Her house overlooked the church, and as the newly married couple had slipped out of the side entrance, their hands entwined, hers had been one of the faces staring at them from behind the net curtains. But not in disapproval! How she'd envied them: the bride beautiful, the groom tall, strong and handsome, as they followed their path to happiness; the kind of happiness that, up to then, had eluded her. She was afraid it always would.

After her father's death she had closed her house and travelled, accompanied by a maid, and sometimes by an aunt, her mother's sister, who was an accomplished painter and linguist. She had died too, after which Euphemia found herself completely alone in the world except for her books, her sizeable fortune, safely invested, and her memories.

Euphemia Monk was not a pretty woman, but she was comely. She liked to dress well and was highly thought of in the town. Gradually her shyness seemed to evaporate, but still she kept herself to herself, a single lady without any vices and few close friends. She had two maids, a cook, and a gardener who doubled up as coachman; but the carriage was scarcely ever used. Occasionally she made forays to Blandford, Wimborne or Dorchester, or as far afield as Bournemouth or Bristol; but most of the time she remained at home, reading, sewing, or working in her garden. She was extremely fond of gardening and knew a lot about plants.

Miss Monk fell into that indefinable class that was not society, not aristocracy, not of yeoman stock, and certainly not working class. On the social scale, had there been one, she would fall somewhere between the Woodvilles and the Yetmans; respectable middle class rather than gentry.

She had last had a real conversation with the Yetmans at Guy Woodville's wedding, but apart from that it was the occasional encounter at church, the occasional passing the time of day: 'good morning', 'good afternoon' or 'good evening'. But one night in the year 1884 there had been a terrible storm in which her chimney fell down, causing damage to her roof. The next morning she sent her maidservant for Mr Yetman and, to her surprise, Mr John Yetman came in person, as his son was busy on other damage that had been caused by the storm. He wore a frock coat, a striped cravat and carried a silver-topped cane. He was, once again, extremely agreeable and paid her compliments, and she offered him coffee. He was also very knowledgeable about the damage to the roof and said he would send his son to estimate for a repair.

Very gradually Euphemia was introduced to the Yetman family and their world. She had found Ryder Yetman just as agreeable, and even more knowledgeable than his father; efficient, too, for the roof had been repaired within a very short time. One day she had seen a striking-looking woman standing outside her garden gate and immediately recognised her as the notorious Eliza Yetman – still spoken of by some in the parish as the woman who had fallen into sin.

Mrs Yetman had been looking, innocently enough, for her husband. One of her children was unwell, the servants were all occupied, and she wanted him to fetch the doctor. Mr Yetman, however, was not there; it was his men who were working on the roof. Miss Monk offered to send her own coachman to summon the doctor, and the beginnings of a friendship with the family were formed there and then.

Eliza, looking from the window of the children's nursery, observed her father-in-law walking with sprightly step up the drive. He saw her at the window and raised his hat as she waved. On the lawn the nursemaid was playing with his two eldest grandchildren while Hugh, the baby, slumbered in his perambulator. John stopped for a word with his grandchildren: he loved them dearly, and they loved him.

Eliza was doing her morning round of the house, a tour of inspection that took her from the top to the bottom, from the servants' quarters to the kitchen. In the children's room she lingered longest because there were tiny things that had escaped the attention of the two nursemaids whom she employed to look after them.

From the window Eliza couldn't see the big house where she had been born and brought up. Her view now overlooked the Wen, which flowed through the bottom of the garden and, on the far side, the wood where her husband, his brothers and sister had played as children. She was glad that Pelham's Oak was not a constant visible reminder of her past, because it always brought a pang of regret that, in loving one man, she had lost her family.

She still saw her uncle Prosper; she saw Margaret and the children, but she never saw or heard from Guy and her mother and, because they were her own flesh and blood, she missed them.

From being a headstrong, impulsive, romantic girl, Eliza had turned into a practical, philosophical young woman. Her brief experience of the harshness and unfairness of life had brought her maturity. She had quickly learned how to manage a large house and servants, and how to have accomplishments of her own, though she would never be any use with a needle, she was too impatient. Whenever she could, she liked to accompany Ryder as he travelled round the countryside on various projects; daily she exercised Lady and a pony, Ned, which would be trained for the children.

She stood for a while watching her father-in-law fussing over Laurence and Dora. He seemed curiously elated. Finally he kissed the tops of his grandchildren's heads and then hurried towards the house, arriving at the porch just as Eliza got there to greet him.

'My dear,' he said, kissing her cheek, 'I have some very happy news for you.'

'I *knew* there was something,' Eliza said, taking his arm and leading him into the drawing room. 'You fairly skipped up the path . . . rather like a man in love,' she finished with a sparkle in her eye.

'I *am* a man in love, my dear,' he said, sitting next to her on the sofa and placing his hand over hers. 'I think you know who she is.'

'Euphemia!' Eliza burst out, scarcely able to contain her own excitement and pleasure.

'She has just agreed to be my wife. She has asked me to call her Effie. Oh, Eliza, I can't *tell* you how happy I am. There is no man in the world happier than I at this moment.'

The romance had been a subject of family speculation for two years, but it was no rushed affair, as befitted a couple who were not in the first flush of youth. Because of the difference in their ages few people took much notice of their rare promenades about the town, down to the river or to the cattle market to look at the livestock. They dined together quite frequently, but never alone, always with Ryder and Eliza, or one of John's other children. It was a slow burgeoning, rather than a swift falling in love.

'Oh, Father, that is wonderful news,' Eliza said, squeezing his hand. 'I so hoped it would happen.'

'I never dared *hope* she would accept me. I am not well born, and I have retained my country manners as well as my accent. She is a gentlewoman. I am wealthy, but so is she. I am twenty years older than Euphemia, a man set in his ways, with grandchildren. She, bless her, owns that *she* is set in her ways too; but we think we shall be happier together than apart.'

'I'm sure you will. I *know* you will. She is perfect for you. Not too young and not too old. You could have another family, Father.' She looked at him, her eyes dancing.

'Effie *would* like it,' he said shyly. 'We have discussed the matter, as befits older people. Oh, Eliza, you have *no* idea what a truly wonderful woman she is. She has been on her own for a number of years and yet she has conducted herself with such dignity. There has *never* been a word of scandal about her, or even criticism.'

'She is much liked in the parish,' Eliza agreed. 'When is the wedding to be?'

John Yetman's face lost its beaming smile for a moment.

'There *is* a small point of dispute between my love and me. I said I would never enter St Mark's again after the way the Rector addressed you on your marriage, and I never have. Effie, on the other hand, is a regular churchgoer, a friend of the Lambs. You know I occasionally attend the Methodist church, though I am not a Wesleyan.'

'The wedding *must* be at St Mark's,' Eliza said firmly. 'We shall behave as though nothing had happened to upset us five years ago.'

'Oh, my dear, I'm *so* glad. I thought if we were married there you and Ryder might not come. If you agree, there is not a cloud in the sky.'

'Now go and see your fiancée and say she has our blessing,' Eliza said, rising. 'And ask her to dine with us tonight. There is a lot to celebrate.'

'My dear,' John said, still hanging on to her hand, 'there *is* one thing more. Effie would like me to move into her house. It is quite large enough for two, even three or more if we are blessed with a family. She is much attached to the house and would not wish to move. I have no objection, because I would like you and Ryder to have this house as my way of thanking you for the happiness you have brought a lonely man over the past five years. Had it not been for you, my courtship of Effie would not have been so easy. We were able to entertain and be entertained because you were always there, and I want you to know, my dear Eliza, that I love you as my daughter and could never have wished for a better wife for my son.'

'Thank you, dear Father,' Eliza replied, giving his hand a last squeeze. 'Now I must go and find Ryder to give him the good news.'

While John Yetman turned back to tell his fiancée that their engagement had his family's blessing and to invite her to dinner, Eliza went down to the kitchen to give directions to the cook for the celebration dinner. However, the large, cool room was silent except for a pot bubbling on the stove, as though preparations for lunch were in progress. The door into the yard was open, and Rover, one of the large red setters, lay basking in the sun while, provocatively, a couple of hens clucked inches away from his nose, as though daring him to snap at him. The dog, having chased elusive rabbits all morning, was far too tired and never even opened his eyes.

Suddenly there was a furtive movement by the pantry door and two figures sprang guiltily apart.

'Beth!' Eliza exclaimed angrily. 'What *are* you up to?'

Another figure, this one male, made as if to beat a hasty retreat through the open door, but Eliza, as agile as he, grasped him by the shirt collar before he had time to reach the door and dragged him back.

'Oh, Albert *Newman*, is it? I might have known.' She gave him a sharp smack across the face, her dark eyes blazing, and the man cringed while, in the background, Beth, her cheeks aflame, screwed her apron up into a tight ball.

'I have told you, Beth, Albert,' Eliza went on severely, 'that I will have no courting here in working hours. Now, off you go, Albert, and if I catch you again I'll have your father after you . . .'

'I was just fetchin' the saddle we repaired for Lady, mum,' Albert, the son of the saddler in the High Street, mumbled.

'I don't care *what* you were doing as long as it is not seducing my servants in the time I pay them for. Or any other time,' she added as an afterthought.

'I left the saddle in the stable, mum,' Albert said ingratiatingly. 'It fitted beautiful.'

'Now you just get out of here, Albert Newman.' Eliza pointed angrily to the door, and as he scuttled out she turned to Beth, whose eyes were now brimming with tears.

'Now, Beth,' Eliza said, wagging a finger at her. 'I have told you once and I'll tell you again, I will have *no* courting in my kitchen in working hours. If I have to tell you again you'll be packed straight back to Farmer Frith . . .'

'Oh *no* ma'am, please, *please*,' Beth twittered, very different from the bold, amorous creature she was now considered to be by a few fortunate men in Wenham. 'I beg you, ma'am. I will *never* set eyes again on Albert, if you say so, ma'am . . .'

'Or Ted?' Eliza demanded, still trying to pretend she was angry. 'I thought you were going to *marry* him?'

'I can't decide, to tell you the truth, ma'am.' Beth stepped forward a little more confidently. 'Or there is Benjamin Sims at the mill . . .'

'You are an absolute disgrace, Beth.' Eliza tapped her foot on the floor in mock anger. 'I bring you here, rescuing you from a life of slavery, give you a good home, pay you well, feed you, clothe you . . . and yet you betray my trust and confidence in you.'

'Oh, *no*, ma'am, please.' Beth suddenly sank to her knees, convulsively clutching the hem of Eliza's dress.

'Beth, don't be ridiculous!' Eliza was now scarcely able to prevent herself from bursting out laughing. 'There is *no* need for this performance, which I know is quite artificial. Get up please.' As her servant struggled to her feet, Eliza went on: 'You have got yourself a reputation in this town which greatly displeases me. There are at least *two* men who have proposed to you, and I don't know how many more with less honourable intentions. Now I warn you, Beth, if I find you in the family way it will be *out*!' Thoroughly enjoying her role, Eliza pointed to the door, where even Rover, his curiosity aroused by the noise, had opened an eye. 'You will be sent to the poorhouse in Blandford, or back to Farmer Frith. I don't know which is worse.'

'Oh, I *beg* you, ma'am . . .' Beth screwed her apron right up to her chin, clutching it as a child clutches a favourite piece of cloth. 'I *promise*, ma'am. But I am only twenty, I don't feel it is the time to be wed now, ma'am. Besides, I don't want to leave you.'

Beth looked at her with such trust, such love, which in a way, was mutual, that her mistress decided to forgive her. She pointed to a chair and, as the trembling girl sat down, she sat next to her.

'Now look, my dear. I am very fond of you, you know that. I don't want to lose you. But I'd rather you were happily settled than an unwed mother. Now who is it to be Ted or Albert . . . or neither?'

'Well, ma'am.' Beth's face became even more contorted. 'I

like Ted. He was so kind to me when he brought me from Ennerdale. I *love* him, I *think*. But Albert . . . well, I like *him* too. I think he has better prospects, ma'am. He is a trained saddler and will succeed to his father's business one day with his own shop. I would be nearer you then, ma'am, but, truthfully, I would hate to leave you. I would like to work for you all my life.'

'Oh, *Beth*.' Impulsively Eliza threw her arms around the young woman she regarded almost as a sister. It would have been impossible to have had a more loving, loyal and devoted servant; but she did have this weakness . . . On the other hand had not she herself had it too? If anyone should understand the stirrings of the flesh it was she, Eliza Yetman.

'I'll tell you what, ma'am,' Beth said suddenly. '*If* I married Ted maybe the master would employ him here to look after the stables?'

'And what would Lady Woodville say to that? She values Ted as much as you do.'

'But Ted loves *you*, ma'am. You know that. He has never quite took to Lady Woodville, kind as she is. Being foreign, they don't understand our ways, ma'am, if you'll forgive me saying it.'

'I know what you mean.' Eliza got up and, going over to the stove, lifted the lid and sniffed the broth cooking there for lunch. 'However, I am very *fond* of my sister-in-law, and I wouldn't want to start a quarrel with her. But let me see if I can have a word with her about Ted . . .'

'Oh, thank you, ma'am.' Beth grasped Eliza's hand and kissed it. With difficulty Eliza freed herself and pointed to the stove.

'If you can give me some of this good broth in a billycan I'll take it out to my husband, who is working nearby, and exercise Lady too.'

Although popular and well liked by the people of Wenham, Ryder Yetman was also regarded as a rather odd, even eccentric character. He was a loner, and did not mix too well with his

243

fellow men. He belonged to none of the clubs or associations which proliferated so that the menfolk could get away from their wives. He was too much of an animal lover to hunt or shoot, and he rarely frequented public houses. He was known to be devoted to his family and his work, possibly in that order.

And at both he excelled. He was a devoted father and husband, and in five years he had built up his father's business so that it now covered three counties.

Yet, although undoubtedly he was now wealthy, he did not show his wealth or behave like a wealthy man. Apart from Blandford his branch offices were small, usually in the high street of a town, and so was his staff. He employed craftsmen to do his building and had rapidly acquired a reputation for excellence. People would wait to have their houses built by Yetman rather than another builder in the area, because they knew it would be a first-class job.

Ryder, who was an expert, taught the art of thatching to his apprentices himself and would often either start them off on a job or complete it on his own. As Eliza, riding on the back of Lady, sought him out she knew that he was finishing the ridge of a house that he'd just built on the far side of the river for one of the town councillors.

Ryder was just about to climb down the ladder, having completed the morning's task, when he saw Lady crossing the bridge with his wife on her back. He remained where he was and, folding his arms, watched their steady progress up the path that ran from the river bank to the new house. Eliza was still the slim, beautifully formed young woman he had fallen in love with in circumstances not so very different from the one today, except that now they had been married for five years and had three children.

But he still had the same passionate awareness of her; still couldn't believe that she was his wife and would remain so until the day – God grant that it was far off – when death would part them.

Eliza had acquired a radiance and assurance with her maturity, and yet she was still only twenty-four. She had seemed to be concentrating on the narrow path, when suddenly she looked up and saw him staring at her.

She, in turn, caught her breath, because standing there on the roof he reminded her of when she first fell in love with him – chest bare, fair hair gleaming against the canopy of the sky. She waved and quickened her pace, and by the time she arrived in front of the house Ryder had climbed down the ladder, put on his shirt and was awaiting her.

He touched Lady's nose, and she nuzzled up to him, greeting him as a familiar. Then he helped Eliza down and enfolding her in his arms, gave her a long, deep kiss.

When he released her she gazed up at him, aware of the desire that was never very far from the surface.

'I've come to bring you good news,' she said, breaking the silence.

'You are with child again?' He put a hand on her belly.

'No,' she laughed and shook her head. 'Would that be good news?'

'Yes. Very.'

'But we already have *three* children, under five.'

'Let us have another.' He leaned suggestively towards her again, the expression in his eyes not difficult to fathom, but she neatly sidestepped him, putting the billycan carefully on the ground.

'Ryder, one of your workmen will see us!'

'None are here today. I am just finishing the ridge and then the job is done.'

Styles of thatching varied from county to county. In Dorset the ridges tended to be round and flowing; further west they were flatter and rounder. In other parts of the country they were steeper and more angular. A master thatcher, like Ryder, had his own style, and other experts could identify which roofs had been done by whom, rather as particular styles of sculpture or painting could be attributed to an individual artist.

'Here, I've brought you some hot soup,' Eliza said, opening

the lid of the billycan. 'Though it's a warmer day than I thought.'

'It's still welcome though,' Ryder said, putting the edge of the billy to his mouth. 'Well, what is your good news?'

'Father has finally proposed to Euphemia.'

'And she accepted?' Ryder put down the billy and wiped his mouth on his bare arm.

'Of course. She must have been waiting and hoping for this for a long time.'

'But he's a lot older than she is.'

'I don't expect she minds. It's been clear for some time, as you know, dear, that she loved him.'

'Well, I think it's splendid,' Ryder said with satisfaction, and began drinking from the billy again.

'So do I. What's more, she wants to live in *her* house. Your father wishes to give us his.'

'Really?' Ryder looked at her with interest. 'And would you like that?'

'Of course, wouldn't you?'

'I thought I might build us a fine, big house one day.'

'But I want to live where your family has lived since you were a boy, by the river. I love Riversmead and I'm happy there.'

'I am too.' Ryder finished the soup and, replacing the lid on the billycan, handed it back to her.

'Would you like to come inside?' he suggested.

'Why?' She looked puzzled.

'I've something to show you.' His expression was mysterious and, catching her by the hand, he drew her into the house which, although almost ready for occupation, was unfurnished, with bare wooden floors.

'What *is* it?' she asked, holding his hand tightly as they stood in the hall.

'This,' he said, turning to kiss her again and very gently lowering her to the floor.

They must have dozed, because when they awoke the sun was at a different angle, whereas when they had made love they had lain with a bright, warm beam upon their backs.

246

'Oh, *Ryder!*' Eliza cried, sitting up. 'What time is it?'

Ryder squinted out of the window at the sun. 'About two o'clock.'

'But I've missed the children's lunch.'

'What do we have nursemaids for?'

'They might be worried about me.'

'They won't worry.' He pulled her down by him again until he could lean over her once more, smothering her face with kisses.

'Ryder, I really *must* go.' She wriggled away from him and, pulling her dress towards her, slipped it over her head. 'If someone had come in . . .'

'I knew no one would come in . . .'

'I've to see if Effie's coming for dinner.' Playfully she pushed him off her. 'I have *all* kinds of things to do and you appear to have only one thing in your mind.'

'Well . . .' Reluctantly he let her go. 'I suppose you're right. I'll just finish trimming the ridge.'

He got to his feet and then helped her up. She quickly finished dressing and ran a hand through her hair. Hand in hand they went through the door and stood outside in the sun, suffused by a deep sense of well-being.

'I would like to learn how to thatch, you know, Ryder,' she said, gazing critically at his new ridge.

'Are you serious, Eliza?'

'Yes, why not? I'm still young. When we complete our family I may be able to help you in the business. The more I know, and learn, the better.'

'You're an amazing woman,' he said, stealing another kiss, 'in every way. Are you serious?'

'Perfectly serious.'

'But you can't climb the roof in skirts.'

'Why can't I?'

'I might want to make love to you again.'

'Then I shall have to wear breeches,' she said, smiling at him.

'You'll scandalise the neighbourhood.'

'I think it would be more scandalous if we were seen making love on the roof!'

Lady, who had been contentedly munching grass by the roadside, suddenly looked up at them knowingly, almost as if she understood.

12

The man removed his shiny top hat and, with a polite smile, skilfully edged in sideways past Abby while she was staring at the card in her hand. He wore a half cape, known as an Inverness, attached to his coat, and looked like a bailiff's man. Pomphrey Blood was the name printed in elaborate italic script and then, in the left-hand corner, an address in Lincoln's Inn Fields.

'If you would present the card, and my compliments, to the lady of the house, I should be *most* obliged.' Mr Blood's plummy overtones did not completely conceal his Cockney origins.

'Might I ask the nature of your business?' Abby said, trying to look severe.

'Just present it to your mistress,' Mr Blood replied sharply, 'and say it is in connection with a legal matter.'

'Oh!'

Instructing Mr Blood to wait in the hall, Abby disappeared, and within a few minutes she was back.

'Follow me, please.'

'Thank you,' Mr Blood said, all smiles again.

Lally did not rise to greet her visitor, but remained lying on the chaise-longue which faced the French windows leading into the pretty garden. She extended a languid hand, which Mr Blood shook gingerly. He seemed unsure of his welcome.

'What do you want?' Lally asked, with complete absence of ceremony, staring at his card again.

'If I may, Mrs . . . Woodville, is it?' The name was uttered delicately, almost in a whisper.

'No,' Lally replied. 'The name's Mrs Bowyer.'

'Ah!' Mr Blood seemed to make a mental note.

'Please take a seat and state the nature of your business.'

'Well . . .' Mr Blood perched on the very edge of his chair. 'It is about this property, ma'am.'

'What about this property?' Lally looked at Abby, who, as instructed, was hovering on the threshold of the half-open door.

'I am acting on behalf of a client who is interested in purchasing it.'

'As far as I know it is not for sale.'

'How do you mean, "as far as you *know*", Mrs Bowyer?' Mr Blood's voice trailed off.

'It is not for sale. I live here,' she replied. 'Now kindly take your leave. I have not been well.'

'I am very sorry to hear that, ma'am. Very sorry.' Mr Blood nervously rubbed a bald spot on the crown of his head with his index finger. 'Is . . . may I ask . . . that is to say . . . is the property in your name?'

'And what business is it of yours?'

'My client is very persistent . . .'

'Mr Blood, if you do not take your leave this instant I'll . . .' Lally made a feeble effort to rise.

With considerable agility, Mr Blood got out of his chair. However, he remained standing, hands clasped in front of him, looking sorrowfully down at her.

'Mrs Bowyer, believe me, ma'am, I do *not* wish to distress you; but I have reason to believe this property is not in your name, but in the name of Sir Guy Woodville. You see, there are records in these matters, ma'am. The purchase of property is a legal affair, and I am a solicitor's clerk. My principal has despatched me to find out to whom the property belongs so that he might make an offer to the proprietor, on behalf of his client.'

'And why should *anyone* want this, my home, so much?' Lally enquired in a withering tone.

'It is a very attractive house, ma'am, in a very *desirable* part of town. I have no idea why my principal's client should wish to live here, nor is it my business to enquire. I was merely asked to look into the matter on his behalf.'

'Well, now you know. It is *not* for sale.'

'But could you confirm that the owner is Sir Guy Woodville?'

'As you already seem to know, why should *I* confirm it?'

'And your position with Sir Guy Woodville is . . .' Mr Blood put a podgy finger to his mouth.

'Tenant,' Abby said from the door, seeing that Lally was at a loss to describe herself. 'My mistress rents it off 'is lordship.'

'Ah, thank you for making it so clear, my good lady,' Mr Blood said with a polite bow. 'That is all I wish to know.'

Lally sat back against her cushions as though she were exhausted and closed her eyes, waving her hand vaguely towards the door.

'Get out,' she said in a voice hardly more than a whisper, 'and don't *dare* come here again.'

Julius Heering was thirty-nine years of age when his wife, Sofia, died of puerperal fever, having failed in her fifth attempt to give him a living child.

Julius – a middle son – had always been an earnest, hard-working, industrious man. His life would have been rounded off by the sort of family circle that his brothers, all prolific breeders, and his sister, Margaret, enjoyed. He had given Sofia everything that money could buy: a lovely home, plenty of servants, the best medical attention. She could not give him a child, and he could not save her life. He found he was unable to forgive himself for this.

He took solace in the prosperous Heering concerns, and even though it was thought impossible that he could increase his work load, he did. He never stopped, and his home became a kind of hotel, seldom visited.

It was Julius who had come to London to cement the already good relations between the Martyns and the Heerings, and to assume his position as a fulltime partner in the firm. It was he who, at his sister's request, had instigated the investigations into the house in the Vale of Health. She felt she could trust him where she could trust nobody else.

When he got the report from his solicitors, he reflected that he had already known the answer for some time. His brother-in-law, as well as everything else, was an adulterer. It did not surprise him. The investigations were now proceeding into 'Mrs Bowyer'. Every little fact was being dredged up because the Dutch were a thorough people, though, rather like the Reverend Lamb, they would not be among those to cast the first stone.

But when as much as was known was revealed at a secret board meeting held in Threadneedle Street, with only the senior partners present, Prosper Martyn was able to supply the additional information that Lally was a former music-hall artiste, a dancer. He had only seen her once, years before, but he had not forgotten her face.

It was curious that no one found out about the baby, who had been spirited away to a small house in Kentish Town to the care of Abby's sister, already the mother of five and in need of extra cash.

The decision was taken to tell Margaret about Guy's liáison; after all, she had surely guessed enough already. The facts should be laid clearly before her and she should be permitted to make the decision. Did she want to live with an adulterer, or did she want a divorce? Did she somehow wish to punish her husband and his mistress, or was she the type to forgive?

Julius pondered the question as he made his way to Dorset at the beginning of 1887. It was not the sort of mission he liked to be entrusted with, but it was decided that he was the only one to do it.

Brother and sister were near to each other in age and had always been close. Julius had been against her marrying Guy, even at the risk of her remaining a spinster. He was a careful man who did not wish to see Margaret's wealth melt away, as he knew it would. But his father and he had devised a scheme to ensure that Guy didn't get it all. Now, with the advent of the new Married Woman's Property Act, Margaret was more in command of her own fortune.

He didn't think she would be too surprised by what he had to tell her. But she was. She lost her breath and seemed unable to speak.

Julius, who had left the announcement until they were seated by the fire after dinner, got up and tried to make her comfortable on the sofa, putting a cushion under her head and unbuttoning the top of her dress.

Then he knelt by her side and stroked her brow.

'Shall I call the doctor?'

'Fetch the laudanum,' she gasped. 'There is some in the drawer of my bedside table.'

Seriously alarmed, Julius ran through the silent house, up the stairs and down again when he had found what he was sent for. Back in the drawing room he put a few drops in her handkerchief and held it under her nose.

'Margaret, my dear. Had I known . . .'

She took a few rapid breaths, blinked her eyes several times and then, opening them, gave a great sigh and her breathing became more regular.

'An attack of palpitations,' she said, clutching her chest.

'I was much too blunt, too abrupt . . . But did you never *suspect*? I thought I was merely confirming something you guessed already.'

'Never!' she said, fluttering her handkerchief in front of her face.

'But what did you think Guy did with his time, his money?'

'*Never* with a woman! I never thought, you see . . .' Her face crumpled, and her expression, usually so self-confident, strong, and sometimes even arrogant, looked like that of a lost child.

'He is always very *attentive* to me when he is with me. You understand what I mean?' She coloured slightly as he nodded. She then laid her hand on her stomach and, looking at the ceiling, closed her eyes. 'I am once more expecting a child. How *could* I suppose . . .'

'Oh, my dear. I am so very sorry.' Julius got up and stared into the fire. Had he known the circumstances, he thought, he probably would not have told her. But it was too late.

'Guy must get rid of that woman,' Margaret said with sudden, unexpected firmness in her voice. 'And *you* must dismiss him from the business.' She sat up as if she were her old resolute, decisive self again.

'Are you serious, Margaret?'

'You know he is useless at it. Tell him to come and live back here where he belongs, and you can be *very* sure that I will keep an eye on him. Very, very sure.'

'You could divorce him, return to Holland.'

'And be an object of pity?' She gave her brother a withering look. 'No, thank you. I would rather live here as Lady Woodville than admit I couldn't keep my husband. I would rather live in enmity with Guy than suffer the humiliation of returning to my father's house. But I do not *intend* to live in enmity with Guy.' She rose and looked at her reflection in the beautiful gilt Empire mirror over the marble mantelpiece. 'I will be a good wife. I *am* a good mother. We shall enjoy the delights of country life together: hunting, visiting, entertaining. I think Guy is getting off very lightly . . .'

'Oh, *very* lightly,' Julius said with heavy irony. 'How fortunate he is to have you as a wife.' He leaned towards the fire and, taking a spill, lit a cigar.

'Fortunate indeed. He may realise that. Guy has a duty to me *and* our children. Had he spent his money, *my* money, on anything else I don't think I should have minded so much. As a matter of fact,' Margaret turned her back to the fire and gazed at her brother, '*I* thought he was a gambler – I didn't approve, of course – but a womaniser . . . never!' She crumpled her handkerchief in her hand and her expression was spiteful. 'Let him pay for it.'

'He might not agree.'

'What do *you* think he would do?' Margaret's tone was contemptuous. 'Live in sin with her? Never. She's penniless, don't forget. Guy likes his comfort. He does not like work and never has. He was not brought up to it. I intend to make it *very* agreeable for him to live here. He will have everything he wants, all the comforts, *but* he will have to account to me for every penny he spends, and every move he makes.'

'I don't think you will keep him very long,' Julius said quietly.

'You don't know Guy,' Margaret replied with a confident air. 'Not in the way that I do.'

Guy said: 'My dear, that is absolutely splendid news,' and blew his wife a kiss.

'I'm so glad you're pleased, Guy.'

'Of course I'm pleased.' He rubbed his hands together. 'To be the father of a large family is admirable.'

'Then we may have more?' Margaret lowered her eyes modestly.

'Most certainly.' He looked across the dinner table at his wife. 'Don't you wish it?'

'I do not wish to kill myself, like poor Sofia.'

'My dear, she never had a living child. You are very good at it.'

Guy seemed very satisfied with himself, and after dinner he took her arm as they strolled along the hall to the drawing room, where a large fire leapt up the chimney.

'I'm thinking of retiring from the business.' Guy's voice was low, his manner offhand as he began to light his cigar.

'Really?' Margaret pretended to be surprised as she took her seat by the fire. 'Is that wise?'

'I think so. It is not something I enjoy, you know.'

'Oh, I know *that*,' she said with a smile.

'As it was your brother Julius who suggested it,' he looked at her sideways, 'I thought you might already know.'

'I knew he was to spend more time in London.'

'He is going to live in London permanently. He is already looking for a house. In fact,' Guy tipped the ash of his cigar into the fire, 'one might almost think you'd *planned* it, Margaret.'

His pleasant smile had gone and the expression on his face was enigmatic.

'That's most unlikely.' She began to feel uncomfortable.

'But you *do* know about my friend . . .' It was almost as though he were accusing her.

'Your *friend*!' Margaret leaned her head back. '*That's* a nice thing to call her. I'd like to know her name.'

'I wonder you don't – you know everything else. You, your brother and my uncles have conspired against me. Well, if you think it makes me feel foolish, it doesn't.'

'I never meant it to do that, Guy,' she said quietly. 'I merely wished to remind you that you are married to me and we are a family. We have two children and are to be the parents of another.' She held up a hand, but he didn't take it, remaining cold and aloof. 'And besides, how can I countenance your continuing to see another woman?'

'I was tired of her anyway, to tell you the truth,' he said in a voice that was suddenly weary, seating himself opposite her and thrusting out his legs. 'I'm glad that the deception is over and that everything is out in the open, I truly am. She – I shan't tell you her name, it's unimportant now – was a pretty little thing I picked up, and she had become a burden to me. The business, as you know, I have never been suited to. Now, if your father and brother want to pay me to stay at home, I shall. Gladly.'

He reached over and gave her his hand.

Tentatively, Margaret grasped it. Now that she had him, she wasn't *quite* sure it was what she wanted after all. She had thought she had him in the palm of her hand – but had she? Life would never be quite as simple and carefree again.

Early in the new year Euphemia Monk, spinster of the parish, became a married woman. She was nearly thirty-nine and, in deference to her age, she didn't wear white or drive through the town in an open carriage.

The wedding was a quiet, dignified but very happy affair,

256

and the reception was held at her husband's old home, which he had now made over entirely to his eldest son.

Margaret Woodville used her pregnancy as an excuse not to attend, but all John Yetman's children and grandchildren were there, including his daughter, Agnes, who, despite much earnest endeavour, was still unmarried.

Agnes had soon tired of living with her aunt. When she had first gone to London, five years before, it had seemed like the adventure of a lifetime; but her aunt seldom moved outside the house, preferring to entertain at home, and finding it necessary to be attended by Agnes at all times. Agnes's chances of finding a suitable mate were even more remote than they had been in Wenham. Finally, she went to a family as a governess and, to her surprise, found she enjoyed the work.

The Agnes of today was not the Agnes of yesteryear. She was twenty-seven, an age at which most women considered themselves completely on the shelf if they were not married. Agnes had never thought it would happen to her, but it had. Instead of despairing about her situation, however, she became cynical. She would go to great lengths to make herself attractive, to ogle surreptitiously the husbands or elder sons of her employers. Thus, inevitably, she found herself changing her employers at an alarming rate.

One advantage of her growing cynicism was that Agnes had become less censorious about the weaknesses of others. With hindsight, she decided that, in her place, she might have done what Eliza had done. Indeed, given half a chance she might do it even now.

Agnes returned home as though she had never been away; never acquired a niece and two nephews, or a new stepmother. If Eliza remembered why she had gone away, she appeared conveniently to have forgotten it. The two women got on so well that Agnes decided to stay a while and see what opportunities, if any, presented themselves. Maybe she would not look so askance at some clodhopper of a Dorset farmer now.

One day about a week after the wedding, Eliza was busy

grooming Lady in the stables at the back of the house, and thinking about the events of the week, when there was a movement behind her, so stealthy that it startled her. She turned quickly to see the tall figure of her brother standing in the doorway gazing at her. How long he'd been there she didn't know.

'Guy,' she gasped, 'you startled me. How long have you been there?'

'A few minutes,' he said, advancing diffidently into the stable and removing his hat. 'How are you, Eliza?'

'As you see,' Eliza said, the grooming brushes still in her hands.

'You look very well. It's been a long time . . .'

'You can't blame *me* for that.' Angrily Eliza turned back to Lady. The horse seemed to recognise Guy; she gave a whinny of greeting and stamped a hoof on the ground.

'Hello, Lady,' Guy said affectionately, throwing his arm round her neck. Lady nuzzled him, and with a note of triumph in his voice he cried: 'She remembers me, she remembers me, Eliza!'

Eliza's emotions were in such turmoil that she could scarcely speak. She and her brother had not met for over six years. They had once been good friends, confidants. Now they were like strangers.

'You know I'm back for good?' Guy said.

'No more City of London?' Eliza looked surprised. 'Did they kick you out?'

'More or less, thank God,' Guy said with a laugh. He sat down on a bale of hay and seemed more at ease. 'I have been sent to look after my estate in Dorset.'

'I thought Margaret was doing that most efficiently.'

'She is having another child. The truth is,' Guy continued after a pause, 'I am not suited to City life. I never was.'

'Then what life *are* you suited to?' The hostility still in his sister's eyes surprised him.

'Why, Eliza . . .'

'We can't just continue where we left off, you know, Guy,'

she said angrily. 'I was eighteen and I am now twenty-four. *You* abandoned me, denied me access to my home. My mother ignored my letters and then burnt them.'

'You shamed your family.' Guy's voice was reproachful. 'That made Mama ill. It has taken us a long time to get over it.'

'It has taken *you* . . . what about *me*!' Eliza threw the brushes down on the floor and, folding her arms, gazed defiantly at him.

'My dear sister, *you* were the one who offended. What you did was something few people would be prepared to overlook, or forgive – ever. Now I have come here, though it is hard for me to do so, because I really want to be friends. I have missed you . . . I love you. I have forgiven you completely now.'

. 'But have I forgiven *you*?' Eliza retorted.

'My dear Eliza.' Guy got off the bale of hay and dusted the seat of his pants. 'Please don't throw the olive branch which I hold out to you back in my face. I know you like Margaret and you see a lot of her. If I am to live here permanently and you and I are not on speaking terms, it will be hard for her. I think it will also be hard for you.'

He looked so earnest, so sincere, that she remembered the brother she had loved so much, and because she was an impulsive, generous woman she suddenly held out her arms. Brother and sister embraced, each close to tears, and for a long time they said nothing.

'I have *missed* you,' she said at last, leaning against his shoulder.

'And I you. I have always asked Margaret for news of you. Besides,' he paused and glanced quickly down at her, 'I did want to see you years ago. I wanted to forgive and forget. But Mama made me promise . . .'

'And what made you change your promise now?'

'I think Mama would like to see you too.' Guy's voice had a wistful note. 'She is not a young woman any more, Eliza. Would that be possible, for you and Mama to forget the past and forgive each other?'

'I *would* like to see Mama again.' Eliza, overcome by emotion, was on the verge of tears. 'More than anything.'

'She wants to see her grandchildren, and I my nephews and niece. We have so many things to talk about. Oh, Eliza, may we bury the past?'

'Let it be buried,' she said. 'Everything, except our happy youth together, will be forgotten. Now, come up to the house and meet the children.'

Eliza seized Guy's hand, and together they walked across the yard and into the house by the kitchen door.

The cook, standing at the table rolling pastry, stared at the gentleman but went on with her work. Beth stood at the sink, suds up to her elbows, washing the pots and pans from the morning's cooking.

'This is my brother, Sir Guy Woodville.' Eliza linked an arm through his, and Cook curtsied, while Beth, in her confusion, lowered her face so that her nose nearly hit the water.

Guy and Eliza passed through the green baize door into the hall. Just as they were about to enter the drawing room Agnes, reading a book, emerged from the library and almost cannoned into the animated pair.

'Oh, *pardon*!' Agnes swiftly removed the gold-rimmed spectacles through which she was perusing the printed words. 'Why, Sir Guy. It *is* Sir Guy, isn't it?'

'It is indeed.' Guy, a pleasant smile on his face, extended his hand.

'How do you do, Miss . . .'

'This is my sister-in-law, Agnes Yetman.' Eliza told him. 'She was at your wedding.'

'Of course.' Guy did not attempt to conceal the admiration with which he was regarding Agnes.

'You would scarcely remember me, Sir Guy, on an occasion like *that*.' Agnes's tone was a little coquettish.

'I never forget a pretty face, Miss Yetman,' Guy replied. 'I hope I see you again.'

'Agnes will soon be going back to London,' Eliza said. 'She has been staying with us for her father's wedding. But

I dare say you will be down again in the summer, won't you, Agnes?'

'Perhaps,' Agnes said nonchalantly and, with another glance at Guy, made her way along the corridor to mount the stairs.

'What a charming girl,' Guy remarked as they reached the drawing room. He stationed himself with his back to the fire and rubbed his hands. 'This is a very cold house, Eliza. Did you know we now have heating installed throughout Pelham's Oak?'

'Yes; you have to thank Margaret and her fortune for that.'

Guy missed the significance of her remark. He still seemed preoccupied by the pleasant Miss Yetman. 'Tell me, she is not married?' he asked.

'Who? Oh, Agnes? No.'

'She looks about thirty.'

'She is a little older than me, twenty-six.'

'I wonder then that she is not married. I suppose there are few men around here who appeal to her.'

'She's been a governess in London.'

'Really? And yet her father's a man of wealth also, I understand.'

'It is her choice. She doesn't want to be idle.'

'That's why she had a book in her hand. A bluestocking, I expect, though she does not look like one.'

'She is *not* a bluestocking, but she likes to read. Why must you put labels on people, Guy? *I* was a fallen woman . . . Agnes is a bluestocking.'

'Oh, I put labels on *women*, but not people in general.' Guy gave her a teasing smile, and she remembered how they used to banter when they were younger, each trying to score points off the other.

'I don't know what Ryder will say about this,' Eliza said after a moment's thought. 'I must be honest.'

'About what?' Guy reached towards the fire and warmed his hands.

'About our reconciliation.'

'You mean *he* might not want me in his house?'

261

'It's possible. He's a very determined man.'

'And also, I hear, a very rich one. Congratulations, Eliza, on making such a good match. As I told Mama, times have changed.' He crossed the room and sat down next to her. 'It is not enough now to be a gentleman. One has to work, and I was not brought up to work. If it hadn't have been for Margaret's fortune, its true, we would be in a *very* sorry state at Pelham's Oak . . .'

'Which brings me to your news,' Eliza said, 'that you are no longer to work in the City. It disturbs me.'

'Why does it disturb you, my dear? My fellow partners recognised that I was not a man of business. Margaret's brother Julius, who is a very considerable and successful one, takes my place on the board. I am absolutely delighted with the arrangement.'

'But what will you *do*, Guy?'

'I will enjoy myself the way I was meant to.' Guy looked towards the door. 'Will Miss Yetman be joining us again, do you think?'

Guy had gone by the time Ryder returned home, and Eliza did not quite know how to tell him the news. As it was, the matter was taken out of her hands, for as they sat down to dinner Agnes said:

'How *excited* you must have been to see your brother today, Eliza. It is some years since you last saw him, is it not?'

Ryder, who was holding Eliza's chair out for her, paused and looked at her.

'Is it true? Guy was here?'

'Yes, dear.' Eliza cast a reproachful glance at Agnes.

'But why did you not tell me?'

'I was about to. Agnes took the words out of my mouth.'

'Oh, so *he* has forgiven you then, has he?' Ryder's voice was heavy with sarcasm as he walked round to his own chair and, sitting down, shook out his napkin.

'Don't take it like that. Much water has flowed under Wenham Bridge since I ran away from home, and I think it is time for forgiveness. Besides, he is my brother, and my mother wishes to see me too. I didn't think you would be exactly pleased, but . . .'

'I am very displeased, Eliza,' Ryder said wrathfully. 'Have you no pride?'

'I cannot continue to be alienated from my family, Ryder.' The colour rose in Eliza's cheeks.

'But you have a new family now – one that has loved you and *always* accepted you.'

'Agnes did not accept me . . .' Eliza began.

'Oh, but that was a *very* long time ago.' Agnes sounded agitated.

'It is only recently that you have started to visit again, and to see your father, I think, not us.' Eliza gazed calmly at her husband's angry face. 'We must *all* learn to forgive, Ryder. I have.

'It is true that I have a new family, and I love them dearly, you above all. But Guy and my mother – all my childhood memories are of them, and my dear father. Now that our relationship is restored you must realise how much pleasure it gives me.'

'Well . . .' Ryder leaned back in his chair and thoughtfully tapped his fork on the table.

'You must see Eliza's point of view,' Agnes said, glancing at her sister-in-law. 'I think Sir Guy is delightful. How *fortunate* she is to have him as a brother.'

Guy lost no time in arranging the meeting between his sister and their mother, and a week after his reconciliation with Eliza he called to take her and the children to Bournemouth.

While he waited for them by the carriage he walked up and down, smoking thoughtfully. As Eliza appeared with the two eldest children, and Beth behind her carrying the baby, Guy threw away his cigarette and went to greet them, kissing his sister and then each of the little ones.

'No Miss Yetman today?' he asked casually, looking round.

'No.' Eliza was surprised. Handing up Laurence first, she started to climb into the carriage. 'Did you expect her?'

'I thought she might come to help with the children.'

'She went to see about a situation. The Mounts are in need of a governess. Margaret seemed to think Agnes might be suitable.'

'Well, that is *very* convenient,' Guy said with a smile, jumping up to sit beside his sister.

'What do you mean, "convenient"?' Once they were all seated and the coachman up on his box, Eliza looked at him sharply.

'The Mounts are such great friends, aren't they? That will mean we shall see more of Agnes. As well, of course, as more of them. How pleasant.'

He called out to the coachman and the carriage began to wend its way along the drive, out of the gate and down the road towards the river.

It was quite a long drive to Bournemouth, and by the time they arrived the children were tired and the baby crying.

Eliza saw her mother's face at one of the windows of the house, but as soon as Henrietta saw her looking up, the face withdrew. Eliza felt a constriction in her chest and wished she had not come. But in the hubbub of arrival, the children's relief at being out of the cramped conditions of the carriage, she had no chance to be nervous and was swept along by the excitement of arrival.

The door was opened by the butler, and a liveried footman appeared on the steps to help with the children. Beth bustled about in the background while the coachman sprinted after Laurence, who had made straight for the garden, from which he could glimpse the sea.

Guy took Eliza's hand and, smiling comfortingly at her, led her up the steps.

'Lady Woodville is in the drawing room, Sir Guy,' the butler intoned but, at that moment she appeared, standing in the hall as still as a statue, as if frozen into immobility.

Then, as she spontaneously opened her arms, Eliza opened hers, and the two women flew towards each other and embraced.

'Oh, *Mama!*' Eliza at last rested her chin on her mother's shoulder.

'Eliza,' Henrietta said caressingly, stroking her daughter's beautiful hair. 'Oh, my dear daughter, my darling child. Can you forgive me in your heart?'

'Can *you* forgive me, Mama?' Eliza took a tentative step backwards and studied her mother's face.

'You have given me three beautiful grandchildren.' Henrietta indicated the two elder ones, who stood shyly with their fingers in their mouths gazing at her, and at little Hugh, fast asleep in Beth's arms. She took a peek at the baby first, kissed his forehead, and then threw out her hands, which were immediately clasped by Laurence and Dora. Guy and Eliza, exchanging happy glances, took their place in the procession, bringing up the rear. There was a lot to talk about. Seven years was nearly a quarter of Eliza's life, and she was no longer the girl she had been. Henrietta too had changed. She was smaller, she was more wrinkled and, though she would never let her hair go grey or her cheeks remain untouched by rouge, she was beginning to look her age.

Towards the end of the visit she took Eliza alone into the garden, and as they sat on a bench surrounded by wisteria and roses, clasping hands, they felt instinctively that they were closer now than they had ever been.

'I so regret the past,' Henrietta said. 'Had I not been so stupid I would still have been in my home.'

'Maybe it's not to late to return?'

'I would never return to Pelham's Oak,' Henrietta said proudly. 'You I love because you are my flesh and blood. I can never love Margaret, and she will never love me. No, I learned from my mistakes too late.'

'But what I did at the time *was* very wrong, Mama,' Eliza said with unaccustomed humility. 'I see it now, and I realise why you behaved as you did . . . but still I am glad *I* did what I did.' She turned large, wondering eyes to her mother, who thought that Eliza had never looked more beautiful. 'I have a wonderful husband, whom I love. We have three adorable children. And Mama – ' Eliza put her arm round her mother's neck and her warm tears stung her cheeks ' – the joy of being reconciled with you again almost makes the misery of our parting worthwhile.'

Prosper Martyn stood outside the stage door of the Alhambra looking carefully at the faces of the people as they emerged. It was very late and the alley was a dark one. In twos and threes the artistes hurried away, and as they were reduced to a trickle Prosper wondered if his quarry had left by another door. But suddenly there she was. Glancing to right and left, she began to raise her umbrella against the fine drizzle before making for the direction of the square with its welcome lights.

'Mrs Bowyer?' Prosper said, stepping forward and quickly holding his own umbrella over her head for protection.

'Oh! You startled me.' Lally's hand flew to her breast.

'You startled me too,' Prosper replied. 'I thought that you had left by another way. I see you don't remember me?'

'I have never seen you before in my life, sir.' Lally looked closely at him.

'I think you have, but you have forgotten. May I give you supper, Mrs Bowyer, and then perhaps escort you home?'

Home was not the house in the Vale of Health, which had been sold after Guy left town. She had been given one week to quit, and the day she moved out the furniture removal van arrived and the place was stripped bare. From Guy she had heard not a word. He had said he would provide for her, but he had nothing to provide her with.

She was very lucky to find work again so soon to give her money with which to support her child. She thought that if the year did not go well she would be forced to put him in a foundlings' home and that would be that.

Lally was almost permanently hungry, and she hurried through her dinner saying very little. The meeting with

266

the gentleman who called himself an old admirer was a mystery; but there was no doubt that a gentleman was what he was. He also had an air of great wealth, which was especially attractive to a woman on the verge of destitution. Lally took Prosper up the creaky stairs of her former lodgings in Drury Lane, only this time she had a slightly better room on the second floor. As she flung open the door she declared: 'It is not what I am used to. I had a beautiful home in Hampstead and was protected by a titled gentleman.'

'And what happened to the gentleman?' Prosper enquired politely, removing his hat.

'He abandoned me. He had no money. His wife controlled the purse strings.'

'How *very* unfortunate.' Prosper gave a convincing shudder. It was true that the beautiful face he had glimpsed once and remained haunted by ever since was a little more lined, more careworn. Her figure was fuller, but she was still beautiful. However, if she were not careful she would soon lose her job as a dancer. Whereas before she had been in the front row of the chorus, now she had been relegated to the back.

He had given her a good dinner, and she had told him a little about her life. They talked mostly about the theatre. Maybe the wine had had an effect, because as soon as she had removed her coat she raised her leg as if also to remove her stocking, lifting her skirt up over her knees.

'Oh, please, madam.' Prosper stretched out a hand in alarm. '*Please* don't misunderstand me. I am not here to take advantage of your situation.'

'Oh!' Looking confused Lally replaced her garter and hurriedly pulled down her skirt. 'What *are* you here for, then?'

'I am here to offer you protection.' Prosper took out his cigar case and slowly, with an expansive smile, lit one. When it was drawing to his entire satisfaction he blew out the match and threw it away. Then he leaned back on the rickety chair and gazed at her. 'I would like to take the place of the man who treated you so badly, Lally, and provide a home that is fit for you to live in.'

13

Newman's the saddlers had been in the High Street ever since Wenham had begun to evolve from a village into a town, probably some time in the middle of the eighteenth century. The skills of saddlemaker had been passed from father to son, and Albert Newman, the latest heir to the business, was well on his way to becoming a master saddler like his father.

Albert used to sit in the room above the shop where the stitching was done, ostensibly working the machine that sewed the pieces of leather together, that joined the thongs to the buckles and stirrups, but he spent more time than he should have looking out of the window in the hope that his eyes might alight on that woman who so inflamed his senses: Beth.

Beth had no surname. If she arrived at Farmer Frith's with one she had long since forgotten it. For legal purposes she was known as Beth Yetman, but everyone just called her Beth.

Beth had settled down in the Yetman household and had immediately assumed the role of faithful servant, companion and even friend to the inmates of the house. She was especially devoted to Eliza.

Treated with kindness and no longer half starved, Beth was very different from the pathetic little creature who had come from Ennerdale with Ryder when he brought back Lady. She possessed a sexual allure that, while it would have astonished her betters, was well understood by the young men of the parish. She had developed a big, provocative bosom and wide hips, and the thought of what lay between them stirred the blood of the many males who lusted after her.

Beth's reputation was well known in a town where most of the unattached young men at one time or another tried to engage her favours, which was not difficult. By some stroke of luck she had escaped the consequences of her behaviour, and ever since Eliza had given her a talking to and threatened to send her back to Cumberland, she generally avoided the ultimate act by a mixture of teasing and banter which drove all the young men mad. She was also a swift runner, so that her encounters in the dark passages of the town or among the bushes by the side of the river were seldom consummated.

Albert Newman was an impressionable lad who had taken Beth more seriously than most of the others, with the exception of Ted. Albert, the son of respectable parents who were ardent Methodists, and Ted, the groom at Pelham's Oak, were thus the most persistent suitors of this unlikely creature who had the morals of an alley cat; and between them there grew up a rivalry, the flames of which Beth undoubtedly enjoyed fanning, dallying first with one, then with the other.

In time Albert's father realised that his son was neglecting his work at the sewing machine. He was forever glancing out of the window hoping for a glimpse of Beth coming up the hill, her heavy bosom swaying, her basket tucked comfortably over her arm against her generous hips.

No amount of common sense could be talked into Albert. He could not see the damage that would be done to the good name of the family should the stupid girl agree to marry him.

He grew more careless about his work, more and more obsessed with Beth, more jealous, until he took to avoiding Ted, with whom he had always been friendly since they were schoolboys together. They had boxed, played cricket and rugby, enjoying all forms of sport, as both were well-built, strapping men, fond of country pastimes.

On a fine morning in June Albert was sewing together some reins that were to be delivered eventually to Lord Mount at Moreton Park. He had been told to take extra care with the job as his lordship was very particular and only the best was good enough. At last, his eyes sore and his limbs aching, he went over to the window to smoke a cigarette. He stood for a few moments puffing away, observing the people passing the ornate wrought-iron drinking fountain outside the shop, which had been erected in place of the village pump by Albert's grandfather, William, to mark the accession of the Queen in 1837. This was still much used by horses and the thirsty cattle who were driven through the town on market day.

Albert saw the new bank manager, Mr Troup, in his dark pin-striped suit, a gold watch and chain strung across his stomach, about to enter his bank. Mr Troup almost collided with Miss Fairchild, who had a leather bag in her hand, and they stopped on the steps to pass the time of day before the manager gallantly stood back and, opening the doors for her, begged her to precede him into the bank.

She was followed by the butcher, presumably also with the takings from the day before. Then Annie McQueen appeared as if on cue in front of the Baker's Arms, as she invariably did just before opening time, to make sure that the pavement was clean. After a careful look round, she applied herself vigorously to her task with the aid of bucket and mop.

In accordance with the strict Methodist principles of his family, Albert was a teetotaller, but his other passions were not so restrained, and Annie McQueen, with her fine looks, her generous and mature curves, did much to stir a young man's fancy. As if reading his thoughts, she looked across the road, caught his eye and waved. Albert blushed and backed into the room, pretending he had not been looking. Had he gone a step or two further he would have missed the sight of Ted, who rode up the brow of the hill and paused for a moment or two to give his horse a drink at Newman's fountain.

Albert hurried over to the window and, throwing it up, was just about to hail Ted when he saw Beth, her basket on her arm, hips swinging, strolling along the pavement in Ted's direction. Trust her to choose that time.

'Hello!' Albert called in an attempt to divert Ted's attention in the forlorn hope that Beth would pass by. 'How is it with you Ted?'

270

'Oh, hello, Albert,' Ted doffed his hat. 'I'm just getting some last minute things before the christening today. Cook has run out of sugar. A great "do" we're having up at the big house.'

'I'll be seeing you then, Ted,' Albert said, slamming down the window.

'Right, Albert.' Ted was just about to turn, his horse having assuaged his thirst, when he saw Beth. Politely he raised his hat but Beth came close up to the horse and, leaning against it, smiled at Ted in a way that infuriated Albert, who had had his nose pressed to the window pane, but who now abruptly and angrily turned away. His blood boiled so furiously that he felt like seizing the stitching machine and throwing it out of the window. However, when his temper had cooled and he strolled back again there was no sign of them.

For the rest of the day Albert's mind was not on his work. His father was not satisfied with the bridles he stitched for Lord Mount and told him at supper that night, that if he went on at that rate he'd never become a master saddler. He said the cost of the new leather to replace the straps Albert had ruined by his sloppy workmanship would be taken from his wages.

Albert didn't care. He had brooded all day about Beth and Ted, about the glances they'd exchanged by the fountain, and the suggestive way she'd rubbed herself up against his horse. It implied an intimacy he'd suspected but never proved.

But as this was the very day of the christening of the latest child to be born to Sir Guy and Lady Woodville, Albert decided that the coast would be clear for him to try and make some encounter with Beth while festivities continued at Pelham's Oak that night which would be sure to preoccupy Ted.

'I can't understand the boy,' his father observed to his wife as Albert hurried out, his supper only half eaten. 'Something's got into him and it do worry me. If he goes on at this rate he'll *never* make a master saddler.'

'I think it's love that's got into him.' His wife cast her eyes sadly towards the door. 'Love for the wrong woman, if you ask me.'

'God help us,' Mr Newman said piously, and got down the Bible from its shelf by the kitchen stove to see if he could find in that good book some words of comfort for himself and his wife.

Ted had spent all day at Pelham's Oak helping with the preparations for the christening, but by evening, when the family party started, his work was done. The family would not be needing his services again, and he was invited to go and celebrate in the large marquee that had been raised on the lawn for the servants and townspeople.

But he heard the sound of the revellers and knew that the parties were in full swing, Ted mounted his horse and, taking one of the bridle paths across country, set out for Wenham. When he got to the town the streets were deserted, the only light coming from the top window of the saddler's, where Mr Newman was trying to make up for the bad work his son had done that day.

Ted went down the street and entered Riversmead by a side gate. He tethered his horse to a tree and went stealthily towards the kitchen door, which stood a little open, casting light from the oil lamp on to the stone flags outside.

He prayed that Cook wouldn't see him. She was as bad as Mrs Yétman, and would have sent Beth upstairs to bed if he so much as put his nose through the door.

Very carefully he peeped round the door, but the kitchen was empty. Its stone slabs and wooden boards wiped clean, the pots and pans in their places, all shining. Not even the kettle bubbled on the range. Everyone was either in bed or at the christening party.

Ted was about to go in a little further when he felt something sticking into his ribs. Turning sharply, he saw, in the light from the kitchen, the grinning, mischievous face of Beth, her fingers pointed towards him.

'Thought you'd come,' she murmured as he lowered his face to hers. 'I've got a little something put by in one of the stables where we won't be disturbed.'

'I want more than a "little something",' Ted said amorously as he tried to thrust his hand down her blouse. But Beth gave him a sharp slap, and giggled. Then, taking his hand, she put her finger to her lips as they crept round the back of the house towards the stables.

The night was very still except for the occasional call of a bird or the whinny of a horse. There was a crackling sound nearby, and Ted, whose ears were very sharp, stopped.

'Did you hear that?' he whispered.

'No,' Beth whispered back.

'I think there's a prowler.'

'Go on. Everyone went to the christening party up at the Oak. It's probably Peter taking his dog for a walk.'

They reached the stable door, and before they opened it Ted took Beth in his arms and crushed her to him.

'I love you,' he said when, after a long, passionate kiss, he released her. 'What do you say to that?'

'I'll have to think about it,' she replied coquettishly. 'You're not the only one. There's *Albert* says he loves me too. I'll have to toss for it.'

Ted curled his fist and grunted.

'Albert . . . If I see Albert so much as *touch* you, I'll . . .'

There was a sudden movement behind him, and as something crashed hard down on his head his eyes rolled upwards, showing only the whites, as he slumped senselessly to the floor.

In the dim light from the kitchen door Beth saw the face of Albert Newman staring down at the man she thought he'd killed.

'Oh, oh, oh!' She started to scream. 'Oh. Oh . . .'

'Hush,' Albert snarled, trying to put his hand over her mouth. 'I told you, Beth . . . I told you that if I so much as saw him *near* you again . . . I warned you, didn't I?'

At that moment windows above them began to fly open as those members of staff who were too old or too amorously inclined to go to the party had their slumber or love-making disturbed.

'Ain't you got nowhere to go?' Peter the gardener called out crossly. Then, looking down, he saw his cousin Ted supine on the floor, blood oozing from a gaping wound in his head.

'Oh my God,' he cried. 'Oh my *God.*'

Albert pushed Beth away, threw the club with which he'd felled Ted to the ground, and fled.

'I baptise thee Matthew Julius Carson Woodville,' the Rector pronounced in a sonorous voice as he poured water over the baby's head. 'In the name of the Father and of the Son and of the Holy Ghost.'

'Amen,' answered the large congregation which had packed into the church of St Mark for the baptism of the youngest son of Wenham's most important citizen.

Matthew Julius Carson Woodville, who had been sleeping happily in the experienced arms of his godmother, Eliza, emitted a lusty cry as the cold water trickled over his head and down his face, and wriggled so much that Eliza nearly dropped him. He was a large baby whose birth nearly brought his mother to grief. As she had laboured her mind had dwelt terrifyingly on the fate of her late sister-in-law, Julius's wife, poor Sofia. But she was determined not to let Guy enjoy all her money without the disadvantage of having her nearby to guard it, so she struggled with all her might against the odds, and she and her baby remained alive.

Vigour and strength, rather than sensitivity, plus his mother's tenacity, would be his characteristics, and he would always be known by his last name, Carson.

It was many years since so many members of the Yetman and Woodville families had been gathered together, and one of the rare times that Ryder and Eliza had stepped into St Mark's Church since the Rector had preached about the woman taken in adultery, at their wedding. The other godmother was Lady Mount, and the godfathers were Prosper Martyn and Julius Heering, chosen in the hope that they would be able to look after their godson from a materialistic point of view.

After the ceremony the doors of Pelham's Oak were thrown open. The guests were entertained indoors, where a lavish buffet had been prepared. A small string ensemble played tuneful airs in a corner of the drawing room, and from the comfort of the reception rooms some people found it amusing to look out on the lower orders drinking themselves into insensibility or dancing their hearts out on the lawn below.

The little Woodville and Yetman cousins, scampered around, supervised by their nursemaids. Baby Hugh was just about able to toddle, but sat for most of the time on the knee of his doting grandmother, who was thrilled to see her family again so soon after their reconciliation. Laurence and little Dora were not far away, dressed in white like their small Woodville cousins.

'Are you all right with Baby Hugh, my lady?' Nancy, the nursemaid, asked solicitously. 'If he is too heavy for you I could take him for a while.'

'Don't you think I love seeing my grandchildren?' Henrietta replied, hugging Hugh close to her. 'I have been deprived of them for too long. But if you *could* find my daughter and ask her to come and see me I would be grateful.' She looked anxiously at Hugh and touched his cheek. 'See here, he has a little spot. I do hope it's nothing contagious like the measles.'

'Oh, have no fear, my lady,' the practical nursemaid replied. 'Hugh often has little spots like that. Maybe the milk is too rich. I do assure you . . .'

'Nevertheless I would like to see my daughter to reassure myself,' Henrietta said firmly. 'At *once*.'

'Very well, my lady.' Nancy turned sulkily away and took her time about finding Eliza, who was standing with Guy and Margaret and some acquaintances while Ryder, his back turned to her, was talking to Prosper.

'Mrs Yetman.' Nancy gave a little bob. 'Your mother would

like to see you. She says "at once".' Nancy gave a disapproving sniff.

'Is there something wrong, Nancy?' Eliza looked at her in surprise.

'Master Hugh has a tiny spot, ma'am.' Nancy indicated, with her fingers pressed close together and by almost closing her eyes, just how minute that spot was. 'She thinks he has the measles.'

'And you told her, of course, that he did not, that Hugh does get spots.'

'I *told* her it was probably the richness of the milk, ma'am.' Nancy folded her hands over her stomach, a look of outraged virtue on her face.

'Well, go and tell her,' Eliza gestured about her, 'I will come when I can.'

'I'm afraid I *dare* not return without you, madam. Her ladyship looked vexed.'

'Oh well,' Eliza said with an air of resignation, 'maybe she feels neglected.' She turned to Ryder, who was still deep in conversation behind her.

'Dearest, do come and meet Mama. She wants to see me, and I'd like you to say "hello".'

'Has your mother *asked* to see me?' Ryder raised an eyebrow. 'That is the point.'

'Ryder!' Eliza stamped her foot. 'You are both too stubborn.'

'You have to meet, you know,' Prosper remarked in amusement. 'This feud can't go on for ever. Come,' he put an arm through Ryder's, 'I'll accompany you to give you courage.'

'I don't need support, thank you.' Ryder still looked thunderous, but under the good-humoured gaze of Prosper he appeared to change his mind. 'Oh, very well, maybe I do if I am to meet the Gorgon.'

Henrietta was busy showing her grandson off to some friends when the family party joined her, arranging itself in a semi-circle until the admirers finished their flattering remarks and moved away.

'Eliza I wanted . . . Oh!' As soon as Henrietta saw Ryder she stiffened. 'It was *you* I wanted to see, Eliza.' She enunciated the words very carefully. 'You.'

'And I wanted you to say "hello" to Ryder, Mother, and bring this silly feud to an end.'

'There is *no* feud as far as I am concerned.' Henrietta turned her face away. 'What nonsense.'

'Come, Henrietta,' Prosper said, 'you have never accepted Ryder. *Now* is the time for forgiveness . . .'

'Forgiveness,' Ryder spluttered. 'There is nothing to forgive . . .'

'That's what *you* think,' Henrietta snapped. '*You* seduced my daughter – or have you forgotten?'

'Please, Henrietta!' Prosper hissed, leaning towards her. 'Everyone will hear.'

'I will not listen to another *word* of this,' Ryder said wrathfully, and, breaking away, he strode across the room. Eliza ran after him.

Prosper looked anxiously after them. 'Now, Henrietta what have you done? I thought you and Eliza had made up your differences?'

'We have. I have no quarrel now with my daughter: she was only eighteen and knew no better. But *that* man,' she said, indicating Ryder, the baby wobbling precariously on her knee until the nursemaid swooped down to prevent him falling, 'is no better than he should be. When I forgave Eliza, I did not forgive *him*.'

'You have created a very awkward situation, Henrietta,' Prosper said reproachfully. He looked up as Guy, having seen the disturbance from across the room, joined them.

'Something wrong?' Guy asked.

'Very wrong,' Henrietta said.

'Eliza brought Ryder over to be re-introduced to his mother-in-law.'

'Well, it is high time he was,' Guy said with a laugh. 'They have three children.'

'That is *not* the point,' Henrietta said stiffly. 'I love my daughter and I forgive her. But I do not love *him* – and as for forgiveness, it is right out of the question.'

'Well, I must go and see if I can smooth his feathers,' Prosper said and went in search of the offended party.

'Tut tut, Mother,' Guy muttered. 'I thought we were all friends.'

'I am friends with Eliza only,' Henrietta repeated stubbornly, 'not *him* – and the sooner he realises it the better.'

'Oh, I think he realises it all right,' Guy said. There was a pause. Then he yawned and said: 'Would you look over there at those men.' He indicated a crowd in the corner consisting of Julius and Willem Heering and his Martyn relations. 'They never stop talking business, even on an occasion like this.'

'I wish *you* were prepared to discuss business, Guy,' his mother said sharply. 'You would have more independence. Instead I hear you've given it up – forsaken it all for a life of idleness in the country.'

'I have only contempt for men of business, Mother,' Guy replied loftily. 'I consider them a loathsome breed, manipulating people by their cunning and deceit. I am proud to be known merely as a gentleman – with a name and a title that no one can take away from me. I would not be one of *them* again for anything.'

'But what if something happened to Margaret, Guy?' His mother glanced at him. 'Supposing she had died in childbirth, as I hear she almost did? You have married well. You might not be able to do so again.'

'Oh, I think Agnes Yetman has a little money,' Guy replied, a note of amusement in his voice.

'What are you talking about?'

'Making a joke.' Guy glanced at his mother, then at Eliza's pretty sister-in-law, who was talking to Lord and Lady Mount nearby.

'I should hope you are,' his mother said frostily. 'Agnes Yetman's wealth is nothing compared to the Martyn-Heering fortune, and the Yetmans are a low breed of people.'

'But she *is* a very pretty girl, Mother.' He glanced at her slyly. 'Were poor Margaret to have another bad labour as you suggest, who knows?'

'Really, Guy!' Henrietta's cheeks had flushed and she looked shocked. 'I don't like that sort of talk.'

'But you have no liking for Margaret, Mother. You never had.'

'I don't say I have, but neither do I wish her dead.'

'Mother, *I* don't wish her dead either.' Guy, said, then whispered in her ear: 'But *if* it were to happen . . .'

'*If* it were to happen that's something else. I say you are better off as you are. Margaret leaves you alone.'

'On the contrary, she *never* leaves me alone. She watches me like a schoolboy: "Where are you *going* Guy?" "Where have you *been*?" ' He imitated Margaret's heavily accented Dutch voice so well that his mother was forced to smile.

'Then you must *train* her better, dear. You are in absolutely no position to do anything else.'

'We'll see,' Guy said and, winking at his mother, he walked casually over to greet Lord and Lady Mount, who frequently came to dinner parties at the house.

'Of *course* you know Miss Yetman,' Eleanor Mount cried. 'She's Eliza's sister-in-law. We are hoping she will come as a governess to our children.'

'What an excellent idea,' Guy replied. 'Miss Yetman is very well qualified. And how pleasant it will be for Eliza to have her again in the district. Well,' he looked at Eleanor Mount and smiled, 'when will your new governess be taking up her duties?'

Lady Mount looked uncertainly at Agnes. 'It's not quite decided. Miss Yetman has yet to consider the matter and accept.'

'I think you can take it I will accept,' Agnes said, beguiling her prospective employers with a modest smile.

'In that case,' Lady Mount said effusively, stooping to embrace her slim shoulders, 'we cannot believe our good fortune.'

From the other side of the room Eliza was watching her brother anxiously. He seemed to flit around the room like a moth round the flame of a candle. Although he pretended to be happy, she knew he could not be, subject as he was to the whims of people he professed to despise. She knew he did not love Margaret, and it was clear that Margaret was no longer as enamoured with him as she had once been.

The proximity of Agnes worried her: the talk about staying in Dorset, working for the Mounts, who lived only five miles away. She wished Guy would find an occupation. Though he lived in the country, he had no real interest in country matters and not enough to do.

Meanwhile her father-in-law was showing off his newly pregnant wife. At thirty-nine Euphemia was enchanted by the prospect of being a mother, but her health was not good and she was forced to take care of herself.

The shock of marriage and almost immediate pregnancy had taken its toll on one delicate from birth, and nurtured and cosseted all her life. Even though it was what she had wanted most in life, it seemed there was a price to pay.

Every now and then she was forced to pause and sit down, and John would stand protectively by her side.

Eliza smiled across at Euphemia, but she still looked distracted. Ryder had gone off in a sulk after her mother's rudeness. He had refused to talk to her when she tried to make peace, and deliberately joined the Heering and Martyn men grouped in a corner earnestly discussing business. When she tried once more to speak to him, he briskly motioned her away.

She felt hurt and unhappy, but she still found a smile or a friendly word for the many people who greeted her. The days of ostracism were over now that she had been fully restored to the bosom of the Woodville family. For this – and especially to Margaret, to whom she knew she owed such a lot – she was grateful.

Her mother had now retrieved Hugh from the nursemaid who stood protectively by, and eventually, Eliza joined her again. She stopped to inspect the spot on the baby's face.

'It is nothing,' she said shortly.

'You don't take proper care of your children, Eliza,' Henrietta rebuked her.

'Mother!' Eliza exclaimed. 'How *can* you say that?'

'They are running all over the place. Laurence seems to do exactly as he pleases, helped, no doubt, by George, who has a will of his own. I would like to see you taking more control . . .'

'And *I* would like *you* to mind your own business, Mother,' Eliza said sharply. She was close to tears: nothing had really changed between them after all. 'And as for your *rudeness* to Ryder, I find it unforgivable. You were not only rude to *him* but to Uncle Prosper. The two men didn't know what to do with themselves.'

'Oh, they will recover,' Henrietta said with a careless toss of her head. 'Men always do.'

'I don't think Ryder will *ever* speak to you again.'

'That won't worry me.'

'But Mother, you can't accept *me* and my children but *not* my husband, who is also their father.'

'I don't see why.'

'I find you very *stupid*, Mother.' Eliza stamped her foot. 'And I . . .'

'Now now!' Guy, who had returned from a brief flirtation with Agnes, was just in time to hear the last part of the exchange. 'This is no way to behave on the occasion of my youngest son's christening. Please stop your quarrelling, Mother and Eliza. I did a lot to bring you together. It would greatly distress me if you were to part again. 'Now – ' he looked around for a neutral subject of conversation ' – do you not think Euphemia looks well?'

'Who is *Euphemia*?' Henrietta lifted her lorgnette and peered through it.

'You remember Euphemia, Mother.'

'Oh, Euphemia *Monk*.' Henrietta's face cleared. 'I thought it was her, but I could not believe how *fat* she has got.'

'Mother, she is married and is to have a child,' Guy explained with a smile. 'She married Eliza's father-in-law, John Yetman. You know she did. It was a great romance. Everyone was very pleased for both of them, and I'm sure you are too, Mother.'

Henrietta did not look convinced. She searched her brain for something unkind to say, and at last she found it.

'You mean that old man by her side is her *husband*? I thought he was her father.'

Guy, still in high good humour, began to laugh to humour his mother, but Eliza continued to look annoyed.

'It is true there is twenty years between them. Yet they are newly married, expecting a child and extremely happy. It is simply that you can find nothing good to say about the Yetmans, Mama.'

'You can't blame me,' her mother said. 'There is little good *in* them. Now I do recall poor Euphemia Monk, never strong and always looking for a husband. Never did I realise she would stoop as low as that!'

'I find you *most* offensive, Mother.' Eliza had gone pale with anger. 'You must know the effect your words are having as I, too, am a Yetman. I can't understand what has got into you today.'

'*You* are a Woodville,' Henrietta said, in a voice so loud that a few people turned to stare at her.

'Oh, Mother, do desist,' Guy said, giving her a warning look, 'or you and Eliza will not talk for another ten years.'

'I would never give up Eliza or my baby Hugh.' Henrietta gazed fondly at the child sleeping in her arms, then at her daughter. 'I'm sorry if I offended, Eliza. I know I let myself be carried away. You must pity a poor, lonely woman neglected by one and all.'

'I'll go and get Effie. I'm sure she'd like to see you again.'

Eliza crossed the room, though in her progress she was stopped by so many people that it was some time before she returned with the newlyweds.

'My dear, how nice to see you again,' Henrietta said to Euphemia with a palpably false smile. 'And my daughter tells me you are *enceinte*.'

'Thank you, Lady Woodville.' As John quietly brought up a chair, Euphemia sank thankfully into it. 'I am not, alas, in the best of health.'

'I hope you have a good doctor – although they are all rogues, believe you me.'

'Lady Woodville.' John Yetman bowed before her. 'We have not met since your son's wedding, ma'am.'

Henrietta gave him a chilly smile. 'How long ago that seems! My dearest Eliza was still a girl, at home with me.'

John Yetman did not feel at ease in Lady Woodville's presence. He shifted from one foot to the other, sensing – accurately – an innuendo in everything she said.

Euphemia was aware of his discomfort and, rising, put her hand on his arm.

'I think we should be going soon, dearest. I am a little tired.'

'Of course, my love,' John Yetman said solicitously. 'I will call for our carriage.'

He bowed to Lady Woodville, who inclined her head and, putting out a hand towards Euphemia, looked at her anxiously.

'Do take care of yourself, my dear, and be *careful* of the doctors.'

Without another word, John Yetman hurried his wife away.

'What an *alliance*,' Henrietta murmured *sotto voce* to Guy. 'God knows what sort of monster *they* will produce.'

'Mother do let me introduce Agnes to you,' Guy pleaded. 'I think you will like her.'

'Go and fetch her then, for goodness' sake.' Henrietta gave her darling boy an indulgent smile. 'But do be careful, dearest. That wife of yours watches you like a hawk.'

In a moment of freedom, between passing from one group of people to the next, Margaret paused to look with satisfaction at the crowded cream and gold drawing room which, for the christening of Carson, could be seen at its best. The beautiful, ornate plasterwork and cornices, part of the original eighteenth-century decoration of the room, had recently been regilded. From the oval painting of Diana the Huntress in the centre of the ceiling hung a magnificent chandelier, made up of thousands of tiny pieces of crystal which, mirroring the bright sunshine outside, twinkled as they turned and twisted in the breeze wafting in from the open windows.

The Wilton carpet had been part of the refurbishing before the marriage and, specially woven for Pelham's Oak, had worn well. The priceless furniture, much of it purchased from the Continent in more affluent days before the family had begun to decline, had now been restored to its original magnificence: burnished mahogany, rich ebony, walnut and cedarwood, intricate marquetry, shone with the patina of age.

It was an assembly, in a setting, that one could be proud of. Margaret would have liked to grace it with her husband attentively by her side; but he was like a will-of-the-wisp, here one moment, gone the next, never where she thought he was or where he should be. And why was it that Guy was invariably seen talking to women and not to men? And why did all the heads of the women turn as, with varying degrees of success, they tried to catch his eye?

She saw that he had returned to the Mounts; saw the special, almost intimate smile Eleanor Mount gave him – but of course she was a very old friend – then watched as he drew Agnes Yetman from their group and took her over to his mother, talking animatedly to her all the while.

Yes, Agnes Yetman was a pretty woman; but perhaps just a little overdressed, a little too eager and coquettish, trying too hard: a spinster in the making if ever there was one.

Margaret gave an involuntary shudder. Women like Agnes reminded her of what she herself might have become had it not been for Guy Woodville.

Maybe she should let him have a little licence after all. To be seen with a pretty woman was not necessarily to make love to one.

By five most of the guests had gone; but there was to be a family dinner. There the important gifts would be made to the baby; the promises of sums of money to be realised at such and such a time. They had been made to George and Emily, and they would be made to Carson. They would not amount to much, but it was a way, neatly devised by the family, of circumventing giving money to Guy by putting it in trust for his children. By keeping Guy comfortable, well fed, but short of money, Margaret intended to keep him at home. Prosper Martyn, who strolled about rather like Guy among the prettier ladies, had already announced his gift: a hogshead of port which would mature in twenty-one years' time and some shares in the Martyn-Heering Bank.

Before dinner Prosper detached Ryder from his family, ostensibly to discuss business; but first he had something else on his mind.

'You mustn't take any notice of my sister. She is not as bad as she seems,' he said.

'She hates me – ' Ryder scowled ' – *and* she will never forgive me. I can't be expected to accept that sort of rudeness from her, and I will forbid Eliza ever to invite her to our home.'

'You must try and understand how *she* feels,' Prosper pleaded.

'What happened, happened a long time ago,' Ryder said. 'I think everyone agrees that I have done my best for Eliza and made her happy. We have three fine children. I have worked very hard to enable her to live in the style she was used to. It was this, and this alone, that was behind my determination to rebuild the Yetman business to what it once was. And I have succeeded. I will not allow my mother-in-law to demean me; to hang on to the bitterness which made my wife so unhappy and may well do so again. Eliza saw her mother against my wishes. I said she should agree to see us both, but Eliza persuaded me differently. Now her mother insults me in my brother-in-law's home. I tell you I will not lay myself open like that again.'

'Dear friend, try and be generous when Henrietta is uncharitable,' Prosper urged. 'You will be rewarded, I promise you.' Prosper briefly touched his arm and then, as they resumed their walk, he said: 'Your business acumen has impressed me and my colleagues. Your work is of high quality and renowned. However, I'm sure that a man like you has ambition to go even further than you have already. For instance, we have great opportunities for investment.'

Ryder seemed surprised.

'I assure you,' he said, 'I know nothing about the City. My business is on a very much smaller scale. I would feel quite out of place dressed in a frock coat all day and walking to work wearing a top hat.'

'I am not asking you to be there *all* the time,' Prosper said jocularly. 'In fact you need come up no more than two or three times a year . . .'

'Oh . . .' Ryder drew on the Havana cigar Prosper had thoughtfully provided him with and stared down at the ground.

'My company is anxious to extend its own interests into the building industry . . .' Prosper continued.

'I have plenty of work . . .'

'But wouldn't you be interested in expansion?'

Ryder stopped and looked at Prosper.

'In a way, I would. I am ambitious, and I have enlarged my father's business in the years I have been in charge.'

'I know that.' Prosper put a hand on his shoulder. 'And I have admired it because you have done it virtually by yourself. What do your brothers do?' He looked at him curiously.

'My brothers are professional men – one a lawyer, the other a banker. They have ample money of their own. In addition to what they earn, father settled on each of them a considerable sum when they married which they have invested wisely. I am not close to my brothers – our interests diverge – and the families do not see much of one another. However, they are still on the board of the company and are entitled to a share of the profits.'

'Maybe we could change the structure of Yetman's?' Prosper suggested.

'How do you mean?'

'Buy them out so that *you* are in sole control.'

'Oh, we don't need to do that.' Ryder waved his cigar

dismissively in the air. 'It would cause more trouble than leaving them where they are, because they would begin to suspect something is amiss. I'll give your proposals some thought, Prosper. I'll discuss them with my wife.'

Eighteen people sat down to dinner round the long table in the rococo style which had been purchased, along with other pieces of furniture, by an eighteenth-century Woodville ancestor from the workshops of Thomas Chippendale in St Martin's Lane. Guy Woodville sat at one end, his lady at the other. Between them were six elaborate silver candlesticks, each holding lighted candles, and in between them bowls of choice blooms especially cut that morning from the greenhouses and gardens and arranged by Margaret, who numbered flower arranging among her accomplishments.

The Woodville silver had been supplemented by Margaret as part of her dowry, and the dinner service, also from her, was by Meissen. The servants had been trained to serve dinner punctiliously and on time, a stream of them issuing from the kitchens as the various courses were served and cleared away. There was salmon from the Tay to begin with, consommé of beef, with roast woodcock, from the Woodville estate, as the entreé. Syllabub, fruits and sweetmeats followed, and the finest French Burgundy, red and white, accompanied each course except for a Sauternes, Château d'Yquem, served with the sweets, one of the finest vintages of the century.

Afterwards there was dancing to the overworked string orchestra, and enthusiastic revellers kept its perspiring players active until nearly three in the morning. After that the carriages made their way in leisurely fashion down the hill from Pelham's Oak to their various homes, through the dawn.

Ryder and Eliza sat for a while without speaking. They were tired but keyed up by the activities of the evening, both aware of a constraint between them, caused by Henrietta's ferocious attack on her son-in-law.

'I'm sorry,' Eliza said in a tense voice as the carriage went slowly down the drive, part of a long procession of homegoers. 'My mother didn't change after all.'

'You must not blame yourself for what your mother said,' Ryder commented stiffly. 'And people rarely do change.'

'Nevertheless I'm sorry.' Her hand stole into his and she was aware of him unbending. 'I should not have brought you over. It should have been done some other way.'

'She will never accept me.'

'Well, if she doesn't I won't see her any more. It's as simple as that.'

'You should not have gone in the first place. I did warn you.'

For a while Eliza sat silently looking out of the carriage window at the landscape shimmering peacefully in the light of the setting moon. Already in the east the sky was growing lighter at the approach of dawn.

'I wanted to see my mother. She *is* my mother. There is a bond. I also wanted to make Guy happy.'

'You care more for your own family than me.'

'That is not true.' Eliza realised that, perhaps because of the tensions as well as the excitement of the evening, she felt close to tears. She rested her head on his shoulder. 'I love you, Ryder. I love you and the children best of all, and if you desire it I will not see my mother again, until she improves her temper and her attitude towards you.'

'My darling,' he murmured, 'I know how much that sacrifice means to you.'

'But I will do it, to show you just who is the most important person in my life.'

She turned to him and their embrace lasted some moments, lulled as they were by the even pace of the horses trotting towards Wenham. It was as well that they knew their way, for the weary coachman dozed in his seat.

Eliza murmured into Ryder's shoulder: 'I feel very, very happy now.'

'I'm happy too,' he sighed, and leaned back against the seat. 'We have cleared the air, my darling. By the way –' he looked at her with a smile ' – Prosper has made a business suggestion to me that I find quite attractive.'

'Oh?' Eliza smiled lazily at him. 'Is he going to build a house? I had heard that he wanted a country residence.'

'It's better than that. He wants me to be a partner.'

'Oh!' Slowly Eliza withdrew her hand and stared straight in front of her. 'You refused, of course.'

'No, as a matter of fact I didn't. But I said I would consult you, of course, before making up my mind.'

'I would scarcely think *that* necessary, my dear,' she said. 'Surely you knew that I would be very much against it.'

'No, I didn't.' He looked at her in surprise. 'Why should you be?'

'Because you have more than enough to do.'

'It is not *more* work. In fact I may have even less, because I shall have partners who will share the burden with me.'

'And look what trouble partners cause! Look what happened to poor Guy.'

'Oh, my dear, you can hardly blame Prosper and the Heerings for what happened to Guy. He had only himself to blame.'

'I'm not so sure about that.' Eliza's voice rose. '*That* is not the story I heard from Guy. They used *his* name as a baronet to get business, and then they got rid of him.'

'Well, *I* never heard that version. I think it's preposterous. Guy admitted to everyone that he had no head for business. He didn't like it and he resented it. You know that as well as I do, Eliza. He told you that story to save face. But please, dear, let's not quarrel about this matter.' He laid his hand over hers, but she snatched her hand away.

'Well, whatever the truth is, it did Guy no good, and I'm sure it will do *you* no good either. You are too much of an independent spirit, Ryder. You like to make up your own mind what to do and not be guided by others.'

'I will still have my independence, my dear. You exaggerate too much. *I* shall be in charge of Yetman's, but I will have more money to spend on expansion. My partners will expect to be consulted, but I will still be in control.'

'Well, I'm against it,' Eliza said flatly.

'That is just because you are annoyed about your brother.

He is your flesh and blood after all – more important to you than I am, obviously.'

'Ryder!' In the dim light of dawn she stared at him aghast. 'How can you possibly make a statement like that? It is a ridiculous thing to say.'

'No,' he said tetchily, 'I understand it. You grew up together . . . I didn't realise how badly you felt about the treatment of Guy.'

'I feel badly because there is much good in my brother, whatever people say. Guy is a gentleman. He is a gentle, kind person – look how anxious he was to make up with me. He was humiliated by those men of business, who, after all, have nothing to do with our family, the Heerings and the Martyns.'

'Nonsense, Eliza! The Martyns are your mother's brothers. They *have* something to do with your family.'

'I meant to say the Woodvilles . . .'

'Oh the "aristocracy"!' Ryder said with a slight sneer. 'The people who ground the faces of folk like mine into the mud, who lived in large houses yet could not afford to maintain them. I see whom you really identify yourself with, Eliza . . .'

Suddenly his head shot back, and the sound of the hard slap she'd given him reverberated around the carriage.

The coachman abruptly woke up and reined in the horses.

'Hoa there, hoa!' he called, and, obediently, they came to a stop just before Wenham Bridge.

'Go on, go on,' Ryder called out of the window, his hand nursing his stinging cheek. He then drew the window up and sat back, gazing angrily in front of him. Eliza too stared straight ahead, as if in a state of shock.

But she could not apologise. She dared not. Yet, even as they proceeded in frosty silence towards the house, she didn't quite know why she had acted as she did, or what demon had driven her to do it.

As soon as the coach stopped in front of the house Ryder, who had the door half open, jumped out. With a stony face he put out his hand to help Eliza, and she had just reached the ground when there was a terrible commotion from the side of the house and, to the astonishment of her employers, Beth rushed round, fully clothed, her hands to her cheeks, shrieking at the top of her voice.

'Oh, ma'am, sir,' she cried, sinking dramatically to the ground, 'something terrible has happened. Poor Ted has been attacked and left for dead.'

'Where is he?' Ryder demanded.

'In the kitchen, sir. On the floor, breathing his last.' Beth, her cheeks streaked with tears, looked piously towards heaven.

'Fetch the doctor quickly,' Ryder commanded the coachman. Then he turned to Eliza. 'Come, we must see what has happened. Maybe it is not too late to save him.'

Half dragging the hysterical maid between them, they took her round to the kitchen door, while the coachman set off to fetch Dr Hardy, who lived on the far side of the town.

The kitchen presented a scene of confusion and chaos, for all the servants had been raised from their slumbers by the rumpus which had, apparently, occurred not too long before in the grounds of the house.

Cook in her flannel nightdress was bending over the supine form of Ted, who had been laid on a blanket on the floor, while one of the scullerymaids, not immune to his manly charms, held his head tenderly in her arms. This infuriated Beth, who made to fly at her until restrained by Eliza. Attention also had to be paid to the parlourmaid, who had swooned and was being revived in her chair by Eliza's personal maid, who seemed to be one of the few to have kept her head in the affair. From upstairs could be heard the screams of the children, who had also been disturbed, but Eliza was told that Nancy, the head nursemaid, was already pacifying them. One of the gardeners, who slept over the stables, was trying to fan to life the embers of the fire in the grate, while the head housemaid was endeavouring to boil the kettle with little success.

'Goodness me.' Eliza, having transferred Beth to the restraining arms of the bewildered footman, dropped to her knees on the cold stone floor beside Ted. She gently drew up one of his lids and inspected his eyes closely. To her relief his pupil immediately appeared, and momentarily Ted seemed to recognise her before losing consciousness again. From his mouth issued a thick trickle of blood which had already stained his shirt and dribbled on to the floor. His hair was matted as though he had been hit with a blunt instrument, and there was a deep wound from the top of his right eye to beyond his ear.

Frantic with grief, Beth struggled free and threw herself full length on the floor beside Ted. Clasping his legs, she moaned: ''E's gone, ma'am. 'E's gone.'

'He has *not* gone,' Eliza snapped. 'Now get up and pull yourself together, you silly girl. Get me a bowl of hot water and a clean cloth. He has concussion and, I hope, little else.'

In fact the wound was more superficial than at first seemed to be the case. Eliza thought the doctor would confirm concussion and a deep but superficial scar. Hopefully Ted's skull was not broken.

The doctor, who came within a remarkably short space of time, confirmed her diagnosis and commended her nursing skills.

'Don't forget I am a mother of three *and* had a boisterous brother,' Eliza said with a strained smile. 'Will he be all right?'

'Oh, he'll recover, ma'am,' the doctor said, getting to his feet. 'A couple of days in a warm bed and he will be as right as rain. But who is the one who perpetrated this foul deed? He must be caught and punished.'

Eliza looked at Beth, who gazed at the floor. But Peter, the gardener, told them what he knew.

He had been asleep when he heard voices raised in anger and then the sounds of a struggle. He heard a grunt, looked out of the window and saw a figure running through the wood at the back of the house while, just below him, Ted lay slumped on the ground.

When he had finished his story, Dr Hardy looked grimly at Ted and said: 'Then *he* must know who did it.'

'*She* was there, zur.' Peter looked sideways at Beth. 'She was skulking in the shadows too . . .'

'Beth!' Eliza said in an authoritative voice, rising to her feet. 'Tell us at once who it was.'

'Oh, ma'am, I durst not,' Beth said, quaking and burying her face in her hands. ''E will kill me.'

'*I* will kill you if you don't,' Ryder snarled, 'or, rather, it will be back to Farmer Frith. I'm sure *he* would welcome your return . . .'

'Oh, sir.' By now Beth was shaking all over, but seemed too numb to speak.

''Twas Albert Newman if you want to know,' Peter said in a surly voice. 'I'd know him anywhere.'

Albert was immediately arrested and taken to the Baker's Arms, which also served as a magistrates' court. He was locked in a bedroom for the night and guarded by one of the strong McQueen brothers in case his temper should make him lose control again.

But there was no fear of that. Poor Albert was too upset, too humbled, because he knew that he had ruined his life, and not just as far as Beth was concerned. His strict Methodist father would allow no brawling son who had dishonoured the family name to carry on the business started over a hundred years before.

The following day the temporary court held on the first floor of the Baker's Arms was thronged with people all agog at the spectacle. The magistrate, Mr Leach, who was also the verger of St Mark's, sent him for trial at the County Court and Albert was taken to Dorchester in chains.

A few weeks later Albert was sentenced to eighteen months' hard labour at a trial which only his sorrowing father and Ted, who had to give evidence against him, attended.

Ted was a reluctant witness, loath to help send down a man who had once been a friend. But their love for the same woman had put paid to their friendship, and there was only one winner.

It was nightfall when Ted returned, having journeyed to Dorchester on horseback along the narrow lanes and bridle paths which, as a countryman born and bred, he knew so well.

Lights burned in the big house, but the stables were in darkness and so would be his room over them. He dreaded the thought of spending the night there, for he was certain he would be haunted by the memory of Albert's face as he was taken down to the cells.

As Ted wearily dismounted, there was a movement in the shadows, and fearing some act of vengeance – though he knew not from where – he covered his head with his hands to protect himself.

''Tis only I,' Beth said shyly, emerging into the moonlight.

'You startled me,' Ted said gruffly, and then he led his horse into the stables and lit the lamp before starting to feed it and rub it down.

'Mistress sent me.' Beth followed him and, in the light of the newly lit lamp, he saw that her face was pale.

'*Mrs Yetman* sent you?' asked Ted in surprise.

'Mistress thought you would be unhappy, and a word from me would make you feel better.'

'She'm a good woman,' Ted said, removing his horse's saddle.

'She said . . .' Beth paused and wiped her nose on her sleeve. 'She *said* that I was to tell you as she'd had a word with her ladyship.' Beth gestured towards the house. 'That is, that if *you* wus willing, you could be groom at Riversmead. And we . . .'

'Groom at Riversmead?' Ted looked startled.

'*If* we wus wed,' Beth said, wiping her nose again. 'There, I've said it.'

'Well, I'll be blowed,' Ted said. But he was not an impulsive kind of man – indeed, he was a little slow – and only after he'd fed and watered his horse, rubbed it down and stabled it for the night did he give her a reply.

'I'll be blowed,' he said again. 'First time I ever heard of a woman popping the question.'

'Well, it's done,' Beth said, throwing up her arms helplessly.

'You know it's done,' Ted said, a little more gently, putting out his hand to touch her before gingerly feeling his head. 'A blow well worth having, to my mind, to get such a reward.'

Euphemia Yetman, who had waited so long for marriage, found in it all the contentment and fulfilment that she had desired. Though her husband was so much older than she, he was the kindest, most considerate and loving of men. He reminded her of her own dear father.

Euphemia was, by nature, calm and tranquil. She looked forward to her confinement with a certain amount of dread, but with an unswerving faith in God and his goodness.

She knew that at forty she was considered old to have a baby, and her pregnancy had not been easy, which gave her a measure of foreboding about the outcome.

Euphemia went into labour just after Albert Newman was sent to prison. During the early stages, she remained in the drawing room doing her tapestry, her feet resting comfortably on a stool and an expression of serenity on her face. Her contractions were light and frequent. John sat next to her reading a book, but he was anxious and he would often put the book down on his lap and look soulfully at her.

'I do love you, my darling Effie. You have made me the happiest of men,' he said.

'Dearest.' Effie put down her work and reached for his hand. 'Don't sound as though it's all in the past. It is only the *beginning*. This blessing of a child of our own will enhance our love.' She touched his face gently and gazed into his eyes. 'But *should* anything go wrong, I want you to know, John, that this has been the happiest year of my life. Whatever happens I have never regretted marrying you, and I am grateful to you for the love you have given me.'

Later, when Effie went to her room, Eliza came up to the house to be with her while Ryder talked to his father and tried to allay his fears.

'She *is* old to have a child,' John repeated again and again, clutching at the pipe in his mouth for comfort.

'Father, you are upsetting yourself needlessly. Euphemia will be all right, but you won't. Come, let's take a stroll outside.'

'Oh no, I couldn't do that,' John protested, 'in case she needs me.'

'When we come back it will all be over.' Ryder looked out of the window and saw the doctor hurrying up the path. 'See, here's Dr Hardy.'

He went to the door but found that Eliza had already gone to greet the doctor and was talking quietly to him in the porch.

'Is anything wrong?' Ryder enquired in a low voice after he had joined them.

'She is *very* weak and distressed. I asked the doctor if he had forceps.'

'It may not be necessary,' the doctor said, patting his bag. 'Come, Mrs Yetman.'

'I thought I'd take Father out . . .'

'Good idea,' Eliza said, looking over her shoulder at Ryder as she mounted the stairs behind the doctor. Then, appearing to have second thoughts, she silently shook her head.

'Is everything all right?' John Yetman asked anxiously when Ryder returned to the drawing room.

'Of course, Father, have a whisky,' Ryder said, going over to the cabinet and pouring out a large measure for each of them.

Upstairs, after examining Euphemia, the doctor opined that everything was in order. But after he had listened to her heart through his stethoscope he seemed less happy, though none of this was discernible to Euphemia, who seemed almost insensible to what was happening.

Dr Hardy put his ear against her abdomen and listened to the baby's heart beat. He seemed satisfied with this.

'We shall just have to wait,' he said to Eliza. 'Send one of the servants for the midwife. I may have to administer chloroform and deliver the baby by Caesarean section.' Then, putting his mouth close to Eliza's ear, he whispered: 'I don't like the colour of her face. It is too blue.'

At two o'clock in the morning Dr Hardy decided to deliver the child in an effort to save it as well as the mother. He made a swift, neat incision and, within seconds, drew from Euphemia's womb a girl child who at first sight appeared to be dead. She was completely blue and lay lifelessly in the midwife's arms.

By this time Eliza was downstairs with her husband and father-in-law but, summoned by one of the two maids who were assisting, she went back upstairs.

She looked with horror at the scene in the room, the midwife trying desperately to staunch the blood that issued from the open wound; the inert child now lying in the arms of the doctor, who had inserted a tube down its throat and was sucking hard.

'You must baptise this child,' he said to Eliza between mouthfuls of air. 'There is no time to send for the Rector.'

Without a word Eliza took a little water from one of the jugs in the room and put it in a cup. Then, though she was trembling and could hardly speak, she poured the water over the head of the new-born infant, naming her Constance. The doctor then placed the child in Eliza's arms and, going over to the bed, began to stitch up the hole in Euphemia's belly.

Eliza cradled the baby and hugged her to her.

'Live, *live*, little one,' she murmured, wishing with all her heart that she had the power to work a miracle. The water from the baptism was still on the tiny furrowed brow and, tenderly, she wiped it off. Then, forgetting everything else that was happening in the room, she sat on a chair with her back to the bed, hugging the baby and, softly, she began to croon to it.

After a while, though it seemed almost fanciful to imagine it, she thought she observed the baby's eyes flicker; and then she knew they had. The tiny wrinkled hands were moving as though the baby were trying to stiffen her fingers, and suddenly she coughed and spluttered and began to cry.

The doctor turned round, a look of astonishment on his face; the midwife gave a cry of joy.

But for poor Euphemia it was too late.

14

Agnes Yetman awoke with a start to hear birds singing. She rubbed her eyes, but it was still dark. The sounds were coming from the grounds of Moreton Park, home of Lord and Lady Mount.

'Quick,' Agnes whispered, pushing the man slumbering beside her. 'It is already morning. You must go!'

'Mmmm,' Guy Woodville murmured, too sleepy to move, but then his arm encircled Agnes's waist and drew her down to the bed again. 'Too late if the birds have started to sing.'

'But you can't stay *here*!'

'I am safer here than creeping through the house when the servants are about. Then some time in the morning I'll saunter forth and no one will be any the wiser.'

'You might be seen *then*.'

'My dear little girl,' Guy said, sliding his hand between her thighs, 'don't be always worrying about what *might* happen. Let us enjoy what is left of the night.'

As always she was overwhelmed by his demands, and, as always, she gave in, putty in his hands. He was her first and only lover, and for the last three years she had been in thrall to him. Those years had coincided with her time as governess to Laetitia, the youngest daughter of Lord and Lady Mount. They had been the most exciting, the most dangerous, the most rapturous of her life.

Guy had become her lover shortly after she had assumed her position of responsibility in the household. It had not been easy. Not only did his wife keep a close watch on him, but the Mount house was full of servants, few of whom were particularly well disposed towards Agnes, whose manner was haughty and distant.

She knew what the servants thought about governesses, who were usually poverty-stricken members of the genteel classes. In her opinion she was too good to be one. She had money and if not born a lady she had been brought up as one. Her father had paid for her to be well educated. Except for Ryder, she and her brothers spoke the Queen's English, their Dorset vowels erased by good schooling. It was just sheer bad luck that, with so much going for her, she had not found her place in the marriage market.

Agnes Yetman had been enamoured of Guy Woodville since she was a young girl and had seen him riding through the town in his scarlet coat after a day's hunting. He was then about nineteen and she was five years younger. He was now thirty-four and she was thirty.

Snatching opportunities to meet was so difficult that it added a spice to their relationship, which was one of the reasons it had lasted so long.

On this occasion Guy was supposed to be in London, on a flying visit – this time not supervised by Margaret – to see his tailor. Margaret still permitted visits to the tailor, the shirtmaker, the bootmaker and hatter, though if possible she liked these visits to coincide with a time when she was able to travel up with him too. Then she would visit her dressmaker and milliner, her furrier and jeweller.

But all the children had the measles, Carson particularly badly, and Margaret, the good mother, had not wished to leave them. Guy did his business in record time and stopped off in Blandford on the way back, booked a room at the Crown Hotel and hired himself a horse. He had left the horse at the local inn in the village of Moreton and walked the two miles to Moreton Park. He had loitered near the house until after dark and a light came on in Agnes's room.

It was all very difficult and exciting. It was the spice of life. But for Agnes it was getting too much. Guy had initiated her into the delights of love, but one couldn't live on love alone. She had wanted more, and what she wanted above anything else was to be Lady Woodville. She thought she deserved it. Everyone knew Guy didn't love his wife and she no longer loved him. Moreover, she treated him like a child, kept him constantly short of money, which was why he enjoyed these boyish escapades.

As Guy lay on top of her, his heart thudding against hers, she wriggled uncomfortably beneath him.

'Guy . . .' she began.

'I know, my dearest.' He slid off her and drew the bedclothes over his shoulder. 'Just a little sleep, and then I'll go.'

'It isn't *that*, Guy.' Agnes's tone was querulous. 'I just can't go on like this. The Mounts . . .'

'The Mounts haven't found out yet, and why should they?'

'We can't go on *for ever*.'

'I don't see why not.' Thoroughly awake now and a bit irritated, he put his arms behind his head and gazed at the ceiling. 'All right then, if you're tired of me tell me.'

'It's not *that* . . .'

'Then what is it?' By now it was daylight, and he looked at his watch by the side of the bed. Maybe he could creep out of the house without being seen and get away from this tiresome woman. They were all the same. It always came down to marriage in the end. Maybe Agnes had made the mistake of thinking he loved her more than he did, equating passion with love. He would have breakfast in Blandford and then go to the station to await collection. He was supposed to be arriving from London in the afternoon.

Actually he was a little tired of these escapades. In a way they were becoming more dangerous, and Agnes was turning into a shrew. Nag, nag, nag . . . Better use her continual complaining as an excuse to break with her altogether.

'Right,' he said, sweeping back the bedclothes and swinging his feet on to the floor. 'I'll chance it.'

'Don't be silly, Guy.' She put a restraining hand on his arm.

'I can't bear all this nagging, Agnes. You might as well know. My wife is a nag and you are a nag. It is a bit too much.'

'I only nag because I *love* you, Guy,' she pouted, feeling a little frightened. If she lost him . . . '*If* we were married it would be very different.' She paused as if wondering whether to continue. 'I *do* have money, Guy. I don't think you realise that.'

'My dear!' Guy exclaimed, walking naked across the room to where he had left his clothes. It was freezing cold in the bedroom and he hurriedly shrugged on his shirt and coat. The huge modern Palladian-style house had been built with the latest central heating system, but only downstairs. It was considered that the English upper classes like to keep a cold bedroom.

He sat on the chair and pulled on his socks. Opposite him Agnes sat up in bed, her small neat breasts appearing over the top of the sheets. It excited, but slightly repelled him. He'd never seen Margaret naked. If Agnes really were a lady she couldn't behave in this manner. Fancy considering herself good enough to be his wife! He thought the fact that his sister had married her brother sometimes gave Agnes delusions of grandeur. Guy liked Ryder, but he considered him a rustic all the same – no fit spouse for a Woodville.

'It's not a question of *money*,' he said roughly. 'I am married to Margaret and we have three children. Marriage is an institution, and I approve of institutions. It is the fabric of society. I couldn't divorce Margaret and marry you even if I wanted to.'

'And *do* you?' She seemed on the verge of tears, and her voice quivered.

'Of course, dearest.' He went over to her and sat on the bed to give her a kiss. 'Other things being equal I would.' His hand rubbed her nipple and then he squashed it flat against her chest.

'Ouch!' she cried indignantly, 'that *hurt*. *If* you wish to marry me . . .'

'Let's talk about it when we meet again,' Guy said. 'I'll give the matter some serious thought.'

He then shrugged on his topcoat and, with a finger to his lips, gently opened the door and stole silently down the corridor of the huge house.

Sally was the housemaid who was always first up in the morning to light the fires and clean the grates. She stole into the bedrooms of the master and the mistress, then into the children's rooms, but she was never allowed into the bedroom of Miss Yetman. Sally knew why.

If she had seen Sir Guy Woodville creep out of it once, she had seen him a dozen times in the past few years. She knew quite well who he was because he came to dinner with his wife, and though his children were younger than the Mount children, in the summer he would bring his family over and they would play on the lawn, sometimes with his sister's children, or be taken rowing on the lake.

In common with the rest of the staff, Sally didn't like Miss Yetman, yet she was a little in awe of her. The staff all knew about Sir Guy's visits because Sally was not one to keep explosive information of this sort to herself. Even that high and mighty eminence, the butler, knew. He had a direct line to Lord and Lady Mount, but he had warned the staff that the scandalous conduct of the governess must never reach the ears of their employers. Lady Mount was a gentlewoman through and through, her father an earl, and the shock might well kill her. Though they would have liked to inform on the governess, with her airs and graces, and have her ignominiously dismissed, they were all fond of her ladyship and could not risk upsetting her.

As Sir Guy went to the door that led to the servants' staircase Sally, who had just emerged from the room of Laetitia Mount, Miss Yetman's pupil, flattened herself against the wall and stayed there, scarcely daring to breathe, until he had opened the door and disappeared.

Eleanor Mount was a pretty, graceful woman in her mid-forties, the mother of four, and a loyal and loving wife. She was a woman of some distinction. She could draw, sing and play the piano, some said almost to a professional standard. Her watercolours had been exhibited in London and had been favourably compared to the works of distinguished contemporary artists.

Her husband, the first Baron Mount, was fifty years old, and had recently been appointed a circuit judge following a career as a successful barrister. He had commanded high fees, and there was money in his family and hers, so the Mounts lacked for nothing. They were a close and, to all appearances, happy family.

As a circuit judge Lord Mount was often away from home, and once the three boys were all at boarding school he would sometimes take his wife with him. As he sat at the various Assizes Lady Mount would get out her easel and watercolours, or even pencil and paper, and while away the time in the countryside surrounding whichever county town they happened to be in.

The Mounts felt very confident about leaving their treasured only daughter to the care of Miss Yetman, that pleasant, reliable girl who had come to them three years before. They treated her as one of the family, an elder daughter of the house. They were aware that the staff considered her a bit uppish but they attributed this to the fact that maybe her upbringing had not been as liberal as theirs, when one was taught to value the services of staff, to treat them courteously at all times and never to regard them with contempt.

Gifted and pleasant though Miss Yetman was, she had not the same leisured, affluent, cultured and upper-class background as Eleanor and Geoffrey Mount and they made allowances for it.

Lord Mount was away on circuit, the boys were at their schools, but Eleanor had stayed at home because, with the summer approaching, there would, as always, be a lot to do in the house. The Mounts loved entertaining and, besides, Eleanor, in addition to her other accomplishments, was a keen gardener. At this time of year, the end of the winter and beginning of spring, she preferred being at home to travelling around with her husband.

When her husband was away she usually took breakfast with nine-year-old Laetitia before lessons began. When the judge was at home he and she breakfasted alone. Otherwise family meals, which included Agnes, were usually the rule. Frequently there were guests for dinner in the evening; sometimes the Woodvilles, sometimes the Sudburys or the Abbots, or Eliza and Ryder Yetman, Agnes's brother.

It was a delightful way of life lived in the midst of a most tranquil and beautiful part of the country. Nearby was Milton Abbey, the home of the Hambros, and not far away was magnificent Kingston Lacy where the Bankes family, who owned a good slice of Dorset, kept a hospitable table.

Laetitia was a dark, rather solemn girl who took after her father the judge rather than her pretty, fair-haired artistic mother. At nine Laetitia was scholarly for her years, a bookworm. Unfortunately she had to wear spectacles on account of her poor eyesight, and Eleanor often compared her with her three handsome, outgoing brothers and thought it was a pity that she had not been born a boy too.

Laetitia never gave anyone the slightest cause for complaint. She was a model child; a good and loving daughter, an assiduous pupil. Between her and Agnes there existed a fond, rather than close relationship. Agnes was a good instructor and Laetitia a good learner, but otherwise they had little in common. Laetitia liked her own company; Agnes was secretive and enjoyed walks on her own.

Because of her undoubted intellectual ability, it had been decided that when she was eleven Laetitia would also be sent away to school, to Cheltenham Ladies' College, that enlightened place of learning founded by the redoubtable Miss Beale. Until then the Mounts hoped that Agnes would remain with them.

Eleanor was already seated at table, opening her post, when Laetitia came into the breakfast room and, after kissing her mother, sat opposite her, unfolded her starched linen napkin and tucked it under her chin. A footman almost immediately entered with the lightly boiled egg and toast which Laetitia always had and, his eyes questioning, turned to the chair normally occupied by Agnes.

'Yes, where is Miss Yetman?' Eleanor asked, looking up from her letter.

'She's not well, Mama,' Laetitia said, carefully knocking the spoon against the shell of her egg.

'Not well *again*? Dear dear, we must get Dr Brothers to see her. This must be the second or third time this month.'

The footman discreetly exited from the room, and Eleanor, who enjoyed a copious correspondence with people all over the world, thought no more of the matter and went on reading her post.

A short while later Agnes, looking pale, entered the room and apologised for her indisposition.

'Yes, indeed,' Lady Mount said. 'I thought I should ask Dr Brothers to call. You have been quite unwell lately, Agnes.'

'I have suffered from migraine all my life, Lady Mount.' Agnes passed a hand across her forehead, a pained expression on her face. 'I assure you it is absolutely nothing.'

'Nevertheless I think . . .'

'I *beg* of you, please not. It will pass. It always has.'

'I must say you've never complained of migraine before.' Eleanor peered at her closely.

'That's because I've concealed it from you, Lady Mount, not wishing to worry you. It comes and goes, I assure you.'

'Oh, very well,' Eleanor said as the footman again entered, bearing a plate on which were grilled kippers, which he placed before Agnes with a slightly malevolent smile. Immediately her hand went to her mouth, and she turned away from the table to retch.

'No, please, I beg of you.' She barely managed to indicate the offending plate. '*Please* take it away.'

'May I bring you something else in its place, Miss?' The footman swept the plate away and stood with it poised on the palm of his hand.

'Just tea, please,' Agnes said, sitting upright again though her eyes were streaming with tears brought on by her exertions. 'Thank you, Ralph.'

Later that morning Eleanor, wearing an old linen hat and an overall, repaired to one of her greenhouses to prick out the little seedlings which were now appearing as a result of her labours in the winter months.

It was a beautiful March day, the wind a little blustery, but the sun, beaming through the glass, made it seem quite hot and Lady Mount, though keeping her hat on, removed the cardigan she wore under her overall. The park was full of trees of great age and beauty – vast oaks, tall poplars, broad ash and cedar trees – and the tiny leaves, beginning to burgeon, seemed to invest the scene with a shimmering gossamer web full of light, through which darted insects in search of pollen.

Lady Mount, conscious of a feeling of happiness, began to hum a little song as she proceeded delicately and quickly with her task. The time seemed to fly by.

After a while she was interrupted by the head parlourmaid, Jessie, who knocked timidly on the door.

'Come in,' Lady Mount called cheerily. 'Yes, Jessie?'

'Would you like coffee in the conservatory, my lady, or in the greenhouse?'

'I think I'd like it here,' Lady Mount said. 'I have a thousand and one things to do, and once I go indoors . . . I really must remember to call Dr Brothers and get him to take a look at Miss Yetman. I've never known her so frequently indisposed in all the time she's been here, have you, Jessie?' Eleanor, frowning, looked sideways at the maid.

'No, my lady.' There was something in the maid's tone of voice as she turned to go that made Eleanor summon her back again.

'Jessie?'

'Yes, my lady?' Jessie looked innocently at her.

'Why do you say it like that? As though you really *do* know?'

'Well, my lady, it's not for me to say, is it?' Jessie appeared commendably diffident and, dropping her head demurely, folded her hands in front of her.

'To say *what*, Jessie?' Eleanor, beginning to think the unthinkable, pulled a stool towards her so that she could sink on to it.

'Well, it's like . . .' Jessie paused, as if her limited education made it difficult for her to find exactly the right words. 'It's just what my mother was always like when she was expecting, and there were twelve of us, my lady.'

Lord Mount gazed at Guy Woodville with an expression of the utmost severity.

'You are a villain and a scoundrel, sir. If I had the powers I'd put you behind bars for good.'

'Just as well you haven't, then.' Guy feigned insouciance, though in fact he'd been very frightened indeed by his lordship's news. That was the first intimation he'd had of Agnes's condition.

The meeting took place, at Lady Mount's urgent request, in the gracious cream and gold reception room which had been the scene of Carson's christening and a lot more parties and entertainments since. The Martyn-Heering business was doing well, and part of the profits was flowing into the Woodville coffers.

'Don't you give me any cheek, young man – ' Lord Mount wagged a judicial finger at him ' – or I will find ways to have you apprehended. As one of Her Majesty's judges I have certain prerogatives, you know.'

'Geoffrey,' Guy said, pointing graciously towards a chair, 'do please sit down, and let us try and take the heat out of this matter.'

'I don't see how you can, sir, and I prefer to stand.' Lord Mount was a large man, twice the girth of Guy, who, however, was much younger and fitter looking. It was, though, a psychological battle rather than a matter of fisticuffs. 'This poor girl has been seduced, most vilely, by you – and in *my* house. *That*, Sir Guy, I consider a gross betrayal of friendship.'

'That "poor girl" could have been seduced by anyone, anywhere,' Guy said contemptuously. 'She laid traps for me around every corner, and for any other man as far as I know.'

'She has told us everything.' Lord Mount stuck his nose in the air. '*You* seduced her at Moreton Park about three years ago, a short time after she came into our employment. Scandalous, sir, scandalous.' By now the judge's face was puce; his whole body quivered and shook with rage.' For *three* years you have been skulking into my house, sleeping with a woman of previously good character, I understand, and skulking out again. Maybe I could sue you for trespass, yet publicity would bring even more disgrace on a woman who is suffering deeply already.

'It appears that practically the *entire* staff knew of it. How little regard they had for Miss Yetman as a result, you may imagine. How they must have sniggered behind their hands at the gullibility of her employers, though they profess to have wished to save us pain. And then, when the truth became apparent and Miss Yetman was trying to disguise it as a "migraine", my wife had to hear the awful news from a servant. Poor Eleanor, what *she* has been through . . . And what that poor girl has been through, too, frightened to death, ignorant of her condition . . . Now, what are *you* going to do about it, Sir Guy?'

'What can I do?' Guy said, shaking his head. 'It's done, sir, and I am very, very sorry. I can offer no excuse except that Miss Yetman did set her cap very deliberately at me, and as I have found life in the country somewhat tedious I was easy prey.'

'She says that you told her you wished to *marry* her; that you and your wife were incompatible and that Lady Woodville was going to leave you and return to Holland.'

'I think she is exaggerating, sir.' Guy blenched at the thought that Margaret should hear even a word of this. 'I, of course, had to pacify her a little – the matter was on her conscience – but I never promised marriage. If you ask me, Geoffrey, her condition may have been engineered to try and trap me. After all, in three years she never became pregnant before.'

He gave the judge a knowing look, as one man of the world to another, and Lord Mount appeared somewhat mollified. Finally he accepted the seat that had been offered to him, his temper abating a little, and began tapping his knee with a finger.

'What is to be done, Guy?' he asked.

'I will, of course, make provision for her.'

'She cannot stay with us a moment longer – it is out of the question. I dread even the thought of my young daughter learning of the situation.'

'Naturally.' Guy drummed his fingers on his knee too. 'My sister,' he said, with the expression of one suddenly inspired. 'Eliza will know what to do. Eliza is, of course, Agnes's sister-in-law.'

'What a good idea.' Geoffrey Mount also looked relieved. 'Eliza is a very clever woman. She *will* know what to do.'

'But word of this must never reach the ears of my wife,' Guy murmured *sotto voce*. 'I cannot answer for the consequences if it does.'

'As long as the matter is *quietly* and *compassionately* dealt with, your disgraceful secret will be safe with me,' Lord Mount said in his most judicial tone of voice and, rising, he extended his hand to Guy. 'I leave it in your hands.'

'I will deal with it immediately.'

Riversmead was a sanctuary of domestic felicity and security. It was ten years since Eliza and Ryder had eloped, and it was difficult now even to think of that event, or the trouble it had caused. Their children were aged eight, six and five. There had been no more, but Eliza was quite happy with two boys and a delightful girl, Dora, whom her father idolised. Laurence, the eldest, was wiry and clever; Hugh the antithesis. He was tall for his age, well built rather than tubby, and at ease with the world. It seemed that, unlike his brother, he would never be competitive, and he was universally popular, whereas Laurence made youthful enemies by virtue of his cleverness.

Dora was like a fragile doll, as fair as her mother was dark. Both boys took after Eliza, with olive skin, brown eyes and black hair, but Dora was a Yetman, fair-haired with bright blue eyes.

Eliza had become the pivot of much that went on in Wenham. Except that she eschewed anything to do with the church, she was into everything else. There was a Townswomen's Guild which she presided over, and many charitable causes devoted to the care of the poor, the sick and the elderly. If anyone was in trouble they went to Eliza. It was thought that, as she had had her share, she would lend a sympathetic ear and, invariably, she did.

Everything that happened in Wenham Eliza either knew about or was consulted about. She could hardly walk in the High Street without being stopped by a dozen people. It was by now almost completely forgotten by the people of the parish that she had been born a Woodville, so completely had she become one of them. She was loved, and Ryder was respected.

Beth had by now been happily married to Ted for three years and was the mother of a little girl, Jenny, who was two. Beth had entirely forsaken the ways that had earned her such a deplorable reputation, and had become not only an exemplary wife and mother but an even better servant than before. She no longer went into fits of giggles or hysterics at the least provocation.

Beth had matured into a person with responsibility. She had assumed the role of housekeeper and ran the house under the guidance and direction of Eliza. She was younger than most of the staff, yet she bossed them about. She had acquired an authority which might have seemed incredible to those who had known her a few years before.

Eliza loved her and took her into her confidence over every issue that concerned the house, the children or various souls in difficulty who had come to her for help.

And now in this, the biggest crisis in her married life, worse even than the death of Euphemia, Eliza once again turned to Beth for help.

'Oh Lordy,' Beth cried, putting both hands to her head,

when the story was finished. 'Oh, that wicked brother of yours, ma'am. What *shall* the poor girl do?'

'Poor girl, indeed.' Eliza rose sadly to her feet. Crossing her arms, she went to the window and, for a few moments, watched the river rolling by on its slow, timeless course to the sea, taking with it the flotsam and jetsam that had been flung into it by the winds. It was a bleak March day and it seemed to augur a bleak future. Bleak for poor Agnes, who was about to be cast adrift.

'We cannot possibly have her here.' Eliza turned a tormented face to Beth.

'Of course not, ma'am. It would be scandalous.' Beth pursed her mouth with all the virtuousness of a former sinner.

'It would have such a bad effect on the children,' Eliza went on. 'It would get us all talked about in the town. And of course it would get to the ears of my sister-in-law, and Guy is quite terrified of that.'

'Do him *good*,' Beth muttered. 'Get him flung out on his back, I don't doubt.' The idea seemed to give her some satisfaction.

'No, she wouldn't fling him out. I doubt if she'd even leave him. She must know what he's like – everyone else does. But who would ever have dreamed that Guy would have gone after Agnes, or that *she*, who was so censorious of *me* and Ryder, would have succumbed?'

'It's always them that knows best as behaves worst,' Beth said smugly.

' "He that is without sin among you, let him first cast a stone," ' Eliza murmured almost to herself, thinking how awful those words had seemed nine years before but that now, in another context, they seemed curiously apposite. It had been Agnes then who had been so disapproving, who had told her father that she could not live in the same house as her sister-in-law. Well, Agnes had learned something from life. If nothing else, it might have taught her some charity. 'Beth,' she went on, 'I am going to ask a great sacrifice of you.' She walked over to the woman she considered a friend rather than a servant and put a hand on her shoulder.

'And what is that, ma'am?' Beth asked cheerfully.

'I want *you* to look after Agnes.'

'Oh, ma'am, how can I do that?' Beth put a hand to her mouth.

'It will only be for five months as she is four months gone, or thereabouts. I know I am asking a sacrifice of you. It will mean leaving Jenny and Ted for a while . . .'

'Oh, ma'am, I could never . . . even for you.' Beth regretfully shook her head.

'If you like you may take Jenny with you,' Eliza insisted. 'I am only asking you to go as far as Weymouth. We have had a long family conference – Mr Yetman senior, my husband, Sir Guy and myself – and we have decided that the best thing is to send Agnes away. We shall take a house for her where she will live until she has had her baby. But you see, Beth, she needs company. She does need you.'

'But, ma'am, is there *no one* else?' Beth screwed up her face in anguish. 'Ted . . .'

'Ted will be all right. He will go down and visit you. It's not far. But we want to send Agnes away before the news gets out, and you are the only person we can trust. Will you do it, Beth? If Ted agrees, will you do it?'

'Oh, Ted will agree,' Beth said as if she had suddenly become conscious of the responsibility her employer was giving her, and was even flattered by it. 'Ted will do what I say, ma'am. And *I* will do what *you* say.'

'Oh, Beth!' Eliza exclaimed, throwing her arms around her. 'You are so marvellous. You are the only one I could turn to, and I *knew* you wouldn't let me down.'

'Never, never, ma'am,' Beth assured her and, for the first time in her life, she returned her mistress's hug, embracing her too. She felt now that she was no longer a mere servant but a fully-fledged, trusted, responsible member of the family.

Agnes Yetman left Moreton Park, which had been her home for three years, without saying goodbye to anyone except Lady

313

Mount, who professed to forgive her indiscretion and still to have some affection for her.

'What you have done under the roof of people who were so hospitable to you was a *dreadful* thing, Agnes,' Eleanor told her, more in sorrow than in anger. 'But I want you to know that I was fond of you, I remain fond, and I'm grateful for what you did for Laetitia over three years. I wish you well.'

She then gave the departing governess a chilly peck on the cheek, after which one of the footmen took her luggage to the carriage where Beth already awaited her.

There was no farewell to Laetitia, who had been sent to stay with an aunt the moment the news became known, as if the susceptibilities of one so young might be corrupted by the mere proximity of the sinner.

Eliza had previously gone in person to Weymouth to find a suitable house to rent – for her widowed sister-in-law, she told the estate agent. So tragic, so sudden: a young husband lost at sea.

The agent quickly gave the news to the neighbours, who were sympathetic too, so that when Agnes arrived dressed in deep mourning, her maid similarly clad, they all peeped from behind their curtained windows to take a look.

Weymouth was a resort on the south coast not far from Dorchester, and much favoured by sick or elderly people for the mildness of its climate, its bracing sea air. There were rows and rows of detached, or semi-detached, houses which all looked alike. The people who lived in them were mostly of the lower middle class and worked in the town as shopkeepers, sales assistants, insurance brokers, bank officials, solicitors' clerks, corporation officials. With their wives and families, and possibly one maidservant, they led sober and respectable lives and would do so, uneventfully, until the end of their days.

Not so Agnes Yetman. She seethed with rage at what had happened to her: her betrayal by Guy, her ignominious expulsion from Moreton Park, her strict segregation while family councils took place without her to decide her fate.

Eliza had been the nearest, and the warmest, the most sympathetic; but her father had been chilly, too incredulous to believe such a thing of his daughter, and there had even been glances of disapproval from Ryder. What a short memory *he* had.

Agnes Yetman was a proud, complex young woman who, having gambled with fortune, felt she had lost. What name she had was now ruined. No one would marry her, even for her money, were it known that she had borne a child out of wedlock.

She felt no love for the baby in her womb, and had she known how to rid herself of it she would gladly have done so. As it was, she had to endure what she had to endure, this agony of shame and rejection, until she gave birth to a child she already hated.

As one who was, ostensibly, in mourning, Agnes found it easy to keep away from the neighbours. She knew, from the tone of the district, she would heartily dislike them, and their prying eyes and false, sympathetic smiles were a source of intense irritation to her.

She was a difficult charge, and her innate snobbery prevented her from making a friend of Beth, who was strictly confined to the kitchen and to the cold, bleak room set aside for the servant in the attic. There had been no question of her being allowed to bring Jenny.

Every morning just after eleven, and every afternoon at about three, Agnes used to emerge, warmly clad against the cold, and walk down the road which led, ultimately, to the sea front with its hotels and its boarding houses, most not yet open for the season.

It was a desolate time of year to be in Weymouth, and the grey seas and chill winds did nothing to cheer Agnes's dejected spirits. She would sometimes have a cup of tea or coffee in the lobby of a hotel, but even then she was stared at: a pregnant woman out on her *own*? Not done, not done at all. Soon she could no longer stand the icy stares she got from the other patrons in their comfortable twos and threes, the familiarities of the waiters, so she gave up taking tea or coffee and confined herself to walking along the promenade to the end and then back up through the town to the dreary little house where Beth would be awaiting her, full of warmth and cheerfulness, despite the way Agnes treated her.

One day as Agnes reached the door after her customary afternoon walk Beth flung it open and cried: 'Oh, Miss, I have a surprise for you.'

'A surprise?' Agnes's heart gave a great leap of joy. The only surprise she longed for was a visit from Guy. It had been hard for her to admit that she still loved a man who had behaved so badly to her, who had abandoned her without a single word of remorse. But she did. She loved him and she missed him. A single moment in his arms, and everything would have been forgiven, especially if he had whispered that he loved her and would leave his wife to marry her. She put a hand to her belly. Then, *then* she might come to feel affection for that *thing* inside her. But even as her thoughts ran on, her hopes were dashed.

'Mrs Yetman is here, Miss. Your sister-in-law.'

'Oh!' Agnes's brief feeling of elation turned to apathy, and she put her hat and gloves on the hall stand. When she looked round Eliza stood in the doorway, her arms extended.

'Agnes!' She moved as if to embrace her sister-in-law, but Agnes merely brushed past her and, going into the cheerful drawing room, bent over the fire to warm her hands.

Beth, with a knowing look to Eliza, said: 'I'll just fetch the tea, ma'am, and leave you two to chat.'

'I'm sorry you don't seem very pleased to see me.' Eliza closed the door and took a seat opposite her sister-in-law.

'Why should I be?' Agnes replied. 'It was *your* idea to send me to this dreadful place.'

'My dear – ' Eliza gazed at her solemnly ' – what alternative was there? You couldn't stay with the Mounts. For obvious reasons you couldn't come to us. What else *could* we do?'

'I could have gone to my aunt in London.'

Eliza shook her head regretfully.

'No, I'm afraid you could not.'

'Surely Aunt Emma didn't refuse?'

'She did. You must remember a woman of her age is very easily shocked. She said she would prefer not to have the responsibility.' Impulsively Eliza got up and, crossing the room, knelt on the floor beside Agnes and put a hand on her arm. 'I *do* think we've done the right thing. This is a congenial house, and Beth is a dear . . .'

'Beth is only a servant with whom I have nothing in common,' Agnes burst out. 'I'm nearly going mad, here on my own. There is *no one* to talk, *nowhere* to go. I can't even have a cup of tea or coffee at the hotel because people *stare* at me. I . . .' Suddenly her face crumpled and she burst into tears. 'I hate it here, Eliza. Please, please take me away.'

Eliza took her in her arms and cradled her head on her breast, stroking her fine, silky hair. Her heart went out to her in pity and love.

'My dear, dear Agnes,' she murmured, 'don't think *I* don't feel with you in your predicament.'

'How can you? You've *never* been in it.' Agnes sobbed as if her heart were breaking.

'I have in a way. I never told you before but when Ryder and I were in Ennerdale I was expecting a baby.'

Agnes gave a choking sound and her tears stopped abruptly.

'You *what*? What happened to it?'

'"It"!' Eliza too seemed to be choking back tears. 'It was a boy, who died at birth. He was not, however, a full-term baby. We baptised him, but we had to bury him in unconsecrated ground. In the condition I was in then, I could never have come back to Wenham, so I do know how you feel.'

'But *you* h-h-a-ad Ryder.' Agnes started to sob again and feebly clasped at her sister-in-law's chest.

'Yes, I did. Thank God for that and, believe me, I *wish* I could be here with you . . .'

'Then . . . st-stay.'

'I can't, my dear.' Eliza leaned back and looked at the tear-stained face in front of her. 'I really can't. Little Hugh isn't well, and now Connie has the measles. Your father can't really look after his little girl on his own, you know, and he needs me to go up to the house several times a day.'

'Serve him right, getting married at that time of life,' Agnes said spitefully, and with a pang Eliza thought how very much her poor sister-in-law still had to learn.

'Well, right or wrong he has got a little girl whom he loves. We all adore her, as you know, but she *does* need a mother . . .' Gravely Eliza looked into Agnes's eyes. 'Just as yours will, Agnes dear. Have you thought of that?'

Whether or not Agnes had given the matter much thought, she looked disturbed. She pushed Eliza violently away from her.

'How do you *mean*? You don't expect me to *keep* the baby, do you, Eliza?'

'But what will happen to it?'

'There are many people seeking to adopt children.' Agnes's tone was defensive.

'You don't mean you would let it go to an orphanage? Your own flesh and blood?'

'Where *else* is there for it to go? I shan't want it. It will ruin my life.'

Slowly Eliza, who was still on her knees, rose, and then she too went over to the fire and warmed her hands as though the chill outside had entered her soul.

'You never *really* thought that I would keep a bastard child foisted on me by your brother, did you, Eliza?' Agnes burst out, her tone so harsh, so ugly, that Eliza found it almost impossible to control her own anger. She spun round to face Agnes, her hands on her hips.

'*Please* don't let me hear any more stupid talk like that, Agnes. My brother was certainly at fault, but so were you. You were not a young woman. You were gently reared and well educated, and if anyone should have known better it was you. You were also very prudish. Look how you behaved towards Ryder and me. You didn't want to live under the same roof, you said.

'You have abused the hospitality and trust of the Mounts, and you have embarrassed us. There now, I've said it and I'm sorry, but really, Agnes Yetman, you are in many ways the most ungrateful creature I have *ever* known.'

Later, on her way home, Eliza had time to reflect on her outburst and regret it; but by then it was too late to go back.

In midsummer Agnes gave birth to a baby girl at the house in Weymouth. It was a swift, easy birth with only Beth and the midwife in attendance.

She was such a beautiful baby that Beth adored her from the moment she saw her; but when she tried to put her in the arms of her mother, Agnes refused to let her.

'I want absolutely nothing to do with it,' she said. 'Take it away!'

'It's not an "it", it's a "she",' Beth reprimanded her tartly and tried again. 'See how pretty she is. Just like you.'

'Take her away I say.' Agnes turned her head away, and the midwife, who was washing her, looked at the new mother in surprise.

Later, as Beth was paying the good woman for her services, the midwife commented on the attitude of the child's mother.

'Oh, take no notice,' Beth said with a confidence she was far from feeling. 'She'll come to love her. She still grieves for her husband, you know, as was lost at sea.'

'Oh!' The midwife, with a sceptical look, pocketed the shillings Beth put in her hand. 'You'd think she'd want her, if only as a reminder of her husband.'

'She'll come round to it. It'll take a day or two.'

Agnes remained in bed for a week, refusing resolutely to feed, or have anything to do with, her daughter. She said the baby's crying got on her nerves and Beth should take her up to her own room under the rafters.

Eliza was sent a telegram, but was unable to come as she was down herself with a severe attack of influenza. It appeared that no one else, her father or her brothers, wanted to see Agnes.

It is perhaps understandable that, in her loneliness and misery,

319

feeling rejected by her own family, Agnes should reject a child she had never wanted in the first place.

When she was able to get up and dress, she remained in her sitting room, closing her eyes and ears to the rest of the world except to eat and go to bed. In fact she ate very little and slept very badly. Occasionally she went to the end of the road for a glimpse of the sea, but no further.

Beth began to regard the baby, who was as yet unnamed because her mother refused to have anything to do with her, as her own. She had engaged a wet nurse to feed her, a woman who had just weaned her own child and whose milk had not yet dried up.

Beth used to sit and watch the baby, poor rejected little thing, and she felt a bond almost as strong as if *she* had been her mother. She didn't dare mention it to Agnes, but she called the baby Elizabeth after Eliza and herself, whose own names were a corruption of the new baby's. Eliza: Beth: Elizabeth. She used to croon to the baby and talk to her, sitting by the wet nurse while she fed her, wishing that it was something she herself could do.

In the afternoons she used to tuck Elizabeth up in warm shawls and, placing her in her pram, walk down the road with her and along the promenade. Neighbours, stopping to peek at the infant, would ask about the mother. They were told she was not well.

One afternoon Beth came in from her walk with the baby. As soon as she closed the door she knew something was wrong. There was a chill in the house, an emptiness, as though it had not been lived in for a long time.

On the table in the hall a note was propped against a vase. She snatched it up and opened it. Beth could read only with difficulty: Ted had been painstakingly trying to teach her for years, without much success. She would protest that she was no scholar, and she was right. But by diligent spelling out she recognised the words 'Gone away' and she knew for certain that Agnes had left.

Her room was empty, the wardrobe bare. All the trinkets

had gone from her dressing table, her jewellery and underthings from her drawers.

Gone away. It was so strange that, in a road where nobody ever seemed to miss anything, where curious eyes were perpetually peering from behind lace curtains, no one had seen her go, noticed no cab come to collect her. Agnes had simply disappeared. She had gone out of her daughter's life – perhaps for ever.

15

Lally rushed up the stairs to the first-floor drawing room and threw herself into the arms of the man sitting there waiting for her. He had obviously been impatiently watching the carriages come and go in Montagu Square, because his seat was slightly turned towards the window.

'Oh, darling, darling, *thank* you!' Lally cried, covering his face with kisses. 'The *most* exquisite, the most wonderful present. *Why* are you so good to me?'

'Because I love you, Lally,' Prosper replied, tenderly enfolding her in his arms. 'I love you very much. You have become indispensable to me.'

'But it is such a beautiful gift!' Lally ran her fingers round the necklace, sparkling with diamonds and sapphires, at her throat. 'I couldn't think what Garrard's *wanted* when they asked me to call.'

'I wanted to make sure it fitted you, my darling,' Prosper said, running his own finger lightly over the jewels which, cut and honed by masters, were worth a fortune. 'I saw it and liked it so much. I thought it would be a surprise . . .'

'You are *too* good to me, too generous, Prosper darling.' Lally curled up coquettishly on his lap, one hand around his neck, the other still fingering her necklace. 'Sometimes I feel so happy that I . . .'

'What is it, my dear?' he enquired solicitously as she brushed a real or pretended tear away from her eye with the dramatic flourish that she still retained from her days on the stage.

'I feel it may not last, Prosper darling,' she whispered, her

luscious mouth against his ear. 'That something will happen:
you will tire of me, fling me out on to the street, like . . .'

'Never. Never, my dearest.' Prosper kissed her lips to prevent
her speaking the name they both knew, but which was never
mentioned between them. Then, very tenderly, he helped her
to a standing position while, from the pocket of his waistcoat,
he drew a small velvet box which he began to open very, very
slowly. Lally, a hand on her cheek, opened her mouth as if to
say something, but remained speechless.

It was many years since Lally had graced the boards of the
Alhambra or, indeed, any other London theatre, thanks to the
generosity of her protector. Prosper Martyn had removed her
from the squalor of Drury Lane to a pleasant town house
in Montagu Square, conveniently near Baker Street, Oxford
Street, Hyde Park and, most important, the shops which Lally
loved. For the sake of appearances Prosper maintained his own
house in Hill Street ten minutes' walk away, but over the years
he had spent more and more time with Lally, whom he had
slowly, carefully transformed from a pretty young dancer with
an undeniably common streak to a lady of fashion, with a touch
of class.

Lally had nothing to do all day except please herself and
her lover. By pleasing herself she pleased him, because he
loved to see her looking not only beautiful, which she was
naturally, but fashionable, *du bon ton*. He took her to Paris for
couture clothes, and to Rome and Spain for jewels. They
holidayed in Venice, where he taught her something about the
great Renaissance masters of painting, and the architects of the
past. He would rent a palazzo on the Grand Canal where they
went in the season to entertain, and be entertained by, the
cosmopolitan community that flocked to that great city. He
took her to Florence, where he introduced her to the great
masterpieces in the Uffizi Gallery, the Fra Angelico murals
in the convent of San Marco, the marble Bellini tombs of
the Medicis and, of course, the shops that straddled the Ponte
Vecchio where he bought her even more jewels. He felt he
could afford it.

It was a time for the acquisition of great wealth by those who were prepared to work hard for it, and Prosper did work hard. He took long holidays, but he put in many hours at his office, and when he travelled abroad in the company of Lally he always contrived to do business in each of the cities they visited.

By the time the ring was out of its box Lally had still not said a word. It was a single huge diamond surrounded by tiny sapphires, the whole cluster set on a platinum band. It was the same design as the necklace which Lally had only just picked up that morning. One delightful surprise led to the next. It was always the same with Prosper.

Lally's mouth silently formed the single word 'Oh' as Prosper reached for her left hand and, effortlessly, slid the ring on to the third finger.

'I want you to be my wife, Lally,' he said gravely, raising her beringed hand to his lips, his eyes gazing into hers. 'Will you?'

What else could the answer be? She slipped an arm round his neck and, to his surprise, replied with tears.

'There, there, my dear.' He gently took her head between his hands. 'Is it such a terrible thing? A sentence for life?'

'Oh, Prosper . . . I can't believe you *mean* it.'

'Of course I mean it, and the tangible evidence is there for you to see.' He indicated the ring on her finger. 'Shortly I will place alongside it a wedding band, and then we will be man and wife and this pretence can all end at last.'

When they travelled abroad it was as man and wife. Yet many people knew they were not married. Some of his Continental business acquaintances were rather shocked and would not introduce them to their wives. Lally was perforce frequently left in the hotel while Prosper went out to dine.

He pressed his mouth against hers and, his hand still on the back of her head, embraced her. Then he led her across the hall to the bedroom where, slowly, he divested her of all her garments, leaving her clad only in the diamond necklace and matching ring. He looked at her for several moments as she stood unblushingly before him, thinking how the exquisite nude body and the beautiful jewels complemented each other.

And everything – jewels, body and the soul within – belonged to him.

Without him she was nothing.

'Prosper is getting *married*!' Eliza exclaimed as she read through his letter at the breakfast table.

'Oh?' Ryder, an eye on the clock, gulped his breakfast, listening at the same time to the chatter of Dora, who sat next to him.

'She's a widow of independent means. A Mrs Bowyer.'

'Well, that's very nice.' Ryder sat back and wiped his mouth on his napkin. 'Now I must go.' Rising, he planted a kiss on his daughter's head. On his way to his office he would drop Laurence off at the dame's school. 'Why don't you ask him to bring her to our anniversary party?'

'What a *good* idea,' Eliza said, raising her own face for a kiss. 'That way the whole family can meet her.'

She got up to see her husband and son to the door, where Ryder's carriage was waiting with Ted in the driver's seat.

'Morning, sir,' he said, removing his hat. 'Morning, ma'am.'

'Morning, Ted,' Eliza called out. 'How are the children today?'

'Little 'un baint so good, ma'am.' Ted frowned. 'I think Beth will be asking for the doctor.'

'I'll go round and see her straight away.' Eliza waved as the carriage set off, and then she hurried round the outside of the house to the pretty little cottage that, in the past year, Ryder had built for Beth and Ted and their growing family.

Eliza knocked at the door and then gently pushed it open. By the fire sat Beth with the baby in her arms, while little Jenny crawled happily about on the floor playing with a frisky kitten. Beth was gently rocking the baby and crooning to it while, with one hand, she dabbed her forehead with a cloth.

Eliza quickly crossed the room and bent over the baby, putting a hand on her brow.

'She's very hot.'

'Yes, ma'am, a fever,' Beth said prosaically. She never fussed or became alarmed. A sensible country woman learned from life the hard way. 'I'm bathing her head and face with cold water.'

'Ted thought you might want to see the doctor?'

'If it gets any worse I thought I'd ask you, ma'am. It's your decision.' Beth gave her an imperturbable look.

'How long has she been like this?'

'All night, ma'am. I hardly had a wink of sleep.'

'Then I think we'll get Dr Hardy. When Ted comes back . . .'

'Ted'll be gone all day with Mr Yetman, ma'am.'

'Then I'll send someone else.' Eliza stood up and looked fondly down at Elizabeth. 'We can't take any risks with my precious little niece.'

When Beth had returned with a baby after an absence of several months, naturally questions were asked. Tongues even started to wag. However, Ted and Beth were known as a devoted couple, despite their past history, and her explanation that the baby belonged to her dead sister was readily accepted by the community. No one knew how many sisters Beth had, or even if she had any. The wilds of Cumberland were a convenient distance away for someone who wished to cover up her past.

To Eliza, who hated deceit and would have loved to adopt the baby into her own family, it seemed the logical thing to do. Whereas Beth could provide a ready excuse for adding to her family, she and Ryder had none. Besides, Ryder's feelings towards his niece were equivocal. He was a loving and, in many ways, enlightened man; but he was also the product of his age, and the baby was a bastard, the issue of sin. He had a short memory too.

Ryder would have been in a dilemma if Eliza had insisted on having the baby in her home; but Eliza was too wise. Beth loved children and, living nearby, gave the best opportunity for Agnes's baby to have a chance in life despite the fact she had been deserted by her mother.

326

As for her father, like many men Guy had the ability of shutting out unpleasant truths. He had to his knowledge fathered two children by two different women outside wedlock, and he had not the least interest in what had happened to them. He was grateful to Agnes for disappearing so conveniently, presumably with her baby.

Little Elizabeth was much loved by her adoptive mother and her aunt, however. She wanted for nothing, and as she grew older would share the education of her cousins. In the meantime Beth was expecting a second child of her own, and when, later that day, Dr Hardy came to look at Elizabeth he had a look at Beth as well and reported his findings to Eliza over a cup of tea.

'The baby has a touch of fever,' he said, 'probably from her ear. I have suggested hot camphor oil three times a day. Mrs Yewell is in very good condition. A hardy woman of hardy stock.' Unaware of the pun, he sat sipping his hot tea and took a cake from a plate which Eliza held out to him. 'That little Elizabeth doesn't seem to come from the same stock at all,' he muttered, shaking his head. 'A sister's child, you say?'

Eliza said nothing, but poured the doctor fresh tea and passed him his cup with a smile.

'But then one didn't know the sister, did one?' she enquired. The doctor shook his head with a grimace.

'What the eye doesn't see the heart doesn't grieve over,' he murmured. 'And, talking of children, what a dear little girl Connie Yetman is. I saw her the other day. How proud her mother would have been of her. Very brainy, I understand.'

Eliza felt a special affinity with Constance Yetman, because she felt she had saved her life. Or, rather, thanks to divine intervention she had saved her life. Eliza was not a religious woman and seldom attended church, but she could so vividly recall that day when she had held the dying Euphemia's baby in her arms and *willed* her to live with all her might, rubbing the water of the baptism into her forehead as though it were indeed the life force.

And Connie had not only lived, but thrived. Dr Hardy had

pronounced it a miracle and had taken a special interest in the child ever since.

'She's also very gifted musically,' Eliza said with enthusiasm. 'She can already read and, in many ways, is as advanced as my Laurence, yet she is only four. Her father pronounces her a genius, and as she is pretty as well as clever he is not averse to having a bluestocking in the family.'

'And you, Mrs Yetman, how are *you*?' Dr Hardy asked with a kindly glance. 'Coming up to your tenth wedding anniversary, I hear.'

'Yes, a big party on the lawn. You and Mrs Hardy are invited, of course. The whole town will be here.'

John Yetman sat with his head thrown back, eyes closed listening to the scales being played on the piano by his small daughter with the facility, so many people said, of one much older. Up and down over the keys her agile fingers went and then, at intervals, there was a pause and the gentle voice of Miss Fairchild could be heard either in encouragement, reprimand or explanation: 'Too quick, too fast, Constance dear,' or 'Too *slow*.'

After the scales there followed a simple piece prettily played, an adaptation of a work by Schubert which was a favourite of Connie's. The clear, pure notes seemed to strike the air in harmony with the hum of bees, the sigh of leaves, the scything of the hay in the field behind the house interspersed with the chatter and, sometimes, the laughter of workers.

Since the death of his beloved Euphemia Connie had been the world to John, who gave her everything he possibly could to make up for the loss of her mother. Accordingly father and daughter were as devoted as two people could be.

Connie's normal music teacher was a Mrs Proud who had a number of pupils, most much less gifted, in the vicinity. However, she was at present confined to her home expecting her third child and Miss Fairchild, who found she had time on her hands now that the shop was sold, was willing and, certainly, able to fill in.

However, so far she had declined to visit Connie preferring to see her at her own home. John, the soul of tact himself, knew quite well why. Christopher's name would erect a barrier between them.

The music stopped, interrupting his reverie and, after a pause, Miss Fairchild appeared on the threshold of the door her hand lightly holding Connie's. Immediately John got to his feet and went over to greet her.

'It is *very* good of you to come, Miss Fairchild' he said extending a hand. 'Good of you to take the trouble; but, as Connie has the slightest touch of a cold I felt that . . .'

'Oh it's *no* trouble at all to see dear Constance.' Miss Fairchild beamed delightedly taking the hand of the brother of her erstwhile suitor. 'And very nice to see *you* again, Mr Yetman. After a long time,' she murmured hesitantly.

'Indeed,' he shifted his feet awkwardly. 'Won't you run into the house and get your shawl, Connie?' he asked anxiously. 'You are supposed to stay indoors you know.'

'But Papa it's so *warm* . . .' Connie protested.

'Do as I say, dear,' he said a little sternly and, like the obedient daughter she was, she ran off, both of the adults following her with their eyes.

'I'm *devoted* to little Constance,' Miss Fairchild burst out in an unexpectedly emotional tone.

'And she's *very* fond of you,' John Yetman replied warmly.

'For one so young she is very talented.' Miss Fairchild's eyes positively blazed with enthusiasm. 'Why, she can master quite complicated pieces.'

She turned, her blue eyes shrewdly appraising him. 'And yet I'm glad to find you firm with her, Mr Yetman. She is a spirited child and lack of discipline would turn her into rather a spoilt one, I fear.'

'You need *not* fear I will spoil Connie,' John said firmly. 'I know quite well to what you're referring, Miss Fairchild. An indulgent father could spoil a daughter who has lost her mother. I . . .' he stopped and looked searchingly at her. 'I have seen Christopher . . . though I suppose you're not interested . . .'

329

Miss Fairchild didn't answer but gazed sternly in front of her.

'He's bearing up to prison well. You can imagine how he repents of his past . . . especially towards you.'

Miss Fairchild seemed about to reply just as Connie appeared, draping her shawl casually round her shoulders. Miss Fairchild flicked a tear away from her eyes as she drew on her gloves and straightened her hat. 'Well I must prepare to depart,' she said briskly, 'I have promised Mrs Lamb to help her make strawberry jam. It always helps to be *busy*, you know' she said as if she were, by implication, referring to the part of the conversation that had touched on Christopher. Then, as Connie and John stood watching her, their hands tightly clasped together, she gave a little wave and hurried along the path towards the gate. 'See you on Thursday, Constance.'

'She always calls me "Constance",' Connie said in a slightly rebellious tone as they watched Miss Fairchild follow the path away from the house towards the Rectory.

'Don't you *like* the name Constance, my darling?' John drew her arm through his and they walked slowly back towards the house.

'I prefer Connie, Papa. Connie sounds more . . . fun,' she burst out at last.

'Fun!' He stopped and looked anxiously at her. 'My poor child, I don't think you have enough fun, do you, with an old father . . .'

'Oh Papa, don't *say* that.' Connie stamped her foot on the ground and her tight ringlets seemed to fly above her head. 'To me you are not an *old* father; you are a wonderful, lovely father and I want to live with you, and only you, until I am a very old lady . . .'

And, as she impulsively threw her arms around him, obviously completely unaware of what she was saying, his own arms enfolded her and his tears moistened the top of her silky hair.

After a while he raised his head, hurriedly wiping his eyes on his cuff.

'Now, my darling,' he said in a normal tone, once more

clasping her hand. 'We have a lot of preparation to do for Ryder and Eliza's anniversary. Ten years married, and a *big* party at the house. That will be fun, won't it. Eh Connie?'

'*Fun*, Papa,' Connie concurred, bursting into excited laughter and, without even looking at him, she began to skip along the path ahead of him, her arms floating up and down in imitation of the action of a bird.

He thought that, if she could, she would fly – so infectious was her happiness and enthusiasm. At that moment she was the embodiment, the very spirit of her dead mother, and the picture of her so attuned to nature, so happy with the world, was a sight that would remain in his heart until the day he died.

Eliza woke up on the morning of her tenth wedding anniversary and glanced at her spouse slumbering beside her. As luck would have it, it was a Saturday and there had been no need to get up at dawn, the usual hour of rising. She could hear the children playing in the nursery, and there were sounds of life from the garden. Ted might have taken Laurence out on his pony, because her elder son adored riding; and maybe Dora rode behind Ted, because she, like her mother, loved horses.

Hugh might be standing at the window or, under the watchful eye of the nursemaid, be playing on the lawn with Jenny.

Eliza, revelling in a sense of peace and well-being, lay with her arms under her head and thought back to that day ten years before when she had gone to the church with John Yetman and walked up the aisle towards Ryder, who was standing waiting for her. She would never forget the look in his eyes, though she had seen it many times since: love, devotion, admiration, even a form of worship. He had promised to worship her, and she felt he did.

They had been loyal and devoted friends and lovers ever since. Would God be so good and allow it to continue for ever?

Suddenly she was filled with an inexplicable feeling of apprehension, but then she decided it was because when one considered how fortunate one was, it was a little like tempting fate. Besides, her Ryder was a healthy, strong, robust man, not yet forty. She gently prodded him and his eyes flickered, then opened wide.

'Happy anniversary,' she said, leaning over him.

Fortunately she was already naked.

When they came down to breakfast there was already an air of festivity in the house. The staff greeted them with bobs and bows at the bottom of the stairs, and the children had presents for them which they presented at table. Beth brought Elizabeth with a posy and a special hug for Eliza, and John Yetman and Connie came with more flowers and stayed for lunch.

There was to be a big marquee on the lawn, tables and chairs scattered about, and a troupe of entertainers from the circus, which had recently encamped outside Blandford, arrived after lunch and began practising their acts.

There was a sword-swallower, a man who could eject flames from his mouth twenty feet high, a juggler, a clown, a negro who could break out of an iron cage into which he was padlocked, and three Russian dancing bears who arrived chained together.

The lawn resembled nothing so much as the annual Wenham Fair, when all these turns, and more, would be seen again. The Yetman children were joined for lunch by the Woodville children, and they all spent the afternoon enthralled by the many different spectacles as the various acts began their rehearsal for the evening's entertainment.

At five a troupe of gaudily dressed Morris dancers arrived complete with tambourines and streamers and, casting rather hostile jealous glances at the Russian bears, who were going through their paces with their trainer, they started dancing between sticks, arms held high in the air, to the accompaniment of three fiddlers who had also been engaged for the general dancing which would follow.

A fire had been lit by the river, well away from the revellers, over which an ox was being slowly roasted on a spit, watched over by Ted to ensure nothing went wrong.

Among the first to arrive were Guy Woodville with his

wife, and Julius Heering, who was staying with them for the weekend. Then all the notabilities of the town and surrounding countryside began to trickle in, the ladies in their finery and the men wearing their best suits.

Dr and Mrs Hardy were here; the dentist, Mr Few, with his wife and grown-up daughter. The chairman of the Parish Council had come, and all the local shopkeepers with their wives. Even Mr Newman the saddler was there, because Albert had long since been released from the county gaol, but had emigrated to Australia. There would be no successor for his father at the saddler's shop. Among Ryder's employees there were stonemasons, bricklayers, carpenters, roofers and thatchers with their wives.

His head man, Perce Adams, who was a bachelor, always on the lookout for a wife, was roaming the field, keeping an eye out for pretty unattached girls. The Reverend Austin and Mrs Lamb came with Sophie, their daughter, docile, well-behaved and very clever. The Mounts, although invited, did not come, because the business with Agnes had cast a shadow over relations between the families, and they also wished to avoid Guy.

The bank manager, Mr Troup, was there with his wife and three daughters. Miss Bishop accompanied Miss Fairchild, who still felt nervous about visiting the Yetman house because of the memories it awakened of Christopher, now serving seven years in prison for bigamy.

Miss Fairchild had recently sold the haberdashery store to a young, newly married couple called Goodison. Mrs Goodison was a fine hand with a needle and thus very suitable to take Miss Fairchild's place. Both she and her husband were there, making a nervous entry to Wenham society.

When the Morris dancers had finished their performance to great applause, the general dancing began, while Ryder ceremoniously began to carve the ox still turning slowly on its spit.

In the marquee, as well as a variety of meat, fish and game dishes, salads, sweetmeats, fruits, pies and pastries galore, there was a plentiful supply of wine, beer and spirits, and several people began to show the effects quite quickly.

At about seven another carriage drove up the drive, and Eliza, who was talking to Miss Fairchild and Miss Bishop, suddenly excused herself and ran quickly up the lawn as Prosper Martyn descended and then reached up to hand his lady from the carriage. A gasp of admiration went up from the crowd who were standing nearest as Lally alighted, dressed with an elegance that was better suited to a Mayfair drawing room than a field in Dorset. She wore a closely fitting dress of fine organdie with a matching hat, in the middle of which lodged a stuffed bird which looked for all the world as though it were alive and had recently laid an egg. Her silver shoes, extremely unsuitable for the terrain, were fastened with fine little pearls, and as she reached the ground she rested one hand on her parasol, the other on the arm of her fiancé.

'May I introduce Mrs Bowyer?' Prosper beamed with pleasure and obvious pride as Lally and Eliza shook hands.

'You are very welcome,' Eliza said. 'I am so glad you could come.'

She thought that Mrs Bowyer looked at her with unusual interest, as though she already knew her, as she smiled and said: 'I'm delighted to be here. I've heard a lot about *you*.'

'Have you?' Eliza looked bemused.

'All good, I assure you.' Despite her appearance of tremendous calm, almost *hauteur*, Lally was anxious and uneasy. She had not wanted to come, but Prosper insisted. He regarded the Yetmans as part of his family, and as he and Lally were soon to be married they would be part of hers too. But Lally was surreptitiously looking around for Guy and wondering what his reaction to her appearance would be. She imagined that Guy would want to forget the past as much as she did; that the risk of seeing him was worth taking, for to have refused point-blank to come would have looked most suspicious. Nevertheless it was with a feeling of acute apprehension that she had journeyed down and now that she was here she was more frightened than ever.

334

'May I introduce my husband, Ryder?' Eliza said, bringing him forward. Ryder was sweating and still wiping his hands on a rag.

'Forgive my appearance,' he said, making Lally a deep bow. 'I've been carving – our guests are hungry already.' His eyes seemed suddenly transfixed by her dainty flimsy shoes. 'Do please sit down,' he said. 'I'm afraid you'll have trouble walking on that lawn. It has been raining for days.'

'Oh, I shan't venture on the grass,' Lally said in horror. 'I didn't realise the party was to be outdoors or I should have worn boots! Oh!' She suddenly gave a scream and clasped a dainty hand to her mouth as the Russian bears were led past her by a man carrying a pole with which he scattered the crowd to clear a way through to the centre of the lawn.

'They are quite tame,' Ryder assured her as she backed towards him. 'They're circus bears.'

Lally watched in fascination as, at a command from their trainer, the bears began mournfully to dance in a circle to the music of the fiddlers, aided by the encouraging handclaps of the enthusiastic crowd.

In a way it was a melancholy sight – these poor old bears, their coats lacklustre, their eyes dull and bewildered, dancing in a circle like marionettes. Every now and then when one faltered he received a sharp prod from the pole.

Eliza found it a distasteful spectacle and turned away when the crowd roared approval and the trainer, wiping his sweaty forehead, gave fresh commands for the dirge-like routine to begin all over again.

The footmen, some of them borrowed from Pelham's Oak, dressed in shirts and breeches, scarves knotted round their throats, began to circulate with trays. Ryder summoned one of them and offered Lally and Prosper champagne.

'To you.' Prosper raised his glass. 'Ten happy years.'

'Thank you, and to *you*,' Ryder replied, and all four of them toasted one another. 'When is the wedding to be?'

'As soon as we can,' Prosper said. 'It will be conducted very quietly in London, as Lally is a widow. We are not having any guests, but we shall have a party on our return. Incidentally, Ryder, I would like to take this opportunity of talking to you again about joining our firm . . .'

'Oh, not *now*, dearest.' Lally gave her sweetest, most persuasive smile. 'Not business on a happy day like today.'

'You are quite right, my love.' Prosper inclined his head as if to acknowledge the wisdom of her remarks, and was astonished to see a look of acute apprehension, even terror, on her face.

Happily at that moment there came a roar from the crowd on the lawn as the man who swallowed fire belched a great arc of flame which seemed to flash across the river like a huge, translucent, orange rainbow. For a moment there was silence as everyone stared at the exhibition, with the possible exception of Guy and Lally, who were gazing at each other.

'May I present my fiancé Mrs Bowyer?' Prosper said smoothly as Guy stooped, wooden-faced, over Lally's hand.

'Lally, Sir Guy Woodville.'

'How do you do, Mrs Bowyer?'

'How do you do, Sir Guy?'

'Lady Woodville.'

Margaret cordially shook hands with the younger woman, who had risen from her seat to greet her.

'I am delighted for you, Prosper, to have secured such a charming and attractive bride,' Margaret said with a gracious smile. Then, once again, the crowd's attention was diverted by another orange arc, this time even higher and longer than before.

'I hope he doesn't burn the wood,' Prosper remarked to Guy.

'It is all an illusion,' Ryder assured him. 'Or so I'm told. So I *hope*.'

Eliza was drawn into the conversation with Margaret and the bewitching Mrs Bowyer, and Guy, putting a hand on Prosper's arm, murmured in his ear: 'A word with you, if I may.'

'Certainly,' Prosper said, knowing quite well what was to come.

The two men strolled towards the river, amiably enough,

chatting about nothing in particular until they were well out of earshot of anyone who might have had the remotest interest in hearing what they had to say. They stopped just on the far side of the fire-eater, near to the marquee where such a hub bub of noise arose that their words would be drowned anyway.

'Yes, Guy, what is it?' Prosper turned to him, a lighted cigar in his hand.

'What I have to say might distress you, Prosper, but I thought it better to tell you now, before you are under any further misapprehension as to the nature of the lady you say you intend to marry.'

'Oh, indeed?' Prosper casually blew a spiral of smoke into the air which, though not competing with the skill of the fire-eater, was probably equally expressive of his feelings, of the contempt beneath that pleasant and equable façade.

'I *know* Mrs Bowyer.'

'Really? How interesting.'

'Or rather,' Guy hastily corrected himself, 'I knew her many years ago. I am sorry to tell you that she is *not* a wealthy widow as you suppose, but a common little dancer. A woman of ill repute . . .'

'Really?' Prosper, his eyes narrowing, said again. 'Is that so? And how do you come by this knowledge, Guy?'

'To tell you the truth, *I* had a liaison with Mrs Bowyer – or Lally as we know her – myself. I'm afraid she must be got rid of as quickly as you can, Prosper. You must despatch her back to London forthwith.'

Prosper continued to smoke his cigar quietly for a moment or two, looking towards the river in which were reflected the myriad lights of the gas lamps, the burning sconces which were being lit now that it was getting dark.

He then threw his cigar into the river with a gesture of unexpected violence and, turning suddenly towards Guy, caught him by the lapels of his coat and shook him so hard that Guy imagined his teeth were rattling. Then, as quickly as he had seized him, Prosper let him go again in case his violent gesture was observed. Instead he put his face to within an inch of Guy's.

'Now listen here, young man, and listen well. I am quite aware of Mrs Bowyer's past, *and* your part in it. The intelligence, I may say, never came from her. Not once has she mentioned your name to me. She has no idea that *I* know, either, but thinks we met by chance. But I did know her. Do you remember I once suggested that you might pay more attention to your work than to the ladies, as you were a married man? I already knew what you were up to. It happened that one night I was passing through Leicester Square with a lady of my acquaintance of whose charms I was tiring. In the glow of the street lamp I happened to see you escorting from the stage door of the Alhambra the most beautiful woman I had ever seen. She had her head turned towards the light, and the way she held her head, her gossamer veil scarcely hiding her eyes, entranced me. Her presence so filled my heart that I felt like a man suddenly and unexpectedly transformed.

'But I knew it could not be. You were my nephew and I could not expect, or hope, to take your place. Not yet.'

Prosper took a deep breath like a man in the grip of strong emotion. His eyes shone with a fanatical gleam.

'Some time after you left her I sought her out, meeting her as you had that night outside the stage door. The magic returned. It seemed like a dream; everything was the same, and if she had aged a little it was scarcely perceptible. Maybe I was like a boy playing games; but I knew that it was a game I could win because I had everything necessary to satisfy Lally in material terms. In addition I could bring her real, lasting love, which you could not.

'The fascination never left, but she has become in fact the love of my life; the woman I was always looking for and have found. I have delighted in teaching her and discovering that she has natural discernment and taste.'

Prosper suddenly became solemn and pointed a finger threateningly at his nephew.

'Listen, Guy, and listen well. If anybody in this family, or neighbourhood, no matter who, ever hears the truth about this woman I intend to make my wife, I will see that you suffer for it. The news about the unfortunate Agnes Yetman will immediately be relayed to your wife, as will every other indiscretion of yours I have ever heard of. Do I make myself clear?'

'Why, er, yes.' Gingerly Guy massaged his Adam's apple. 'I *never* intended for one minute, Prosper, I assure you . . . I was thinking that if *you* . . .'

'That is all I have to say to you,' Prosper said in the same low, harsh voice. 'And remember, Guy, it will be the end of you. *Not* the end of me, because I have resources sufficient to protect Lally and myself from any breath of scandal. You have none. Understood?'

'Understood,' Guy muttered feebly, and as his uncle strode off in the direction of his fiancée Guy remained by the river bank, staring glumly in front of him, his hands clasped behind his back.

The day after the party, everyone in the Yetman household was up early, clearing up the debris from the celebrations the night before. With outside help the marquee was rapidly dismantled, and all the remnants of food and drink put into sacks and loaded on to carts which were trundled off to the rubbish tip outside the town. The grass was badly trampled, and parts of it deeply scoured and blackened to show that the fire-eater was no trickster. Not only did he eat fire, he *had* expelled it too. A miracle-maker indeed, but now he had gone on his way with the dancing bears and the sword-swallower, the clown and the juggler, to dazzle people in other towns and villages around the country with their magical skills.

Eliza and Ryder were sitting over a late breakfast watching the servants and their helpers finishing their work, when they saw a horseman approaching the gate. After letting himself in, he walked with the horse up the drive. Seeing him, one of the grooms ran over to take the bridle from the visitor and lead the horse round to the stable to rub it down and water it.

'It's Julius Heering,' Ryder exclaimed, getting to his feet. 'I wonder what brings him here?'

Eliza didn't reply but watched Julius, dressed in riding clothes, as he took a leisurely look round at the scene of the previous night's party before turning towards the house. She knew very little about Margaret's brother, except that he was a widower and had greatly strengthened the Heering-Martyn fortunes since he had taken Guy's place at the bank. 'Taken Guy's place' was, however, a misnomer, because whereas Guy had no business ability at all, Julius had a great deal.

He was a tall, reserved, distinguished-looking man just a little older than Margaret, and not unlike his sister in many ways. What was ungainly in a woman was strength in a man, and his solid Dutch looks, his dignified, erect bearing and rather grave manner gave him an air of authority, the demeanour of one used to giving orders and instantly being obeyed.

Eliza rather liked him, although she didn't know him very well, and as he came towards the door she rose and went out with Ryder to greet him.

They shook hands warmly, and after thanking them for the party he looked round the lawn and commented on the complete change of scene from that of a few hours before.

'A very efficient organisation you have here,' he said.

'Well, it *is* our home, not a fairground,' Ryder replied with a smile, politely indicating that Julius should precede him into the house.

'It was a wonderful party,' Julius said. 'It had all the best qualities of a fair *and* an entertainment. We have such things in Holland, with strolling players and a variety of acts and diversions.'

'We're having rather a late breakfast,' Eliza said, explaining the disorder around them. 'Ryder never thinks anyone can do anything without him, so he was up first thing this morning giving orders.'

'It *is* quite true,' Ryder said. 'Had I not been there they would just be about to pull down the marquee.'

'A man after my own heart.' Julius slapped him on the back. 'In fact this is just the sort of thing I wish to talk to you about.'

340

'Oh, *you're* planning an entertainment?' Ryder gazed at him in surprise.

'Not *exactly*,' Julius laughed. 'I'm planning to build a house, and I think you're the man to take charge of it for me.'

'I think then that you probably wish to discuss business by yourselves,' Eliza murmured as they entered the sun-filled morning room, where the remnants of breakfast lay on the table. 'I'll have coffee sent in.'

'Please, Mrs Yetman – ' Julius put an arm out to stop her ' – I would like you to be present at the discussions too.'

'But how can *I* help?' She looked surprised.

Julius's expression was enigmatic.

'I would like you to hear what I have to say. It concerns you too,' he said.

'Very well.' As the maid appeared at that moment Eliza gave orders for coffee. Julius Heering refused anything else.

'Just coffee for me, please,' he said. 'And *do* finish your breakfast which I've interrupted.'

'I think we've finished.' Ryder sat down at the table. 'Now what plans do you have in mind, Mr Heering?'

'I think we know one another well enough for Christian names, don't you?' the Dutchman said with a smile. 'After all, Eliza and I are practically related by marriage.'

'How long are you staying at Pelham's Oak?' Eliza asked.

'A few days. I like to see my sister, nephews and niece, and of course I have been looking at property in the area. However, as I have found nothing suitable I've decided to build. I think I have got a good piece of land about ten miles from here.'

'In which direction?' Ryder asked with interest.

'Between Sherborne and Dorchester.'

'Oh, well within my sphere.'

'I understand that your concern has grown quite large. I'm sure you're the man to do it for me.'

'And if it has a thatch he will do it himself,' Eliza said with a smile. 'It's his hobby. He is a master thatcher.'

She looked up as the footman entered with the coffee on a tray and cleared the table in front of her so that she could pour.

'I think the roof will be too large to thatch,' Julius replied. 'I have in mind a substantial house made of brick and tiled. But that we can discuss by and by. If you're interested, Ryder, we could drive over and see the site I have in mind before I purchase it.'

'Excellent.' Ryder rubbed his hands together.

'And maybe you would like to come too, Eliza? Your opinion would be invaluable.'

'I have too much to do,' she said. 'Really. But I'm flattered you asked.'

'Do you want to go now?' Ryder enquired, leaping up.

'Why, do you have the time?' Julius looked excited.

'I could *make* time. If we take my carriage and pair we shall be there in half an hour.'

'Then maybe you'll come back to dinner?' Eliza was giving the signal to the maid who had entered to clear the table.

'Well, it's most kind . . .'

'It would give you the chance to talk more business, if you agree upon the site.'

Eliza then smiled at them and left the room.

'I like your wife *very* much,' Julius told Ryder after she'd gone. 'She is so practical, yet she's beautiful too.'

'I'm a lucky man,' Ryder agreed, beginning to fill his pipe. 'Sometimes I wonder if such happiness can last.'

'Well, whatever you do, – ' Julius produced his own meerschaum and began lighting it ' – make the most of it. Happiness is short.'

The sadness in his eyes left Ryder in no doubt that he was thinking of his dead wife, and the brief time together that was all that had been granted them.

Later at dinner the two men were so excited about the site Julius had shown Ryder that they had already begun to sketch plans for the house. The offer for the property had gone in immediately they arrived back together, and as Julius had an option to purchase there was little doubt that the deal would soon be completed.

The men were bubbling with ideas and seemed scarcely to notice the excellent meal set before them. The walnut table in the dining room, lit with candles and decorated with flowers, was the setting for the fine but simple fare that Eliza had ordered as soon as her husband and his guest had set out. Home-made soup, a leg of lamb from the butcher in the High Street, vegetables freshly picked from the garden, newly baked bread, apple pie and cheese, two bottles of claret.

Julius's would be a large house – a magnificent one if the sketches were anything to go by. It had a Dutch look about it, which was perhaps inevitable. Built of red brick with gables and turrets, it would have ten bedrooms, four reception rooms, stables and outbuildings, with grounds occupying all in all about fifty acres.

'Why is it you love Dorset so much?' Eliza asked, leaning over the table to see the sketches.

'It reminds me of my home.' Julius sat back and sighed. 'It is also not too far from London.' His expression was melancholy. 'Ever since the death of my dear wife I have been a restless man, constantly moving back and forth, but reluctant to return to Holland for too long because it is full of sad memories, of her and the happiness I have lost.'

'Maybe you will, in time, marry again,' Eliza suggested, hoping not to offend him by her remark.

'If it is the will of God,' the Dutchman said piously. 'But so far it has never crossed my mind to replace my sweet Sofia. It would seem like a betrayal of her memory to marry again. But who knows . . .'

'Why such a large house then?' Ryder voiced the question that Eliza had toyed with too in her own mind.

'Well, it is an elegant house, is it not? Not too large to be uncomfortable, yet big enough to entertain the many business friends and acquaintances I have made in the City. The shooting, they say, is excellent, and there is fishing at the bottom of the garden. It is a house for a gentleman, and I shall be proud to live there.'

Coffee was taken in the drawing room, where once again

343

the plans were spread on a table and studied by the two men while Eliza sat in the background. Julius was usually grave and unsmiling, no matter what the occasion. Eliza had never seen him so animated, and she felt that probably the reason was that at last he had found a hobby, something to take his mind off the death of Sofia. When he was animated he looked quite different from the City financier with little small talk, his chief concern being money matters.

Now, as he described his new house, one saw a man of taste and imagination, and when he began to dwell on the pictures he would hang in it from his collection in Amsterdam he revealed himself to be a connoisseur of art as well.

She thought he held a certain fascination, and wondered that he had evaded for so long the temptation to marry again: there must have been a number of women pleasing enough, and eager to be his wife.

Her thoughts turned to Prosper and the bewitching Mrs Bowyer. Maybe Julius, too, had a secret mistress in London and the house was to be somewhere where he could entertain her. It was a temptation to talk about Mrs Bowyer, whom Eliza had liked, but it seemed indiscreet until Julius brought the matter up himself when the plans of the house were finally laid aside.

'And how do you like the future Mrs Martyn?' he enquired, eyebrows suggestively raised.

'Oh, Mrs Bowyer,' Eliza said a little guiltily, wondering if he had been able to read her mind. 'We thought her charming. Had you met her before?'

'Frequently. She acts as his hostess when he entertains. I don't think she knows much about cooking herself, but she presides most gracefully at his table. She is a great asset to him.'

'Did you know her husband?' Ryder asked without thinking.

'Husband?' Julius looked vague.

'Prosper said she was a wealthy widow.'

'Ah!' Julius endeavoured to look discreet. 'No, I don't think I had the pleasure. I believe he passed away some years ago.

Now – ' he started to rise ' – there is just one thing. I should have thought of it before, but it has been such a pleasant day, and I'm afraid I was so full of my own concerns that I almost forgot.' He sat down again, clearing his throat. 'Ryder, the mention of Prosper Martyn reminds me that I believe he asked some time ago if you would be interested in joining the board of our company?'

'Yes, he did,' Ryder said, with a glance at Eliza, 'and I refused.'

'Is there any point in asking you again?'

'No,' Eliza said emphatically and then, a hand to her mouth, looked at Ryder. 'I'm sorry, my dear, but you know how I feel . . .'

'Ah, *you* are the one against it, Eliza?' Julius gave Ryder a shrewd look. 'On what grounds?'

'On the grounds that we are happy as we are. That we have enough money and the business is doing well. Why should he want to travel up to the City?'

'We could do with his brains. He is an excellent man of business. I knew that from Prosper, but it was confirmed today. He grasps very quickly everything one says. It would be to our advantage as much as his. Are you *still* opposed to it, Eliza?'

'Yes. I feel now just as I did then.'

'And Ryder?' Julius looked at him enquiringly. 'Are you governed by what your wife says?'

'No, not *governed* – ' Ryder seemed on the defensive ' – but guided. It is her life too, after all. She is quite right in saying that we have sufficient for our needs, and that I can do without the problems of a large business.'

'They would be shared.'

'My brothers are also included,' Ryder went on. 'They each have a share in the company.'

'Each has a share?' Julius said in alarm. 'So if it comes to it you are outvoted?'

'No, my father has a share. We are two and two; but usually my brothers leave the business to us and just help themselves to a share of the profits or the dividends.'

345

'But if something were to happen to your father, or even to you, your brothers would control the company?' Julius appeared genuinely concerned.

'If they wanted to, yes.' Ryder looked puzzled. 'But it is not likely to happen. We do not fight. They are content, and so are my father and I. I am, thank God, in good health, able bodied, not likely to die just yet, and there seems no reason to change the structure.'

'As a man of business,' Julius said, pressing his hands together in an attitude of prayer, 'I would be most anxious if that structure were to continue. It leaves your family in a very vulnerable position. If your father dies or, God forbid, if something were to happen to you, your brothers could snatch away the business, sell it, dismantle it, or do what they liked with it. If Eliza were widowed she could be left very badly off.'

'Oh!' Eliza cried, getting briskly to her feet, irritated by the turn the conversation had taken, 'what a *gloomy* way to end the evening. Can't we talk of something else?'

'I'll think about it,' Ryder promised Julius. 'We'll have plenty of time to go into the pros and cons in the next few months if we are to build your house.

'I can't tell you how much I am looking forward to it.'

16

Ryder Yetman was a happy man, a fulfilled man. Sometimes he felt he lacked for nothing, and wondered why he had been so blessed; why had *he* been singled out for such good fortune? In many ways, despite his love for his wife and family, he was a solitary man, a countryman, and in his travels around the county inspecting his various projects and building sites he had much time to ruminate upon his life.

He was married to a woman whom he not only loved but who was a companion and partner. He had three healthy children of a happy disposition, he had all the work that he needed, no debts and no known enemies.

Why then was there this feeling, which increased as the years went uneventfully by, that there was something lacking in his life? Was it that at times his fortune seemed *too* good and something – just a little something – was needed to spoil it so that he could appreciate it more?

Ryder Yetman would never knowingly have put himself in the path of temptation, or ever attempted to cause the smallest amount of distress to his wife. Yet he was human and he was the son of Adam. And as Adam fell, so he was tempted to fall too. At the time, however, he didn't know it; nor could he possibly have foreseen what it would lead to.

Maybe it was Eliza's implacable opposition to an expansion of his business that made him conscious of her possessiveness, her power over him, and he came to resent it. It was as though she were the leader, the man of the family, and not him.

It happened very gradually over many months, even years,

while he was building the magnificent house that Julius Heering would name after his native city. Amsterdam Hoos might seem a rather misleading, indeed even comical, name in the middle of the Dorset countryside, but after it was built and Julius had moved in, everyone would soon come to realise what it was and, above all, *where*. There would never be any problems about finding him or directing people to him.

'Amsterdam? Why, zur,' would reply an enlightened yokel, ''tis foive miles beyond Dorchester just off the Sherborne Road.'

The house took quite a long time to build. Even when its shell was finished, there were a number of things Julius wished to be done to the interior that postponed the time when he could even contemplate moving into it. Armies of decorators, designers of all kinds, descended on the house from London, or came over from The Hague or Amsterdam, bringing with them wallpapers, patterns, swatches of cloth, ceramic tiles, catalogues, and ideas for an interior that would be unusual enough to rival anything in the county of Dorset, possibly even the whole of the south of England.

Of course, it would not be to everyone's taste. Many people considered it too modern. Gone were the trappings of Victoriana, and in their place was the lightness and airiness of an altogether different style, the flaccid elegance of *art nouveau*. Heavy walnut, oak and mahogany were replaced by softer woods like beech, afromosia and cedar. The interior had more of the clarity and sparseness of a painting by Vermeer. Some people liked it and others didn't. But as it took shape it was much talked about, and people came from all over the county to try and get a glimpse of it.

In the basement, before such things were thought possible even in the homes of the rich, was a magnificent Turkish bath complete with swimming pool, hot and cold cabinets and icy showers from faucets in the walls. The water came from a nearby well which was considered to have special healing properties and to have been venerated for centuries. Dorset was peculiarly rich in wells with alleged magical and curative properties, and Julius was fortunate to have secured one on his land.

The land he had bought had once been part of a farm, and when building on Amsterdam began most of the remnants of the farm had been obliterated. There were, however, one or two remaining edifices that had been stables in the old farm, and it was Eliza, looking over the almost completed property with Julius and Ryder, who suggested it should be turned into a cottage for ground staff, maybe with a thatch.

Julius was delighted with the idea. After all, this was Dorset and thatching was part of the county tradition. The architect was asked to design a cottage based on the existing buildings complete with a thatch roof. As a sign of his affection and gratitude to Julius, Ryder undertook the thatching of it himself, and promised to begin work as soon as the exterior of the cottage was finished and the roof beams were ready, felted and battened.

By the year 1895 everything was nearly ready. The decorators and designers, after quarrelling bitterly among themselves, had perfected their marvels on the interior of the house; the curtains were in place, the carpets – some of them priceless – laid, and the furniture, much of it specially commissioned from celebrated Dutch, Belgian or Spanish cabinetmakers such as Van de Velde and Antonio Sandi, was ready to be delivered.

One by one the craftsmen working on Amsterdam Hoos gradually completed their tasks and departed, until just a skeleton staff remained to do odd jobs, make a few repairs and finish the cottage ready to be thatched.

Often, after work, Ryder rode back to Wenham with as many of his men as he could take in the carriage – some standing on the outside steps and hanging on to the sides – and, towards the end of the completion of the job, he became accustomed to taking them into the Baker's Arms for a pint or two of best Dorset bitter.

The Baker's Arms was an ancient public house that had stood in the High Street since Wenham was merely a cluster of dwellings round the village pump. It was a low, two-storeyed building that sometimes served as a magistrates' court, as had happened with Albert Newman.

Ryder was in his element among working men. He always had been. He thought of himself as a craftsman, a man who worked with his hands, and his dress and demeanour showed it. Civilised he was, but no gentleman. His hands were thick and rather coarse, and he had never lost the accent of his boyhood. He had the respect of his employees, but also their affection as one of them. Any job in the building trade they could do, he could do. He could put his hand to anything: plumbing, bricklaying, carpentry, plastering and, above all thatching. In this he was an expert; a master thatcher.

Ryder enjoyed being surrounded by the men, swapping stories, some of them rather rude, and quaffing beer. Sometimes on Friday nights, when he had taken the men their pay, he treated them to several rounds and some had a bit too much to drink. Then, one after the other, they slowly went home, the less drunk supporting those who had had too much.

Ryder was a slow drinker; he had a good head but knew his limitations and seldom got drunk. On Friday evenings after the men had left, he found himself spending more time chatting to Annie McQueen who usually served them. She was a comely woman of about thirty-five whose husband, the drover, had by now left her with three children to clothe and feed. Her mature charms were coveted by more than one man in Wenham.

She had moved back into the public house with her mother and father, and her contribution to the household was to work every evening in the bar, and sometimes during the day as well.

Annie was buxom, full-breasted, but not fat. She had brown curly hair which cascaded over her shoulders, and she always wore a rather low-cut dress or blouse. There was a directness, a friendliness and a simplicity about Annie that appealed to Ryder. Moreover, in her brown eyes there was a sympathy, a ready understanding, which suggested that, whatever bad experiences others had, she could cap them with worse stories of her own. She was a woman, above all, who had lived.

But Annie was also full of laughter. Those brown eyes that could be so sad could also break into merriment. Annie, one felt, understood everyone and everything. It was no surprise that she was popular among the men, most of whom had wives with none of her winning attributes.

Gradually, over the weeks and months that went into the finishing of the Amsterdam Hoos, Annie became a confidante of Ryder, a true and trusted friend; one, moreover, he felt he would not like Eliza to know about.

Annie's eyes always lit up when she saw Ryder come into the saloon and move towards the bar. Her manner became more animated, slightly flirtatious, and gradually she moved along until she stood opposite him. As she leaned over, her full breasts seemed to be supported by the top of the bar, and the deep cleavage between them became visible. Ryder knew that, again and again, his eyes strayed towards that provocative sight, and his loins stirred with crude and impulsive longings.

Annie was so voluptuous compared to Eliza who, despite three children, still had the figure of a boy: small-breasted and slim-hipped. Annie was overtly sensuous, whereas Eliza couldn't be thought of in the same terms. He realised then that life with the same woman could be a little dull, however much one loved her. A mild adventure now and then rejuvenated a man, doing him, surely, little harm?

Ryder knew that, in his mind, the idea of an adventure with Annie was forming. It would be that, and nothing more. For a married man who had been faithful for fifteen years it would be a change, something to remind him of his former virility, the success he had had with all kinds of women in his bachelor days.

Ryder began to be wholly obsessed with Annie, and if she wasn't there when he entered the bar he would leave quite soon afterwards and not stand drinking. But if she were there he stayed for hours. Some of his men noticed it and it became a joke among them. But hadn't any number of them also cast lascivious eyes in the direction of the buxom Annie? Perhaps they were merely envious.

Annie knew that Ryder was married, and to whom. She had never been introduced to Eliza. Such a woman, a lady of refinement, would never be seen entering the doors of a public house. But Annie knew who she was. Sometimes when she was sweeping or washing the pavement outside the door of the pub she might see Eliza on the other side of the street greeting an acquaintance as she went about her errands. Annie would lean on her broom handle and gaze surreptitiously at her, because Eliza was the kind of woman that others could not but help admire, perhaps even envy a little.

But Annie knew she would envy her no more once Ryder was her lover.

Annie and Ryder stalked each other for several months like a couple of dogs on heat though, naturally, not so obviously. But the intentions were the same. They would eye each other across the bar, sending silent signals. Then the other men would slowly drift off and they would be left alone. Ryder could see right down her cleavage and imagine the great splayed nipples at the tips of each milky white breast. He imagined Annie taking all her clothes off and himself pressing against her. Sometimes the thought was so vivid that he suspected she could see it there, reflected in his eyes: that she knew.

'I hear that house is nearly finished,' Annie said to him one night, just as he was thinking it was time he went home or Eliza would be asking him why he was so late every Friday night. 'They say it's beautiful,' Annie went on. 'One of the wonders of the world.'

'Oh, nothing like that!' Ryder smiled at her and moved a little closer. His gaze travelled from her cleavage to her eyes, and he saw the naughty, mocking smile as if she did indeed know what was going on in his mind; lustful, evil thoughts. 'It's quite unusual and very modern, but certainly *not* a wonder of the world.'

'Worth seeing, though,' Annie added speculatively, moistening her lower lip with the tip of her tongue.

'Oh, worth seeing.' Ryder picked up his glass and finished

the contents. Then, almost reluctantly, he put it on the bar and gazed into it.

'Another half?' Annie said, in such a suggestive voice that Ryder could have imagined she had said something else. Their secret game was getting complicated.

'I don't think so. Not tonight.'

'I have a nephew,' Annie began and, so that no one else could hear what she was saying, she leaned so far over the bar that it squeezed her breasts into the shape of two great balloons. You couldn't have put a hair down her cleavage, never mind a finger or a hand, Ryder thought. 'I have a nephew,' Annie said again, 'who is *very* interested in the building business.'

'Really?' Ryder said, straightening up.

'He's done a bit of carpentry, that sort of thing. He'd like to be a thatcher.'

'Is he apprenticed to anyone at the moment?'

'No he's not.' Annie looked meaningfully at him. 'Now I know *you're* a master thatcher.'

'But I scarcely ever do any practical work these days.' Ryder's voice held a note of regret because it would have been nice to have done Annie a favour. Maybe she might have rendered one back.

'Perhaps you could just see the boy and talk to him?'

'Gladly,' Ryder said, clutching at a straw. Then, as if an idea had suddenly struck him, he went on: 'I'm going to do some thatching very shortly. There's a cottage attached to the big house you were talking about. I'm going to thatch it myself. As a matter of fact I could do with an assistant. Most of my men are busy on other work. Why doesn't your nephew . . .'

'And *I* could perhaps come along with him and have a peep inside that house at the same time,' Annie said, all wide-eyed innocence.

A few days later when Ryder arrived at Amsterdam Hoos at the appointed time he saw a pony and cart standing outside the gates of the house, but no sign of the occupants.

He had ridden over on horseback by himself, and with a

feeling of excitement mingled with guilt he tethered his horse to the tall new wrought-iron gates and, pushing them open, walked up to the front of the house. There he saw the solitary figure of Annie, dressed rather decorously and formally as if out for a visit – no hint of that enticing cleavage now – with her coat buttoned right up to her throat and her hat, looking rather like an elaborate bird's nest, perched on her head.

'Well, well,' Ryder said, feeling a shade inadequate now that the moment of truth had arrived. 'Did you come alone?'

'Oh no.' Annie pretended to seem shocked. 'My nephew Billy has gone round to take a look at the cottage you are to thatch. I said I'd wait for you so that you'd know we were here.'

She smiled at him, and then, as Ryder didn't move, she said suggestively: 'Shall we take a peep inside?'

'I'm not sure it's open – ' Ryder began to fumble in his pocket ' – but I think I have a key.'

He knew, of course, that he had a key; but now that she was here, and the dream was about to become reality, he didn't know quite what to do. He had not slept with a woman other than his wife for fifteen years, and he loved Eliza, he truly did. If she ever found out about Annie he knew how much it would hurt her.

He doubted whether she would be as tolerant as Margaret was about Guy. It could kill their marriage.

Ryder made a pretence of looking for the key, finding it, and when he had it in his hand and put it to the door he found he was trembling. Suddenly the cool hand of Annie closed over his and, taking the key from him, she said: 'Here, let me,' and with a deft turn unlocked the door and pushed it open.

The hall was vast and, with a sharp intake of breath, she stood and gazed at the high ceiling, which had a skylight in the roof. The hall was shaped like an atrium, and there was a round staircase that curved up three floors right to the top. It was, in every respect, a breathtaking conception based on a design of classical antiquity.

'And *you* built this?' Annie gasped, mouth hanging wide open.

'Yes.' Feeling composed, a little smug, more confident, Ryder took the key from her and smiled. 'That's why it's taken such a long time – over four years. It would have taken longer, but my client is a man who likes to get things done, impatient of delay . . .'

'He sounds a bit like you,' Annie said, nudging him and moistening her lips with the tip of her round, wet tongue.

'Well, we are a bit alike,' Ryder admitted, overcome once more with a feeling which he thought must be akin to stage fright – a rapid beating of the heart, an overpowering, almost overwhelming sense of fear . . .

He watched as Annie slowly undid the top of her coat. Beneath it, to his astonishment, her breasts were bare: two enormous orbs, as he had imagined, with the wide brownish nipples splayed across, even larger than he had expected.

'Oh!' he gasped.

'You like them, don't you?' she said and, her hands under her breasts to lift them, she pressed herself against him just as, so many hundreds of times, he had envisaged that, one day, she might. With the palms of both hands he squeezed her breasts, feeling the large nipples harden to his touch. Then her tongue was in his mouth, and he undid the rest of her coat rather clumsily but found to his disappointment that, from the waist down, she was fully dressed: a corset, a skirt and a long, long pair of drawers.

His hand came away from between her thighs, and his expression, when he looked at her at last, was so comical that she laughed.

'Now *now*,' she said. 'We can't have it all at once, can we? Not *here*.'

'*Where*, then?' His voice had a note of desperate urgency, and his eyes travelled upwards as he thought of all those bedrooms leading off the main staircase, some of them already furnished.

'We'll have to think, but my nephew will soon be back.' She moved away from him and, with practised fingers, rapidly did up the buttons of her coat again. He knew that his eyes registered their disappointment as the objects of his intense desire were ruthlessly hidden from view.

'There are some bedrooms upstairs,' he whispered frantically.

'*Are* there?' She gave him a vampish look. 'Well, maybe another time. One day you can give me a *proper* look around the house. I'd like that. And then I'll give *you* a proper look too.'

'Come without your nephew if you can,' he said in a voice thick with frustrated desire to which Annie replied:

'Of course. Doesn't do to corrupt the young.'

Annie's nephew, Billy, was sixteen. He had little practical ability and, in Ryder's opinion, little inclination to be a thatcher. He wondered if the whole thing had been engineered by Annie because she wanted to make love to him too.

So anxious was Ryder to possess Annie that he began thatching the very next week, but Billy was clumsy and held him back so, in the end, he gave him the job of fetching the bundles of old English wheat and heaving them up the ladder. About a hundred bundles or more would be needed for the roof, and although he tried to show Billy how to place the spars against which the bundles rested, and how to smooth them into place with the leggit, he knew that he was wasting his time.

Dull-witted Billy was a slow learner.

'How's Billy getting on?' Annie enquired at the end of the second week, when Ryder was again in the pub with the men after paying out the wages. Ryder gave her a look.

'I thought you *said* he had a practical bent?' he said.

'I thought he had.' Annie looked puzzled.

'Well, I don't think he has.'

'Oh dear, what a pity,' Annie answered. 'My sister will be so disappointed, though I must say Billy always has been a bit of a disappointment. Maybe she tried too hard.'

'Never mind,' Ryder said with a cheerful smile. At least it had given him a chance to feel her breasts.

'Tell you what,' Annie murmured, leaning over to give him

356

a better look as the customers began to drift away, 'I've got an afternoon off tomorrow. Perhaps I could come over and take a look at the rest of the house. It will soon be occupied, won't it?'

'What a good idea.' Once again he was overcome by that wild, irrational, irresponsible feeling of excitement. 'Shall I meet you there?'

'But how will I get over?'

He couldn't possibly take her. Even in a closed carriage anyone might see.

Such was her womanly perception and intuition that it seemed she could sense every dilemma he faced, was aware of every tortured, tangled emotion.

'I'll get Billy to run me over,' she said, putting her mouth close to his ear. 'We can get him out of the way, give him a job to do, and then take a look at those rooms.' Slowly she winked at Ryder. 'He'll never say a word. He's a bit slow on the uptake, as you know.'

That night Eliza said: 'How's the house coming on? I'd love to see it.'

Ryder felt a terrible pang of guilt, and again the stage fright, the fear that she too had a woman's uncanny intuition and his base desires were about to be revealed.

'It's nearly ready,' he said. 'Some of the furniture is in.'

'How about tomorrow? Can I come over with you tomorrow?'

They were in their bedroom preparing for bed. Ryder was glad that he could turn his back to her, because he felt she would see right through him into the dark murkiness of his unfaithful soul.

'Oh, I shan't be there tomorrow,' he said, pulling his nightshirt over his head. 'I've got to go to Dorchester.'

'Just as well. There's a meeting of the Needlework Guild. Let's leave it until some time next week.'

'It will look even better then,' he said, and he sat on the bed and opened his arms for her.

357

She came towards him very slowly, an enigmatic look in her dark eyes, a half smile on her face.

He felt that she already knew, and he wanted to get down on his knees and beg her forgiveness. He took her in his arms, pulling up her nightdress and squeezing her small, firm breasts. But immediately there came into his mind the memory of Annie's breasts, as soft and pliable as the udders of a cow when his palms pressed against them. He tried to block the vision from his mind and, putting a hand between Eliza's legs, found it was warm and inviting, moist and welcoming, open and yielding.

They made love for an hour that night, husband and wife thrashing and rolling, groaning and grunting like youthful lovers amuck in the hay. Fantasies of Eliza were blended with fantasies of Annie, the one with voluptuous, milk-bearing breasts, the other with a moist, dark, infinitely mysterious interior. There lovemaking was so sweet, so rapturous that, when it was over, he lay wrapped tightly in her arms.

He vowed then that he would have nothing more to do with Annie McQueen.

How near he had come to the brink of the precipice.

The following day he drove over to the house full of good intentions, his speech all prepared.

'I love my wife,' he would say, 'it would hurt her so much if I did anything to destroy that love. I like you, Annie, and thank you. I . . .'

The pony and trap was in front of the house, but the boy was standing by Annie's side waiting for him. He had his knee pads on and was carrying his leggit to smooth down the bundles of reeds. He looked very businesslike.

Maybe he would make a thatcher after all.

'Billy thought you could start him off,' Annie said with a wink, 'and then maybe come over and let me have a peep at the house.'

'I . . . good idea,' Ryder said, but he thought he could tell by the look in her eyes that she had already guessed. He was very bad at hiding his feelings. He thought he saw her own expression change from excitement to disappointment, but he couldn't be sure. 'I don't have my key today,' he said, feeling in his pocket. 'I must have left it in the office.'

'Oh *dear!*' Annie said with heavy sarcasm as her mouth tightened into a hard line. He knew she didn't believe him. 'What a waste of time,' she went on, in the tone of voice she used to say 'Time gentlemen, *please!*' 'I could have gone with Father and Mother on a shopping trip to Yeovil. What a waste.'

'I'm very sorry,' Ryder said. Then, turning his back on her, he put an arm round Billy's shoulders.

'So, young man, you want to do some proper thatching, do you?'

'Yes, zur,' Billy said, tightening his hold on his leggit.

'*I* might as well come and watch,' Annie said sulkily. 'Maybe I can learn something *there.*'

Ryder gave Billy a little push and sent him off towards the cart with the golden bundles stacked high upon it.

'I am sorry,' he said to Annie.

'Changed your mind, didn't you? It's your wife, I suppose?' She stopped and looked at him. 'Does she *know*?'

'Of course not! It's just . . . that I love her.'

'I see.' Contemptuously Annie looked him up and down. 'Well, *next* time you change your mind, dear, do try and let me know. If there *is* a next time . . .'

Billy was waiting for them by the cart. He had Ryder's knee pads in his hands, and as Ryder knelt down to put them on Billy began to get the bundles out of the cart and heave them up the ladder to the roof.

'You could sit by the cart,' Ryder said, feeling a little ashamed of himself. 'I *am* sorry, Annie . . .'

But she spun round and took no more notice of him, shaking her shoulders in an offended way.

Ryder felt full of remorse and unhappiness as he began to climb the ladder on to the roof, where Billy awaited him with the bundles he had already stacked.

The sun was hot, and Billy and Ryder removed their shirts while, beneath them, a look of supreme boredom on her pretty face, Annie sat in the shade of her parasol.

Ryder felt humiliated but also strangely happy. He had made a vow and he had kept it. He had been tempted and, to a certain extent, he had succumbed. But he had not given in. He had beaten the devil.

'Get thee behind me, Satan,' he thought, and his mind dwelt on the frenzy of desire he and his wife felt for each other the previous night, and the repose and happiness he'd known as he lay in her arms.

'Maybe I could go and get a drink,' Billy said after a while. 'It's terrible hot.'

'Yes.' Ryder, also panting, paused and looked towards the ridge of the roof. The job was half over, and he would be very glad when it was completed and his inadequate assistant, unwanted and, now, no longer necessary, could be sent on his way.

For a while, too, there would be no more visits to the Baker's Arms. He would take his custom, and that of his men, to the Lamb and Flag on the other side of Wenham Bridge.

He looked down at Annie sitting rather dejectedly under her parasol in all her finery. He felt that he had treated her badly and was sorry. He had aroused in her hopes of something that had not happened. She was a good woman, a sad woman and now, maybe, a wiser one.

As Billy put down his leggit and went towards the ladder Ryder stood, arms akimbo, looking down at her, and just then she put aside her parasol, looked up at him and waved. He thought she had forgiven him and waved back.

He turned abruptly to heave another bundle up the roof and shake it into place in its set, when suddenly from behind him there was a cry. Turning, he saw Billy, who had missed his footing on the slippery reeds, grab the edge of the thatch with both hands as his legs frantically searched for the ladder.

Swiftly Ryder moved down the roof and reached out just as one of Billy's hands flew up in the air. Ryder managed to clasp it, but Billy's desperate flailing and the weight of his body propelled Ryder forward.

Then, just as Billy got a foot on the ladder, Ryder flew over his head, did a somersault in the air and landed with a thud on the ground below.

Eliza sat in the yard behind the house with Beth, Elizabeth and Beth's new baby, Jo. All her own children were now at school, and it was that pleasant time of the afternoon when she could take it easy, do a little gardening, read a book or chat to Beth before it was time to go and get the children.

Elizabeth was now nearly old enough for school. She was a good-natured, even-tempered child and, although no one could see it but Beth and Eliza, like her father to look at.

Eliza loved her very much. Although she slept at Beth's, she lived among her cousins as much as was possible and frequently had meals with the family. But Ryder always seemed to resent Elizabeth a little, as though she had come between him and his own children, as though she had no right to be there. It was not true at all, but Eliza knew that Elizabeth was a tiny bit afraid of Ryder, which made her often prefer her home with kindly Ted and Beth to her visits to the big house. In many ways, however, she showed that she felt she belonged to neither.

Beth still suckled Jo, although he was nearly eighteen months old. He was a large baby and toddled confidently about, but he would climb on his mother's knee to feed at her breast, and now, he lay curled up in her arms, his large knowing eyes looking at her every now and then while Beth dropped kisses on his cheeks or held him even closer.

'Oh, I do love you,' she said, squeezing him to her.

Eliza had a book on her knee, but she was not reading. Lazily she looked up at the sky through the trees and felt an overwhelming sense of stillness, of the greatness and peace of the world. She felt she was on the verge of an experience of some magnitude, but she had no idea what it was. She had no intuition of alarm or apprehension at all.

Her eyes already half closed, she was about to nod off when they heard a commotion from the front of the house, voices calling and the noise of wheels on the gravel.

As Eliza flew out of her chair Jo started, opened his eyes and, beginning to cry, tried to push his mother's nipple away from his mouth.

'Whatever be it?' Beth, also half asleep, rose, startled, the baby still in her arms.

At that moment, her face ashen, her hat awry, her eyes already swollen from weeping, Annie McQueen ran round the house. She collided at the corner with Eliza, who clasped her by the shoulders and shook her hard.

'Whatever is the matter, Mrs McQueen? Whatever has happened? What a *state* you're in. Is there something wrong at the Baker's Arms?'

'Oh, ma'am,' Annie cried wildly, clutching at Eliza's hand, grasping her dress. 'Your husband's had a turrible accident. Fell off the roof, ma'am, and – ' her free hand clutched her stricken face and, drawing her sharp nails right down her cheek, she fell full length at Eliza's feet, her hand still in her frenzy clawing the ground ' – I do think 'e be dead.'

The streets that had been empty for Ryder's wedding fourteen years before were thronged on the day his funeral cortège wound its way from his house by the river to the church a third of a mile away. People, many clad in black or with black armbands, stood with bare heads bowed. Women wept openly, and the muffled bell of the church tolled mournfully as the black-draped hearse, drawn by two of Ryder's favourite horses, stopped outside St Mark's and the pallbearers – his brother-in-law Guy, his brothers Robert and Hesketh, his wife's uncle Prosper Martyn, and Julius Heering as a close family friend – shouldered the coffin and carried it into the church for the funeral service.

The same Rector who married him buried him, not a very different man from the one who had preached the offensive sermon about the woman taken in adultery; but, perhaps, a little wiser. He was well aware of the respect and affection with which Ryder was now regarded in the parish, so he chose his words more carefully. His funeral oration drew both tears and murmurs of appreciation from the congregation that not only filled every pew but stood in the side aisles and at the back of the church, and even formed a column down the middle.

The Reverend Lamb took as his text I Samuel Chapter 3 verse 18. 'It is the Lord: let him do what seemeth him good.' What had happened to a man who was well liked and respected in the community, a man in his prime, was shocking and incomprehensible. It seemed, the Rector suggested, completely to defy any rational explanation, because Ryder was, above all things, a master thatcher, a man of great skill in his trade.

If there was any comfort for his family it was in the mysterious workings of God, and in the *sight* of God what had happened to Ryder was good. God had taken him to his bosom, although no one doubted that he left a grieving family behind. But it was the only explanation that one could offer; in the wise words of the Bible also: 'To every thing there is a season, and a time to every purpose under the heaven.'

For Ryder Yetman, difficult as it was to accept this, his time had come. It was good in the sight of the Lord, who wanted him for his own.

Eliza, listening with bowed head, Dora's hand tightly clenched in hers, found little comfort in the Rector's words; only rebellion and rage about what had happened. Such a stupid, unnecessary accident, and one, moreover, brought on by someone else – a young lad who should never have been up on the roof at all.

But that day, and for many days afterwards, she behaved as Ryder would have wished her to behave. Her face hidden behind a dark veil, she carried herself erect, with dignity, and even stepped forward resolutely, while those gathered round the grave were snivelling into their handkerchiefs, to cast the first clod of earth upon his coffin. Ashes to ashes. Dust to dust.

A huge reception at the house followed, and only at the end

of the day could she sit down and weep; weep, she felt, as no one had ever wept before.

Prosper and Lally were staying at a hotel nearby. Julius Heering was with his sister. The following day they would all gather around her again to support and comfort her; but that night was hers to mourn, to be alone with the children, to try and explain to them the mysterious words of the Rector, the comfort he had vainly tried to give:

The Lord had done what seemed to him good.

Laurence Yetman was thirteen years of age when his father died. He had been coming home from school when he saw the pony and trap go helter-skelter into the drive of the house and only later did he realise that the object lying in the back covered with a cloth as though it had been carelessly tossed there had been the body of his father. This shocking fact lingered in his mind for many years and would be the subject of recurring nightmares. He recalled glancing casually into the cart, noting the long object, and then he stayed for a few minutes to stroke the head of the pony, an animal he knew because it belonged to the Baker's Arms and grazed in the field next to Riversmead.

The fact that his father's body must still have been warm, that he could have reached out with his hand and touched it, even seen it, perhaps revived it, preyed on his mind and turned him from a carefree young boy to someone with the burdens of a man. He was now the head of the family. He found he was able to become his mother's support in her time of trial; together with his brother and sister he seemed to understand not only her need for them, but her need to be alone too.

That night after the funeral, after the guests had taken their leave, they all went up the hill to the newly dug grave and prayed there for a while silently, together. Eliza wished, as far as possible, to be alone with the children, to go about her daily tasks and, above all, to look after her father-in-law, who had suffered a minor heart attack on the news of Ryder's death and now lay in his bedroom watched over constantly by little Connie.

The family at that time seemed of paramount importance:

her family and John. But Ryder's brothers were people she did not particularly wish to see, and when, a few days after the funeral, they announced their intention of paying her a visit, she thought it was to see about the stone, the situation of their father and the various matters pertaining to Ryder's estate.

She received them alone in the drawing room, still dressed in deep mourning. She kissed each of them – rather cold unemotional men – perfunctorily on the cheek and offered them coffee or sherry, whichever they preferred. It was eleven o'clock in the morning, ironically a bewitching summer's day and, sad though she knew they were, she was glad that the children could still play in the garden, temporarily forget their grief and relieve the gloom with the sound of their laughter.

Eliza had only seen her brothers-in-law, Robert and Hesketh, about a dozen times since her marriage, at family christenings and similar occasions. The two had so little in common with their elder brother that it was difficult to believe they had sprung from the same seed, or issued from the same womb.

Coffee was duly brought, Robert had a glass of sherry before-hand, and all three stood rather awkwardly by the window exchanging platitudes about the weather, the sadness of the occasion, the shock of their father's ill-health – a double blow – and so on.

'I suppose you've come to see your father,' Eliza said, taking her cup to a nearby chair and sitting down to ease her aching limbs. Her whole body seemed to have seized up with shock, and she ached literally from head to toe.

'As a matter of fact, we've come to see you, Eliza,' Robert, the middle brother, said, while Hesketh buried his face in his cup. 'It concerns the disposition of the business,' he went on.

'What disposition?'

'The disposition of shares.'

'Ryder saw no need to change things.' Eliza suddenly had a moment of apprehension, of panic, and she could see Julius as he begged Ryder, years before, to take the controlling interest and buy out his brothers. Because of her he had not done so.

'But things have changed with his death.' Hesketh felt

emboldened enough by his brother's opening remarks to remove his face from his cup. 'Ryder has left his share of the business to Laurence, his elder son, and Laurence is a minor. He can therefore take no part in it until he is twenty-one. What will happen to the business *now*, Eliza?' Hesketh concluded, sitting down and crossing his legs.

'I thought it would go on as it is.'

'How?'

'Ryder had some very good men working for him. I thought the foreman Perce Adams could take over.'

'Adams is a yokel,' Robert said sarcastically, examining his nails.

'But *you* have never taken any part in it,' Eliza exclaimed. 'Do you mean to tell me you intend to do so now?'

'Yes, we do.' Robert looked at her in surprise. 'We intend to take a *very* active part in it, or it will go to the wall. Father has built up a very good business – '

'*Ryder* built up a very good business,' she replied angrily.

'Ryder, Father, whoever.' Robert waved his hand in the air. 'Alas, *not* very satisfactory in the current situation. Father is ill, Ryder is, alas, no more . . . and I don't suppose *you* could run a building business, could you, my dear?'

'I don't suppose *you* could either,' Eliza retorted. 'You never have in the past.'

'That's because it was well taken care of. We were able to employ our fortune doing other things. In the last few years Yetman's has expanded so that it was run to capacity. God *knows* what Ryder was doing on a roof *thatching*. If he had been seeing to his proper affairs, managing as he should and not performing as a *labourer*, he would never have been killed.'

'*If* he had been in Dorchester, as he said he would be,' Eliza thought to herself, that question mark that had tormented her since his death forming in her mind again. What *was* he doing up on the roof? And why was Annie McQueen watching him?

'He was showing an apprentice the trade,' she said, repeating what she had been told. 'You know what happened. The young lad lost his footing and, slipping backwards, grabbed at Ryder's hand.'

'We know what happened, my dear,' Hesketh said with a note of compassion in his voice. Rising, he crossed the room and put a hand on her shoulder. 'Don't distress yourself by telling it all over again. The point is now that we are here to help you. We – Robert and I – virtually control the business. Laurence is too young to have a vote – the shares are held in trust for him – and Father is too ill. Naturally you have no vote at all.'

'Not even a *say* in my husband's business?' Eliza asked angrily. 'One I helped him build up, encouraging him all the way?'

'Alas!' Robert shook his head in an unconvincing attempt at sympathy. 'None at all. However, we will be generous with you, you can depend on that. We intend to make you an allowance and let you keep this house, for the time being . . .'

'It is a house my own wife was always fond of.' Hesketh looked around him casually. 'She thinks a lot needs doing to it, but . . .'

'Don't you *dare* try and take my house from me,' Eliza stormed, jumping to her feet. 'The house belonged to John Yetman, who gave it to *us* when we married.

'My dear sister-in-law,' Robert said in a patronising tone, 'it was *not* Father's to give. The house belongs, and has always belonged, to the company. In the early days, when the business was not doing too well, it was used as security against a loan at the bank. That was never revoked. The house belongs first to the company and then to the bank, that is how things stand. Father *could* have had the house back once the company was in profit, but he never asked for it. Pity.' Robert examined his nails again. 'Had he done so it would have been his to give. He can't have realised the situation, and I don't suppose poor Ryder even knew it.

'The house now effectively belongs to us, but we have considered the matter compassionately and we have decided that you may continue to have the use of it, at least until the children are a little older. It would be unfeeling to ask you to leave now. There, we can't say fairer than that, can we? Everything else is controlled by us, and we move into the main office in Blandford tomorrow with our advisers.

'I'm afraid there is very little you can do about it, my dear. Ryder, of course, never thought he would die. If he had, he would have left a much cleverer will. You never know the hour, nor the day, do you?'

Henrietta Woodville led a solitary, and somewhat bitter, existence in the house that was not too big and not too small, not too humble and not too grand, overlooking the sea at Bournemouth. All winter she had been ill, troubled by her chest and a number of interesting ailments which the doctors put in the category of 'nerves'.

Lady Woodville's 'nerves' were a great source of revenue to the Bournemouth physicians who were called upon to attend her, and they took them very seriously. She was continually being prescribed various pills and potions that necessitated a visit from the doctor and a new prescription each time. It all amounted to quite a lot of money, and the Bournemouth physicians blessed the day that her ladyship had come to live among them.

Henrietta was a woman who found it hard to live alone, and in her isolation she had taken refuge in the hypochondriacal symptoms which were such a source of revenue to the doctors of Bournemouth. Illness made people take notice of one to whom independence had never been attractive. The Martyn relations danced attendance, physicians came and went. One was never alone when ill, or even pretending to be ill.

She was, in a sense, her own worst enemy, because she was not yet old and still had the beauty and the wit to attract people and make friends; but she did just the opposite. Except for her long-suffering Martyn relations she scarcely saw anybody except Guy, who made regular and dutiful calls with his children and, occasionally, Eliza's.

Eliza saw her mother once a year. It was like a solemn

religious occasion, and about as mournful. She usually called on Henrietta's birthday and stayed a short time, just long enough for her mother to upbraid her, and unleash on her all her pent-up misery and frustration that instead of being allowed to grow old in Wenham she had been condemned to a life of boredom in provincial Bournemouth.

Margaret never saw her mother-in-law at all. She had none of the ties, the dutiful feelings that still bound Eliza to her cantankerous parent. So when Henrietta did see her daughter she had to listen to a double lot of complaints; about Margaret and about herself.

When she returned home it was invariably with a headache, and Ryder would upbraid her for her sentimentality, disguised as filial affection. Ryder had hated her mother and never spared her. Now he was gone.

The letter arrived not long after she had got over the shock of the visit from Ryder's brothers. Reluctantly, knowing from whom it came, she sat down and opened it:

Dear Eliza (it ran),

I write to you to offer my condolences on the death of your husband. I would have attended the funeral as a mark of respect and to show the family solidarity, which is always expected of the Woodvilles, but I was too ill. My chest has been troublesome and I have pains in my legs. Dr Worsthorne forbade me to travel and has instead prescribed rest, new medicines and, perhaps, when I am fit to travel, a visit to Bath to take the waters.

My dear Eliza, in my mother's heart I grieve for you, knowing only too well what it is like to lose a husband in the prime of life. But my husband, your dear father, was a good man who never did a bad deed in his life.

Maybe I should not say it but, as I am your mother, I must tell you frankly that I feel Ryder's death is a judgement from God for transgressing His laws. You may have thought you made up for it; but God's judgement is always there, His vengeance. He . . .'

Eliza read the letter with mounting horror. Then she screwed it into a ball and threw it violently into the fire, watching the flames slowly consume the paper, the rest of her mother's words forever unread. Beth, coming in a short while later, found her in an uncharacteristic pose: sitting sobbing her heart out.

'Oh, ma'am, what *is* it?' Beth sank to her knees beside the weeping woman.

'It's my mother,' Eliza sobbed. 'She has written me the most awful letter. She says Ryder's death was a *punishment* . . .'

She raised her tear-stained face and, drawing Beth close to her, buried her head on her shoulder while Beth put her arms tightly round her as though she were a child.

'There, *there*, ma'am,' she said 'don't take on so. You'll make yourself ill . . .'

Eliza gazed at her again, her face still stricken.

'Beth, sometimes I have nightmares. I feel my mother may be right . . . What we did *was* wrong, and in the end we were punished for it.'

PART THREE

The Fabric of Society

17

Maybe it was because of her happy childhood, the love lavished upon her by her parents, that Victoria Fairchild had been able to overcome – not at once, but eventually – her disappointment over the treachery of Christopher Yetman. For many months following the dreadful revelation of his character she had scarcely known how to cope, had gone about her tasks mechanically and slept badly; but, aided by her friends Miss Bishop and Mrs Lamb, she had survived. Indeed, the Rector's wife had shown qualities of understanding and compassion that surprised all those who up to then had considered her a rather hard, unemotional woman, following the letter of the law rather than its spirit.

But Miss Fairchild realised eventually that, whatever the healing benefits of work, she was tired of the life of drudgery at the shop. Some part of her life had gone out of her – maybe because of the hope she had long ago cherished of sharing the business with Christopher. In due course she sold the shop to the Goodisons, retaining, however, the freehold. Mr Troup, the banker, gave her excellent advice and she thus found herself a woman of means; but she had no heir, no one to leave it all to. When she died her fortune would probably be dispersed among the people of the parish who were in most need.

The Yetmans, and John and Eliza in particular, had not abandoned Miss Fairchild after the sad affair of Christopher. But a needless feeling of responsibility for what had happened made them reticent, and it was only gradually that Miss Fairchild plucked up the courage to return their hospitality, to reciprocate their good intentions.

John Yetman was particularly kind to Victoria, but after he became a widower again he felt a little nervous. Enough harm had been done to that good woman already by his family, and he did not wish to encourage her into thinking she could one day take Euphemia's place.

However, encouraged by Miss Bishop, whose house she used frequently to visit, Victoria began to form an attachment to little motherless Connie Yetman, and the bond grew stronger as the years passed. In time Miss Fairchild began to see in Connie the child that she and Christopher might have had. In appearance his niece resembled him, and the older she grew the more the likeness fascinated Miss Fairchild.

This bond was strengthened by a mutual love of music, for which Connie showed talent at a very early age. She could play simple pieces on the piano from the age of three, and at five began to learn the violin.

As Victoria had whiled away many lonely hours in the comfort of music and playing the piano, she was delighted to find someone so gifted who could not only play duets with her but sing with her too. They both sight read, and Miss Fairchild had a beautiful voice, so that when she sang not only her voice but her heart, her soul, were lifted and she could imagine those soaring notes reaching to the heavens where everyone was beautiful and there were no physical blemishes or imperfections.

Once or twice a week, Connie began to go to Miss Fairchild to make music, and in time an affection developed between the two that was not unlike that of mother and daughter. Over the years Miss Fairchild watched Connie blossom into an accomplished vocalist and pianist and she was proud of her. She also realised something more: she loved her.

This feeling was given some substance by a sad event which occurred only a few months after Ryder's death.

John Yetman, who had been ailing since his son's sudden departure, died in his sleep. The servant coming to wake him in the morning found him lying peacefully, with a smile on his face as though God had taken him in the middle of a happy dream.

Little Connie was now an orphan, and Miss Fairchild decided to do something rather bold; to take a step that she would never have dreamt of taking before. After allowing the family time to come to terms with their loss, she made an appointment to see Eliza.

Eliza came to the door to welcome Miss Fairchild and, after shaking hands, took her over to the fire because it was a cold day.

Miss Fairchild had not seen Eliza since John Yetman's funeral, and her appearance shocked her. Her face was pale, her fine eyes too hollow. Always slim, she now looked unbecomingly thin. She could have been called haggard. Eliza drew a hand across her brow and gave her a wan smile.

'I know what you're thinking, Miss Fairchild,' she said, sinking into a chair and inviting her guest to do the same. 'But I am *not* ill. It is simply that life has not been too kind to me since my husband died, and there are occasions when it shows.

'I have so many responsibilities that sometimes I wonder how I cope, yet I do. It is the coping that makes me tired, and of course the death of my father-in-law, a man I loved and respected, has been a grave setback. In addition there is the worry about little Connie. She can't stay alone in that big house, and yet she refuses to move. She is looked after by her old nurse and a small staff. What am I to do with her? A girl of eight is completely unfit to live on her own. She is, of course, a strange child. She has always been solitary, a bookworm, musical as you know.' She paused to look at Miss Fairchild, who had become rather agitated, playing with her bag, dropping her gloves and fiddling with the large hatpin stuck through her hat.

'May I offer you tea?' Eliza asked, thinking she had forgotten something.

No, Miss Fairchild would not accept tea. She was too nervous, too excited on account of what she was about to say; a momentous decision for her, for *any* woman in her sixties who had never been married or had a child and who had spent the last twenty years on her own. And Mrs Yetman, all unknowingly, had prepared the way for her. She moved to the edge of her chair looking like a small, bright bird on a branch.

Her manner worried Eliza more and more.

'Is anything *wrong*, Miss Fairchild?' Eliza asked, leaning anxiously forward.

'Nothing w-wrong,' Miss Fairchild replied, stumbling over the word. 'Not w-w-rong,' she repeated herself. 'I do not quite know how to put this, and I must confess that I'm nervous, because what I have to say is quite i-im-portant. I think, dear Eliza, that you know I am *very* fond of your little sister-in-law.'

'And she of you,' Eliza assured her. 'I have always regarded her with a special love because of the circumstances of her birth. She was not expected to live, you know, Miss Fairchild, and I held her tightly in my arms wishing, even praying, that I could breathe life into her inert little body . . . And then, suddenly, she coughed, and the doctor said it was a miracle.'

'Oh!' Miss Fairchild's eyes suddenly filled with tears. 'What a *beautiful* story. It explains so much about her. She *is* like a gift from God. But – ' she paused dramatically, one of the beautifully kept fingers held high ' – a very *lonely* young girl, in that large house, as you say, all by herself.'

'Well, she won't come and live with us,' Eliza felt a little annoyed, as if Miss Fairchild had come to reproach her. 'I have asked her, *begged* her. She prefers to live there in the care of her old nursemaid and a handful of servants. I . . .'

'*I* would like to take care of Constance, if you would permit it, Eliza.' Miss Fairchild's speech impediment was more pronounced when she was excited, and now she stumbled over almost every word. 'I would like *her* to come and live with *me*. I have a house large enough for both of us, and I am lonely too. Connie and I understand each other very well. There is such a bond between us.'

Suddenly she looked self-consciously at her polished black shoes, and her pale face grew a little pink.

'I think you know, Eliza, that I was once very fond of Connie's uncle.' Bravely she lifted her head and met eyes which were brimming with sympathy. 'Many people thought me a fool, doubtless a silly old fool, to be taken in by a charmer who was after my money . . .'

'Oh *no*, Miss Fairchild, really . . .'

Victoria held up her hand.

'Let me finish what I have to say, Eliza. I fell in love but once and was kissed but once. Christopher Yetman brought a new happiness into my life. He gave me a taste of what – had things been different – I might have known. He was a man of great charm, and for a while he made me feel beautiful, wanted for myself as a woman, like other women.'

Eliza found herself fighting back tears and, crushing her hands in her lap, she nodded.

'In a strange way, although I would have been too old to have children even had I married Christopher, I have come to think of Connie as my daughter. Even before her father died I felt a strong affection for her.'

Miss Fairchild sadly shook her head.

'I have *never* lost my affection for Christopher, and if he were to appear on the doorstep I might be as silly as I was years ago. But I know he will not. He is in New Zealand, isn't he?'

'Somewhere like that,' Eliza murmured. After leaving prison Christopher had fled the country because the many creditors seeking him might have attempted to put him behind iron bars again.

'No matter.' Miss Fairchild gave a dismissive shrug. 'It is with Connie I am now concerned, not her uncle.' She clasped her hands together, and there was in her eyes the expression of one who has been vouchsafed a glimpse of the divine. 'I *think* she would be happy with me, and I know I should, I should be ecstatic. It would at long last give some meaning to my life.'

Eliza, feeling absolutely dumbfounded, gazed at her visitor, wondering if she could possibly be serious. But of course she was. A woman like Miss Fairchild would never be anything else in a matter of such importance.

'Have you spoken to Connie?' she asked after she had recovered from her surprise.

'Oh, of course. I would never have dreamt of approaching you otherwise. I asked her if she would like to come and live with me. She replied that she would, very much. If you would permit it I would like to adopt her as my ward, as she is an orphan, and make her my heir. I would leave her my house and all my money. My fortune is not insignificant,' she said with some pride. 'My parents' business was a good one, and I sold it at a profit, retaining the freehold of the shop, valuable property in the High Street. I have never been profligate with money . . .'

'Miss Fairchild,' Eliza interposed gently, 'please don't think for a moment that I consider you incapable of looking after my sister-in-law, or that your fortune is of any importance. It is Connie's happiness that counts. If Connie is happy to come and live with you, if it's what she *really* wants, then, as her legal guardian, I can see no objection. Whether it would be wise for you to adopt her officially I am not sure. I should have to take advice.'

'Of course.' Miss Fairchild leapt to her feet, clasping her hands in front of her as if in prayer. 'Oh, *thank* you! Of course I understand, and whatever is right for Constance shall be our only consideration.' She went towards Eliza and grasped her hands. 'My dear, dear Eliza, you have no idea how happy this makes me. I have always longed for a daughter. This, really, must be the happiest day of my life.'

Connie moved into the home of her adoptive mother within a very short time after Miss Fairchild's conversation with Eliza. There was, after all, no impediment. The legal situation had yet to be thoroughly thrashed out with lawyers, but in the meantime everyone was happy; above all, Connie was happy.

Connie was a precocious, rather delicate child who, having

been used to the protective love of one person, had felt very deprived since the death of her adored father. She did not fit in very well with her rather boisterous nephews and nieces, who were all older than she was, and she had been given to bouts of melancholy and weeping until Miss Fairchild had had her first serious talk with her, and then another, and had then put the matter to Eliza. Now Connie had found someone who would cherish her as her father had done.

Eliza was happy in the knowledge that Connie, beloved Connie, was provided for. Financially, of course, she already had more than enough money. She was a well-off little girl with a house of her own, for the not inconsiderable fortune of John Yetman had been left exclusively to her.

Maybe if he had thought a little more about it he would have altered his will after Ryder's death, so that some of his fortune went to his son's widow and children. But by that time he was a sick man, anxious about his young motherless daughter, his mind already on the afterlife.

In the months after Ryder's death Eliza grappled with the difficulties of her life as a widow, a woman of small means with a household she was entirely responsible for.

Margaret tried to help, but Eliza would never accept money from the Woodvilles. Prosper Martyn offered help, but she was even less inclined to take charity from him.

She cut down her staff by three-quarters. There was now no need for a butler and footman, and two maids would do where there were four before. Cook was indispensable, and so were Beth and Ted, who, in any case, were part of the family. Beth offered to take in washing for other people and Ted to do odd jobs, but Eliza wouldn't hear of it. She got rid of a carriage and several horses.

She then set about thinking what else she could do to make ends meet.

Eliza was left a widow at the age of thirty-three. It seemed a very long time from now until the grave, which was sometimes where she wished she could be, lying alongside Ryder. Like

Queen Victoria she felt she would never get over the death of her mate, a man so beloved that he still occupied her thoughts night and day.

Her bedroom was a lonely place. The bed was especially solitary. Sometimes she would lie there imagining that he was by her side, and she would reach out in the hope that the dreadful thing that had happened had been a dream, that his comforting form would be there. But the place beside her remained cold and empty, and that was how it would be for evermore.

Also like Queen Victoria she blamed herself for that premature death as though, by some act of foresight, she could have prevented it.

One morning shortly after Connie went to live with Miss Fairchild Eliza lay in bed listening to the sounds of birdsong in the garden. It came filtering through the window, the plaintive song of the blackbird, the cheerful chatter of the chaffinch. Often at that hour in the morning she and Ryder would make love because it was a quiet tranquil time of the day, a good time for them to be together, before the house came alive and all the bustle started.

Eliza felt very lonely in her large bed, and she wondered if the whole house were not too big for them. If it might be wiser to live elsewhere, and let the brothers do as they would. Their shadow would be permanently over her. Whatever they said, she did not trust them. Tomorrow, or next year, or in five or ten years, they would want the house back.

But no, to move would be to give in. She raised her head as she heard a tap on her door, and called out cautiously 'Who is it?'

'It's Laurence, Mother.'

'Come in, darling,' she called and held out a hand from the bed as he crept across the room towards her in his nightshirt. 'Oh, *darling*,' she said gazing at his wistful face.

He stood looking at her shyly, and then, impulsively, she flung back the bedclothes and with a whoop he leapt into bed beside her. Laurence was a tall, well-built boy and the bed shook so much that, for a moment, Eliza feared it was in danger of collapsing.

It was a long time since he had crept in in the small hours of the morning and stood by the door, finger in his mouth, watching, waiting, trembling a little with fear while his parents slept. Sometimes when they woke up they didn't know how long he'd been standing there and shivering, blue with cold, and he would be helped into their bed and would snuggle up between them to get warm.

Now, much older and the man of the house, he lay very timidly beside his mother. Eliza put her arm around him and drew him towards her.

'What is it Laurence? Are you unhappy?'

Silently he nodded, and in the light of dawn she could see how pale and grave his face was, a suspicion of tears in his eyes.

'What is it, darling? Anything in particular?'

'It's about going to school,' he said.

'What about it?' She pressed him even closer to her and laid her chin on his head.

'I would like to stop going to school, Mother, so that I can be of help to you. Some boys leave when they're fourteen, and I nearly am.'

'But Laurence – ' she pushed him slightly away and looked at him in dismay ' – you can't leave school at fourteen! Your father would be horrified.'

'Father's not here, Mother, is he? I can see you're worried about money. Half the staff have left. We haven't much to live on, have we, Mother?'

'No, we haven't,' she said after a pause, aware that her son, despite his youth, was now conscious of his responsibilities, aware of his duty to take his father's place. 'But I don't want it to worry *you*. We have enough if we live carefully. It certainly mustn't affect your education.'

'But I don't *like* school, Mother.'

'You always did.' She looked at him doubtfully. 'I thought

you were going to be the scholar of the family. Are you just saying this to try and help me?'

'No. I mean I would like to try and help you, but I really *don't* like school.'

'Then what would you like to do?'

'I'd like to learn the building business, like Father. I'd like to start up Yetman's again and make it successful.'

'Would you like to work for your uncles?' she enquired with a note of irony in her voice.

'You know I wouldn't like that, Mother,' Laurence replied gravely. 'But maybe we can rescue something from them? Maybe we can build up the business and make it successful like it was before.'

Eliza leaned back against the pillow, and suddenly a great burden seemed to have been lifted from her.

Her son was a man, and they would survive.

Julius Heering looked round the empty hall of his large house, aware of the echo of his footsteps every time he moved. He could even hear himself breathing, the thump of his heart in his chest.

He had walked from the bottom to the top, gone round the circular gallery and then slowly down again, entering some of the bedrooms, the modern bathrooms, the large, beautiful reception rooms with the hand-built furniture and works of art, the airy, well-appointed kitchens.

He had sat in the conservatory admiring the hothouse flowers that grew in its south-facing aspect, and then he had been to the basement and toured the cubicles of the Turkish baths, the hot and cold water jets waiting to be turned on.

It all seemed now, in retrospect, the folly of a madman. Was that because it had cost a human life?

He had stood for a long time looking at the roof of the cottage from which Ryder had fallen to his death only a few months before. It was not hard to imagine that bright summer day, the two men working on the roof, the boy falling, the older, experienced man reaching out to help him . . .

Suddenly he turned on his heels and flung open the great front doors. He walked resolutely on to the pillared porch with its fine view of the curving drive, the great wrought-iron gates a: either side.

Then, putting on his hat, he closed the doors firmly behind him, locked them with the key which he popped into his waistcoat pocket, and ran lightly down the stone steps.

He knew he would never visit the place again. He would put it on the market, or keep it as an investment. Just now he wasn't sure which. He was in no hurry.

Julius's carriage was awaiting him in the drive, and he was about to enter it when he saw a movement in the wood behind him. He stood still, expecting the figure, lurking behind the trees, to appear.

But no one came forward, and thinking it was a poacher Julius was about to give his driver the command to proceed when he had second thoughts.

He jumped out of his carriage and, telling the driver to wait, strolled towards the wood, hands in his pockets. Still there was no movement, but he knew it had not been an illusion. Then he felt a prickle of fear. He was unarmed, unprepared . . . He looked behind him, but his coachman, who was elderly, was dozing in his seat.

Suddenly from behind a tree appeared a familiar figure who, cap in hand, stood awkwardly in front of the owner of the house, obviously aware that he was trespassing.

'Good morning, Mr 'Ering, zur,' the man said. 'Forgive me, zur, for being on your premises.'

'Why, it's Adams,' Julius said, putting up a hand to shade the sun from his eyes. 'What the devil are you doing here?'

'I was looking around the place, zur,' the man said. 'Thinking of old times. I like to come here occasionally and look at the cottage where the master died. I like him to know that I'm thinking of him.'

'Well —' Julius awkwardly put a hand on the man's arm '—that's very good of you, Adams. I'm sure Mr Yetman would appreciate it wherever he is.'

383

'He'm up there, zur,' Perce Adams said, pointing to the sky. 'Of that I have no doubt. Despite what people do say, *I* think he was a good man. I know it.'

'What do you mean "despite what people do say"?' Julius looked at him curiously.

'I didn't mean to speak out of turn, zur. Fact is I have no work to do, and I does a lot of thinking.'

'You've no work to do! You mean you're unemployed?'

'I haven't worked since Mr Yetman's brothers took over, zur, and ran the business into the ground. There is no business now. No Yetman's left. And they did that in such a short time, zur, only a few months. They sacked all the workers; they stopped all the building as was in progress.'

'Is the business up for sale?' Julius asked. He beckoned to Adams. 'Come and sit in my carriage for a moment and we can talk there.'

Perce Adams put on his cap and followed Julius, their feet crackling over the dead twigs and leaves until they came to the gravelled drive where the carriage still stood, the solitary coachman and his solitary horse still slumbering in the sun.

Perce Adams had been Ryder's right-hand man – an indispensable worker, ally and friend. Perce had drunk on Fridays with him at the Baker's Arms and not infrequently had to be escorted home to bed. He had been inconsolable when his master died. Like Ryder he had trained as a builder and could do every job he asked his men to do. He had been with John Yetman since he was a boy, and he was now a man of about forty-five, tough, weather-beaten, used to hard work: a Dorset man, a countryman through and through.

Julius got in first and Perce climbed in after him, thoughtfully dusting the bottom of his trousers so that he did not soil the plush seat. He was clearly ill at ease, and sat very stiff, cap in hand, waiting for Julius to speak.

'Now, Perce,' Julius said, 'what you say is very interesting, also very sad. There is no business left, you say?'

'Soon won't be, zur. They be selling everything like hot

cakes. They be selling the buildings, and taking the money. 'Tis a terrible sorry state of affairs, zur.'

'It *is* a terrible sorry state of affairs,' Julius reiterated in his soft, Dutch-accented voice. 'A good business gone to ruin. Now –' he paused and his eyes narrowed thoughtfully ' – what's this that you're saying: "*despite what people say* about Mr Yetman he was a good man." What does that mean, Perce? I presume you mean Ryder and not John Yetman?'

'Oh yes, zur,' Perce said earnestly. 'I baint never heard nothing but good of his father.'

'And you hear bad of him?'

'I *heard* bad of him, zur, and I didn't believe it. I still don't, though there was the evidence of me own eyes . . .'

'For goodness' sake, man,' Julius exclaimed irritably, 'can't you be more specific, whatever it is you're trying to say.'

'I can't speak no ill of the dead, zur.'

'Then why did you mention it at all?'

'It slipped out.' Perce shut his mouth firmly as though to indicate that his error would not be repeated.

'How would *you* like your job back, Perce?' Julius said after a pause during which, hand on the top of his cane, he had sat gazing moodily in front of him.

'How do you mean, zur?' Perce's hat went from one hand to the other like a ball.

'Would you like to be in the building business again?'

'Would I not, zur!' Perce's eyes gleamed excitedly.

'When Mr Yetman was alive I tried to persuade him to come into partnership with me and his wife's uncle. There was no secret about it; but Mrs Yetman, Eliza, was against it. The matter was only broached once more a short time before his death. Alas, if it had only happened . . .' He looked sharply at the man next to him. 'Now what's this about Ryder Yetman? I must know or else I can go no further. You understand that, don't you?'

'I understand it, zur.' By the expression on Perce's face he seemed to be undergoing the torments of the damned. 'It is just that I don't like to hear no gossip of the dead, zur.'

'What *is* it, man?'

'Well, zur . . .' Perce went bright red. 'They *say* Mr Yetman was after the barmaid at the Baker's Arms, zur – Annie McQueen. That it was on account of her that he died, and that she is having a child . . .' Perce paused thoughtfully for a moment. 'They *do* say the baby she's carrying is his.'

Eliza sat with her hands folded in her lap; her face, though pale, was composed. Julius, who had probably been a little in love with her for a long time, felt that too often recently he had seen her unsmiling, stricken. She had not recovered from the death of her husband or that of her father-in-law following almost immediately upon it. And now this – perhaps the cruellest blow, the unkindest cut of all.

'I *am* sorry to bring you such bad news,' he said, 'but I thought it better you should hear it from me than as gossip from the village.'

'It is *still* gossip from the village,' she said bitterly, kneading one hand into the palm of the other. 'That's *all* it is.'

Yet as she spoke, those fears that had resided in the dark, nethermost reaches of her mind seemed to surface. Annie, who had brought the news of Ryder's death; Annie, who had stood clad in black from head to foot, her face tear-stained, at the back of the church during the funeral service. As the hearse passed her she and Eliza seemed to look deep into each other's eyes, the one asking a question, the other unable, or unwilling, to answer it.

'I questioned Perce *very* closely.' Julius longed to take her hand in his and comfort her, but did not dare. 'He said that Ryder had become accustomed to going into the bar of the Baker's Arms every Friday after he had paid his workmen. He would take them for a drink and he was often the last to leave. He and the barmaid, Annie McQueen by name, spent a long time conversing with each other. The men would joke about it among themselves.' He paused, and looked at her gravely.

'Gossip or not I can't say, but *they* thought he was having a flirtation with Annie McQueen. They seemed to have very little doubt about it.'

'I find it most despicable that you should indulge in this kind of talk with my late husband's employees,' Eliza said, brusquely turning her face away from him.

'My dear, I consider myself a member of your family.'

'You are *not* my family,' Eliza replied with emphasis. 'You may be related to my sister-in-law and my brother, but *not* to me.'

'Oh, I see. Forgive me.'

'And forgive *me* if I sound unkind,' she said, turning round. 'I did not mean to be; but you can imagine how humiliated I feel hearing news of this nature from you.'

'Please *don't* feel humiliated.' He went towards her. 'I *am* a friend. I have only your interests at heart. Now, if you hear this news from elsewhere you will be prepared.'

'You don't know Wenham,' Eliza said with a bitter laugh. 'Everyone will know, or think they know; but they will not tell me, and I will not ask them. Annie McQueen has a bad reputation in this town, and I refuse to believe Ryder was the sort of man who would ever have associated with such a person. Now, please, never refer to this matter again.' She rose as if to dismiss her caller, whose unwelcome news had in fact caused her deep distress. But he had taken up an attitude by the window, hands deep in his pockets.

'Very well,' he said, 'but there is one other thing, and this I hope you will not take exception to. Perce Adams also told me that he would like to go into the business again. The Yetman name will fade altogether as your husband's brothers dispose of the assets. I told you they would.'

'Oh, you know everything, don't you, Mr Heering?' Eliza exclaimed bitterly. 'Is there anything you don't know, or is there more to come?'

'I merely offered,' he stammered, shocked almost to speechlessness by her outburst, 'that is, *if* he would like the capital to start up again I am willing to provide it.'

'And the next thing you will tell me is that you warned us

ages ago about all this. You said if *anything* happened to Ryder it would be bad for me, and, of course, you were right. You are a *very* clever man, Mr Heering. No wonder you are so successful in the City. What *must* you think of us country bumpkins?'

Almost as soon as she had spoken she regretted it, but it was too late. Julius went across to the far side of the room where he had put his hat and stick and, picking up both, he turned to her and bowed.

'Good day, Eliza. Forgive me for offending you. I am deeply sorry.' He seemed about to go and then changed his mind. 'I do mean it when I say that if ever you need me you have only to ask, and, please, forgive me for bringing you such grief today. God, how I *wish* I had not spoken, because then I would still be your friend.'

The children and the rest of the household were long in bed, yet still a light burned in the drawing room. Beth, who always looked in last thing at night to be certain everything was all right, stood timidly for a long time outside the door before knocking on it.

There was no reply and she knocked again, then, thinking the room was empty, she gently turned the handle and peeped inside. She saw Eliza curled up on the couch looking as though she were asleep, and, going over to her, she put a hand on her shoulder. She was even more alarmed when she saw that Eliza's eyes were wide open and she was staring in front of her.

'Ma'am,' Beth said anxiously, 'are you all right?'

Eliza gave a deep sigh but said nothing.

'You look terrible *ill*, ma'am,' Beth cried. 'Shall I send Ted for Dr Hardy?'

Beth's worried words seemed to rouse her mistress, who shook herself as though she had no idea where she was, rapidly blinking her eyes.

'I was dreaming, Beth,' she said, sitting up and putting her feet on the floor. 'Daydreaming. Yet you can still have nightmares even when you're not asleep.'

'It was Mr Julius upset you, ma'am. I could tell by the

way he left that something had happened. His face was ever so stern. He jumped into his carriage and cried "Drive off" in such a thunderous voice you would have heard it in the marketplace.'

'He is *not* a man I like very much after all,' Eliza said slowly.

'I thought you *did* like him, ma'am, you and the master?'

'Well, no longer.' Eliza blinked her eyes again and looked at the clock on the mantelpiece. Then she got up and rubbed her hands together, because lying still for so long had made her cold. 'Do you know Annie McQueen, Beth?' she asked suddenly.

'Huh,' Beth said contemptuously, 'not what you'd call "know", ma'am. No thank you, is what I say. Someone I would *never* have anything to do with.' Beth sniffed. 'Anyway she ain't here any more.'

'Oh?' Eliza looked at her in surprise.

'She left the town some weeks ago, ma'am. No one seems to know for where. Good riddance I say. Gone and best forgotten.'

Shortly after, Eliza and Beth left the room, turning off the gas lights and blowing out the oil lamps which, with their soft rays, illuminated the large, pleasant room that had always been used for family gatherings and was full of happy memories . . . Oh, what memories, Eliza had thought, lying there, almost too sad now even to recall them.

Guy had electric light at Pelham's Oak, and there was electricity in the valley, but most of the people of Wenham considered it a luxury they could do without. Ryder as a forward-thinking man had found the idea attractive, but had not lived to put it into practice. Eliza felt that now it was like so many other things – something she could no longer afford.

She kissed Beth affectionately on the cheek, and then her old friend and servant stood at the bottom of the stairs, her hand clasping the newel post, as she watched her beloved mistress slowly make her way to the top.

Sorrowfully Beth turned towards the kitchen, putting out the hall light as she went.

She wondered if, after all, Eliza knew.

18

With the passage of time Guy Woodville could be said to have mellowed, even to have improved. No longer the wild young roué, he had settled down and become a country gentleman. He had, in his time, sown plenty of wild oats, but the affair with Agnes Yetman and its tragic consequence had unnerved him. It had shown him he was no longer the man he used to be. Nowadays he never seemed to stray, though the maids tried never to be alone in the room with him.

Guy had grown a little more portly, due to his love of good food and wine, and sat uncomfortably upon a horse. He had nevertheless become a horse breeder of some renown, and he ran his estate under the careful, but unobtrusive, guidance of his wife. Like his father before him, he had become something of a scholar. He read a great deal, and had begun to organise the Woodville archives with a view to writing the history of his distinguished family.

The knowledge that he had fathered two children outside wedlock without having the slightest idea what had happened to them may have had a sobering effect on him. Agnes had disappeared and, with her, her child, or so he thought.

George was very different from his father; his Dutch inheritance was very clear in him; he was thrifty, precise and hardworking. Carson, on the other hand, was a Woodville through and through. He seemed to have all his father's faults, though on a smaller scale. Of course he was still very young, and there was plenty of time to develop.

George was several years older than Carson and took life

much more seriously. At heart he was a Heering and, with their Dutch piety, every Sunday at Eton he diligently attended not one church service but two, or even three if he could manage to slip into the St George's Chapel in Windsor as well as the services he attended at the college.

This piety was unnerving to one who had led a dissolute youth and who only entered church for special occasions: weddings, baptisms, funerals and the like. However, George was very lovable and, above all, kind. It was hard not to feel the presence of God more palpably in George than in other people. He was not over-virtuous so that he put people off, as some deeply religious people tend to be, but the joy of his belief showed in his face, his demeanour, his very love of life.

Emily was her father's pet. She had always been so dainty, fragile and lovely, like a little porcelain figurine, with a bubbly personality and a sense of humour. Just to observe Emily was to feel more alive, and Guy attributed much of his change of character to the way he venerated his darling daughter, his desire to be with her and, above all, to be a model to her – someone of whom she could be proud.

And Emily, though she could be wilful and stubborn, recip-rocated. She was every bit her father's girl. They enjoyed walking and inspecting the fields and hedgerows; he taught her to ride so that she promised to be every bit as good as her Aunt Eliza. He taught her the love of the schoolroom and books, and instructed her himself in the periods when her governess was away. He loved her so much that he wanted her always near him and she was never sent to school.

Margaret, inevitably, was a little jealous of his idolised daugh-ter; but it was so difficult to find fault with her. She loved her too, and if Emily kept her father contented and at home then Margaret was contented too.

Since Guy had changed his ways and stayed at home there had been very few visits to London. Guy began to have his clothes made locally, indeed to be even rather indifferent to their cut or quality. He preferred to loaf about in an old jacket and trousers, his shoes slightly scuffed, his waistcoat frequently stained with snuff or tobacco.

By his early forties Guy had assumed the air of a good-natured buffoon, a somewhat eccentric character who was loved, but also slightly derided, by those who knew him or worked for him. People tended to smile behind his back at his casual attire, his absent-mindedness, his awkward seat on a horse, his garrulousness. Occasionally drink still got the better of him. But in a few short years Guy had been transformed from a philanderer into an adequate husband, an earnest and loving father, and his children, each in their different ways, adored him.

Margaret, on the other hand, though universally admired, was loved by scarcely anyone. She was too virtuous, too efficient, too lacking in faults for anyone to be able to identify with her. Despite the devotion of her parents she had never valued physical love, and she found it hard to give it; to kiss or fondle her children when they were babies, or even to see very much of them. They grew up thinking of her as a rather remote mother, who was quick to find fault but sparing with her caresses. None of them could recall ever being cuddled or fondled by her; whereas the all-embracing, all-encompassing love of Guy, especially after he settled down and found happiness with his family, bound them all together.

Carson grew up to be a problem. Everyone said he would change, but they waited in vain. He was as handsome as Emily was pretty; fair, blue-eyed and very tall. He soon turned into a bully at his preparatory school, and his parents were asked to take him away because of physical violence towards a younger boy. For a time Carson was tutored at home. Even here he was beyond even the most patient of tutors, and it was only his elder brother, George, who seemed to have any control over him.

Maybe it was the many hours he spent with Carson, talking patiently to him, and then praying about him in church, that helped make George reach a decision about his future which was to have momentous and unexpected implications for his family.

In the summer of George's seventeenth year he seemed restless and, because he was normally such a settled, even complacent, young man, no one could understand what was the matter with him. He spent hours locked up in his room reading; he was polite but mainly silent at meals. He spent further hours in earnest conversation with Carson, who began to try and avoid him. He even lectured Emily about the sin of vanity: she spent too much time looking at her pretty little self in the mirror.

On Sunday he went to church three times: in the morning, in the afternoon, when he attended the children's service to which he forced his brother and sister to go, and then he was back again for Evensong.

The Reverend Lamb was not much liked by the Yetman and Woodville families – a dislike which went back to Eliza's wedding and also the perfunctory, not to say offhand, manner in which he conducted all the baptisms for the family. Poor Carson had bawled for hours after being drenched by the Rector when he was baptised, and his nurses averred that the shawl of delicate Brussels lace in which he had been wrapped, and which had been in the Woodville family for generations, was ruined.

In the old, irascible Rector who had served Wenham now for many years George found a kindred spirit, a true man of God who concealed his vocation, his sense of the divine, beneath a stern exterior.

Had the Reverend Lamb been of another persuasion he might have been better as a monk attached to an order of silence, for he communicated badly. He found it difficult to express himself or show his true feelings and the real spirit of God that lay beneath.

That summer George spent a great deal of time at the Rectory discussing spiritual matters with the Reverend Lamb, who was astonished and startled to find a young man – and a Woodville to boot, nephew of the repentant sinner Eliza – of such deep and genuine piety.

George Woodville was lean, tall, bookish with, already at the age of sixteen, a pronounced stoop. He was attractive rather than handsome, mildly myopic, with dark hair and the grave features of his mother's side of the family. He was closest of the three to his mother – her chilliness did not upset him – and like her to look at.

He was not the least athletic, and at school he had been renowned only for his scholarship and his piety. He had made few close friends because he was not like other boys, unruly, rumbustious and preoccupied with worldly things. Above all, George had never shown the least interest in or curiosity about the opposite sex. On the other hand, neither had he experimented with that sin against the Holy Ghost which tainted so many of his fellow students: sodomy.

No, from a young age George Woodville was virtuous, his mind set on a much higher plane: on a knowledge and understanding of God, and obedience to His word.

It was with the encouragement and the stirring words of the Reverend Lamb in mind – 'Go forth and spread the word of God' – that, one summer's afternoon, George stood looking at his parents, who were sitting in the gazebo in sight of the oak that Pelham planted. Margaret, industrious as always, sat embroidering, and his father, an open book on his lap, his head on his chest, hands linked across his stomach, was fast asleep.

It seemed such a peaceful, harmonious scene that George was loath to disturb it. As the eldest child he could remember the times when things were not so good between his parents, when there were many harsh words, even at table, but especially behind closed doors.

Margaret, seeing George standing hesitantly on the lawn, put down her needlework and gave him an encouraging smile.

'Hello, dear,' she said, beckoning to him, 'going for a walk?' She raised her face and sniffed the air. 'What a lovely day. Shall I come with you?'

'If you like, er, well, Mother.' George kicked his heels on the ground and looked searchingly at his father. 'Is Father likely to wake up, do you think?'

'Oh, he'll wake up *sometime*,' his mother said, looking at her eldest with a fond smile.

'It's just that I'd rather, er, like to talk to both of you together.'

'Now?' Margaret looked surprised.

'If that would be convenient, Mother.'

'Any time is convenient to me,' his mother said and gave a loud cough in the direction of her husband. 'Guy,' she called.

Guy snorted, sat up, dropped his book, blinked his eyes and looked rapidly round as if he had not the slightest idea what day it was, where he was or with whom.

'Er, er,' he began, shaking himself like a dog fresh from a good swim in the river.

'George would like to talk to us, dear.'

'Er.' Guy blinked again, and as his son retrieved his book from the ground and placed it on a table beside him he said, 'Talk? Talk about what, George?'

'If it's not inconvenient, Father.' George perched nervously on a chair between his parents. The gazebo was full of old, comfortable furniture, and Margaret occupied the chaise-longue made of cane which enabled her to put her feet up.

Guy sprawled in a low cane chair covered with a rug, his back supported by cushions. The front of the gazebo was open to the air, the sides enclosed by glass. Protected from the wind it was an ideal spot on a sunny day, even a chilly one, and much favoured by the family.

About a hundred yards away Emily sat under Pelham's Oak with a friend from a nearby grand house, Sarah Wills. Sarah Wills was the same age, and the pair were intimate friends, seldom apart if they could help it. Sometimes Sarah joined in lessons with Emily's governess. Sarah and Emily were drawing a horse that stood in the field nearby looking rather enigmatically at them over the fence.

Suddenly the two girls put down their books and began to play with a skipping rope until they were breathless. There was much laughing and, for a few moments, her parents and brother watched, spellbound by the energy, vivacity and sheer beauty of the young Emily as, her long curls flying, she vied in turns with the much quieter Sarah to skip the greatest number of times.

'Now, George,' Guy said, reluctantly turning his head away, 'I am *fully* awake. What is it that is important enough for you to interrupt my afternoon nap?'

Although Guy's expression was severe, his voice was bantering, even light-hearted, but it was enough to discourage George, who, in view of what he was going to say, wished to get his parents, especially his father, in their most receptive mood.

'Oh, well, Father,' he faltered, standing up, 'maybe it doesn't matter. Another time.'

'No, boy, no, I'm joking.' Guy held out a hand. 'Sit down.'

'Of course he's joking.' Margaret eyed Guy severely. 'Do go on, George. I'm all agog.'

'Well – ' with a show of reluctance George resumed his seat, stretching his long legs out before him and adjusting his gold-rimmed spectacles which helped to give him an appearance of such earnestness ' – I actually want to talk to you about my career.'

'Career!' Guy looked surprised. 'But you are the heir to Pelham's Oak, George. Thanks to the husbanding of our fortune by your uncles, there is no need to worry about a career. None at all.'

'Or does he wish to go into the family business?' Margaret looked up with interest, neatly cutting a thread with a pair of small, sharp silver scissors. '*After* Cambridge, of course.'

'No, Mother, nothing like that. The whole sordid subject of commerce and profit-making rather disgusts me. I do not mean to be offensive, Mother,' he said hastily, pressing his glasses up upon his nose.

'I'm not the least offended, but, my dear, please do go on.' Margaret abandoned her sewing altogether. 'You have me quite worried.'

'I don't think *you* will worry, Mother, when you know, so

much as Father.' George turned to his father, who was now sitting upright looking at him in comic disbelief.

'Go *on*, George,' he said, tapping his fingers on the arm of his chair. 'Do get it over with, man. It can't be *that* terrible.'

'Well, Father, Mother.' George stopped, choked, and then continued in a rapid voice. 'I feel I have been called to the service of God. I can interpret my feelings in no other way. I have discussed this not only with the chaplain at Eton but with the Bishop, and also the Rector of Wenham. They *all* feel that I have a vocation.'

'A *what*?' Guy said peevishly, scratching his nose as if he didn't properly understand. Then he looked across at his wife for clarification. 'Do *you* understand what he's saying, dear?'

'I think,' Margaret said a little faintly, as if fully aware of the impact George's announcement would have, 'I *think* our son is telling us that he wishes to enter the ministry, dear.'

'The ministry?' Guy barked. 'The *Church*, do you mean?'

'Yes, Father.' George choked again, for he could tell from his father's expression that his deepest fears were about to be realised.

'You mean you want to be a vicar – *you*, the heir to the Woodville fortune, title and estate? Out of the question.'

Guy sank back as if the effort had cost him a good deal and, taking up his book again tried, with trembling hands, to find his place.

'Guy – ' Margaret leaned towards him ' – that is *no* way to treat George's announcement. You can at least discuss it with him. You can see how difficult it was for him to tell us.'

'I should think it was difficult.' Guy thumped down his book again. 'A vicar! A species I detest.'

'I know that, Father. That's why I dreaded telling you. The Reverend Lamb has been nothing if not good and helpful. He urged me to tell you.'

'Ah, he's the one who's behind it all, is he?' Guy cried, raising a finger in the air. 'I shall have him dismissed from his living. I'll personally speak to the Bishop.'

'Guy, *don't* be absurd,' Margaret said calmly. 'George, your eldest son, is trying to have a proper conversation with you, something he very rarely does now, by the way. He is obviously seeking our guidance and advice, as his parents, and you are doing nothing but uttering threats.'

'They are *not* threats,' Guy muttered. 'I simply will not have my eldest son, my heir, corrupted by the *Church*.'

'I am not being corrupted, Father.' George's voice grew heated too. 'I am answering a voice, *the* voice of God, which has been speaking to me persistently for a number of years.'

'Rubbish,' Guy said and, picking up his book, pretended to read even though it was upside down.

'You must listen, Father, because I am going to do it.' George, driven beyond endurance, snatched the book out of his father's hands.

'You *can't* without my permission,' Guy said, trying to snatch it back.

'After I am twenty-one I can do what I like.'

'You will be very foolish if you do, my son. I can make life very unpleasant for you. The Woodville fortune is not as clear-cut as you might think. Much of it remains in the hands of the Heering family . . .'

'Who, I'm sure, would support me being far nearer to God in their estimation than you, Father.'

'Don't you *dare* be impertinent to me, sir.' Guy jumped with surprising alacrity out of his seat. 'I'm telling you you cannot be a vicar. I do not want you to be one, and you must put such a ridiculous notion from your mind. Sir George Woodville, a parson!' Guy snorted with laughter and abruptly sat down again.

'Anyway, dear, you are going to Cambridge,' Margaret said a little nervously, surprised by her husband's vehemence. 'You are studying Classics, and that will give you time to think about it. You may feel very differently in a few years' time.'

'I should hope so,' Guy said, appearing mollified.

'I thought I'd change my studies to include Theology, Father,' George said boldly.

'Well, you won't,' Guy snarled. 'Classics it is, and Classics it will remain. Now let's stop this conversation, George, and please don't ever bring it up again. Get rid of the notion once and for all, or you will no longer find yourself welcome here.'

The girls, who had moved with their hoop and a ball to the end of the field, were now seen walking slowly back towards the house. Sarah looked as though she were tired, or had somehow been hurt, and Emily's arm was around her protectively. Her governess, who was still reading under the tree, put down her book and went quickly over to her charges. She put her head close to Sarah's, who appeared to be weeping, and began talking to her earnestly.

Margaret put aside her tapestry and went over to the girls, leaving the men staring stonily ahead, mouths tightly pursed as if all communication between them had ceased.

'What is it, Sarah?' Margaret asked anxiously.

'Sarah is not very well. She says she has a headache,' Emily said.

'Oh dear.' Margaret put her hand on the girl's brow and then rapidly withdrew it.

'Goodness me, she is *very* hot. We must take her home at once. I'm sure she has a high fever. Did you not feel well when you came, dear?'

Sarah shook her head, but seemed disinclined to say anything more.

'She likes coming here,' Emily explained. 'She thought her mother might stop her if she said she had a headache.'

'Well, that's very silly of you, Sarah,' Margaret chided the stricken girl. 'Anyway you'll soon be home.' She looked up at the governess who had closed her book and appeared concerned.

'Would you go with her, Miss Phillips, and tell Mrs Wills I think she should call Dr Hardy? I fear Sarah has a *very* high temperature indeed.'

Margaret and the governess, supporting the by now weeping girl between them, went rapidly back to the house, while Emily resumed her game with the ball and, throwing it high in the air, began dancing about the lawn, her terrier Spot yapping excitedly at her feet. She was such a picture of joy and innocence in her pink dress, long white socks and white shoes, her fair curls blowing in the wind, that Guy's parental heart filled with love for his darling: someone he knew would never fail him or distress him, as George had. He wished that she would never grow up, and remain as she was now: a lovely young girl, neither a child nor a woman.

'Come over here, darling,' he called out to her, and she ran happily over to him, and flinging her arms around his neck.

'You would *never* upset your papa would you, darling?' he asked, looking into her eyes.

'Never, Papa, never,' she said smiling. 'Why?'

'George wishes to be a minister.'

'A *what*?' Emily's voice seemed to throb with amusement.

'Like the Reverend Lamb.'

'Oh *that*!' Emily put her hand to her mouth and, trying unsuccessfully to suppress her giggles, looked askance at her brother. 'The *Reverend* George Woodville,' she said in a mocking tone, and began to laugh so much that her father joined in. To the sound of their cruel, echoing laughter, George rose abruptly and made his way across the lawn towards the stables in order to saddle a horse that would take him to his aunt's house in Wenham.

'I'm sure your father will come round to the idea,' Eliza, said, looking at George with sympathy as she passed him a plate of cakes across the table of the conservatory where they were having tea.

George and Eliza had always enjoyed a close relationship. From childhood he had been a sensitive soul, rather a difficult boy to understand and although she knew Guy loved him, he didn't always see eye to eye with him.

'Your father loves you very much,' she said. 'I wonder he didn't think you might enter the Church before.'

'Why?' Guy looked at her in surprise. 'Did you?'

'Yes, I did. You have always been religious, gone frequently to church, got high marks in Bible studies. I am not the least surprised you consider you have a vocation. I am only surprised your father didn't think of it before.'

'I only realised it myself this summer,' George said. 'I have been feeling I had a call for a long time, but Mr Lamb helped me. It was he who encouraged me to confide in Father and Mother.'

'Oh!'

'You don't like him very much, do you, Aunt?'

'I don't consider him the *most* saintly of men,' Eliza said, 'but what he did to me was a very long time ago. I am sure he has changed since then, and his sermon at your Uncle Ryder's death was very fine . . . a great comfort to us all . . .' Her voice trailed off, and her expression was one of grief. George leaned towards her and grasped her hand.

'*That* is what I want to do too; to be of service, bring comfort to the afflicted . . .'

'And I am sure you will do it very well, George,' she said gently. 'Now why don't you go for a ride with your cousins? They see little enough of you, and they admire you. And would you tell Connie to come in and see me? You might find her in the orchard playing with the others, and George – ' she let go his hand as he stood gazing down at her ' – cheer up. I'm sure it will all come right.'

From inside came the sound of the piano, a piece by Mozart or Schubert, Eliza wasn't sure which, played expertly, even thrillingly, and she could imagine little Connie's long, beautiful fingers running with mesmerising speed up and down the keys.

'Oh no,' she said to George, 'she has started her piano practice inside.'

It really was a miracle to have such gifts, Eliza thought, watching George go round to the stables in search of a cousin to go riding with, and then she turned to enter the house, walking slowly in the direction of the music room while all the time the music grew louder and louder.

She stood for a while on the threshold watching the little girl – for she was still only ten – perched on the high piano stool playing without music, the stand empty in front of her. Her little head followed the direction of her skilful fingers – to the right towards the high notes, left towards the base.

Suddenly Connie seemed to sense that someone was watching her, and she stopped, her hands still poised over the keyboard, her face turned towards the door.

'Oh Eliza,' she cried, jumping off her stool. 'I'm sorry, I should have asked permission.'

'But you don't *need* permission to play the piano in this house,' Eliza said, stooping towards her. 'Please don't stop. What is it?'

'Sonata in C by Mozart. One of my favourite pieces.'

'And you play it so beautifully, Connie. You have a great talent.'

'A gift of God,' Connie said, a pious sentiment of which George would have approved. It was all the more remarkable because Miss Fairchild was not a regular churchgoer. It was suggested that she blamed God for her affliction and didn't see why she should spend her life on her knees thanking Him for it.

Connie, however, did go to church and was a particular favourite of Mrs Lamb, who was musical too, teaching her to play the organ. Connie, with her lovely voice, sang in the choir and was often given solo soprano parts.

'Go on playing, Connie,' Eliza urged, giving her an encouraging push towards the piano, but Connie shook her head.

'I just wanted to play a few bars. Aunt Vicky will soon be here to fetch me.'

'Come and have a cup of tea in the conservatory. Maybe Miss Fairchild will join us when she arrives.'

That seemed to satisfy Connie, who, although she was shy, retiring and undersized, was possessed of a formidable will of her own. However, when they reached the conservatory George had returned and was sitting by the tea tray. The sight of him seemed to throw Connie into immediate confusion, and she turned to go back into the house again.

Eliza held out her hand, which Connie quickly grasped, and

as she drew the young girl gently into the conservatory Eliza thought that the trouble with living in such close proximity to an elderly spinster was that one became like one, especially a young, withdrawn, socially unaware child like Connie. Clearly she was frightened of men and didn't mix easily with her young relations.

'Hello, Connie,' George said rising as the two females entered the conservatory. 'I heard your playing. It was magnificent.'

'Thank you, George.' Connie blushed to the roots of her hair and stared fixedly at her shoes.

'Shall you take it up professionally?'

'Oh *no*,' Connie said hastily. 'I don't think so.'

'You mean she could teach the piano, George?' Eliza enquired, pouring fresh tea.

'Or play it,' George said, resuming his seat. 'Clara Schumann was a *very* accomplished pianist who performed in public.'

'Oh, I don't think I should like *that*!' Connie said, nervously screwing up her handkerchief in her hands.

'But why not?' George asked kindly.

'I'm too shy,' Connie replied. 'I hate playing at school, or singing solo in the choir. I hate it, but sometimes I must do it.'

'That's a good child,' George said gently, and then he sat looking speculatively at her for some time as though seeing aspects of her he had not been aware of before.

Connie was no beauty; she took after her mother, whose looks had not been her strong point. She had straight brown hair which her maid nightly put into rags in order to try and beautify her. She wore steel-rimmed spectacles and yet her eyes were perpetually screwed up as though the optician had prescribed the wrong prescription and she couldn't see properly. The consequence was that her face wore an expression of perpetual bewilderment which made her seem dull, or even slightly retarded, which was far from the case.

'Aren't you riding, George?' Eliza enquired.

'None of them want to come, and I have to return home soon anyway.'

'Oh well, I'm sure your father will have got over the shock and you will find him in a better disposition.'

'I hope so.' George drained his cup and got up. He bent over to kiss Eliza on the cheek and then turned to Connie, who shrank back in her chair.

'Goodbye, Connie.' George didn't attempt to kiss her but stood gazing at her again. 'You know that "Amadeus" means beloved by God? I'm sure it applies to you as well as to the divine Mozart.'

At this compliment Connie blushed violently, and squeezed her eyes together as though she could obliterate herself from their sight.

Eliza gave George a knowing smile – Connie's bashfulness was well known in the family – and, rising, took his arm as she saw him to the door.

'Sometimes she's so nervous and bashful I fear for her. Even the company of her contemporaries upsets her.'

'That's why she's so happy with Miss Fairchild,' George said. 'She is no threat to our dear Connie, who is so unaware of her gift that she feels threatened by other children. I'm afraid she will be a spinster like Miss Fairchild, but who knows? I am very fond of Connie and wish I could draw her out more.'

'Maybe when she's older you will,' Eliza said encouragingly, patting his lapel. 'Now *don't* let your father upset you.'

'I'll be going to Cambridge next year anyway.' He stood with her at the front door, his hands in his pockets. 'Mother insists on that, and I agree.'

'You will definitely drop Classics for Theology?'

'Yes I will, or I may combine both. A knowledge of the Scriptures in the original languages will be of great benefit to me. Thank you for your support, Aunt Eliza.' He kissed her again.

'I'll have a word with Guy if I get the chance,' Eliza said, and as Ted brought round George's horse she watched him mount it and ride away.

When she returned to the conservatory Connie appeared to have recovered her composure and sat there drinking tea.

'What is George afraid *of*?' she asked, looking at Eliza.

'He wishes to become a minister of the Church and his father is unhappy about it.'

'Why?' Connie chose a cake from the plate, carefully examining it with her myopic eyes as if inspecting it for imperfections. She seemed quite happy and at ease now that she was alone with her sister-in-law.

Eliza resumed her seat next to her. 'He is his father's heir. One day he will be *Sir* George.'

'But he can still be a minister, can't he?'

'Oh yes; but supposing he is sent to an industrial parish or somewhere far away, perhaps overseas? I think it likely that, by the time his father dies, George will be quite happy to serve in the parish of his ancestors. Guy is a comparatively young man.' Eliza suddenly looked as though she had had a good idea. 'I shall put *that* to Guy when I have the chance to speak to him. It doesn't mean that George will leave Pelham's Oak for ever, or be unable to look after the estate. Guy was very young when he inherited. Our father was a sickly man, but Guy is robust. For that reason George may be quite old when he succeeds to the title.'

Connie screwed up her eyes as if choosing her words with great care. 'I find it very difficult, Eliza, to think of *you* as a Woodville, growing up in that huge house.'

'Why is that?' Eliza said laughing, but she could already guess the answer.

'You are so unstuffy. I like Lady Woodville well enough, and she is always most kind to me; but I can never forget *who* she is or *where* she lives. With you I never think of it. But I love you,' she added, and the spontaneity of the remark went straight to Eliza's heart. She leaned across and took Connie's hand in hers.

'And I love you,' she whispered. 'Tell me, are you happy, Connie? Are you really happy with Miss Fairchild?'

'Oh, I love Aunt Vicky,' Connie cried, clasping her hands together. 'I am *very* happy with her. But,' she folded her hands, and her eyes filled with nostalgia, 'but I do *so* miss Papa. I loved him very much and no one will ever take his place.' She gave a deep sigh and her expression became practical again. 'Aunt Vicky may look odd, and she does speak in a peculiar way, and has a funny lip, but she is the most *beautiful* person inside. Besides her goodness, she is full of fun and understanding.' Connie paused and her expression changed. 'And she is *very* good to me. She understands me. Not many people do.'

'Oh, *Connie*,' Eliza said, abashed.

'You do, Eliza,' Connie hastened to reassure her, 'but you and Aunt Vicky and Mrs Lamb are about the only ones. Miss Bishop is kind, but none of my school friends understand me. In fact I don't think I have any. I never invite them home to tea, and they never invite me.'

'Well, perhaps you should invite them and they'll invite you back,' Eliza said encouragingly.

'But I don't really like them. I think they're childish and silly.'

'Well, that's it then, isn't it? They realise that.'

'Do you think they do?' Connie turned to stare owlishly at her.

'Oh yes, without any doubt. They may be a little afraid of you, and . . . Oh, but here *is* Miss Fairchild.' Eliza got quickly to her feet as Miss Fairchild, driving her own pony and trap, stopped in front of the porch.

Immediately one of the grooms came round the house to help her down, and she was already standing on the ground dusting herself energetically when Eliza arrived, but even then Connie was there first.

'Oh, *there* you are, dear,' Miss Fairchild said, her thin lips breaking into a smile, and as Connie rose on tiptoe to kiss her Eliza realised the strength of the bond was certainly that of mother and daughter.

They had, indeed, found each other.

'Will you come in and have a cup of tea, Miss Fairchild?' Eliza asked, pointing towards the conservatory. 'My nephew George Woodville has just left us, and Connie and I were having a chat.'

'Well, that's *very* kind.' Miss Fairchild turned to the groom who was patiently holding the pony. 'Maybe you'd look after him for me, would you, while I accept Mrs Yetman's kind invitation? And maybe Connie will go with you?'

'Certainly, ma'am.' The groom bowed and led the pony and trap round to the back of the house while Connie, sensing that Miss Fairchild wished to be alone with Eliza, trotted obediently after him.

'That seems a nice young man,' Miss Fairchild observed as she followed Eliza into the conservatory. 'I don't think I saw him before?'

'He is nice, but, alas, he will probably have to leave us.'

'Oh dear,' Miss Fairchild said politely, 'is he going away?'

'I'm afraid I shall have to give notice to most of my staff.' Eliza pointed to a chair. 'My husband didn't leave me well off. Of course, he didn't expect to die.'

'Of course not.' Miss Fairchild clucked sympathetically.

'We have kept quite a large staff, and gradually I've been forced to shed them. The children must learn to become self-sufficient.'

'Oh, I always believe in that, anyway,' Miss Fairchild averred accepting a cake with her tea. 'But I do hope you are not – ' she paused and searched the ceiling for the right word ' – not in *distress*, Eliza?'

'Not in distress, I assure you,' Eliza said reassuringly. 'But nothing is secure in life, is it? This house, for instance, does not belong to us and, although my brothers-in-law say they will give us several years, I always feel they may change their minds. You know how it is.'

'Fortunately I do not.' Miss Fairchild brushed a crumb from her lap. She wore a light summery jacket and skirt with a white blouse open at the neck. Her hat, secured with two large hatpins, was made of straw and had a rakish bow at one side. Her high buttoned shoes matched her bag, both shining brilliantly as though her maid had given them much of her personal attention that morning.

Miss Fairchild always looked prosperous, well turned out

and, since Connie had gone to live with her, much much happier.

'I say "fortunately", Eliza, though I do not wish to sound smug or complacent. But my dear mother and father left me with sufficient money, as I once explained to you. I have never known want or insecurity, but' – she stared mournfully at Eliza for a moment – 'neither have I known the blessing of a happy marriage or children. In fact, but for that singular encounter that you know about, I have never had any romantic contact with a man in my life. So, you see, money is not everything, as I expect you well appreciate. You at least were singularly blessed in your marriage to Mr Yetman.'

'Yes, I was.' Eliza gazed down at her own feet. If Miss Fairchild knew about Ryder she might not envy her so much. There was nothing like the pain of discovering that the husband one so loved had betrayed one.

There was a pause while both women seemed lost in their own private thoughts, and then Miss Fairchild cleared her throat and fidgeted with the large cameo brooch on the lapel of her jacket.

'Dear Eliza . . . *I hope* you will not mind my mentioning this . . .' she began.

'Mentioning what, Miss Fairchild?' Eliza felt a momentary nervousness, wondering if there were something amiss with Connie.

'Well, it *is* rather a delicate thing to suggest, and I *hope* you will not misconstrue it, but accept it in the *spirit* in which it is intended.' Miss Fairchild gave certain words emphasis, and mentally one could see them italicised as in a book.

'Do go on, Miss Fairchild,' Eliza said encouragingly.

'You know that dearest Constance is my heir. She will get every penny I have when I die, in addition to my property which, though not extensive is, I believe, quite valuable. There is also what her father left her, accruing compound interest. She will be quite a wealthy young woman, and never in need.'

'Oh, if you think I am worrying about looking after Connie . . .'

'No, that is *not* my thought at all,' Miss Fairchild hastened to interrupt her. 'But the fact is that Constance has a large house in which she does not live. It is closed and shuttered and may remain like that for years. When Constance comes of age she may wish to sell it, I don't know; but I felt that if, in the meantime, you would like to use it Constance and I would be delighted. With the means at her disposal I'm sure that it could be made over to you legally for as long as you wish. *That* way you would have no worry about being ejected from this delightful place with its fond memories of your dear husband, your long and happy marriage.'

'Oh, Miss Fairchild,' Eliza said with a break in her voice, 'how *very*, very kind of you to think of it.'

Miss Fairchild held out a hand.

'Don't rush. Don't do anything you don't want to. Think about it. After all, did you not once tell me that you believed you saved her life? I can assure you that Constance would be *only* too pleased to return your *own* goodness to her by making over to you indefinitely the use of her house.'

Soon afterwards Miss Fairchild left with Connie sitting beside her in the trap. As they drove out of the gates and out of sight up the hill, Eliza waved, and remained waving even when she could see them no more.

Then she wandered back along the drive and paused for a few moments to gaze at the view: the smooth lawn leading down to the river, the herbaceous borders full of bright summer flowers, the trees in full leaf and, on the other side, Wenham Wood where Ryder and his brothers used to play.

The truth was that Eliza felt at times that she was anxious to be gone from Riversmead, a place that now held few charms for her. She would never at the time of Ryder's death have imagined that this would ever be the case, but it was.

Ever since she had known about Annie McQueen, Ryder's memory was tainted. They'd been together fifteen years by the time he was killed, been through so much, and although no man is ever perfect, to her he nearly was. They had their arguments,

409

their disagreements, as any couple had; but that deep bond of joys and sufferings shared, of children produced, of the terrible loss of their first-born, had seemed to her to forge their love irrevocably.

But no. The fact that he should have chosen to deceive her with a woman as notorious as Annie McQueen had sickened her then, and it sickened her still.

She had once blamed herself for the tragedy that had occurred; but there were times when she wondered if that guilt should be laid at the door of her mother. The constant warfare between her and the son-in-law she refused to recognise had led to rows between Ryder and his wife. Had it, in the end, led him to seek consolation in the arms of another woman?

Maybe what was needed was a fresh start; Miss Fairchild offered a solution and one that could be accepted with dignity. Maybe. Who knew?

Only time would tell.

19

Lally sat very stiff and correct, as she always did when she paid her quarterly visit to the Mountjoy family in Kentish Town. Quarterly, or thereabouts. The year she married Prosper she only saw her son once.

But as he didn't know she was his mother, she assumed that Roger felt no deprivation or loss when she failed to visit him.

To Roger, as to all the Mountjoy family and their neighbours, Lally's visits were a great talking point. They all stood gawping on the pavement and hanging out of the windows when the fine lady appeared in her carriage, which waited outside until her visit was over. Her goodness and generosity to a large family like the Mountjoys, whose father was permanently out of work, was a source of wonder. Why did she do it? No one knew. Few could recall the small baby wrapped in a shawl who had been left there many years before by Mrs Mountjoy's sister Abby.

Edgar Mountjoy had been a railway worker and had lost a leg when a train approaching King's Cross station ran over him while, in a moment of carelessness, he was looking the wrong way when adjusting points at the entrance to the station. Maybe he was talking, or maybe he was drunk – it was never quite decided. By that time the Mountjoys had five children. One more would make no difference, so when Abby suggested that they provide a home for the child her mistress had borne out of wedlock they agreed to take him in.

To have an extra child was no hardship, but the money, the

promise of a regular income, was a great boon. Indeed, it had helped the family to survive over the intervening years when Edgar Mountjoy had not worked at all, and they all regarded Mrs Martyn as a great benefactress.

Roger was brought up without knowing that his parents were not Edgar and Dot, that his real name was not Mountjoy. At his birth he had been registered Bowyer; but he was always known as Roger Mountjoy and he went to the local council school in Kentish Town.

In many ways Lally might have liked to forget about Roger altogether, but there was always a little nugget of affection, a modicum of mother love for the boy she had borne and also for the man she had once loved in a way she never could love Prosper Martyn.

On the occasion of this particular visit the other children, as usual, rushed forward to open the presents Lally always brought them. It was like Christmas and better, because there were never presents at Christmas time, only some nuts and occasionally a chicken and some sweets from their mother's employers in the City where she worked as a cleaner.

Edgar Mountjoy spent much of the day at the public house at the end of the road – the Lord Raglan – resting his good leg on a bar stool. Most of the money earned by his hard-working wife or sent by Mrs Martyn ended up in the cash register of the Lord Raglan, as was quite apparent from the paucity of the furnishings, the general air of poverty and neglect about the house, which stank of the odour and dampness of other people's washing.

Roger was a boy of startling good looks – so startling that he was teased by his schoolmates, who nicknamed him 'girlie'. His looks were, in fact, rather feminine. He had blond curly hair and dark violet eyes, just like his mother, and also her long dark lashes that lay on his cheeks enhancing his pink and white complexion.

'Girlie' he might have been called by his rough schoolmates, but there was nothing effeminate about him; even at a young age he liked the female sex, who liked him. But there *was* something about him that made him seem out of place in Kentish Town. Despite his upbringing, there was a lordly, even aristocratic quality about Roger that immediately singled him out as someone different from the rest.

Lally sat in the parlour, twitching her nose disapprovingly and looking about her. Then she looked at Roger, who stood in front of her, his hands by his side, his bright golden hair plastered to his head with water, his suit darned and his nose well wiped.

Peering at him closely, she tried to remember exactly when she had given birth to Guy Woodville's son. What hopes had she not had then, foolish girl? The son of a baronet – surely that would mean something, a change in her fortunes, a foot on the ladder of respectability?

But no, it had only meant rejection, more years of deprivation, until Prosper Martyn had appeared as if by magic to give her a life of undreamed of riches and respectability.

But he had not given her a child, and although it was something they rarely spoke of it was a source of great sorrow to them both.

'How old are you now, boy?' she asked Roger peremptoririly.

'Eleven, mum,' Roger said with an accent that made even Lally cringe.

'I am not your *mum*, I am your *aunt*,' Lally corrected him sharply. 'Please address me as such.'

'Yes, Aunt.'

'And where do you go to school?'

'Wiv me bruvvers and sisters.'

'Hm!' Lally looked at him searchingly for some moments and then made a gesture of dismissal.

'You may go now, Roger, but I shall see you again shortly. Please ask Mrs Mountjoy to come and see me.'

'Yes, mum . . . Aunty,' Roger hastily corrected himself and slid through the door yelling 'Muvver! The lady wants yer.'

Dot Mountjoy, looking flustered – Lally's visits were always unannounced – came in drying her hands on her pinafore. She was pink and perspiring and her hair lay damply on her brow. Lally supposed she was not much older than herself, yet already her hair was streaked with grey and her face was deeply furrowed.

'Oh, Mrs *Martyn*,' Dot cried with a deep bob, 'I hope as how everyfink is all right, madam. Roger has had a cold and I know he looks peaky. I . . .'

'Mrs Mountjoy, I want you to pack Roger's clothes, and any other belongings he might have.' Drawing a purse from her handbag, Lally began extracting notes and counting them. 'I intend to take him with me,' she concluded, looking sharply at Mrs Mountjoy.

'What, today, mum?' Mrs Mountjoy appeared horrified by the news.

'This very day. He does *not* look well, but, worse, he does not *speak* well. His accent is quite atrocious – just like yours.' Lally's face expressed deep disgust. 'Roger is, after all, the son of a gentleman, and it is time he resembled one.'

'Well, what can you *expect*, mum,' Mrs Mountjoy began to whine tearfully 'with *seven* mouths to feed and a husband wot does *no* work?'

'Then you should *make* him work, Mrs Mountjoy,' Lally said severely. 'Even with one leg, is there nothing better he can do than prop up the bar at the Lord Raglan? I intend to pay you ten pounds in lieu of further board and lodging.' She carefully counted the money into the hands of the speechless woman, who had never seen such a large sum all at once in her life. 'There,' she said, shutting her purse again. 'I shall send you more from time to time to show you I am not ungrateful for what you have done in the years when I was unable to provide for him. However, it is time to take Roger back with me, and make a gentleman of him.'

Lally spoke little to the shy, withdrawn boy sitting nervously by her side during the journey back to Montagu Square. A box with a broken lid tied with string and containing his few belongings had been put on the back of the carriage by the coachman who, in so far as it was his business to wonder anything, did ask himself what his mistress was about.

When they reached the house and a liveried footman ran down the steps to help Lally out of the carriage, Roger hung back, conscious of his threadbare suit, his scuffed and down-at-heel boots, and the fact that he had just had a cold and his nose was red.

He wiped it with a grubby handkerchief put in his hands at the last minute by Mrs Mountjoy (who took it from the pocket of a customer's shirt she had been washing at the time) as the footman, in response to something his mistress had said, looked into the interior of the coach and barked: 'Come out, boy.'

Roger stumbled into the house. By town house standards it was not a large one but, to someone used to the dimensions of the railwaymen's cottages in Kentish Town, it appeared vast. Brightly polished woodwork, soft luxurious carpets, sumptuous furnishings and quantities of flowers glowed in the summer sunshine.

'Take the boy up to his room, Roberts,' Lally told the footman.

'Which room, madam?' the footman asked politely.

'Any room.'

'The *servants'* quarters, madam, I presume?' Roberts said loftily.

'No, not the servants' quarters. This boy is my nephew – left by his mother in sadly reduced circumstances, as you can see. Kindly give him one of the spare rooms for the time being and then we shall see what we shall see. I shall probably send him to a boarding school in September.'

'Yes, madam.' Roberts's attitude towards the stranger, while still distant, was a shade more polite.

'Come with me, young man. Have you a valise?'

'Just me box,' Roger said, passing a finger across his nostrils.

The footman, who had heard many rumours regarding his mistress's origins and her rise to riches, could not wait to discuss this latest development with his peers below stairs.

He showed Roger to a comfortably furnished but not luxurious room at the back of the house and then, shutting the door, he left him.

Roger felt completely disorientated by this experience and was not at all sure that he welcomed it. He had been wrenched away abruptly from what, to him, was a large jolly family despite the frequent drunken outbursts of his adoptive father. He had not even been allowed to say goodbye.

Roger looked at the pathetic bundle of belongings which was all he had in the world and, flinging himself on the bed, boots and all, he gave himself up to an orgy of weeping such as he could not remember since Edgar Mountjoy had last tanned his hide when he returned home one night drunk as usual.

The memory of that night seemed to give Roger pause and he sat up.

Much as he loved the other children, fond as he was of his oppressed, downtrodden, overworked adoptive mother, Edgar Mountjoy he had hated. The whole family was frightened of him. It was easy to remember the good things and forget the bad. But there had been many bad times, and they were mostly associated with Edgar and his beatings.

Roger gazed round the room, which contained a chest of drawers, a wardrobe and a washstand with a basin and jug on it, as well as a bookcase and two easy chairs. It looked like a room kept for not very important guests, but Roger wasn't to know that. To him it was luxury.

He had only ever seen books at school and had never been encouraged to linger over them for long. Certainly if a school book had ever been brought home it was used the following day as fuel for lighting the fire.

Roger was curious about books and the world outside generally, but his horizon was limited not only by what he could see but by what he was shown.

It was a very narrow view of life.

Outside he looked on to a small garden, little better than a yard – albeit a well-kept one, and not hung with washing and filled with litter – which, in turn, looked out on to the back of the house on the other side.

It was not an attractive view; it was a confined glimpse of the London skyline, quite common even in the better parts of

London. Land was at a premium as London grew in prosperity.

A grey tabby cat sat on the high wall, its front paws tucked under its chest, and it gazed at Roger in a manner that, though aloof, was not altogether unfriendly. Roger was quite used to the undernourished cats with their ribs showing who jumped about the roofs and walls of Kentish Town scavenging for any little bits, however unappetising, that were thrown out by harassed housewives.

This was a well-formed, well-nourished, even aristocratic creature, and suddenly Roger thought that, one day, he might have a cat like that for his very own, one he could cuddle in bed. Maybe he could also have a puppy on a lead, like those he used to see being walked by people of affluence in Parliament Hill Fields.

He gently opened the window and, putting his arm tentatively out, tried to entice the cat towards him. The cat looked interested, but remained unmoved, merely blinking its eyes once or twice.

'Puss, puss,' Roger called, flicking his fingers gently in front of the cat's nose. 'Pussy . . .'

Suddenly there was a sharp tap on the door, and the superior voice of Robert was heard saying: 'If you are ready, young man, the mistress will see you in the drawing room.'

In a trice the cat, frightened by the disturbance, had gone and left Roger faced with grim reality: the prospect of meeting again his awesome 'aunt', of trying not to feel inferior in front of the servants. His courage drained away, and his impulse was once again to fling himself down on his bed and weep.

Disconsolately he opened the door to find Roberts waiting outside with a supercilious smile, a hand extended towards the staircase.

'This way please, *sir*.'

Downstairs Roger found that Mrs Martyn had changed her dress. Although she was just as beautiful and elegant, she looked a little less formidable in a long tea gown of some soft shimmering material, and several rows of pearls at her throat.

She was standing by the window, and as he entered she turned and he saw in her arms the cat – the beautiful cat who had sat on the wall staring imperturbably at him. It had obviously just jumped into its mistress's arms as she opened the window. It looked over her shoulder and gave Roger a smug, blank stare before putting its face up to be caressed by its mistress.

'Oh, what a lovely cat!' Roger cried, running up to his aunt eagerly and putting out his hands.

Lally immediately stepped back, a look of disapproval on her face.

'Did you wash your hands, boy?'

'Yes mum . . . Aunt,' he lied.

'Show them to me.'

Roger put them both behind his back.

'I said *show* them to me.'

Roger extended them palms outwards.

'You are *lying*, Roger.'

'I saw the cat,' Roger said, his eyes bright with happiness, the expression on his drawn, pale face ecstatic. 'I was talking to him from my bedroom window. Oh, I'm so glad he lives *here*. I'm so glad he's yours. May I hold him, mum?'

'No, you may not, and he is a *she*,' Lally said coldly, withdrawing even further. 'Her name is Coral and she is a pedigree cat, a very rare breed. Little boys with dirty hands are not allowed to touch her.'

'Oh, I'll go and wash them then, mum.' Excitedly Roger made for the door.

'Roger,' Lally commanded sharply.

'Yes, mum?'

'I am your *aunt*, your Aunt Lally – please do *not* forget it. Now, wash your hands in the cloakroom downstairs and then you may come and stroke Coral.'

Really he was quite a dear boy, Lally thought, hand to her chin, one leg crossed over the other as, for the very first time, she took afternoon tea with her son.

When she had brought him back to Montagu Square she was

acting on impulse. She had no real feeling for him – just a sense of duty, she told herself. That was all it was.

Maybe the weather had something to do with it; the fact that, at the time of her visit it had been raining, although so capricious was the English climate that the sun was now shining brightly. Maybe it was the dark, miserable house; the smell of unwashed clothes or the pathetic look on the face of the child to whom, after all, she had given life, and whose prospects in the circumstances in which he was being brought up appeared very grim indeed.

Roger lay on the floor playing with the cat who, now that she had been properly introduced by her mistress, seemed delighted with her new friend. Quite forgetful of her pedigree, she rolled wantonly about on the Aubusson carpet displaying her soft, furry stomach, all four paws in the air.

'I *love* her,' Roger said, looking up at Lally ecstatically. His face was completely transformed, and the thought crossed her mind that, one day, he might look at her like that.

But did she deserve it? Suddenly overwhelmed with guilt, she stretched out a hand to him.

'Come here to your aunt, Roger, and let me look at you.'

Reluctantly he dragged himself away from Coral, who was not the least perturbed and began to wash herself, particularly where he'd ruffled her fur.

Roger went up to Lally, who touched his face. She had never held him or stroked him since he was a baby. Maybe a peck on the cheek during her rare visits; visits she could scarcely now recall. They had been more duty visits, after all.

'You're a dear boy, Roger,' she said after a while, 'and I want you to know why I have taken you away from the Mountjoys.'

'Yes, Aunt. Am I never to go back?'

'I don't *think* so,' Lally said after a pause. 'I have a husband who is called Prosper. You must call him Uncle Prosper. He is a businessman and very, very rich. He is away at the moment, but he will be back in a day or two, and by that time I shall have purchased for you a complete set of new clothes: new suits, new pyjamas, new underclothes, socks, shoes and hats, new everything. Tomorrow I will send you to a lady who is going to help you to speak properly. You will spend all day with her, and all the day after that, and the day after *that*, until you have not a trace of the vulgar, awful accent you have now. Do you understand?'

'Yes, Aunt.'

'That's better. I want you to be a gentleman, Roger, because you are one by birth, and I want you to impress your Uncle Prosper and be *very* nice to him, correct and most polite. I want him to like you, do you see, dear boy?' She began, very gently, to stroke his brow, brushing back his fair hair, and suddenly her eyes filled with tears.

'Oh, Roger,' she sighed, 'it is *very* important that you get on with Uncle Prosper and that he likes you. Because if he doesn't, I may have to send you away again.'

Roger turned round and looked at Coral lying again on her back, her ablutions finished, but this time she was winking coquettishly at him.

Roger thought of the cat and the house, the soft warm bed all to himself, the lovely smell of Aunt Lally and the sensuous feel of her hand as she stroked his face, the glint of jewels on her fingers.

'I will be *very* nice to Uncle Prosper,' Roger promised, looking limpidly at Lally, 'because I like you and I like the cat, and I feel now that I would like to stay here.'

Dr Hardy looked at the young girl who, her brow bathed in perspiration, her breathing very rapid and irregular, lay tossing and turning on the bed before him. He put a hand on her wrist, feeling her pulse, and noted that her skin was dry and hot to the touch.

At his request Emily's maid drew back the bedclothes and discreetly pulled up the girl's nightdress so that the doctor could examine her. In the background, a hand to her mouth, Margaret waited anxiously.

Dr Hardy stooped and looked closely at the rash on the girl's chest, on her legs and her stomach.

He nodded to the nurse, who drew down her nightdress and tucked the sick girl up in her bed again.

'Scarlet fever,' he pronounced, turning round to the distressed mother. 'How long has she been like this?'

'She began to be ill yesterday, Doctor,' the nursemaid said in a frightened voice. 'I called her ladyship at once.'

'Yesterday she didn't seem quite so ill,' Margaret said. 'Her little friend Sarah Wills is unwell too, and they were playing together only a few days ago.'

'I'm afraid in that case they both have scarlet fever,' the doctor said. 'I will prescribe medicine and hope that the illness takes it course. Above all you must keep down the fever with cold washes several times a day.'

Dr Hardy was shown downstairs and offered whisky by Sir Guy as he gave him and George the news. Margaret remained upstairs with her daughter.

'Any other signs of sickness in the family or the staff?' Dr Hardy asked. 'Is Carson all right?'

'Carson is still at school,' Guy said. 'The term has not finished.'

'Just as well. Scarlet fever is an unpleasant thing.'

'She *will* be all right, though, won't she, doctor?' Guy asked, suddenly sensing that the doctor was less than his usual cheery self.

'She has a bad attack, Sir Guy, I'll be honest with you. Her pulse is rapid, her temperature very high. We must trust in the will of God and hope for the best.'

Guy stood up and with a fearsome expression on his face rushed over to Dr Hardy. He grasped him by the lapels, upsetting the good doctor's whisky all over his waistcoat.

'Don't you *dare* let my daughter die, Hardy. She is my life. If you think there is *any* remote chance of that, you'd better stay here and make sure that she lives. Do you see?'

'Really, Sir Guy!' Dr Hardy stepped back as George pulled his father away. 'Scarlet fever is a most *virulent* disease for which there is no effective treatment. The fever must take its course, reach its crisis, and then, as I say, with God's help the patient will recover.'

'With *your* help too, Hardy,' Guy said, jabbing a finger in his stomach. 'It's no use standing there drinking my whisky and taking my money if my daughter is going to be allowed to die.'

'Hush, Father, hush!' George threw an apologetic glance at the doctor. 'Dr Hardy has done all he can. Threatening him won't help.'

'I'll look in again tonight,' Dr Hardy said nervously, putting down his by now empty glass and taking up his black Gladstone bag. At the same time he vigorously dabbed his waistcoat with a handkerchief, looking both affronted and annoyed. 'You won't do *yourself* any good either, Sir Guy, if you lose your temper so readily,' he said. '*You* should be careful of your own health too.'

'And so should *you*.' Guy made as if to fly at him again. 'If my daughter dies I shall proclaim you a charlatan and a fraud, so when you return you had better bring some more effective medicine *or* another doctor . . .'

By this time Dr Hardy had reached the door, and as he sharply turned the handle and threw it open a servant came tumbling down the stairs and rushed towards him.

'Lady Woodville would like you to come upstairs again at once, sir – Emily is having convulsions.'

Dr Hardy spent the rest of the day at Pelham's Oak, and even Guy admitted that he spared no effort to save Emily. By evening her fever was a little lower and, emerging from her state of semi-consciousness, she opened her eyes and saw her parents and her brother standing anxiously at her bedside. In the background was Dr Hardy, still in shirtsleeves, and, behind him, her trusted nurse Nora.

With overbright eyes she looked at them, and her cracked, dry lips parted in an effort to smile.

'Oh, my *darling*,' Guy said, kneeling beside her and taking her hot hand. 'We have been so *very* worried about you. How do you feel, my precious?'

'I love you, Father,' she said. Then she closed her eyes again, but from the even rhythm of her breast it seemed that she had sunk into a deeper, less fitful sleep.

'Is the crisis over, Doctor?' Margaret asked, standing at the side of the bed opposite Guy and taking up a limp hand to feel the feeble pulse.

'She is certainly a little better,' Dr Hardy said cautiously, slowly rolling down his sleeves. 'I think tonight will be crucial; but tomorrow, I hope . . . I'll look in again first thing in the morning.'

The doctor put on his coat and picked up his bag, once again preparing to depart. George went down the stairs with him to the massive front doors which were held open by two footmen.

'I must apologise for my father,' George said. 'He has been a very, very worried man. You see he so adores Emily, the only girl.'

'I quite understand,' Dr Hardy said a little stiffly, for he too was tired and anxious. A medical man was unaccustomed to being attacked by his patients: usually they were only too grateful for what he could do. However, he had no wish to lose a patient, especially one from a wealthy and well-known family. It did one's reputation no good at all, and as it was there were already too many doctors crowding into the district and setting up their brass plates.

'Your father has always been an excitable man. But it does the patient no good even to *appear* to be worried about them. If they sense the anxiety, inevitably their temperatures soar even higher. Try and keep your father calm, George, away from drink and out of his daughter's room. I'll see you tomorrow.'

'Thank you, Dr Hardy,' George said.

He watched the doctor's carriage depart and when he turned to go back inside his heart was heavy. His sister was so weak and emaciated that he wondered how much fight she had left in her.

Margaret Woodville stayed by Emily's bed all the time, relieved occasionally by Nora or one of the maids. It was agreed that Guy was too overwrought to stay for long in the same room, and George repeated to his parents what the doctor had said: if Emily *felt* the anxiety her temperature would rise. Margaret, on the other hand, was a calm, almost unfeeling presence, going about her sickroom duties as quietly and as capably as she went about everything else. Not that she loved her daughter any the less; but she was a woman, and she was more experienced, had suffered more pain and was also more skilled at concealing her emotions.

'Take your father downstairs,' she said after Guy had got up from where he had been kneeling beside Emily's bed and stooped again to place a longer kiss on her brow. 'And *don't* let him come up again. Give him plenty to drink and see that he goes up to bed.'

'The doctor said *not* to let him drink, Mother.' George looked doubtful.

'I think this is an occasion when we must disobey the good doctor; now do as you're told.' His mother gave him an affectionate pat on the cheek before going back into the sickroom and firmly shutting the door behind her.

George went slowly downstairs, thinking what very different people his parents were: his father mercurial, boisterous, romantic; his mother calm, undemonstrative, reserved, slow to show affection.

Yet Mother had always been the real presence in the house, her reliability a source of strength. His father was something of an enigma to George, who was his exact opposite in temperament. He didn't understand people who drank too much, lost their tempers too easily, or made rash judgements. The talk the other evening about his sacred vocation was quite typical of the kind of reaction he had had from his father all his life; impetuous, ill thought out, irascible. His father had yet to apologise for that, but no doubt he soon would.

When he got to the drawing room Guy was pouring whisky, and as he lifted his glass to his mouth his hand already shook.

He gave George a bleary look and then went to sit in front of the fire.

'She will be all right, won't she, George?' He gazed trustfully at his son, as though only he, with his direct line to God, could give him the spiritual consolation he needed.

'I *thought* she seemed a little better, Father,' George replied cautiously.

'She's less red, not so hot,' Guy nodded. 'Hardy *is* a good man. I was wrong to do what I did, but then, I've been so wrong in so many things, George. I've been a rash, impetuous man, and I've made a lot of enemies.'

George poured himself a very small whisky and, replacing the stopper in the decanter, went over to his father's side and drew up a chair next to him. 'It is no use blaming yourself for what is happening to Emily, Father. It is nothing to do with *you* or your past *or* your life.'

'But it *is*,' Guy insisted, slightly slurring his words, which made George suspect his father had already had a very large amount of whisky in a very short time. 'Don't you see? It *is*. It is the judgement of God for my past life. I have been a bad father, George, worse than you know, a bad husband too. I have been an adulterer, George. I have.' Guy shook his head sadly as though the experience had given him no happiness at all. 'I have been to bed with many, many women. I have fathered at least two children out of wedlock that I know of, and maybe many more that I don't. I . . .'

'*What*, Father?' George looked at him incredulously. Maybe Dr Hardy had been right and he should not have allowed his father to drink. But on the other hand how could he prevent the head of the household from doing what he wished inside it? '*What* are you saying?'

'It's true, George.' Guy threw him a maudlin look. 'I had one mistress who had a son. I don't know what happened to him. There was another woman who became pregnant by me. I don't know what happened to her, *or* her child. I've been a bad, bad man, George, and now God is punishing me.' Guy put down his glass and, pulling a large handkerchief from his pocket, began to cry. 'I have been a wicked man, a sinner, and God will take the thing I love most from me – my daughter.'

'Father! I am not here to hear your confession. Maybe you exaggerate, I don't know . . .'

'Oh, no exaggeration, George, I assure you,' Guy continued in the same lugubrious manner. 'Maybe I have not told you the *worst*. About how cruel I was to your dear aunt, Eliza, refusing to support her when she wanted to marry Ryder. Now he's dead too.'

'Yes, but that's not your fault, Father.'

'I could have been kinder to them, more understanding. And yet see how good Eliza was to *me*? How quickly she forgave *me*; and look how many times has she been here since Emily became ill, thinking nothing of the danger to herself or her own children. That woman is a saint, and I am the opposite of a saint. I think I have something of the Devil himself in me, George.'

'Now look, Father, really.' George eyed his father's glass, wondering whether he should refill it or remove it for good. Maybe one last glass and then he'd take him upstairs to bed and let him sink into oblivion.

'The Devil is in me, George, you should know that.' With tears in his eyes Guy held out his hands to his son, who put an arm awkwardly round his father's shoulders. 'You tell me you have a calling, a vocation to serve God. What do I do? Do I listen as a father should, and give wise counsel and advice? No, I do not. I *threaten* you and *mock* you. Did I thank Dr Hardy and tell him he was a good doctor for trying to save my daughter? No, I did not. I mocked him and called him a charlatan. Oh, George!' Guy cried wildly, throwing his arms around his son's neck. 'How I *love* you, how I regret my outburst against you. Pray, George, pray that God will spare Emily, and I vow to you that from now on I will be a changed man. Like St Paul on the Road to Damascus I will allow myself to be blinded by God's light.'

Guy fell to his knees and, the tears streaming down his face, began to intone the words of the Lord's Prayer.

Silently George dropped down beside him and joined his hands together, convinced he was witnessing a miracle.

Prosper Martyn loved his beautiful wife, and he dearly wanted her to bear his child. Yet after several years of marriage their union remained fruitless, and he was no longer a young man, though Lally was still young enough to bear children.

His marriage coincided with a burst of expansion in the Martyn-Heering business, which was growing into one of the great institutions of the City, employing several thousand people worldwide. There was trade with the East Indies and the West Indies, the Indian subcontinent, Russia and the Baltic States. Ships from the Martyn-Heering fleets sailed to North and South America, and as far away as Australia and New Zealand. The warehouses on the Thames were bursting at the seams, and the bank in Threadneedle Street had expanded so fast that already they were looking for larger premises.

Julius and Prosper were partners, equal in seniority, neither of them young and both without an heir. But as they were both religious men they kept their grief to themselves, ascribing it to the will of God.

In every other way Lally was the perfect wife for a man who had married late, who was settled in his ways, already wealthy, and wanted an intelligent partner, a woman of the world, rather than the plaything that many men seemed to like their wives to be.

So completely successful had been her transformation into a lady that he had almost forgotten that she had once graced the boards of the Alhambra, and walked the streets of Soho and Covent Garden selling her body.

Those days were long past; he seldom thought of them now and as he let himself in through the front door of the house in Montagu Square, after another successful trip abroad, he felt it was good to be home. He relished the idea of dinner alone with his adored wife and then early retirement to the raptures of bed.

It was late afternoon, he was earlier than expected, and the hall was in semi-darkness. It was the time when the servants were usually allowed to rest before preparing the evening meal, though there had been a light in the basement and he knew that Cook would already be at work in the kitchen, labouring for the master of the house. Perhaps Lally, too, was upstairs resting, or making one of her visits to her furrier, her dressmaker, milliner or jeweller. He put down his valise and, on top of it, his hat and coat and, smoothing his grey hair, went into the drawing room to order tea.

In the corner of the room he perceived a youth sitting in a chair caressing Coral, Lally's cat, who showed every sign of enjoying the attention, stretching out her claws in ecstasy and almost smiling in Prosper's direction. This in itself was unusual enough, for if Prosper attempted to touch the cat she leapt a mile and, with an indignant squawk, either rushed out of the room or took cover.

Coral was lying in the boy's lap and the boy was stroking her, apparently unaware of Prosper's presence until he coughed. The boy looked up at last and, quickly putting Coral on the floor, stood up, brushing his thick blond curls away from his forehead.

He was an extraordinarily handsome youth, lithe and tall; one day he would be taller than Prosper. He wore a grey suit with an elegant thin pinstripe, a white shirt with a stiff collar and a tie. He looked embarrassed as he stood gravely contemplating the newcomer, and as he came over to him he put out a hand.

'Good afternoon, sir,' he said. 'You must be Uncle Prosper.'

He spoke with such an atrocious Cockney accent – an accent that completely belied his appearance – that Prosper winced. Apart from this disadvantage the effect that the boy made was charming.

'And who are you?' he asked pleasantly, taking the boy's hand. 'I was not aware . . .'

'Mrs Martyn is my Aunt Lally.'

'Indeed?' Prosper, feeling thoroughly confused, crossed to the fireplace and rang the bell for tea. 'This *is* a surprise to me, I must say. Maybe she will . . .'

At that moment there was a commotion in front of the house as the carriage appeared and Lally jumped out before the coachman, or the footman from the house, had time to open the door. She was laden with parcels, and there were more to follow. He could hear her chattering all the way until, obviously seeing his things in the hall, she gave a small scream and he heard 'Oh my goodness!'

She then came rushing into the drawing room, still in her coat and hat, and threw herself into the arms open to receive her.

'My *darling*,' she cried, 'you're *early*.'

'I caught an earlier train from Dover, my dear,' he said, smiling tenderly into her eyes.

'And there was *no one* at Victoria to *meet* you,' she pouted.

'I caught a cab, and – ' he turned towards Roger, who was standing, hands shyly clasped in front of him, a few feet away ' – what a *surprise* awaited me. A nephew! Fancy.'

'Oh *dear*!' Lally looked embarrassed and confused, but still very charming, her high colour accentuating her blonde beauty.

'I had meant to prepare you, dearest. You knew absolutely nothing about Roger.'

'Absolutely nothing. But we have introduced ourselves,' Prosper said calmly.

'He is my nephew,' Lally explained hastily. 'I had an unexpected call from my sister.'

'I didn't know you *had* a sister, my dearest Lally.' Prosper carefully helped her off with her coat. 'You have never mentioned her before.'

'That's why I wanted to see you, dearest, to explain. Oh!' She threw herself into his arms and hugged him tightly. '*Please* don't be cross with your Lally. Roger is a dear, dear boy and I already love him. So will you.'

'Your cat certainly loves him too.' Prosper gently disengaged himself from his wife's embrace. 'That is most singular. I think it even makes me a little jealous. Do you know,' he said, to draw Roger into the conversation, 'that animal never even lets me *touch* her.'

'She *does* love me, sir,' Roger said with a remarkable lack of tact, and, to demonstrate it, he picked Coral up and pressed his face against hers. 'And *I* love her.'

'I can see your nephew *was* deprived, Lally dear,' Prosper remarked after studying him thoughtfully for a moment. 'You must tell me all about him. Incidentally, how long is he staying?'

'That is what is not certain, dear,' Lally said a little timorously. 'I thought I would discuss it with you.'

'Well, if he is to stay with us for any length of time he will have to get rid of that appalling accent,' Prosper said sharply. Then as the footman came in he gave orders for tea.

Roger stood stroking the cat, aware that Aunt Lally was lying; that she was hiding something, possibly quite mysteriously to do with him and that, despite his politeness, her husband was displeased. Roger, who knew all about this kind of thing, could sense a row in the air.

He suddenly thought of his adoptive brothers and sisters and the warm, ramshackle house in Kentish Town, and he felt a wave of nostalgia overwhelm him.

He liked his aunt, but his uncle was a man to whom he was not drawn and, he was sure, who was not drawn to him despite his politeness. He could sense a rivalry for the affections of his aunt, and he wondered how secure he was in a place he admired but did not love.

Roger felt like a branch cut off from a tree; a possession who was dressed up, mocked for his accent and, he feared, could be punished at the whim of his uncle or aunt.

It was a dangerous, insecure feeling, and he sat down again clutching the cat, as far away as he could from his uncle, who was opening the mail, still with an expression of displeasure on his face. Aunt Lally, meanwhile, disappeared to change into yet another tea gown – she wore a different one every day – to repair the ravages to her complexion after a day out of doors, and maybe to have a word with Cook about the evening meal.

While she was out Uncle Prosper said nothing to Roger but opened the envelopes, with care, one after the other, briefly perusing the contents before discarding the letter on to a table and opening another.

He suddenly stood up with a sharp exclamation and, as Lally entered and put on the lights, looking fresh and beautiful, a bright smile on her lovely face, she saw his expression and stopped, a hand flying to her mouth.

'Is it bad news, Prosper? Your face looks quite awful. You are ashen, my dear.'

'Oh, Lally.' Prosper reached out to the mantelpiece and leaned heavily on it. 'What terrible, terrible news.' He pointed to the letter in his hand and fluttered it in front of her. 'My poor little great-niece, Emily Woodville, is dead, suddenly carried away by the scarlet fever.'

20

Emily was only twelve years of age when she died. She could be said to have made no mark in life except in the hearts of her sorrowing family – especially her father, who was nearly demented by her death. It had happened suddenly in the middle of the night, when she was thought to be getting better. Even her mother had gone, at last, to her bed to rest. She was awoken by a maid, but it was too late.

Ironically, Emily's friend, Sarah Wills, from whom she had caught the illness, made a complete recovery, but was considered too upset to attend the funeral.

Once again the people of Wenham had gathered in the streets, listening to the muffled tolling of the bell, as yet another member of the Woodville/Yetman families made her last voyage to the family church, struck down before her time.

Emily had been too young to be well known by the people of the town. Those who did know her considered her a little too haughty, even for a Woodville; but what did that matter now? Life had been snuffed out, and with it her potential, so that no one would ever know what sort of person she might have become.

She was young, too young to die, and she was mourned. Her only memorial would be the marble figure of an angel in the churchyard with folded wings, gazing in perpetuity towards the family vault.

Eliza felt, as she followed the coffin into the church and then afterwards to the Woodville vault for the committal, that she had seen too many funerals in too short a time. There were too many sad things in her life; too much had gone wrong. Next to her was Guy, shoulders bowed, who seemed in a few short days to have aged ten years. On the other side George, with his strong Christian faith, was endeavouring to give him the strength that only he seemed to be able to give. Margaret, though grief-stricken, was erect, noble and dignified. Eliza thought, as she clung tightly to Dora's hand, that one could not imagine anything happening that would cause that rigid façade to crack.

It was summer but it was bleak; a bleak English summer's day with everyone well wrapped up against the biting wind that blew on the hillside as Emily's coffin was placed in the family vault above that of her grandfather.

The Woodvilles were the only family in the parish with their own vault, which was a huge stone edifice with an iron door that remained barred between burials, and surrounded by a wrought-iron rail.

The Woodville mausoleum housed the remains of the first Woodvilles, their bones now reposing in urns, which was the fate of all the skeletons after a suitable period of time to ensure that there was room for members of the family who followed them.

The names of the interred were engraved on the outside of the mausoleum, the first being Christopher Woodville, followed by his two wives (one after the other); then Pelham, his wife and daughter, and Charles, who completed the magnificent house begun by his father. The last was Sir Matthew, the engraving looking quite new, and the next name would be that of his young granddaughter who did not live to grow old.

Margaret and George followed the coffin into the vault to see it into its place, while Guy remained sobbing in his sister's arms.

Julius Heering, standing next to Eliza, observed her distress at being unable to comfort the grieving father. He caught Eliza's eye, and she saw in his eyes an unexpected depth of sympathy that was directed not just at Guy, but at her too. He was a man who had known grief, he seemed to be telling her, and he understood not only about Emily, but about everything that had gone before. She looked quickly away, recalling the last time they had spoken, the abrupt way she had terminated their interview.

On her other side, tightly clutching the hand of Miss Fairchild, was Connie, not understanding about death but knowing that she would never see Emily again. She hung her head as the coffin was borne aloft into the vault, and wept bitterly.

All the young relations attended the funeral, and all of them, except Connie, managed not to cry, perhaps because they were, by now, getting used to death. Connie had attended neither Ryder's nor her father's funeral and, protected by Miss Fairchild, she was ushered away before the orderly withdrawal from the cemetery began.

After the interment Eliza sent her children back home while she rode with Margaret and Guy in the family carriage. Guy leaned back against the seat sobbing, his eyes closed, his lids swollen with tears. Next to him Margaret held his hand, pressing it from time to time in a mechanical fashion as though she knew it was impossible to comfort him.

The whole house was shrouded in funereal gloom, with blinds drawn and black ribbon and crepe draped everywhere. Feeling the beginnings of a headache, Eliza turned and saw Julius by her elbow.

'I think you have not forgiven me,' he said, handing her the cup of tea which he carried in his hand. 'You seem to be avoiding me.'

'Oh thank you, that's just what I needed,' Eliza said with a wan smile. 'It has been such an awful day that I have a headache.' Thankfully she drank the tea and then, giving the empty cup to a passing footman, looked at Julius. 'Why should I be avoiding you?'

'I think you know why.'

'That was a while ago. I'm sure you meant no harm.'

'I didn't, but I was clumsy. My greatest grief is that I offended you, because I have such a high regard for you, Eliza.'

434

'Please . . .' she said looking at him, the strain on her face showing all too clearly.

'I assure you – ' he put out a hand ' – it is not my intention to refer again to anything that might distress you, and today is certainly not the day, so soon after the loss of darling little Emily. The house still seems full of her. I can't believe she's gone.'

'I don't think any of us can.' Eliza felt a lump come to her throat. 'That she should be taken so suddenly is too cruel. I can't think what it will do to Guy. He adored her.'

Julius stood looking awkwardly at Eliza as if he didn't know how to continue. He was used to meeting people of all kinds and at ease in any company, yet Eliza made him feel tongue-tied. There was something about the composed, dark-haired, dark-eyed woman with her unconventional past that he found increasingly attractive. He wanted to communicate to her some sense of his own needs and desires; to tell her that he thought of her almost every day and often dreamt of her.

If he could have got close enough to her, he would have told her that he thought he was in love with her. But he doubted that she could ever feel the same about him.

'I shall be going away soon,' he said suddenly. 'There is much business in the Far East, particularly in Hong Kong and Shanghai, and I intend to spend some time there; maybe acquire a home and settle.'

'And not live *here* in the beautiful house you built?' Eliza looked surprised.

'Do you blame me?'

'I don't think Ryder's death should deter you from living there. It was not *you* who brought that about.'

'You really feel that, Eliza?'

'Yes, I do. If anything, I think he would want you to live in the house he built, the last thing he did before he died.' She spoke without emotion.

At that moment Prosper and Lally appeared from the crowd, kissed Eliza, acknowledged Julius, and began to talk mournfully about Emily.

'She was such a favourite of mine,' Prosper said sadly. 'I cannot believe it. As for Guy, he will never recover . . .'

Lally looked as though she had been weeping too, as indeed she had. She had wept about Emily, and she had wept about Roger. It was still very early days, but her husband and son were ill at ease and resented each other.

She was a simple woman who liked things to be simple too. She wanted people she liked to get on well; people she didn't like to be mutually antipathetic. Lally's world was full of clear colours; there were no in-between shades of grey and brown.

Lally had been glad to get away even for a funeral, and then she had started to weep all over again at the sight of the sad cortège and the stricken faces of Emily's family.

She threw herself into Eliza's arms as though she were the one who had been bereaved, and Eliza offered her comfort, soothing words, as she had to the various members of the family in the days since Emily's death.

Prosper was looking at Margaret moving quietly among the crowd of people pressing forward to offer condolences.

'She is such a brave woman,' he said. 'She seems intent on giving consolation to *others*, with never a thought for herself.'

'My sister has very great powers of self-control,' Julius said a little sadly. 'People sometimes think that she herself feels nothing, but of course she does. She has to be strong today, especially, because Guy is weak . . .'

'Guy is *not* weak,' Eliza exclaimed furiously. 'He is a completely different sort of person from Margaret. He is nervous and highly strung, and he especially adored Emily as his only daughter. If you had one of your own perhaps you'd know how Guy feels.'

As soon as the words were out of her mouth she clapped a hand to it as though she regretted what she'd said.

'I'm sorry! I shouldn't have said that.'

'I know what you mean,' Julius replied, 'and I shouldn't have said what I did. Maybe we're quits?' Looking at her beseechingly, he whispered: 'And, once again, may we be friends?'

Eliza looked away, but the exchange and its nuances did not escape Prosper, who seemed anxious to change the subject.

'Tell me, Julius,' he said, 'when are you going to move into your fine house?'

'Never, I fear,' Julius replied. 'I was just speaking to Eliza about it. I am reluctant to live there. Now that I have built an Aladdin's cave it no longer charms me. As you know, I am shortly to go to Hong Kong to establish our branch out there. I may settle there for some time, now that we are well staffed in London and Amsterdam, and put my house on the market.'

'But it is a *beautiful* house.'

'I know.' Julius gave a regretful shrug. 'And much thought went into it. But that's the way it is.'

'Are you open to offers?' Prosper asked suddenly.

'I might be.' Julius gave him a shrewd, businesslike look. 'Would you be interested?'

'I might.' Prosper looked at Lally. 'What do you think, my dear?'

'Live in the country?' Lally shook her head in mock horror. 'There is nothing I should dislike more in the whole world.'

Lally said: 'I *told* you I didn't wish to see it. Why waste time?'

'But you must admit, my dear, it's *very* beautiful.'

'If I wished to live in the country – which I don't – I should like to live in an old place like Pelham's Oak. What's the point of living in a modern house in the middle of Dorset? It has no charm or antiquity.'

'But it has every conceivable comfort, in an area of natural beauty.'

Lally, looking very beautiful, very soignée, and completely out of place in the country, looked very obstinate and wilful too. She stared sulkily out of the window of what Julius had intended as the master bedroom on the first floor, with dressing room, bathroom and a balcony which was reached through French windows. There were heavy silk curtains draped at the windows and Wilton carpet on the floor, but there was no furniture, since Julius had never lived in the house he had built so lovingly.

Julius had given them the key, and they had been over the house from bottom to top and then right down to the bottom again. It was indeed a marvel of building and design, and he wanted a high price for it.

'We could live here in the summer and in London in the winter,' Prosper tried again, but Lally moved petulantly away.

'I told you, I don't wish to live here at *all*.' She turned to her husband and gave him the smile that nearly always bewitched him. 'Dearest, you *know* I am not a country woman. I love the city – put me anywhere in London, Paris, Vienna, Rome and I am happy. But the country . . . urrh.' She shuddered and pulled her cape around her shoulders, though it was in fact quite warm.

'It is my native county, Lally,' Prosper persevered. 'I would like *you* to wish what I wish, for once,' he added thoughtfully.

'Well, I don't,' Lally snapped. 'And by now you should have realised *that*, Prosper.'

Ignoring the splendours of the countryside around them, the outstanding views of woodland, vale and hill, she turned on her heel, and was about to leave the room when Prosper seized her abruptly by the arm.

'That is *not* the way I wish to be addressed, Lally. Don't forget what I rescued you from. I am the one you have to thank for being what you are today.'

'Don't you *dare* speak to me like that.' Lally's eyes flashed as she snatched her arm away. 'Have I not given you years of faithful, loyal love? Have I not done *everything* you wished, gone with you everywhere, and entertained for you in a manner you yourself have admitted was good enough for the Queen? Now you dare to bring up the question of my humble origins. I am ashamed of you, Prosper. You knew about them, and now you fling them in my face.'

'I am ashamed of myself,' he said, suddenly chastened.

Crossing to the French windows, he threw open the doors and went out on to the balcony. Then he leaned over the white-painted wooden balustrade and sighed.

Slowly she followed him, aware of her capricious temper, the fact that maybe she had this time gone too far. She put a hand around his shoulder and leaned her head winsomely against his arm.

'Don't be angry with your Lally,' she murmured in the voice of a small girl. 'She knows how much she owes you; but she has repaid you.'

'Oh, you have, my love,' Prosper said, turning to enfold her in his arms. 'And I am a wretch to speak as I have. But . . .'

'It is Roger, isn't it?' she murmured.

'Well, since he came into our lives.'

'You talk as though it were weeks ago,' she pouted. 'It is only a few days.'

'It is simply that you never told me about him. Suddenly you produce a nephew out of the air and expect me to accept the fact that he is to live with us.'

'Only for a time. I think you will like Roger, dearest, once he speaks well and conducts himself like a gentleman. You can see he has the instinct.'

'Oh, I can see that.' Prosper glanced at her slyly. 'Quite remarkable, in fact, for one who has come from the back streets of Kentish Town. But why did you take pity on him now, my dear? Why now, and not before?'

'I felt he was different from the rest – from his brothers and sisters, I mean. I was sorry for him and felt inspired to rescue him and give him a chance.'

'Because he is really your son, is he not, Lally?' Prosper said gently, but he put a distance between them just the same, and moved away.

'The very idea!' Lally cried, flouncing to the other side of the room. 'Why will you not believe me when I say he is my sister's son?'

'It would be more believable if you *had* a sister, my dear.' Prosper's quiet, normally controlled voice had begun to rise.

'But I don't believe you have. You once told me that you were an orphan, without any relations. Perhaps you have forgotten that. What, therefore, *am* I to believe, Lally? Why have you lied to me, if that is not the case? Besides, he has your hair, your colouring, your eyes . . . Did you expect me to be taken in by your story, my dear? If you had been honest with me we could perhaps have rescued the little lad before now. I would have taken him to my heart and brought him up as the son I have longed for. But now . . .'

'But now?' Lally echoed fearfully.

'*Now*, he is a boy who has formed opinions. I can see he is a boy also who has been bruised by life, wounded maybe by your rejection. He is brought into a strange environment, and already I can sense he dislikes me.'

'He hardly *knows* you . . .'

'He hardly knows *you*, either, does he, Lally? As a mother you were not a very regular visitor, were you?'

Lally felt as if all the life, the spirit had gone out of her. She propped her arms on the wooden balustrade as though it could hardly sustain the weight of her heavy, pain-racked body. She sighed deeply and began, in the voice of one setting out to tell a tale:

'It is true, Prosper, that Roger *is* my son, the fruit of a liaison with a gentleman many years ago. I had no money, and his father left me in distressing circumstances. The alternative to a foundlings' home was to leave him with the sister of my maid, Abby, who was a good woman with children of her own.'

She went over to him and tentatively touched his arm, looking at him with her soft, limpid eyes. 'When I met you I didn't feel I could tell you about Roger. I'm sure you understand that. You are such a *good* man, and I thought it might spoil your love for me. I imagined, in any case, that we would have our own children; but, alas, I have failed you there.

'It is true I have visited Roger occasionally, but not often enough. He calls me "aunt", but he scarcely knows me at all. I think he resents both of us at the moment, and perhaps it would be kinder to take him back where he came from. And yet . . .'

her hand tightened on his arm 'you have always longed for a son, dearest. He seems to me to be a bright lad and attractive. With an education, maybe he would be an asset to you. Did you think of that? Who knows, he may be as good in business as you yourself are. As it seems, alas, that we cannot have a son of our own, would you not take Roger to your bosom, and love him as if he were your son?'

Prosper looked for a long time at the landscape he loved, towards the cottage where Ryder died. Like Ryder he too was a Dorset man, and this was his land, his country. The house seemed to him to embody everything that he had ever wished for: modernity, style, opulence.

He was a businessman and used to the ways of the market-place, so putting his arm round Lally he hugged her closely before murmuring in her ear: 'If you make a bargain with me I will adopt Roger and bring him up as my son, as a gentleman.'

'And the bargain is?' Lally began, but she had seen the look in his eyes and she already knew it. One day Roger would be living in close proximity to his natural father, and that was the eventuality that she dreaded. However . . .

'A bargain is a bargain,' she said softly, giving him her hand and kissing him gently on the lips.

Perce Adams stood in front of Eliza, his cap in his hand, yet his attitude was one of defiance rather than humility. Years ago it would not have been like this, and Eliza knew with certainty that times were changing. Men like Perce were no longer content to be subservient. Even though his manner was polite and respectful, his words were strong.

'The fact is, Mrs Yetman, that the Yetman name is doing nothing. I have spent the years since the death of your husband, ma'am, carrying out my trade best as I could. Now Mr Heering has offered to set me up in my own business.'

'Then let him set you up, Perce,' Eliza cried, yet already she knew she was losing ground. 'Use your *own* name. It is an honourable name.'

'But Yetman's has a name for quality, ma'am. Besides – ' he

looked nervously around him, 'there's your son, ma'am, your Laurence. He told me a long time ago he would like to be in the same business as his father . . .'

'My son doesn't come into this, Perce,' Eliza said tersely. 'He is a schoolboy . . .'

'Nevertheless he be always hanging round where we be working, ma'am. He is a ready lad with his hands, skilful too. How would it be if he followed in the tradition of his father and grandfather and headed a fine business again, built up what his uncles have tried to destroy?'

Eliza rose and began to pace the room.

'I'll have to think about it, Perce. I'll have to take advice. I don't want *charity* from Mr Heering . . .'

'But charity isn't what he's offering, ma'am. 'Tis capital, a business proposition. That's a different matter altogether. I tell you, I like Mr Heering, ma'am. He may be forrin', but he is a good and honest man. He has sold his house to his business partner and already he has put work in my way. I have taken over where Mr Yetman left off to finish that house so that Mr Martyn and his lady can move into it. Think of the opportunity, ma'am . . . Think of turning it all away . . .'

Perce opened his arms so wide that they seemed to embrace the whole county of Dorset, and more besides.

When Perce had gone Eliza sat for a long time brooding at the desk where she regularly did her accounts. It was indeed a struggle to make ends meet; every day there was less and less, and it was true that higher education for Laurence, even had he wished it, would have been almost out of the question.

Riversmead was in need of repair; the house – neglected by Ryder while he did other things – was falling about her ears, and yet why was it that Miss Fairchild's offer of Connie's house failed to attract her?

Why was it that she wished to remain in a place where she had known such happiness, but also such sorrow?

After Perce's visit she waited for her sons to come home from school. This was the local grammer school, very different from Eton where their cousin George was and where Carson

442

was to go. Eliza could not afford the expense of boarding school fees, and she had felt, anyway, that it was not what Ryder would have wished for his children. They had agreed on that before his death.

It was the spring following Emily's death, and she stood by the river, her eyes on the road in the distance where she would see Laurence and Hugh trudging home from school.

Dora still went to Miss Bishop's Academy, but she would leave in the summer. Her future had not yet been decided.

Dora had missed her father so much that, for months after his death, she had wandered round the house looking for him, refusing to believe he had gone. Since his death she had become much quieter and more thoughtful. The death of her cousin Emily had depressed her even further, and there was a melancholy strain in her daughter that worried Eliza.

Just then she caught sight of the boys through the trees and she hailed them, going swiftly to the gates to welcome them.

Hugh, always loving, ran to kiss her, but Laurence avoided kisses. He was undemonstrative.

'Tea's ready,' she told them, 'and afterwards I want to talk to you, Laurence.'

'I'd like to finish something for the woodwork class tomorrow, Mother.'

'Nevertheless I wish to speak to you first.'

Hugh talked about school and the day's happenings, but Laurence was silent, seeming preoccupied as he munched his tea. He did, however, ask where his sister was.

'She's gone to tea with one of her friends. What's the matter, Laurence? Bad day?'

'Usual,' Laurence said with a frown, then, 'when can we begin our talk, Mother? My work will take me quite a long time to complete.'

'Let's talk there then,' Eliza said, rising. She bent towards Hugh. 'Will you finish your tea, darling? Be sure to do your homework before going out to play.'

Hugh, who was clever but lazy, rolled his large eyes heavenwards but nodded, and Laurence rose, still eating a piece of cake, and preceded his mother to his workroom, which had once been part of the stables.

Eliza no longer kept a carriage, but used a pony and trap for going around the country. Lady's daughter, Beauty, and her foal, Magellan, were the only horses left in the field. Ted mostly did work around the house, and eked out a further income cutting wood when he could. Eliza still employed a cook and two maids: labour was very cheap, and people would rather be in domestic service than go to the poorhouse.

Eliza seldom went into Laurence's workroom, but when she did she was always impressed by its neatness. Everything was tidy and in its place: all his tools, his instruments gleaming in brackets on the walls.

It was quite certain that he had inherited his father's gift.

On his bench there was a model of a schooner in full sail which she had not seen before, and as she went towards it she cried out: 'It's *beautiful*.' She fingered the delicate sails and intricate rigging. 'How long has it taken you, Laurence?'

'Three months.' Laurence blushed a little.

'And you did everything – the hull, the rigging, the sails . . .'

'Everything,' Laurence replied then, a little anxiously. 'Careful, Mother. Those sails are very fragile. It is for my final-year project. I hope I shall be given first-class marks.'

'I'm *sure* you will. It's very beautiful, and you didn't say a word to me.'

She stood back as he crouched in front of his model and began delicately to paste part of the sail that had not yet adhered to the mast.

She watched him in fascination realising, as sometimes a mother does, how little she knew him. The boy is outstripped by the man who becomes a stranger, and acquaintance has to begin with him all over again.

'Laurence,' she said drawing a chair up to his bench, 'Perce Adams was here today.'

'Oh yes?' Laurence squinted in concentration as if he scarcely heeded her.

'I think you know what he wanted?' Eliza went on.

'Why should I know?' He didn't look at her, his mind intent on his task.

'He *said* you told him a long time ago that you'd like to work with your hands, continue your father's business.'

'But you knew that already, Mother.' Laurence interrupted his work to look at her.

'Is it still true?'

'More true than ever. Besides – ' he stopped working and hoisted himself up on the bench, swinging his legs ' – you *know* that we can't afford to send me to university like George.'

'Yes, but if you would like to go I'm sure I could find the money. I don't like to think of your cousins receiving a better education than you.'

'But where would you find the money?'

'I'd borrow it from Guy, or Mr Heering would lend it to me.'

'Oh, Mr Heering is a nice man. He would gladly lend you the money.'

'Do you see much of him at your Uncle Guy's?'

'Quite a lot since he sold Uncle Prosper his house.' Laurence paused and turned to look at her. 'He asks quite a lot about you, Mother. I do know that. He likes you very much. You should think about marrying him.'

'Laurence!' Eliza felt herself reeling with shock. 'That's a very impertinent thing to say.'

'I'm sorry, I didn't mean to be impertinent. But if he likes you, and you like him . . .'

'I hardly know him.' Eliza sounded doubtful.

'Mother, you've known him for as long as you've known Aunt Margaret. He often talks about you. I like him.' Laurence had returned to an intricate piece of work which was evidently to his satisfaction, because he stood back and admired it. 'We all like him, very much. If he does ask you, Mother,' Laurence looked at her frankly, 'you should accept him. He will look after you and give you a better life.'

'I don't *want* to be looked after,' Eliza said.

'Nevertheless,' Laurence seemed quite adamant, 'I think

you two would get on well together. But it's just as you like.
We don't need his money. I have had a very fine education.
Wenham Grammar School is one of the best in the county. I tell
you, Mother, I *would* like to be apprenticed to Perce. I would like
to run the business as Father ran it, and' – he went over to her,
putting his arms round her neck in an uncharacteristic display
of affection – 'I would like, *most* of all, to see you happy and
comfortable in your life, and free at last from worry.'

Ever since the death of his daughter, Guy Woodville had got
into the habit of visiting the Rectory at Wenham every two or
three weeks to seek comfort from the Rector and to try and
fathom, if he could, God's mysterious ways.

George had gradually convinced his father that the Rector
was not what he seemed. Instead of an angry ogre breathing fire
and brimstone Guy was persuaded, little by little, that beneath
his forbidding exterior the Rector was inspired with the true
Christ-like spirit. He had a deep knowledge and understanding
of the ways of God, and was accordingly able to explain why so
perfect a life had been snuffed out. Why had Sarah, who brought
the infection, been spared and not Emily? Was God fair?

Over the months Sir Guy became well acquainted with the
Reverend Lamb. He came to like and admire him, and also
to depend on him. He would consult the Rector not only on
spiritual matters, but also about his household, his relations
with his wife and sons, with his sister and his by now very
truculent and feeble mother.

Consequently the Rector got to know a good deal more than
anyone else in Wenham about the Woodville family, and about
the Yetmans, the Martyns and the Heerings as well. He knew
almost everything that went on and, of course, he shared this
knowledge with his wife in deepest confidence and within the
sanctity of the marital bond. Consequently it was only to be
expected that, from time to time, she would let fall a passing
remark to one of her acquaintances encountered in the course of
the many good works with which she filled her busy days.

In time everything that happened in any of these households

became common knowledge in Wenham, so that the whole town knew about Julius's romantic interest in Eliza almost before she knew about it herself. Why else, Sir Guy asked the Rector in the course of his conversation about the workings of the Divine Will, did Julius hang about his house but for the purpose of seeing his sister on one of her frequent visits, with or without her children?

The fact was that, in the course of that year, the Yetman children came to know Julius Heering very well; they liked him as a person and, between themselves, they agreed that they would not have objected if he took the place of the father they all still loved and venerated. They knew their mother was lonely, and that she was concealing her perpetual worry about money beneath her usual veneer of calm and good cheer.

Thanks to Guy's friendship with the Reverend Lamb, the town got to know that when he left school Laurence Yetman was going to be apprenticed to a builder who was none other than Perce Adams. The nephew of the snobbish, prosperous Woodvilles was going to be a mere builder's labourer.

The good citizens also learned that Prosper and Lally Martyn had mysteriously adopted a son, who was already at school at Rugby, and being groomed for his new father's business in the City of London? They knew that Mrs Martyn hated the country and only came there for the sake of her husband, who was a Dorset man.

In time the gossip got back to Guy who, forgetting that he was the source – indeed, in its passage around the town the truth was often embellished – would often ask the Rector where the information came from when it was fed back to him. He was particularly exercised that his nephew, who had Woodville blood in him, would, despite a good academic record, become a humble artisan, a thatcher like his father.

When he was at home George Woodville liked to accompany his father on his visits to the Rectory because he found conversation with the Rector's daughter even more enlightening than talking with her father. While their fathers conversed in the drawing room, the two young people would walk in

447

the garden, among the trees in the shrubbery, or through the orchard seeking enlightenment about the ways of God and the meaning and purpose of life.

Sophie Lamb was an exceptional woman. She was by now twenty-three to George's seventeen, and she had already undergone a course of further Bible study at a missionary college in Wimbledon, from where she had hoped to be sent abroad to spread the Word.

However, her parents, thinking, not without reason, this world to be a dark and dangerous place, full of pitfalls for the just as well as the unjust, refused to countenance the idea that their precious daughter should travel so far afield, even in the company of like-minded people; because, of course, she would not go alone.

No amount of pleading on her part would change her parents' minds, so even though she was of age Sophie, who was an obedient, dutiful daughter who would never dream of distressing those she loved, was forced to remain in Wenham. She sought consolation by taking Bible classes, teaching at the village school and, increasingly, delighting in the company of George Woodville. Like her father, he was destined for the ministry, and in time perhaps for the mission fields where she longed so much to venture herself.

Guy Woodville became mistrustful of these encounters between George and the Rector's daughter. Although he liked Sophie well enough, he certainly did not relish the prospect of seeing her occupying, one day, the position now held by his wife.

Yet he found it impossible to talk to George about it, and, as he dared not mention it to Margaret, he decided he would have to await events, and leave it in God's hands.

Guy sat opposite the Rector, his friend the good Mr Lamb, discoursing with him about the ways of God and man. He had his large handkerchief ready in his hand because from time to time inevitably he had to dab his eyes. It was still impossible for him to understand why Emily had been taken: so young, so lovely, so full of promise. Impossible too, despite his efforts, for the Rector to provide him with sufficient reason, except that it lay within the great goodness and mercy of God.

'Think of the *evil* she was spared,' the Rector said, patting his guest's knee, 'the wickedness and degradation of the world. A virgin, glorious in her goodness and purity, she would have been wafted straight to the throne of the Almighty without a sin on her pure soul.'

Moved by the Rector's words, Guy buried his face yet again in his handkerchief. Then, quite inexplicably, he suddenly thought of Agnes, a young woman (although much older than his daughter) whom he had defiled. Suddenly the weight of his guilt for that far-off sin seemed to sit upon him like an enormous boulder, and he wept again.

They were sitting as usual in the Rector's large study, which overlooked the lawn sloping down to the river. In front of them, on a bench in the garden, George and Sophie were deep in conversation. George's good-natured face was turned towards her, and he looked quite animated, the gold of his spectacles gleaming in the sun.

'There there, my friend,' the Rector said, rising. Had he been a doctor, he thought, he would by this time have sent Sir Guy quite a large bill for the number of consultations he had given him. Immediately that man of God banished the unworthy thought. He was on this earth, after all, to comfort the afflicted, not to line his pockets, though there *was* the fabric of the church to think of, the upkeep of the rectory and its large number of servants, the prodigious amount of entertaining he and Mrs Lamb had to do to maintain the goodwill of the wealthier members of the congregation.

'You and Lady Woodville must come to dine with us one night, Sir Guy,' he said, hoping to take the penitent's mind off his misery and, although the Rector did not know it, a fresh attack of guilt. 'I think you will find that we keep a good table.'

'Most *kind* of you,' Guy said, wiping his aching eyes. 'Ah, dear Rector, when will God send me comfort and allow my soul to rest?'

449

'In time, Sir Guy.' The Rector looked surreptitiously at his watch. 'Ah, I think I see Mrs Lamb out in the garden about to offer us tea. Could I prevail upon you . . .'

'That is *very* good of you, Rector.' Sir Guy reluctantly stuffed his large handkerchief up his sleeve, knowing his time was up. 'But I am to take tea with my sister today. I promised her I'd call on the way home.'

'Then at least let us have the pleasure of keeping George with us. He and my daughter get on remarkably well.'

'Do they not?' Guy said, looking with dismay at the young people discoursing earnestly in front of them. Suddenly an uncomfortable awareness came to him of the possible implications if George *were* to become enamoured of the Rector's daughter, whose religious zeal was equal to his own: he and Mr and Mrs Lamb would be related. The Rector would then develop a sense of intimacy that would go beyond the bounds of his calling and perhaps become familiar; he might even wish to address him as *Guy*. Guy believed that every man, and woman, had a station in life, and that's how he liked it: cloth and gentry should not mix. Much as he admired the Rector as a man of God, he would not like to be forced into too close a proximity to the Lambs.

Shaken by the thought, Guy followed the Rector on to the lawn, from where it was possible to see the slate roof of Riversmead some distance below them. A narrow path ran down the side of the Rectory towards the river, but Guy had his carriage waiting for him outside the front door.

'George,' he called out to his son, who leapt up when he saw his father, 'I am going now to see your Aunt Eliza. The Rector has kindly invited you to stay for tea.'

'Most kind,' George said, looking gratified and bowing to the Rector and then to his wife, who was smiling broadly. An alliance between her daughter and the heir to the Woodville baronetcy was, of course, beyond her wildest dreams, their disparity in age made it out of the question, and yet . . .

George saw his father to his carriage, promised that he would follow soon, taking the path by the side of the Rectory, and returned to the lawn, where a table had been laid and a delicious selection of sandwiches, cakes and biscuits were being offered by the servants while Mrs Lamb fussed over the large silver teapot.

The Rector's wife sat there in her hat looking as though she were about to open a bazaar, though in fact she was not going out at all again that day. Sophie had her brown hair arranged on top of her head in a loose bun. Despite the fact that it was a summer's day her long dress was fastened at the throat, though it was ruched prettily with lace at the neck and wrists and was in a summery material, softly patterned so that she did not look at all hot. One could imagine her, strong and serene, with the black natives gathered about her knees longing for the word of the Lord. George thought she looked splendid – capable and alluring: that neat, erect bosom, just a little larger than those of most females of his acquaintance, was certainly something to give a man thought, especially at night.

'How I grieve for your poor father,' Mrs Lamb said, handing a cup to George. 'I have *never* seen a man so bowed down by grief.'

'And yet you, George, thanks to your faith, have come through it well,' the Rector said, looking at him with approval.

'I did not have the same relationship with Emily.' George accepted the sugar bowl with a special smile from Sophie. 'I loved her, of course, but my father worshipped her.'

'That in itself was wrong,' the Rector said reprovingly. 'People are to be loved, but only God is to be worshipped.' The Rector tucked his napkin into the top of his waistcoat and helped himself to several sandwiches at the same time. He was a heavy man and a greedy one; he suffered from gout and bronchitis, but he loved his way of life, the comforts, temporal as well as spiritual, that it brought and he was not afraid to die. 'I think God *may* have used Emily to bring your father to Him. Emily is in heaven, no doubt of that, but your father . . .' The Rector shook his head. 'He was not a God-fearing man. Now he has been touched by the hand of the Lord.'

'How cruel, Father, to think that God would use the death of a young girl to bring about such a transformation,' Sophie protested, largely because she thought she saw a look of anger in George's eyes.

'Oh no, my dear,' the Rector said, his mouth full of sandwich as his hand reached out for more, 'not at all. God works in mysterious ways his wonders to perform. Who are *we* to know the mind of God? By the way,' he went on, looking at George, 'I have asked your father if he and your mother would care to dine with us. We keep a good table. Of course we should be glad of your company as well.'

'How kind of you, sir,' George said, his smile of pleasure directed at Sophie. 'I can think of nothing that I would like better.'

Sophie thought that he was addressing his remark to her, and her heart suddenly seemed to somersault with joy.

Guy sat with his sister on the lawn at Riversmead, enjoying almost the same view as could be seen from the Rectory, only lower down. The fare provided by Eliza was not quite so lavish as that George was partaking of with the Lambs, but Guy's mind was not on his food. He was in a carping, rather petulant mood despite the uplifting conversation he had had with the Rector. Suddenly his mind had become strangely preoccupied with the fate of Agnes, and the child he had left her with.

But there was, as well, the question of the name of the Woodvilles and the respect in the community that had been enjoyed by them for generations.

'Laurence may not be a Woodville in name,' he said to his sister, coming straight to the point with the arrival of tea, 'but he *is* my nephew. How can my nephew become a common labourer? Even the Rector does not approve.'

'Oh, you talk about family matters with him too?' Eliza gave him a scornful look.

'I talk to the Rector about *everything* that concerns my soul, and daily events affect me and my spiritual welfare. I am all for giving aid to the poor, but there is also the question of the station a person occupies in life, and I think no one will deny that is right and proper. George is an Etonian. I *hope* Carson will follow him there too, although I must say at the moment it doesn't seem likely.' He paused to dwell gloomily on his younger son. 'However, my sons have been brought up as gentlemen. How can Laurence, of whom, I must say, I have always been fond, so debase the family name?'

'I don't think being a labourer, as you term it, *debases* the family name,' Eliza said with some asperity. 'Even Jesus was a carpenter.'

'My dear, that is allegory.' Guy dismissed the notion with a wave of his hand.

'Laurence is simply to learn from the bottom.'

'I blame *Julius*, my brother-in-law, for this. He has put up some money so that my nephew can serve an apprenticeship with Perce Adams of all people.'

'And what is *wrong* with Mr Adams?'

'He is nobody. How can my own nephew possibly be apprenticed to someone like that?'

'Because he is very good at what he does.' Eliza gnawed her lips angrily. 'I had no idea Julius had finally put up some money.'

'Oh yes, it is capitalised – not much, but enough.'

'He might have had the courtesy to tell me.'

'I think he tried, but you were against it.'

'Using the Yetman name.'

'Laurence *is* a Yetman. In a few years he will be head of the family. Yet although Julius interferes he has a good heart. He means well. He *is* a very good man, you know, Eliza. He has your family welfare very much at heart.'

'So it seems.' Eliza did not sound convinced. 'But if your family has some money in it,' she went on after a while, 'I can't see why it upsets you, Guy. That should make it *most* respectable. Besides, the Heering/Martyn families are in trade, and building is a trade.'

'It is not the same thing at *all*,' Guy snapped. 'They are millionaires. They are the merchant adventurers of today, as our ancestors were in the sixteenth century. Anyway, Laurence should go to Cambridge or Oxford, I don't mind which. He is doing well at school.'

'We have no money.'

'Julius would have lent it to you.'

'Do you think I could possibly ask him?' Eliza asked heatedly, jumping up.

'No use coming to me,' Guy grumbled. 'Margaret keeps me very short. Her hand is always on the purse strings. Well . . . the estate is in good order now. George will want for nothing.'

'I would never *dream* of coming to you either, you know that.' Eliza sat down again.

'Yes, my dear, that's all very well, but how will you manage?' Guy looked towards the house. 'The place is rotten. It needs *hundreds* of pounds spent on it. Margaret says that she gives you clothes for the children.'

'Yes she does, and I am not too proud to accept. They are hardly ever worn and in good condition. Dora's I make myself. Anyway, as you say, in a few years Laurence will be a trained builder, a master thatcher like his father. He has promised to repair this house.'

'By that time it will have fallen down.'

'What *is* the matter with you today, Guy?' Eliza looked at him keenly. 'You seem more than usually out of sorts. I thought the Rector provided some help and comfort to you?'

'He does, he does.' Guy sighed loudly. 'He is an excellent man, a true man of God. I don't know why, Eliza, but, do you know, today I suddenly started to think about Agnes. I have committed many sins in the past, and she was one of the biggest. I think God took my Emily to punish me for that.'

'Well, *I* don't think he did,' Eliza burst out angrily. 'I think that is nonsense. I don't think God works like that, not any more.' She paused thoughtfully.

She had long since abandoned the notion that Ryder's death was a punishment from God: Annie McQueen had certainly helped it along.

'But you are not a churchgoer, Eliza,' Guy said reprovingly. 'I don't think you are even a believer. How do you know what God does and does not do?'

'How do *you*?' Eliza replied, looking at him.

'Through the Rector. He interprets the will of God for me.'

'And did you tell him about Agnes?' Eliza asked slyly.

'Goodness me, no! I don't think he would consider that a sin that God would ever forgive. Do you . . . do you ever hear from her, Eliza?' His eyes watered a little as though he were again on the verge of tears.

'Never.' Eliza shook her head, but she found that her mind was in a turmoil; the question was so unexpected. She had often wondered what Guy would do if he knew about Elizabeth. But it had not seemed fair to burden him with her knowledge, nor was the time ever right to tell him. She had also thought it would not be fair to Elizabeth to know she had a father she could never visit, and who would never acknowledge her.

'Did you ever ask yourself why God took Ryder from me?' Eliza was anxious to divert her brother's mind from the subject of Agnes.

'No.' Guy shook his head morosely. 'Why do you ask?'

'Well, you seem to have a lot of answers. I wondered if you had the answer to that.'

Again Guy shook his head.

'I don't have all the answers, my dear sister. I became very fond of Ryder. It was a cruel blow and may have seemed to you at the time most unjust. But we do not question the whys and wherefores of God. We . . .'

He stopped abruptly as a child came running around the house, scampering after a puppy who bounded in front of her. In the rear steamed Beth, out of breath with running. Just as the girl reached the lawn Beth caught her by the ribbons that flew behind her from her dress and sharply arrested her flight.

'Now, missy,' Beth said crossly, looking apologetically at Eliza and Guy, 'I *told* you not to let that puppy out. He is untrained and will fall in the river. *Then* what will you do?'

Elizabeth put a fist in her eye and began to cry. She tried desperately to get away from the firm grip Beth had on her sash, but the more she pulled the harder Beth held on to her.

Elizabeth was strong willed and liked her own way. She stamped and bawled and, finally, looked up as Guy who had stood up at her outburst as one mesmerised. He walked over to her and, crouching by her side, put a hand round her waist.

'Now, my little darling, what is it?' he asked.

Elizabeth stopped immediately and looked at him in surprise, her eyes wide open, the tears glistening on her lashes like tiny pearl drops.

'The puppy will fall in the river, as your mother said. Is *that* what you want?' Guy sounded eminently reasonable.

'No.' Elizabeth put her arms trustingly round him, and he pressed her face close to his.

'Then go back with Mother,' he said gently as, evidently deeply impressed by this spectacle and Guy's undoubted authority, the puppy obediently wriggled over to him on its stomach in the hope of a pat on the head.

For a moment Guy clung to Elizabeth while, in the background, Eliza and Beth could merely watch. It was a moment, somehow, frozen in time and they would not forget it.

Then as Elizabeth, released from his embrace, ran back to Beth and disappeared round the corner of the house, Guy slowly returned to Eliza. Sitting down heavily, he leaned his head back and shut his eyes.

'I often wondered why you gave that child a home,' he said without looking at his sister. 'Why you gave her a home, and fed her, when you had so many other mouths to feed . . .' He opened his eyes and looked at Eliza long and hard until the tears that had welled up started to run down his cheeks.

'Now I know,' he said in a weak voice. 'She is Agnes's daughter. For the first time I had the chance to look at her very carefully today and I saw it in her eyes.'

21

Guy returned home very much shaken after meeting for the first time a daughter who had been living for so many years within a few miles of him.

If he had ever doubted the working of the Divine Will, his doubts vanished forever that day. God had *inspired* him, had put the thought of Agnes into his mind and then had produced her daughter. Guy had even felt himself propelled out of the chair towards the little girl as she ran after her dog, and he had looked into her eyes, blue flecked with grey, just like Agnes's. Then he knew.

It was a miracle, indeed, but not one that the recipient wished to be noised abroad. It was a secret which he was forced, for the moment, to share only with Eliza for, however understanding, he could not expect Margaret to receive in her house his daughter born out of wedlock to another woman.

Guy had grown to love his wife in a way he could never have imagined possible when he had married her eighteen years before. Margaret was like a rock: enduring, steadfast, dependable. She had turned the Woodville fortunes round, transformed Pelham's Oak into one of the grandest as well as one of the most gracious, most tastefully furnished houses in the county, and she had made her husband content.

She was as much affected by their daughter's death as he was, yet she didn't show it; her many tears were shed in the privacy of her bedroom at night. People thought her hard, but she wasn't; by her practical common sense she was felt to support the family when they needed her, even through that most painful time.

There was one aspect of family life, however, in which Margaret Woodville did consider herself a failure. She was unable to understand or control her younger son, Carson. He was naughty, he was wayward and yet his charm was so compulsive that even she was hardly able to believe the things she knew he was capable of: the pranks, the escapades, the downright wilfulness.

She daily expected to hear he was being sent home from the prep school where the Woodville sons had been educated for generations; but she knew that he was kept in check by the number of thrashings he got, and the undoubted influence over him of his housemaster. The holidays were a nightmare. He harried the servants, was rude to the maids, broke all the rules of the countryside in his reckless daredevil rides over farmland. He consorted with the gangs of unruly village boys and seemed to go from bad to worse.

Only Guy seemed unperturbed, remembering his own youth and how much he had changed.

'He is a good boy,' he would say. 'You'll see.'

Margaret noticed that her husband was preoccupied after his visit to the Rectory; but she imagined it was to do with the constant exposure of his grief, his embracing religion in a way that she considered excessive.

She thought there probably was a God and that he kept a benevolent eye on His creation, but her faith had been shaken by Emily's death whereas Guy's had been strengthened. It didn't make sense to her.

'Julius was here today,' she called across the long table where they dined every night, regardless of who was there.

'He comes and goes a lot,' Guy said morosely.

'Always hoping to see your sister.'

'Eliza?' Guy appeared to be having trouble with his hearing and leaned forward, cupping an ear in his hand.

'He is very much in love with her. He told me all about it this afternoon while you and George were out.'

'Where is he now?'

'He has gone to Bournemouth to see the Martyn family.

Julius says the company has so much money they don't know what to do with it. They are going to start making charitable donations to worthy causes.'

'Pity he doesn't give some to Eliza,' Guy observed grumpily. During their meal *à deux* the servants left the room and were summoned back instantly by the ringing of a bell which Margaret kept at her side.

'He would *gladly* give it to Eliza,' Margaret said, 'but she will not have him.'

'Has he asked her?' Guy looked at his wife with interest. 'She's very proud.'

'He has not properly *asked* for her hand in marriage because he is sure it will be refused.'

'But why should she refuse Julius?' Guy appeared quite cheered up by the news. 'He is an *admirable* man. Eliza should consider herself very lucky and not be so choosy. Ryder was hardly a fine match.'

'For her Ryder *was* a very fine match.' Margaret's reply was spirited. 'He was ideal. Julius, of course, is my brother and I'm prejudiced. I think he and Eliza well suited. He would give her stability and protection, and of course his fortune is immense. Why is she offhand with him? Could you ask her, Guy?'

'No, I could not,' Guy said firmly. 'I couldn't ask her that sort of thing. Eliza is a law unto herself and always has been. Laurence is going to be a labourer, and she can see no harm in *that!* Sometimes I think Eliza's priorities are completely wrong.'

'He's only going to labour to *learn* the business,' Margaret said, ringing the bell. 'That seems to me perfectly reasonable. I only wish that Eliza would see sense and allow Julius to help her. It is all he wants.'

Guy said nothing but, elbows on the table, continued to stare morosely in front of him as the retinue of servants cleared the plates of the master and mistress of the house and swiftly served the next course.

As soon as they had withdrawn, Margaret leaned across the table and said: 'Is anything the *matter*, Guy? You seem out of sorts today. I think you see too much of the Reverend Lamb. Too much religion is bad for you. I hope you don't mind my saying so but I think it. I do.'

'I *do* mind you saying so,' Guy said sharply. 'He is an excellent man, and no man, or woman, can have too much of God.'

'You and George are always traipsing over to the Rectory. Tonight he is there yet again, at a Bible class.'

'My dear, it was you who persuaded me not to raise any objection to George becoming a minister,' Guy replied. 'Why should you object to his attending Bible classes?'

'Because I think you know why he goes to them.' Margaret gave him a level look. 'It is not *only* the Bible that is the attraction, in my opinion.'

'My dear, if you are talking about Sophie you are talking nonsense,' Guy said uneasily. 'He could not possibly be interested in someone so much older than he is.'

'My dear, *I* am older than *you*,' Margaret replied. 'I think you forget *that*, Guy.'

'I do forget it, my dear,' Guy said tenderly, gazing across at her. 'To me you have never looked younger. The thing is,' – Guy pushed aside his plate, on which dessert had been served, and walked along the table to stand by her side and place a reassuring hand on her shoulder – 'the two young people are drawn together solely by the love of God. I am sure there is nothing of a carnal nature between them.'

'I sincerely hope there is not!' Margaret sounded shocked. 'They can still be brought to love each other through the love of God, however. And would you *really* wish the future Lady Woodville to be the Rector's daughter? I'm sure you don't, if I know you, Guy.'

'Then what shall we do?' Guy slumped dejectedly down in the chair next to her. 'I confess the idea has occurred to me already.'

'We must contrive to send George away for the rest of the vacation,' Margaret said firmly. 'I have given some thought to the matter, because it has been disturbing me. Then, when the school term ends he can take Carson on an extended tour of the Continent. *That* young man has been disturbing me too!

They can begin in Amsterdam and then make a leisurely tour of Europe – just as gentlemen used to do in the old days.'

'My dear, how clever you are,' Guy said admiringly, clasping her hand and bending over it. 'Indeed, a pearl of great price.'

Eliza stood looking at the wallpaper in the corner of the drawing room which hung half way down the wall, displaying a patch of damp right overhead.

Beside her, clucking sympathetically, stood Beth.

'Dear oh dear, ma'am,' she moaned. 'The whole thing will have to come down and be done again. It's not just *here* either. The bedrooms in the attic are unfit for occupation. I think you ought to get Perce here. Charity begins at home.'

'But we're not talking about *charity*,' Eliza said, folding her arms and sinking on to the great, rather uncomfortable sofa that had been part of the furnishings of the house since the days of Ryder's grandfather. 'If Perce works here he is not making money. I cannot possibly allow it.'

'Then what will you do, ma'am?' Beth knew her well enough by now to think nothing of sitting down by her side without being asked. She sank on to the sofa also, her arms folded.

'I think we're going to have to move, Beth.'

'Move!' Beth cried, looking deeply shocked. 'Move, ma'am, did you say?'

'Some time ago Miss Fairchild offered me Connie's house. She knew that this place belonged to the Yetmans, and that they could turn us out any time. Well, let us go voluntarily and they can sell it, though who would want it in this state I don't know.'

'You want it, ma'am,' Beth said firmly. 'It is *your* home, the place where your children were born, where you lived with the husband you loved . . .'

Eliza got to her feet and, arms akimbo, began pacing round the room, her eyes on the floor as if seeking inspiration from those well-worn carpets which had seen the feet of so many generations of her husband's family tread over them. Suddenly she turned to Beth, who was watching her in bewilderment and, pulling up a footstool, crouched at Beth's feet, her arms still folded.

'I have never told you, Beth, my dear companion and friend of so many years, that, since the death of my husband, I have been nursing an even greater sorrow.'

'Oh, ma'am, whatever can that be?' Beth said anxiously, moving closer to the edge of the sofa.

'My husband, Ryder, your beloved master, was not faithful to me, Beth.'

'Oh *Lordy*, ma'am,' Beth put both hands over her ears as if she wished to hear no more.

'I only discovered it by chance, by hearing a rumour as one does in a small place such as this. This information was that he had a child by another woman, and I have not found it in my heart to forgive him as I wish I could; as, for instance, I have forgiven my brother for the birth of Elizabeth. For me it is too personal, too hurtful, and I cannot forget it, try as I may.'

Eliza rose and recommenced her walk back and forth across the worn carpet. 'For the years I was married to my husband I was totally faithful to him and believed he was to me. But – ' she gave a helpless shrug ' – the evidence points to the contrary so, although I love this house and thought I would end my days in it, it is too closely associated in my mind with Ryder and his deception. I feel that once I have gone from here I can begin life again. As for you and Ted, dear Beth, there is no need at all to worry. I – '

Beth jumped up, surprising Eliza as she seized her by the arm and said: 'Ma'am, you *must* tell me who this woman is with whom the master is supposed to have deceived you.'

'No, Beth, I cannot.' Eliza shook her head vigorously. 'If I could take *anyone* into my confidence it would be you; but I have kept this secret to myself, and I intend not to reveal it to a soul.'

Beth let go of Eliza's arm and turned away from her, clenching and unclenching her hands. Then, her eyes lowered, she said:

'Mrs Yetman, I think I know who you're talking about, for I too heard the rumour, ma'am, but kept it to myself for fear of distressing you. I thought that if you had heard it from someone else you would ask me, but you never did. But I can tell you one thing, ma'am: you is *quite* mistook. If you saw the child you would know who his father is, with his bright orange hair and green eyes. He could only have *one* father, ma'am, and that is the man Annie returned to shortly after your husband died, and who she has lived with ever since. He is her husband Philly O'Shea, ma'am, a drover who runs the cattle to the market on Thursdays. You have only to go there for yourself to see and, oh, ma'am,' she cried, going up to Eliza and stroking her arm like a baby, 'put your poor, tortured mind at rest.

'*If* you had confided in me I could have saved you the doubt, the suspicion as has gnawed at your soul all these years.'

On market day Wenham, which was a small town well off the beaten track, away from the main roads and with no railway, came into its own. It had a cattle market of great renown, and beasts were driven from all over the countryside to be bought and sold in its main thoroughfare every Thursday. The pens for the cattle stretched the length of the main street; horses for barter were tethered to the railings, and on either side of the High Street were stalls selling every variety of goods and produce that could be imagined: fresh farm products – cheese, home-cured hams, bacon and newly laid eggs; freshly butchered beef, lamb and pork; there were tinkers' stalls, a haberdashery stall, stalls that sold china and porcelain, fresh fruit and vegetables, clothes of every description new and old, boots and shoes, farming and gardening implements and plants, flowers and shrubs.

The plaintive bleating of sheep and mournful cries of the cattle mingled with the shouts of the vendors, each one trying his best to outdo the others. The good-natured throng who came from miles around jostled with one another along the thoroughfare and pavements, and the Baker's Arms was full to bursting point.

Eliza, wearing a headscarf and a drab coat, the collar turned up, picked her way among the crowd, looking past the cattle pens to the men who stood nonchalantly around, smoking, bargaining, prodding the unfortunate beasts with their sticks or simply passing the time of day.

Thankful for the light drizzle which meant she could disguise her face, Eliza walked from one end of the market to the other scrutinising each pen – the drovers, the buyers and the vendors – but there was no sign of a man with bright orange hair and a child that looked like him.

Of course, it was possible that, for once, they were not there. With sinking heart she made her way back again and then recommenced her tour, stopping longer at each point in the market, but still finding no one who stood out from the crowd in the way described by Beth.

It was nearly lunch time and she thought she would go home and send Beth up to see if she had more luck. She had left her behind, fearing that, together, they would have been too recognisable.

Eliza was about to pass the Baker's Arms, when the doors were flung open and a good-natured crowd issued forth. Eliza stopped in the shadow of Miss Fairchild's old shop and, to her amazement, she beheld straight in front of her a cheerful-looking ginger-haired man, his eyes as green as a cat's and one hand tightly holding that of a boy of about three, who looked just like him. Behind them stood Annie McQueen, who appeared to be taking leave of her father and her mother who still ran the public house. In her arms she carried a baby of about six months, the spitting image of its father and brother. Behind her were three older children, all alike, the former issue of her marriage to the man who had once deserted her.

Eliza bent her head to hurry on but, just then, Annie turned her head and their eyes met.

The expression in Annie's eyes was enigmatic, but Eliza thought she smiled.

Eliza looked round the dark, dusty room that had been the first office opened by Ryder's grandfather in Blandford. The first and also the last. In the intervening years many others had sprung up in other towns, but all had been closed down as the business was split into parts and sold off by the greedy Yetman brothers after the death of their father.

In one corner of the room was a battered desk, in another a cabinet and a shabby chair. The floor was bare and, in the stillness, she fancied she could hear the sound of the mice she had disturbed scurrying beneath the floorboards.

The premises were reached by a rickety flight of outside stairs, and when pushed open the door at the top swung rather drunkenly upon its hinges.

Opposite the door was a grimy window on which the legend 'Yetman Bros (Est 1821)', once proudly inscribed in gleaming gold paint, was just discernible. Eliza went over to the window and, breathing on it, rubbed clear a small area through which she could gaze down into Salisbury Street.

On the shelves along one side of the wall of the Yetman office were rows of dusty volumes: old accounts, specifications, orders for all the essentials of the building trade. Eliza took down one, and a huge black spider crawled hurriedly away up the wall, having taken refuge in the old volume for goodness knows how long. As she opened the ledger she saw that the pages were yellow with age and the ink on them was faded.

'1832 Town Hall Blandford: repairs to be carried out': they were then listed with a modest sum of money neatly written in beside each item.

Gingerly Eliza replaced the volume and then sat down at the desk and leaned her elbows on it, possessed of a strange feeling of excitement, almost of exhilaration.

Ryder had been born thirty-one years after the business was established by his grandfather Thomas Yetman and his Uncle Roger. John had been Thomas's eldest son and had carried on the business. The family had moved from poverty to riches in a comparatively short time, cashing in on the building boom and expansion of industrial England.

In her mind's eye Eliza could imagine the office transformed, cleaned, painted, the shelves and old furniture thrown out and replaced by new, the bare boards covered by a carpet. She imagined opening up the shop downstairs which had long been boarded up and making that the front office where people could come and look at plans, and discuss their requirements with – who?

Why not herself? This was the reason for her change of mood.

She rose and went over to the window to look once more through the clear patch she had made past the faded gold letters.

Her discovery that Annie's child was not, after all, Ryder's had given her a new lease of life. She realised, with hindsight, that too much had crowded in upon her at once, with a consequent lowering of spirits: Ryder's death followed shortly by his father's, the realisation of her financial position, and all her new responsibilities coming at the same time as she was told the rumour about Annie.

She had held it against Julius ever since; but it was rather like the ancient practice of killing the messenger who brought bad news. What Julius had told her must have been speculated upon by half the town. For that she had held a grudge against a man whom everyone respected, whom she herself found attractive though she dared not show it.

Her mother had always called her stubborn and she was – and perhaps a little blind as well.

As for Annie and the glance she'd given her in the street: it told Eliza something. There was no smoke without fire.

Suddenly she heard a brisk footfall on the outside steps, and rapidly crossed the room to stand on a landing outside the door as her elder son bounded up the staircase, two steps at a time.

'Be careful,' she called, 'it is *very* fragile.'

'How long have you been here, Mother?' Laurence asked as he reached the top. 'I know the steps are bad and I was afraid for *you*. Well, what do you think?'

He wore the worn trousers, jacket and shirt of the new apprentice; his face and hands were grimy and his hair matted and tousled. But he looked happy. She had never seen him looking so well, and she knew how he loved his work. He was good at it, too, an eager learner who also put in long hours in his own workroom behind the house.

'I think we shall have a business here, my son,' she said, tucking an arm through his and drawing him into the room. 'We will purchase the freehold from what is left of the Yetman estate – they will not dare ask much for it as the place is in such terrible repair – and we will start up again.'

'But who will run it, Mother?' Laurence ran a hand anxiously over his face. 'Perce and I . . .'

'*I* will run it,' Eliza said. '*I* will be in charge of the office. I will take care of the accounts myself and see to all the orders. *You* will see to the execution. When we make some profits we shall plough back into the business what we do not need for ourselves, and engage more workmen.

'That way we will expand, and that way we will be self-sufficient and will be dependent on *nobody's* charity. We will even repay Julius Heering the small amount of money he lent you.'

Laurence gazed at his mother and, bending towards her, planted a kiss on her forehead. 'I do *love* you,' he said and embraced her.

The rest of the morning they spent excitedly going over plans, making a few preliminary calculations on a blank piece of paper found in the office. The following day Eliza would visit the bank, and very soon the business would be operable.

Eliza drove herself home at lunchtime in her pony and trap, feeling happier than she had felt for years. It was rarely that people were given a second chance, and she was going to grasp it with both hands and make a success of the new venture.

The gates of the house were open and a carriage stood in front of the porch. She drew up behind it, and Ted came running up to her immediately with a worried look as he took the pony's bridle.

'Sir Guy has been waiting for you, ma'am . . .'

'Nothing wrong, is there?' Eliza's heart skipped a beat, and she realised that she had been counting too much on good fortune, thinking that the storms were over and only calm water lay ahead.

She turned towards the house, but Guy had already appeared and ran rapidly down the steps towards her.

'Guy, what *is* it?' she asked anxiously.

'It is Mother, Eliza. She has been taken seriously ill and is not expected to live. I want us to go straight down to Bournemouth in my carriage. Margaret has left already. There is not a moment to lose if we wish to take our leave of Mother.'

Eliza sat in the swaying carriage feeling sad, it was true; but the feeling of triumph, of exultation, had refused to go away. She and her mother had never been close. They were different kinds of people, and her mother's rejection of her at the time of her elopement had damaged their relationship irreparably.

As the carriage sped along the road towards Bournemouth she regretted how little real affection she had for her mother – unlike Guy, whose head nodded mournfully in time to the clatter of the horse's hooves.

'It seems that sadnesses never end,' he said, wiping a tear from his eye. 'First Emily, now Mother.'

'Emily was too young to die,' Eliza said gently. 'Mother is not.'

'Still, she *is* our mother.' Guy looked bitterly at his sister. 'You are a hard woman, Eliza, if you do not grieve at the death of a parent.'

Eliza, not wishing to be a hypocrite, said nothing but let her head sink back against the seat of the carriage. It was indeed a hard child who did not love a parent – and a hard parent who could cast off a child.

Then she pictured in her mind the little office and what she would do to make it attractive.

'I am going into business,' she said to Guy, hoping to take his mind off his melancholy preoccupations.

'What?' Guy sat up abruptly.

'I'm going to revive the fortunes of the Yetman business.

468

Laurence has begun his apprenticeship. Perce is very pleased with him, and they have more work than they can cope with. I am going to reopen the Blandford office and take charge of the orders, the invoicing and the day-to-day enquiries.'

If she hoped that her words would cheer Guy up she was mistaken. He threw his head back and once more shut his eyes.

'Dear God, Eliza,' he exclaimed, 'is there *no* end to the follies you will commit? Do you not realise that by birth you are a Woodville? People remember that, you know, even if you do not. Oh yes, and they remember all the other things you did, too. You will take our family right down in the mire, and we shall all sink with you.'

'What nonsense you talk, Guy,' Eliza said crossly. 'This is nearly the twentieth century. Classes are no longer as divided as they were, women not so protected. We have women doctors and academics, and one day we will have women lawyers and businesswomen and . . .'

'That day I hope I *never* live to see.' Guy sighed loudly. 'And all the time you have a man *very* well suited to you, who loves you and could keep you in such luxury you would never want again.'

'If you are talking about Julius, then you would have me bought as every other woman is bought – something paid for at the altar. No, thank you. Julius Heering I like, but I do not want to marry him. I do not want to be owned or helped by him.'

'I don't understand you.' Guy shook his head wearily. 'I don't understand you at all. Marriage is a partnership. See how well Margaret and I get on.'

'Yes, but things have changed a lot in eighteen years. Women are not so eager now to give their rights away – or their money, if they have it.'

'Any moment now you'll be telling me you are a suffragette,' Guy said ignoring her jibe.

'Any moment you may be right. Maybe I *will* invade the council of Blandford and in time be its mayor.'

Guy pretended to sleep, and Eliza was left to think about their conversation and the very real changes in attitudes between men and women that had taken place in her lifetime.

'Do you know, Eliza,' Guy murmured after a while, 'I would like Mother to see my little Elizabeth. She *is* her grandmother, after all, and I would like them to meet before she dies.'

'I think you are asking for the impossible, Guy,' Eliza said. 'No one would understand why Elizabeth was there, least of all she and Mother. It would hurt Margaret, who would ask herself the same question.'

Guy settled his head back in the seat again while two large tears stole down his cheek. 'I am convinced that God *sent* little Elizabeth to take the place of Emily. He meant me to have her, and to have her live with me.'

'God may understand it, but I doubt that Margaret would,' Eliza said. 'Elizabeth is very well looked after, Guy. Who knows what the future may bring? But I think that, for now, you should be thankful for the family you have, for your good wife who understands you so well, and not cause her further hurt than you have already.'

The family stood about Henrietta's bed as she slowly sank into a state of unconsciousness from which, from time to time, she had moments of illumination. She had seen her brothers, her son and daughter-in-law, her daughter and all her grandchildren. To some she had said a word, to others nothing. She had patted Carson's head and told him that it was important to be good, whereupon that young man had thrown himself across her bed in a fit of uncontrollable weeping. Those present to see the edifying sight earnestly hoped that it might have a lasting effect. With Guy she had quite a long conversation. She merely gazed at Eliza, who bent to kiss her.

George made the sign of the cross reverently on his grandmother's forehead and prayed for a long time over her as though he were an ordained minister of the Church already, while Guy also knelt by her side, holding her frail hand.

Dora and Hugh gave her a dutiful kiss, and her Martyn

nephews and nieces made brief appearances and left quickly. Only the immediate family remained by her bedside until the end.

Downstairs practical Margaret served tea and comfort with the aid of Henrietta's two faithful servants who had been with her since her exile in Bournemouth. If Henrietta knew when Margaret came to say goodbye she gave no sign of it; her eyes remained tight shut.

Eliza remained mostly by the window, looking out over beautiful Bournemouth Bay towards the Isle of Wight.

Eliza had never thought that the prospect of her mother's death would move her, but it did. As she'd looked into her eyes a few moments before, she had seen there the intolerance, the lack of understanding and forgiveness, that had characterised their stormy later years together.

But she could recall how things had been when she was a child, wilful, stubborn, disobedient, but loved. From her mother, and especially her father, there *had* always been love, and perhaps it had never completely gone.

She turned and gazed at the still figure on the bed and wished she could roll back the years – to the time when she was a little girl and her mother a beautiful, stately woman.

Suddenly Eliza longed to breathe life into that body whose spirit was ebbing even as she looked at her; they could start all over again if only perhaps the drama of their lives would unfold in a different way.

Impetuously she left the window embrasure and flung herself on her knees by the bed, her heart overwhelmed with love, remorse and pity. She seized her mother's hand and held it to her lips and, as Henrietta Woodville slipped slowly out of a world that had largely disappointed her, maybe she was ultimately comforted by the presence by her side of her daughter.

Five days later the late Lady Woodville was laid to rest in the family vault beside her granddaughter in the church of St Mark, Wenham.

Although Henrietta was not well-known and was little loved, she was treated with respect by the people of the parish, who lined the streets to say farewell to one of its eminent citizens.

People love a show, and Henrietta Woodville, with her hearse drawn by black horses, followed by a long procession of official mourners with black armbands, provided in her obsequies a fitting climax to her life that the town would long remember.

The muffled funeral bell tolled mournfully, the cortège wound its solemn way to the church and then to the churchyard overlooking the river for committal in the family vault. At the back of the crowd gathered round the mausoleum stood Beth, tightly holding the hand of little Elizabeth, the grandchild who would never meet her grandmother.

Guy noticed Elizabeth and sought her out, approving Beth's gesture with a smile. On his way from the cemetery he was observed pausing and tenderly patting the head of the beautiful, curly-headed child.

The funeral party drove back to Pelham's Oak where, as before, the house was draped in black ribbon and crepe. People spoke in hushed voices, but, really, very few had clear memories of the deceased, who had lived for nearly eighteen years in exile in Bournemouth. But the Woodvilles were an institution, and institutions always deserve respect.

Guy and his sister moved slowly among the crowd, followed a few paces behind by George and Carson, who managed to look quite angelic in black. Laurence, Dora and Hugh, reserved and dignified, showed by their behaviour that they too were almost grown up. A new generation was ready to face the new world, the new century.

It was a sad occasion, but not too sad. Lally and Prosper hovered; some Heerings had come over from Holland and would be taken back to the house built by Julius that had been appropriately renamed Forest House. Weddings and funerals were good occasions for deals and diplomacy, as every good businessman and politician knows. There would be a house party; riding and some shooting, the sort of thing Lally knew so well how to arrange.

Julius wandered restlessly among the crowd, seeking out Eliza. She looked so grave and dignified in her mourning, but so unbearably beautiful that he felt more deeply in love with her than he believed possible. For years he had been a man stuck fast upon the horns of a dilemma. He loved a woman, but knew that she did not return that love and possibly never would. Every time they saw each other they seemed to be at odds, yet he had an instinct that the attraction was mutual.

Very occasionally they met at Guy and Margaret's house. Julius went there often because it gave him a base in the country now that he had sold the home he had dreamed about.

He felt that even now, on an occasion as solemn and sad as this one, they were moving slowly across the room with the object of contriving an inevitable meeting in the middle.

'Condolences on the death of your mother,' Julius said gravely, taking her hand and kissing it.

'Thank you,' Eliza replied, just as gravely and inclining her head.

'It is a terrible thing to lose a parent.'

'*And* a wife *and* a husband,' Eliza replied, looking steadily at him.

'I wonder if you would ever forgive . . .'

'I have already forgotten it,' she said. 'And *you* have much to forgive in me, too. I was aloof and most ungrateful, and I'm sorry.'

'Oh, Eliza,' Julius said in a voice that throbbed with emotion. 'Would you like a turn in the garden to take advantage of the cool breeze?'

'It is warm,' she agreed, not too solemnly. 'It has been a *very* hot and tiring day.'

Detaching themselves from the crowd, they walked through the open French windows on to the terrace. They didn't speak at all, but as they wandered slowly, in perfect accord, towards the great oak planted by Pelham – a symbol of the very Englishness of the Woodville family for over three hundred years – the

Dutchman unobtrusively slipped his arm through Eliza's, and she did not repulse him.

They stood together like that for a long time, looking up through the branches of the tree which, caught by a mysterious breeze, swung back and forth slowly and majestically with soft, whispering sounds.

From little acorns do such big trees grow.